Paper Dolls & Hollow Men

Jeff Morris

© 2019 Jeff Morris
All Rights Reserved.

No part of this publication may be reproduced, stored in a retrieval system, or transmitted, in any form or by any means, electronic, mechanical, photocopying, recording, or otherwise, without the written permission of the author.

First published by Dog Ear Publishing
4011 Vincennes Road
Indianapolis, IN 46268
www.dogearpublishing.net

ISBN: 978-145756-691-2

This book is a work of fiction. Places, events, and situations in this book are purely fictional and any resemblance to actual persons, living or dead, is coincidental.

This book is printed on acid-free paper.
Printed in the United States of America

This book is dedicated to my father, Glenn Morris: Citizen Soldier, War Hero, dedicated Soil Conservationist, and enthusiastic World Traveler. I learned lessons from him as a boy. And I learned even more as a late middle-aged man as I looked back on his life as a younger man, revealed in his letters to relatives back home during World II

The Hollow Men

Mistah Kurtz-he dead

A penny for the Old Guy

I

We are the hollow men

We are the stuffed men

Leaning together

Headpiece filled with straw. Alas!

Our dried voices, when

We whisper together

Are quiet and meaningless

As wind in dry grass

Or rats' feet over broken glass

In our dry cellar

Shape without form, shade without colour,

Paralysed force, gesture without motion;

Those who have crossed

With direct eyes, to death's other Kingdom

Remember us-if at all-not as lost

Violent souls, but only

As the hollow men

The stuffed men.

II

Eyes I dare not meet in dreams
In death's dream kingdom
These do not appear:
There, the eyes are
Sunlight on a broken column
There, is a tree swinging
And voices are
In the wind's singing
More distant and more solemn
Than a fading star.

Let me be no nearer
In death's dream kingdom
Let me also wear
Such deliberate disguises
Rat's coat, crowskin, crossed staves
In a field
Behaving as the wind behaves
No nearer—

Not that final meeting
In the twilight kingdom

III

This is the dead land
This is cactus land
Here the stone images
Are raised, here they receive
The supplication of a dead man's hand
Under the twinkle of a fading star.

Is it like this
In death's other kingdom
Waking alone
At the hour when we are
Trembling with tenderness
Lips that would kiss
Form prayers to broken stone

T. S. Eliot

PAPER DOLL

I'm gonna buy a Paper Doll that I can call my own

A doll that other fellows cannot steal

And then the flirty, flirty guys with their flirty, flirty eyes

Will have to flirt with dollies that are real

When I come home at night she will be waiting

She'll be the truest doll in all this world

I'd rather have a Paper Doll to call my own

Than have a fickle minded real live girl

Composed by Johnny S. Black

History is not about the past;
it is about arguments we have about the past.

Ira Berlin

The Long Emancipation: The Demise of Slavery in the United States

BOOK ONE:

A Tale of Two Towns

Windsor, Ohio was founded in 1819, and Chesterfield, Ohio, was founded in 1834. In sharp contrast to the Quaker stronghold in Chesterfield, Windsor was a quintessential river town, "wet" in more ways than one. The river men of old Windsor created a booming hamlet with a raucous aspect—fueled, for most of the period, with alcohol in various forms—and unfazed by enmity, politically or otherwise. Windsor was content to be a vibrant river town, and there was never much question about where the town fathers would come down on the issue of alcohol. Windsor stayed "wet" nearly continuously until Prohibition. The hamlet of Chesterfield was "dry." Three Quaker men—Dempsey Boswell, Elijah Hiatt and Exum Bundy—all with roots in Chester, England, by way of Belmont County Ohio—bought acreage from the Ohio Company and settled in Marion Township and were intent on establishing a peaceful village where they could prosper in business while doing the work of the Lord.

Windsor also had not had much of any experience with slavery. Slaves had never worked the soil in Morgan County, but many passed through on their way to points farther North. In contrast, the Quakers that settled in Chesterfield felt obliged to do much more than simply not engage in the slave trade or help a few runaway slaves now and then. They were compelled to overtly, but peacefully, fight against the *peculiar institution* that was increasingly tearing at the seams of the Republic. The fathers of Chesterfield presided over a well-organized branch of the Underground Railroad that ran through Marietta, Chesterfield, Malta, McConnelsville, Deavertown, Pennsville, Rousseau, Morganville, Putnam, and points north. These Friends became important links in the Underground Railroad in Ohio. Some acted as conductors and others provided money or housing for slaves as they came through. But whether it was with time, risk, or treasure, the good Quakers provided aid and comfort to runaway slaves without raising their voices or lifting a hand in anger.

The Quaker Church remained a strong presence in Chesterfield, and descendants of some of the slaves that passed through in the antebellum period remained in the area. The Methodists, who settled only a few years after the Quakers and still had a strong presence in Marion Township, went along with keeping the village "dry."

As time passed, the divide between the two towns diminished greatly, along religious and political lines. By the turn of the 20th century, the only issue that still raised a ruckus between the two towns was liquor. The stark contrast in the handling by the two villages of the alcohol issue was still being played out in the second half of the 20th century. To this day, it is not uncommon to hear variations on the following conversation while attending the Barlow Fair, Fleming Reunion, or the Oakland Homecoming:

"Reba, I hear that your Josephine has a young man. Are they getting serious?"

"Well, Effie, I guess they are."

"Do you like him? Does he have a good job?"

"Yes to both those questions."

"You don't seem very happy about it."

"I'm just worried a little. He's from Windsor and works on the railroad. My grandmothers on both sides, good Marion Township folk both of 'em, always warned me about boys from Windsor."

"Amen to that, Reba."

"My grandma said about the same thing. She said that, Windsor boys are go-getters and make a good living, but it doesn't matter how much they make on payday if they turn around and give it all to the bootlegger on Saturday night."

1925

Ross

Charlotte Ross as told by Orpha Foster

<u>July 18, 1925</u>: Adolf Hitler's autobiographical manifesto *Mein Kampf* published.

My Dad, John Foster, bought the farm next to Ross's when I was in third grade. One of my earliest memories of Chesterfield was of Nanny Ross, Charlotte's mom, taking me and Charlotte to the Morgan County Fair to help her. This was a few days before the fair opened, and workmen and folks showing livestock and such were coming in and out. I thought it was exciting, seeing all the people come and go.

Charlotte had other ideas, though. Right after we arrived, Nanny had to run over to the Union Hall Theater to check on something. She told us if anything came up, to give Mr. Bowman a holler. He was just a little way over by where they had the kitchen set up. Well, Charlotte thought that put her in charge of the gate.

"Orpha," she said, "I know most of the folks coming in from Chesterfield and Todds. But if any of those Windsor boys try to get in, they better mind me. My Aunt Minta told me all about them boys from over there on the river. And I ain't lettin' 'em in just on their good looks. I want you to stay with me in case I get any trouble."

As I write this recollection, I wish I'd had a nickel for every time Charlotte got me in trouble over the years.

"Well, Char, I would. But my mom told me to go down to the store and get some sausage for our supper and bring it right back home."

"OK, Orpha, go on ahead. I reckon I can do this alone, but I'd sure feel bad if old Dan Franey found out about how nasty you were when you slept over at my house last week."

"You hush now, Charlotte! That stuff was all your idea anyway."

"OK, I'll be sure and tell Dan you were askin' 'bout him. See you."

"Oh, you are evil, Charlotte Ross. I got to run that sausage up and then I'll be back."

Half an hour later and out-of-breath, I returned.

"Did I miss anything, Charlotte?"

"Not much. Right after you left this smart-alecky boy with his hair all greased back and one of those dots on his chin came breezing out through the gate.

'See you in the funny papers, Curly!' he said."

"Well, I stuck my tongue out and put my thumbs in my ears. And that boy gave me a Bronx Cheer with his thumb on his nose and his fingers waggling to beat the band.

"I watched him head into the store there at Marion and Mill Street. And I started thinking up ways to get back at that joker next time I saw him. We still had folks coming in and out, but I decided if he came back I wasn't going to let him in. About ten minutes later, I see him turning the corner heading right for me. I pulled the gate closed and clipped the pin through the hasp. "Hey, Curly, he said with a big smile. 'I got some candy—a couple Baby Ruth and a couple Bit-O-Honey—haven't opened 'em yet. You're welcome to have one.' "'I don't take candy from strangers. Besides, I'm working here, see." He said, 'Well, OK. If you change your mind later, you're welcome to have one. The put his hand on the gate and pulled it a little. He said, 'You going to let me in, Curly?'"

"I said, 'That'll be two bits.'

"And he says, 'But I'm showing Jerseys at the fair. I'm staying here with my stock.'"

"So, I say, 'Got to have a ticket to get in, smarty-pants!"

"He says, 'Please, I need to get back in to look after my cows. I was just kiddin' around a little.'

"'Bet you won't do that again, will you?'

"'No, ma'am,' but I need to get back to my stock. Please.'"

Mr. Bowman came around to see what was going on. 'Charlotte, what seems to be the problem?' he says.

"Well, this boy is trying to get in without paying.'

"Is that right, son?"

'No, sir. I'm showing Jerseys here at the fair. I just went up to the store to get a couple of candy bars. They said we could get back into the fairgrounds. I just want to get back to my stock.'

"'You must be Big Mitch's middle boy, right?'

"Yes sir, Mr. Bowman. I'm Virgil Thomas. My Pa and Ma will be here tomorrow."

"Well, it'll be good to see them. How is your brother, Little Mitch?

"'He's swell, Sir. He wants to be a train engineer. He's got a job in the yards in Zanesville for the summer, helping and such. Says it's kinder like an apprenticeship

"Glad to hear it. He always seemed to be good with machinery and such. Now, Charlotte, we need to let Virgil get back to his cows. Please open the gate.'

"I will not! Not! Not until my mother gets back!"

"She's back, Nanny said sharply as she walked swiftly toward her daughter. "And you better do as you are told, or you're going to be standing up at dinner tonight.'

"But, Ma!

"None of that. Now, open the gate and apologize.'

She pulled the pin from the hasp and pushed open the gate.

"Thanks, Curly," Virgil said quiet-like."

"'Now, what do you say, Char?'

"Charlotte looked down at her feet and then gave Virgil the evil eye. I got lots of those over my years of being friends with Charlotte.

"No apologies necessary, ma'am Virgil said with a big grin. 'I shouldn't have kidded around with her. She was just doing her job. Part of the reason I went to the store was to get her a candy bar, too."

"'Well that's very nice, young man. What do you say, Charlotte?"

"Charlotte didn't say anything.

"After he left, Charlotte came back over and sat down again and started taking tickets. Her Ma came back and asked her again why she was being so spiteful.

"'What'd you tell her?' I asked.

"I said I just didn't like people making fun of me. And I don't mean to take it when they do! Charlotte made a mean face and hit herself hard on the side of her head with the heel of her hand. 'Orpha, I just hate people. They're always telling me what to do and what not to do. I'll show them, all of 'em. People will learn to steer clear of me if they know what's good for 'em.

"About 15 minutes later the boy, Virgil Thomas, came back over. "Look, 'he said, 'I don't like getting off on the wrong foot with folks. I'd still like to give you two ladies candy bars. I'm not trying bribe you or anything. I'm just being friendly, OK?

"That's sounds good to me, Virgil," I said. "I never had a Bit O Honey.

"He handed me the bar.

"I guess I could take a Baby Ruth, Charlotte said.

"Here you go, little lady. I'll be seeing you.

"I opened my bar, had a bite and smiled. After Nanny and Mr. Bowman started talking, Charlotte went back by the stage. I watched her. She opened one end of the package on her Baby Ruth. She took a little bite and spit it out on the dirt. And then she spotted Mr. Bowman's car—a black Model T. She split the rest of the bar and put half on a sunny spot on top of the trunk and watched it melt slowly until it ran down and formed a small puddle in the dirt. The rest she put smack dab in the middle of the driver's seat. I figured she'd get in trouble. She did. She got a whipping from her Pa after he found out what she did to Mr. Bowman's car.

"It was worth it, she told me a week later after she was finally allowed out of the house. "I was tired of everybody ignoring me and such. I decided right then and there that nobody was going to ever ignore me or treat me poorly from then on. And if they did, they'd better look out. And that went for family, friends, and especially, boys. If they thought they could pull something over on me, well, they have another thing comin'.

"'But Charlotte,'" I said, 'you missed the whole Fair. That boy that gave us the candy bars was askin' about you. I told him you were under the weather.'

"'I don't care about that smart aleck. Next time he's over here in Chesterfield he can give his stinky old candy bars to some of the colored girls and leave me alone!"

"Why are you so spiteful, Charlotte?' I asked.

"None of your beeswax, Orpha. I'll be as mean as I want to be. Minta told me not to let folks push me around. I guess until I get a little older I'll have to mind my folks sometimes, but eventually no one will be able to tell me what to do.'

"'How 'bout your husband when you get older?'

"Don't know that I'll need one of them. But if I do get one, he won't be my boss. No, ma'am!'

"Me and Charlotte grew up next door neighbors until my Daddy passed away when I was a freshman in high school. We sold the farm and bought a house on Marion Street halfway up the hill. Charlotte and I were still classmates, but she started treating me differently, like she was mad at me.

"I asked her one time, early in freshmen year, why she was being so mean to me. She said I ought to be ashamed for abandoning her and moving into town.

"Charlotte,' I said, "My Dad died, and we had to sell the farm. We're still in all our classes together, and we play in the band together and go to the same church and such. It's not like I wanted my Dad to die so I could get off the farm. I miss bein' on the farm.'

"Of course, you do, Orpha.' Nanny came out on the porch and put a gentle hand on my shoulder. 'Charlotte, you should be ashamed of yourself. How would you like it if your Daddy died and we had to move?

"'I wouldn't care if every grown person in this whole world died. Then I'd be left alone to do what I want!"

"Since her wish about all grownups dying didn't work out, Charlotte had to continue staying with her mother, Nanny, father Harley and older brother Penrose. Her maiden Aunt Minta stayed with the family when she wasn't nursing folks in their homes.

The Ross's had a 180-acre farm just outside town with two good barns and a brick house. Her folks were liked by everyone. Nanny did lots of volunteering at the Union Hall Theater, at school, at church, and for the Chesterfield Fair.

"Charlotte's older brother, Pen, could be mean, but he was quiet. He was also a 'good farmer" and that counted for a lot back then. He bought a farm over by Hickerson's Fruit Farm after he got out of the Army in 1945. My first memory of Pen when we were kids was him giving me a Dutch Rub in their barn. He didn't quit until Mr. Ross pulled him off me.

"Mostly, we got along well. Charlotte was what folks called high-strung. She was a lot of fun to be around most of the time. When she was feeling good, people loved being around her. She played clarinet in the school band. And we were both in the Chesterfield Belles, which was kind of an unofficial club. When she was being a pill, though, people learned to steer clear. She surely had some tough luck later in her life that didn't help matters any. But to be honest, I think she deserved some of those hardships. My Dad use to say that lots of times, folks make their own luck. And what goes around comes around. In the end, I think a lot of it she brung on herself.

BOOK TWO

Fear Itself 1926 to 1939

Louise Forest

<u>April 24, 1926</u>: The Treaty of Berlin is signed by Germany and the Soviet Union, which declares neutrality if either country is attacked within the next five years.

The first time I set eyes on Virgil Thomas was that first day of school just after we'd moved to Windsor. We'd had a small farm just outside of Chesterfield by Todds. Dad got sick and couldn't farm anymore. We had moved into the house on East River Road. Anyway, Virg was riding a horse—Blackie—down Keffer Road. He just left his horse grazing in the pasture behind the store. And then he hopped on the train into Windsor.

When he came back for his horse that afternoon, a couple of the Sheets' boys from down the road were making fun of me.

"You two leave her alone, 'less you want me to cut a switch and warm up yer bottoms."

"Why you stickin' up for her, Virg? My cousin in Roosterville says she's part black."

"What's that got to do with anything? For all I know, Ben, you could be part jackass. Now you just leave her alone, boys. 'Cause I'm going to be checkin' up on you. OK?"

"Sure, Virgil," the older brother said. "We didn't mean no harm, Louise."

"You let me know, Louise, if these kids are bothering you. OK?"

"I sure will. But I'll be OK. I can look out for myself, but thank you."

He hopped on his horse. "See ya in the funny papers," he said with a big smile. And then he shook the reins and horse and rider disappeared up the hill.

I thought he was awful cute with that cleft chin, his hair slicked back and those blue eyes. I was starting the sixth grade, so that would put him in tenth grade—he started school a year early. He didn't really pay much attention to me 'til later, though. But when he finally did notice me, look out!

Harriet Forest

The first day of the school year is an exciting time in a small town. Louise, my oldest, was starting sixth grade and Barbara was in second grade when we moved to Windsor in 1926. Merlene started first grade the next year. Opal wasn't even born yet.

It was a trying time, too, with Henry's illness getting worse. We had moved from Chesterfield to Windsor just a quarter mile from Mitch Thomas's store in Roxbury. Mr. Thomas let us rent the house for a nominal charge. My husband, Henry, had developed a bad cough the year before and had to give up farming. He couldn't stand the manual labor himself anymore and he couldn't afford to add hands. With four daughters, the oldest just ten, and no hands to do the work, we were forced to sell the 160 acres Mom and Dad been farming for the past 12 years for pennies on the dollar.

After Henry took sick, Big Mitch Thomas, a fellow Methodist and Mason, offered him a chance to fill in minding the store three days a week and delivering the mail another two. Little Mitch, the Thomas's oldest child, had been doing these two part-time jobs for over a year while he waited to get on full-time with the railroad. Little Mitch got the job a few weeks earlier and was getting ready to move to Pennsylvania.

We figured things would be tight with five mouths to feed one and another on the way. I planned to take in people's laundry as I had in Chesterfield. We also had room for a good-sized garden. Henry and I hoped that we could support our family. We also hoped that between the drug store and Doctor Marlowe there might be some hope yet to find a cure for Henry's lung problems.

I had other worries that I didn't share with Henry—the kind that women have nursed and worried over alone for ages. All our girls were cute and good-natured. Their features favored my family, and their long, shining black hair favored their father. Louise was different. It wasn't just her face or hair, there was something else about her that drew people to her. And some of those people would be men—grown men. And I was worried that some of those men would be wild-eyed and excited. And others might be rough and carnal. When we had our farm, there weren't many strangers coming around. But in Windsor we had folks coming and going to the store and others bringing in and picking up laundry. We also had hobos getting off the train and loafing down by the river.

My older sister, Devona, may she rest in peace, was a striking woman. Louise had that, whatever it was, same as Dee. And I prayed that Louise would not suffer like Dee.

We had five girls in my family and all were raised in Upper Sandusky, and the men just flocked around. And before my folks knew what was happening, Devona had men chasing her—schoolboys, male teachers, strangers, family friends. No one in that small town blamed their sons or husbands or fathers for the trouble that followed. Every man-jack blamed Devona—said she was a temptress and other words I can't even say without blushing. I didn't want this to happen with Louise.

There had been no inappropriate incidents thus far, but the girl was only ten. I worried about what would happen when her body started changing. I'd seen what happened with Devona and had navigated those stormy waters myself when, at 14, I had changed almost overnight into a woman. I have thanked the Good Lord every night in my prayers for bringing Henry into my life. And I hope that Louise, too, will find a good husband someday.

1929

Virgil Thomas

<u>October 29, 1929</u>: The Great Depression begins with Black Tuesday the Wall Street Crash

Virgil Thomas skipped lightly down the three steps from the train to the platform in Akron, Ohio on July 4th of 1929.

"Where can I get a cab, Porter?" he asked.

"Down to the end of the platform, just past those luggage carts, sir."

"Thank you," Virgil said with a big smile as he pressed a nickel into the large dark hand.

"Thank you, sir."

The young man made his way toward the cab stand amid a crush of porters pushing carts full of luggage and people hurrying with children. Folks were smoking as they walked—even women! In the stations at McConnelsville and Windsor, there was a smoking area for men only.

Virgil felt as if he'd landed on the moon.

A soldier in a uniform stood at a pay phone near the cab stand. He looked like a creature from another world, another time, with his leggings and odd doughboy insignias. A small cardboard suitcase sat pitifully at his feet. He was digging in his pockets for change.

The line at the cab stand extended back just past the telephone.

"Ma, it's me, Elmer. I'm in Akron. Our train got held up, and I won't be able to get home after all."

A pause, a series of nods and a string of 'Yeses' followed.

"Yes, Ma. I want to see you, too. Tell all the kids their big brother is thinking about them. And, well, I don't suppose you've heard anything from Mervill, have you?"

The soldier shifted his feet and frowned. "Well, I guess she'll have a time working up in Cleveland. Is she staying with her Aunt Margaret?"

Virg watched the soldier make a series of nods. "Yes, I do remember Wanda, Her first cousin, right? It's just, I sure do miss her, Ma."

Another series of nods followed. "I know, it's just that, well, I'm happy to be a soldier, but folks sure don't seem to pay no never mind to us when we're out in public. I still remember all the hoopla when Uncle Corliss got back after World War On. Nobody seems to care about soldiers during peacetime—might as well be tramps or hobos. Oh well, listen to me gettin' all weepy. I love you, Ma and I'm doin' my best. Better get off now 'fore I run out of change."

Poor bugger, glad I'm not a soldier, Virgil thought, as he watched Elmer walk off slowly with his 50-cent suitcase under his arm

The boy's thoughts quickly returned to the bustling station. He'd never seen so many people or felt so much raw, kinetic energy. This eager manchild, not yet 17 and just graduated from high school, felt like a character in a movie as he threw his suitcase and then himself into the back seat of a taxi.

"Five thirty-one Belmont Avenue, please."

"You got it, boss."

This voyage to Akron marked Virgil's first as a man. He'd started school a year early and skipped sixth grade. At 16, he'd finished high school. Virgil longed to be done with high school friends and life on the farm. Now, a bright future seemed to lay ahead for him. His cousin, Mervyn Usher, worked at Goodyear and had been made lead man on one of the lines making ball bearings. He got Virgil a job for two months. If Virgil did a good job, Mervyn said he'd have a good chance of getting on full-time after Thanksgiving.

In Akron, Virgil enjoyed working on the line and hoped this would be the beginning of a life of excitement and adventure. The money was better than anything he could find in Morgan County, and he hoped he could get on as a permanent employee, for a year or two. It had been exciting working with people of different backgrounds and nationalities: German, Italian, Irish, Negro and even some Jews.

It was honest work that a man could be proud of doing and, more importantly, the pay was good enough to build up a grubstake that would allow him to head West like Mervyn's brothers and his own father had done when they were young men.

This new life was so stimulating that Virgil didn't see it coming; the end, that is.

***

Black Tuesday they called it. He returned home in mid-October. Before the ten cartons of Lucky Strikes and the $65 he'd brought back with him to Windsor were gone— the bottom fell out.

The older folks whispered about their children in Chicago and Cleveland going on reduced hours or losing their jobs.

In a letter to Virgil, Mervyn said he'd managed to keep his own job but at a hefty pay cut. He tried to sound cheerful about Virgil's prospects. Mervyn wrote that after this *Panic* ended, things would get back to normal, and Virgil could probably get on.

Wishful thinking, perhaps. Virgil thought of the signs he'd seen — hobos sleeping rough on the bottom of the steep bank down to the river not far from the Roxbury Store. There had been fires in several abandoned barns up toward Dale. He'd heard his mother, Anne, talking with some of the women at church about strange men coming to the house after Mose, Virgil, and Ralph were out in the fields and Big Mitch was delivering mail. They panhandled and demanded food. Anne mentioned this at supper one night, and Big Mitch was visibly upset. Anne Marie, a tall imposing woman with a friendly disposition, told her husband that she had handled tougher customers.

"I had to ride herd on my three brothers when I was in high school. They gave me more trouble than these poor fellows that come up to the back door. Most of them are just give-out, even the younger ones. They don't have anything to hope for. Least we can do is give them a bit to eat and a kind word."

Between Thanksgiving and Christmas older brothers and cousins not seen in years for more than short visits resurfaced. They returned like birds flocking before a storm seeking, if not security, at least a modicum of safety in the bosom of family in a familiar place.

The dread could not always be articulated, but it was understood— present— lurking nearby like a threadbare stranger at the edge of a gathering or wolves baying on the margin of a dark woods, just out of sight, in some Grimm fairy tale. Some intuitive sense told the end of life as he'd known it was near. These wraiths were harbingers of the darkness to come, foreshadowing a sea change that would affect everyone.

Men returning to Morgan County seemed demoralized. They came from points North: Detroit, Pittsburg, Cleveland and Buffalo; and West: Chicago, Gary, Indianapolis and Texas Particularly the older men in their 30s. There was no work for them, and they'd mostly lost their place in their families. Without hope, they seemed like wounded animals who'd crawled back into a familiar hole, in which to die.

Those without homes to return to stayed in motion, their meager possessions in boxes and bags. Willing to work for room and board, they congregated, rolling off the back of freight trains, hopping off trucks and walking head down on the side of roads, arm extended, jerking, hitching for a ride. If there was no work, many begged at back doors. If there was nothing to be tendered by locals, some men stole.

Those without families or places to go were launched—an Armada of hobos—riding the rails endlessly in search of work or a handout, crossing and re-crossing America *ad infinitum*. Their motion now seemed to be always *away from*, rather than *toward*. Those who survived the initial disaster joined the next breaking wave, cresting the troughs of the Sea of Dirt that daubed the sky through the Dustbowl years beginning in '34. The older men of this first wave, like the soil itself, seemed to dry up and blow away with the wind before things turned around.

Some of the younger cohort would be helped along by New Deal programs—CCC and WPA. The ultimate resolution for this younger group was found only with the advent of war. — 'The War'. Many found purpose and order, as well as three welcome squares a day in olive drab. On the front lines, some would uncover an inner strength and leadership potential they'd never known they possessed. Others discovered a fear labeled *cowardice* that left them paralyzed and likely to become early casualties. But strong or weak, brave or timid, all ran the same risk of losing limbs, perhaps, life itself, when they got their chance, finally, to "see the elephant" That's what the old fellows who had been in the Civil War or in Cuba called combat.

As campaigns in Northern Europe, Italy, and Japan wore on, those familiar with Probability (or Poker) realized their chances of surviving ebbed and flowed. The things they learned along the way, in many cases from watching comrades fall, helped their chances a little. The *bathtub curves* that mathematicians and scientists used to predict new product reliability and wear-out times for equipment were applicable to men as well and were basically accurate in the aggregate in predicting casualty rates.

Men, however, do not work or marry or raise children or finish college in the aggregate. In the end, it was sheer chance that often decided an individual's fate. Those who survived lengthy periods of combat without serious injury knew the element of chance was always present.

Many of those not drafted for various reasons found purpose in the frenetic assembly lines that jumped to life when America became Hephaestus for the Allies, turning out weapons of war with a frightening kinetic reverberation felt around the world. They enjoyed the paychecks. And, flush with overtime, some enjoyed socializing with the wives and sweethearts of GIs slogging their way across Europe and island-hopping across the bitter, black sands of the Pacific.

Those days were still to come.

Meanwhile though, 1929 yielded to 1930 and beyond with no improvement in sight. Virgil, like many of the so-called lucky ones, didn't feel lucky. He marked time on the family farm. As the years rolled by, he chafed at having to sleep in the same small rope bed he'd had since grade school. He set up a little egg business that provided him enough cash for smokes and a little bootleg hooch on the weekends, not enough for a man wanting to sow some wild oats and then return home to marry and raise a family.

Four years into the Depression and approaching his 20th birthday, Virgil stood in the doorframe of the family home, rolling a cigarette of mostly stems and listening to FDR on the wireless promising better times. Any gratitude he had felt for having a place to live with sufficient food to eat had been completely overshadowed by a haunting sense that his life was over before it had begun.

Though he wasn't rich, Virgil's father, Big Mitch, was still a respected man in the community. Before the Depression, this translated into the ability to get a small loan if needed, or the possibility of selling a few head of cattle at a profit. Virgil's two older siblings had found careers. Those possibilities had disappeared, drifted away by the time Virgil and Ralph reached manhood.

Opportunity had dried up like the Oklahoma soil and carried away like the ubiquitous red dust.

During high school, Virgil had been considered among the upper crust of Morgan County society. Any such distinction had disappeared in the intervening years. The Farm and the Store continued to stay in the black, barely. But there was no longer money to replace the car every few years. The farm machinery was kept limping along by Mose, their colored hand. Big Mitch and Anne had always prided themselves on making a good appearance. But his shirt collars were frayed, and Anne's dresses were nearly beyond repairing.

There was no longer anyone to make that loan or buy those extra cattle. The adage, "Neither a borrower, nor a lender, be" took on a new meaning when there no longer seemed to be anyone with two cents to rub together in Morgan and Washington counties.

Virgil's prospects for marriage were marginal at best, unless he was willing to marry a young girl from a large, poor family. Even that would depend on his father running off their long-time colored hand, Mose, and giving Virgil the small house where Mose lived in the hollow behind the big barn.

Virgil shook his head at the thought of marrying any of Darnell Dingess' gaggle of freckled, barefoot girls. He envisioned Sunday visits to the in-laws. His wife would stuff scraps of food into her pockets and take them to her famished siblings. A running joke in Roxbury featured various twists on Dingess off-spring trudging up the steep dirt road from their sodden sand flatter cabin and knocking on Mrs. Thomas' kitchen door asking couldn't they please have 'sumpin' on a sammich.'

The taste of city girls Virgil had sampled in Akron made this interminable Depression worse. Rita worked at the next station on the line after Virgil. They'd gone to several dances. After the music stopped they pulled the hooch in the flask out of her turned-down stockings, then removed her stockings and other accouterment and sealed the deal.

The other girl he dated was no girl. Velma, an older widow in her late 20s, lived in his rooming house. She worked at a drugstore down the street.

And she surely knew her way around teenage boys. They went out to dinner regularly and spent nights together. She taught him things, in her tiny room. Back home in his rope bed, he yearned to feel the touch of her painted nails angling down like hot wires crossing his belly. He was afraid he'd never feel that again.

Since he'd returned home, all he'd had to look forward to was Saturday night dances at Big Bottom or Coal Run. He thought of taking off, riding the rails out West, but the Ushers and his father had always told him that you need a poke if you're going out westering. And Virgil didn't have a cent saved. He had to scrimp and roll his own all week just to buy a pack of Lucky Strikes for the Saturday dances. And all that might get you was a kiss, if you were lucky.

Virgil's idea of a life, well-lived had been formed early on, listening to the Usher boys and his father, Big Mitch, tell tales at the Barlow Fair and the Oakland Homecoming. Those tales of working out West had set him on fire. The three oldest Usher brothers followed work in the oil patch across East Texas and into Oklahoma. They worked hard for 11 months and spent September telling stories at the fairs and reunions in Morgan and Washington counties, showing the kids postcards of Buffalo Bill's Wild West Show as well as sepia-tinted pictures of themselves taken bellied up to zinc bars in ornate Denver saloons.

Big Mitch had taught school in mining camps—Golden and Cripple Creek–just west of Denver. He returned to Ohio after his intended, Anna Marie Usher gave him the ultimatum that she was getting married to someone before she turned 30 Mitch came back in 1905, and they spent 46 years together. Big Mitch died in 1951, and Anna died in 1977 at the ripe old age of 100.

But for Virgil, in his early years of manhood, everything seemed to have come to a stop. Preachers preached gratitude to those on farms, exhorting the flock to feel fortunate to be away from the vice-ridden cities, with at least the possibility of a little food on the table. Older folks with some land and small bank accounts and pensions held them tightly, all the while worrying about their children.

Virgil felt like he was treading water in that deep hole just past the Silverheels Riffle. He was a glorified hired hand on his daddy's farm with no prospects in sight. His older brother, Little Mitch and his sister, Grace, had families and the income to support them. Little Mitch got on with the railroad and was on his way to being an engineer. Grace went to nursing School in Zanesville and married Elmer Robertson from McConnelsville. Elmer and his brothers had a Chevy dealership in Zanesville. The two older kids got started before The Crash and they did all right, relatively speaking. Virgil and his younger brother, Ralph, seemed to be stuck with left hind tit.

1934 to 1937

Big Mitch Thomas

August 8, 1934: Members of the Wehrmacht begin swearing a personal oath of loyalty to Hitler instead of to the German constitution.

Big Mitch Thomas, teacher of children in gold camps, rural mail carrier, school board member, sometimes poet, Methodist, Mason, and gentleman Farmer was not a large man physically. His wife, Anne Marie, stood a full five inches taller at their wedding. At reunions, he was invariably in the front row. As he aged he was often found on a stool or a straight back chair off to one side or the other.

Big Mitch made up for his short stature with a *gravitas* that even his few enemies respected. With piercing blue eyes set beneath massive eyebrows, he was an imposing figure sitting as he sat behind the huge rolltop desk in his office in the back corner of the Roxbury Store. He volunteered to join the local Draft Board in October of 1940 as the only non-veteran. By February of 1941 he was the heading the board.

The moniker Big Mitch first appeared coincidently with the birth of Mitchell Jr. It simply evolved to distinguish father and son. And even his old friends and acquaintances adopted this new appellation.

Respect amongst one's peers doesn't necessarily carry over at home—especially when it comes to adolescent boys on the cusp of manhood. Little Mitch and Virgil tried their father's patience from the moment they were big enough to sneak off on Friday and Saturday nights and engage in the kinds of things that Big Mitch himself had enjoyed at that age.

Little Mitch's season of rebellion was short-lived, but was still disturbing for his father. He was crazy to get on with the railroad, and he nearly failed his final exams in History and Soil Science Senior Year. The principal and Big Mitch came to an agreement that his son would take his exams over again in three days, along with an oral exam with the respective teachers. If Little Mitch passed, he could graduate. He passed.

On his way to a Saturday night dance at Big Bottom on graduation weekend of 1926, Little Mitch rode one of his father's postal horses, Abe Lincoln too quickly downhill around the curve by the Roxbury Store. He left the horse, Ajax was in great distress, but Little Mitch left him tied to a buckboard behind the family Store in Roxbury.

Dragging home on foot the next morning as the sun just touched the eastern sky he discovered Anne Marie and Big Mitch on the porch of the store watching Hank and Harlan Dutro as they pulled a carcass onto a hay wagon with a winch.

"You could have got one of your bootlegger buddies to give you a ride and let us know, about Ajax, son. It's not right to treat an animal that way. Mr. Forest heard the thrashing around in that pen behind the store," Harvey said as he methodically cleaned his wireless eyeglasses.

"Poor fellow stayed with the horse and his oldest daughter walked all the way up to the house to let us know. Henry's about ready to die of consumption, but he did all he could."

"His daughter, Louise, is quite a young lady," Anne Thomas said, fixing her oldest son with an unwavering glance. "Not out of grade school yet, but she walked all the way to the house to let us know. Her pap can be very proud of her. That's a blessing for parents—to be able trust their children—especially the older ones."

Little Mitch had been staring a hole in his ruined shoes while his mother spoke. "Yes, ma'am. I'm sorry. I don't know any way to explain it. There's no excuse for my behavior."

"That's a fact, son," Big Mitch said, pulling up his pants and yawning. "We've got your train fare to New Castle for next month, so you can apply with the railroad. And you've got a new suit. We are still going to give you $50 for a graduation present, but we'd like you to consider using part of that to help compensate Henry and Louise Forest for the time they spent cleaning up your mess."

"We'd also like to think that you could show some genuine contrition to those folks. That family has had a mighty tough row to hoe. And they have taken it all in stride," Anne said with pursed lips and worried eyes. "They're barely getting by. We aren't rich, but the Lord has blessed our family with good health and two businesses that have allowed us to have all the things we need with some left over. Think about what I've said, and we'll talk tomorrow."

Little Mitch gave Henry and Louise the $50. And when he found out they were going to use it to buy a Thor Washer made by the Hurley Machine Company of Chicago, Big Mitch pulled a few strings with the C&O, and arranged for free shipping. Little Mitch gave Virgil $10 to get it off the train and help them set it up.

Virgil picked up the washer from the Malta train station and took it back in the freight wagon his dad kept behind the store. Virgil got his younger brother Ralph and Lon Cheadle to help him unload the washer at the Forest's house on East River Road.

Thus, did Little Mitch's rebellion end. By the time the washer was delivered, Little Mitch had gotten on with the C&O and married Eleanor Teller. The newlyweds were living in New Castle, Pennsylvania.

Virgil's rebellion stretched out longer and caused considerably more grief for both Virgil and his parents. Drinking was involved every time Virgil got a speeding ticket, wrecked a car or landed in jail. He seemed stuck on the farm, caught between adolescence and manhood. Despite periodic attempts to straighten up and fly right, he continued to get into trouble.

"It's the drinking that worries me, Virgil. This last time you spent the night in jail. That worried your mom, son. I'm afraid you'll hurt yourself or someone else. I know that staying here at home these past five years after finishing high school has been tough. You've done a good job with the farm, though."

"I am trying, Dad. I just want to get out and see the world. Like you and Ma's brothers did. I'm sorry, Dad. I'll slow down. If you want, I'll take over the mail route for six months."

"I know you're sorry, son. It's the darned Depression that's making most everybody afraid. But, I think FDR is going to get things going.

They're talking about big programs to put fellows like you to work—rural electrification, building and improving rural roads. I think that if we come up with a good plan, we can make out on this. The WPA will give us the go ahead if we write up a good proposal.

"My idea is to buy some trucks that can be used to haul asphalt and maybe a few school buses that we could contract to school districts to drive kids to schools. After we get better roads around here, they can close some of the dilapidated schools and haul kids on buses, hopefully our buses.

"My idea is that your grandmother, Sarah Jane and I buy the vehicles and you run the day-to-day business. It would be something you could have. Sarah Jane and I will look over the books and we can help in a pinch. Otherwise we'd just be kind of a 'silent partners. "I mean the school board would have to know I was a partner in the business if they were going to use our school buses, just to keep things on the up and up. What do you say, son?"

Virgil took a deep breath and smiled.

"That sounds good, Dad. I'll do better. I don't want to embarrass you or mom anymore."

"What I need from you then, Virgil, is a sign that you are serious about this. Maybe we can split the mail route for the next six months. We could even break Ralph in on it when he's off school. "I'd like for you to think about this. You are a grown man and I can't tell you what to do. But if I'm going to be partners with you in a business, I'd like to see you show that you are ready to get serious. That would mean no more traffic tickets. And as I said earlier no more driving our cars for the next six months. You think on this, and we can talk later. OK, son?"

"Yes, sir."

1935-1936

Virgil

<u>September 15, 1935</u>: The Reichstag passes the Nuremberg Laws, introducing antisemitism in German legislation

"Fellows! Hey, everyone, can I get your attention, please?" Virgil Thomas stood at the gym floor at Windsor High School in Windsor and waved his arms at a group of men seated in the bleachers.

"We've had some good news, fellas. The WPA has provisionally accepted our proposal to provide trucks, drivers and labor for the road building in Morgan and Noble Counties. We've still got to work out a few details, but it looks like she's gonna fly.

"We went over pay scale at our previous meeting. But since then, Big Mitch, Sarah Jane and I have discussed another benefit for all our workers. It's a kind of a deal where employees can get an actual share of the business. The more you work and the better the company does in meeting its objectives, the more vested you become in the business. You can be stockholders, not just hourly employees"

"We'd put money away, this could include bonuses for meeting deadlines and such. And when the work is done it all goes into a pot and is divided among us based on things like hours worked, overtime, and sick time taken."

"OK, fellows, don't get your dander up. I'm not going to be doing the books," Virgil said as he scanned the bleachers smiling broadly at his

A few of the young men stirred at the thought of deferring wages in an economy that still

"We're drawing up the details on this and we'll share 'em with you soon. Our best guess is somewhere around Thanksgiving the paving projects plans will be finalized. We may also be running some school buses next school year.

"Everyone needs to have a good pair of work boots, coveralls, a valid driver's license and be able to get insured if you're wanting to be able to drive. If we can get this started, I think, maybe, we can all have a good year in '36."

"Maybe you'll get to see the world after all, Virgil," a voice shouted from the bleachers.

"Maybe we'll all get to see the world," Virgil shouted back with a big smile.

"Careful what you pray for, Virgil. You might just get it and not know what to do with it," Sarah Jane said in a low whisper to Big Mitch.

Her son nodded solemnly and shrugged.

1936

Sarah Jane Lumley Thomas: from her Journal

August 1, 1936: Summer Olympics opens in Germany

When Doc Marlowe allowed us into the room after Little Mitch's birth. I nearly froze up. Little Mitch was big and dark with huge ears and hands like my father and Mitch's grandfather, Tom Lumley. After he grew up, the boy had a loud voice like my Dad's my father but that was where the resemblance ended. Little Mitch turned out to be a big man, a head taller than Big Mitch, but he was not a brute like my father, Tom Lumley.

I was Tom's favorite child because he thought I had a head for business. He never realized just how much I despised his crude manners and the overbearing treatment of his numerous children and wives.

Truth be told; Virgil was always my favorite. He had a rambunctious streak in him, but he was a good boy. He'd help me out when he was over at our house. And he loved hearing those old stories about characters from Morgan and Washington County. He loved hearing the stories those Usher boys and Big Mitch told about workin' out West and all, too.

And he had a wild streak in him, too. He couldn't wait to get out of high school so he could see the world. But that world kind of closed up shop in October of '29, the year he graduated.

Little Mitch and Grace managed to get careers started and get married and such before the Depression hit. They were able to keep their jobs and get on with livin'. And I didn't worry about Ralph so much. I figured he would be happy staying down here, runnin' the store and such. Ralph had Cloris and he would find work and be satisfied.

Virgil was different—kind of the wild card of the bunch. I'd hoped that he might go to Ohio State and get a degree in Agriculture. But that had to be on hold for a while. When Big Mitch and I got that contract with the WPA, it helped Virgil and the boys his age out. They worked hard, and I like to think it helped 'em stay out of trouble—some of it anyway!

I never tried to push the idea of going to college on Virgil. I figured it should be his idea. Still, when he asked to see me in March of 1937, I was praying that he was thinking about going to OSU. I told him he could come over any Sunday afternoon.

When we finally had that talk about school, I was very pleased. I agreed to pay his tuition, housing, and books for the first year. Tuition and housing in his second year. And tuition his third year.

1937

I never tried to push the idea of going to college on Virgil. I figured it should be his idea. Still, when he asked to see me in March of 1937, I was praying that he was thinking about going to OSU. I told him he could come over any Sunday afternoon.

When we finally had that talk about school, I was very pleased. I agreed to pay his tuition, housing and books for the first year. Tuition and housing in his second year. And tuition his third year.

BOOK THREE:

(1937-1940) Barbarians, Outliers, and Others

The Depression was not over, but for those who'd come this far without losing their businesses, homes or farms the future looked a shade brighter than it had since 1928. More families were relieved of the burden of simply surviving. Industry picked up with the beginning of armament sales to England.

Those under the age of 40 and in reasonably good health approached 1937 with a degree of cautious optimism not seen since before the Crash. Those with jobs had a good chance of getting more hours at a higher pay rate. Many of those who were unemployed since the Crash were finally finding full-time jobs.

Louise Forest

<u>June 11, 1937</u>: Soviet leader Josef Stalin begins a purge of Red Army generals.

Louise Forest was hanging out wash and trying to keep the Callendine boys from throwing their muddy old football over that way when she heard horse hooves on gravel. Just as she was thinking about the first-time Virgil came down Keffer Road, there he was.

"Hey, Louise. My Mom wants to know if you can help with dinner tomorrow night."

"Well, mebbe, wouldn't have to be fending off any of them wild boys from up Oakland way, Louise said with wide grin?"

"Might could. It'd only be one feller in Oakland, though."

"Who could that be? Ralph or Mose?

"They're busy. It'd just be me."

"Well, let's see, 'just me'. I'll check my appointment book." She fussed in her back pocket and pulled out folded up piece of paper Louise squinted at it, folded it back up and stuck it back in her pocket. "Guess I'm free. Could I get a ride up there?"

"Yes, ma'am. You could get a ride to go get some ice cream, too. Right now, I mean."

"I'm helping Ma and I'm trying to keep these wild Injuns over here from throwing that football on my hangin' up laundry. Missus Callendine should be here to pick them up pretty soon."

"You get it clear with your Mom and I'll handle the Injuns with the football. Deal?"

"Deal!"

Harriet Forest was also hanging up laundry on the clothesline, listening to the conversation. When Louise asked, Virgil smiled and said, "Yes!

Louise went to the sink, pumped a little water to wash her face and unbuttoned the top button on her shirt. As she ran a soapy rag around her neck and underarms, she hoped Virgil might notice she had finally filled out. She lingered a bit over the drying, allowing Virgil's blue-eyed gaze to behold her; they did. She felt cold—a case of the chilblains.

Louise paused in the doorframe for a short minute and then ran down the warped steps. young man, and when he looked back again headed straight for done

"I told these yahoos if they behaved and didn't dirty up any of your clean laundry, we'd have a treat for 'em when we got back. Right, fellas?"

"You bet, Virgil," they answered.

"You ready to go, Louise?"

"Yes, sir."

Virgil got up on Blackie and offered Louise a hand up. She grabbed the back of the saddle and jumped up, then put her arms around Virgil's waist tightly.

"Well OK, girl. Let's ride."

The younger boys from the neighborhood came around the house and yelled in unison.

"Weezy's got a boyfriend! Weezy's got a boyfriend!"

"Those little brats. I'm gonna skin them when I get home!"

"They're good kids, Louise."

"I guess."

"And you're good with kids, Lou." Virgil gave Blackie a little dig with his heels and his girl had to grab on tighter. "We haven't ridden like this for a while, Virgil."

"That's the truth. With working in the laundry and helping on the farm and the store. I've missed you, too. Guess we both have changed."

"Lumpier, I guess you might," Virgil said with a mischievous grin.

My face reddened; I was glad he couldn't see me blushing. I contemplated jumping off the back of the horse and running up and the river back home and not stopping until she reached Marietta. "Well, you can drop me off right here and I'll find my way home."

"Please don't be angry. You feel good and I'm sorry if I embarrassed you. It's just, well, you're a woman now. And well—shoot — I was actin' like a bigshot and now *I'm* embarrassed. Could we just get off for a minute and talk?"

"Sure," she answered. We were both still acting kind of shy.

"You know, Lou. When your folks moved here, it seemed like I was much older than you. But now that distance has shrunk. We're both old enough to be treated like adults. I'm 24, and you're 20."

"I reckon that's accurate, Virgil."

"Shoot, if it weren't for the Depression I would have asked—well, I mean, I probably would have asked you to—you know—earlier." Virgil was the one with the red face now.

"Asked what?" I said. "To go get ice cream earlier?" She balled up her fists and pressed them against her waist.

"You've got to know how I feel about you, Lou. I hope you do. See, it's just now I've got some things going for me. I'm making some money and feel like I've got a man's job. Before we got this contract, I was just hangin' around the farm. Like I was waiting for something to happen to me instead of making it happen.

I've got big plans, Lou. I want to go to college and study Agriculture. And then work for the Department of Agriculture, helping farmers. I don't want to be a farmer, but I like being around farms and helping people."

"That's good," she said.

"Very good," Virgil shot back

"And I like you, Virg. Have since I met you. And my folks like you because you are honest."

"Lou, I want a lot more than just friendship with you. I love you, girl—always have, always will."

"You're a good person. Sometimes I feel like I'm not a very good person. Like when I was getting in all those car accidents and losing my license and getting put in jail in Windsor. My folks about disowned me. Wouldn't have blamed them if they had, but I'm glad they didn't. And I sure am glad I'm still here in Morgan County and right here with you, right now, and I sure would be thankful if you'd let me kiss you."

She grabbed the back of his neck and pulled his mouth to hers and thought about the kisses she'd seen in the movies. It never occurred to her until that moment that tongues could take up so much room. But she'd never had two in her mouth at the same time before. At first, it was a little yucky. But after a bit, it felt pretty good.

"Wow, that was nice!" Virgil said as they disengaged.

"You said it!"

"I feel more like a cigarette than an ice cream, Louise."

"You got two?" she asked.

"Yeah, I got a half pack. Do you smoke?"

"Well, not regular. But I have had a few with Velma Shook walking home from Eastern Star."

He shook one up out of the pack and held it close to her lips. And then he pulled one out for himself. She coughed a little on the first drag. and

He looked worried.

"I'm OK, Virgil. In fact, I'm fine as frog hair. And that's pretty fine."

"I never heard that one before, Lou. Where'd you get that?"

"Well, I've got some cousins—Le Foret is their name—from up north on the Upper Sandusky and others in Maumee up by Toledo. They used to come down and help Dad with the farm. That's one of their expressions. French for Forest. My family traces our roots back to French trappers, Indians and slaves— escaped and freedmen. Our side switched to English spelling— Forest— a few generations back. "That first day when I met you and you stood up for me to those Sheets boys? That meant a lot to me at the time. See, I'm not ashamed of my bloodlines. But if those boys had started ragging on me my first day of school and kept it up, I would have been miserable. But after you talked to 'em, they stood up for me with the girls in the class. Because girls can be much worse than boys in situations like that."

The couple finished their cigarettes and got back on Blackie after they got each of the kids a Baby Ruth. They all dug in on the old table by the Forest's house.

"I better check and see if Mom is OK. Can you wait a little bit?"

"I can wait until Hell freezes over for you, Louise Forest."

Harriet needed a little help getting something together for Barb—a school project of some sort.

"Can you come back in an hour, Virgil? I'll be ready by then."

"You bet! See you in an hour, Lou."

Even though he was coming back and she was the one who had shooed him away, part of her didn't want Virgil to go. The day had been perfect up to that point, and she didn't want it ruined.

The young man felt the same way. He walked toward the pasture with a goofy look on his face.

They walked over to the pasture where Blackie was grazing. Virgil put the saddle on and walked the horse to the gate. Before heading home, Virgil came back over and hugged Louise—tight. And they had another one of those kisses. They both still felt like they were in the movies.

Virgil got Louise later that afternoon, and they rode up the hill to the Thomas house. Mrs. Thomas had her Eastern Star group over for supper. Louise carried dishes back and forth. Virgil scraped the plates and sat up in the corner on the counter and looked at the young woman in a way that was different from anything he'd ever known or imagined. It was like something in the movies or a book.

Like all Windsor High teenagers, Virgil and Louise had Miss Oldham for English during their senior years. Miss Oldham taught *Wuthering Heights* every year. Louise had loved that book and the events of this day made her feel a little like Catherine Earnshaw.

"Heathcliff, take me to Peniston Crag and fill my arms with heather!"

"What! Oh Cathy, we shan't be able to do that. But, I can take you to Roosterville and fill your arms with barley and chicken feathers."

Both dissolved in soft laughter and Virgil gave her a third kiss of the day just before they started on the dishes. Virgil had put the water on the stove earlier, and he filled the left-hand sink as Louise checked the dining room for stray dishes.

"Do you want to wash or dry, Heathcliff?"

"Oh, Cathy. I think I shall dry so I can snap my towel against your dusky haunches."

"OK, But, first, fill your arms with the tea tray and set it in the parlor."

When he returned, Louise was reading a yellowed poem that was tacked up inside of the window above the sink.

Pike's Peak

(By Mitchell Thomas.)

Why tower your hoary head so high?
Tis true you are a high and glorious mountain
Your snowy peak seems to reach the sky,
Your lofty head hangs o'er the fountain.
Many come to view you from far, far away
And scale your lofty peak to see the first glimpse of day.

'Tis true you hold a great treasure of gold,
Great depths within you dug by men
For wealth of your treasures untold,
As if to steal and rob you of them.
Yet you are only rock, sand and clay
And nothing of your wealth they say.

To men and mortals comes pleasure,
But you are ever unchanging the same
Always satisfied with your treasure.
But brave Pike who gave you his name
Has long ago gone to his rest
And left you the oldest citizen in the West.

You have been a landmark to guide
The weary traveler out on the plains,
But since people on cars must ride,
They never stop to thank you for your pains,
But ride on past and do not seem to know.
You whose hoary head is white with snow.

> You have seen the red warrior with his tent,
>
> And with him the buffalo has emigrated, too,
>
> Steam engines go where once they went,
>
> And cities stand within your view,
>
> Others may come and others may go,
>
> But you stand ever the same with your head in the

"Is this one of your mother's favorite poems?"

"Yes, it is her favorite."

"Who's the poet?"

"Mitchell Benaja Morris, Junior, Big Mitch."

"Your Dad. Well, that's romantic. What's the story there?"

"My Dad taught school around here for a few years and then went out and taught at mining camps—Cripple Creek by Pike's Peak and Golden, west of Denver, just east of Blackhawk and Central City. "He liked it out there a lot. But, after five years of that, with him coming home for only one month every year, Mom gave him an ultimatum: Come back and marry her before she turned thirty or lose her. So, he came back."

"Interesting. Any regrets?"

"I don't think so. Dad grew up listening to Mom's brothers talking about going out West, and then he went himself. Those Usher boys worked in the oil patch and the mines, and they'd come back and tell tales and such, and that sounded exciting. "And they'd come back every year for a month to loaf and tell stories at the Barlow Fair. That was all well and good. But they never married. And when they got older, well two of 'em stayed at these hotels for old folks. One, Jess, was in Wichita Falls, Texas and Rob was in Gallup, New Mexico. We'd stop and see them on vacations, and they'd still come back in the Fall. At some point, they started looking like sad, lonely old men. Dad was glad he came back. I think—I'm sure of it."

"Wow, that's quite a story. Did you ever want to go roam around?"

"Sure did. I was planning on it, but this durn Depression kind of put the kibosh on those plans."

"Think you could be happy stickin' around?"

"Louise, I think you know how I feel about you. Before we got that asphalt contract, I didn't really have any way to make a living that could put me in position to even think about getting married. Also, you were still in high school, and I know you are an intelligent young lady, capable of far more than just having kids and cleaning up after a family. I want a family and this asphalt job has kind of given me some confidence that I can be more than a hired hand on a farm. But that's not all I want. I'm planning to start OSU in the Fall. My Grandma, Sarah Jane. says she'll pay for my first year—tuition, board, and books. I've got a friend, Neil, who just finished his first year. He's got a place south of campus he shared with a guy who graduated, and he says I can stay with him for 15 bucks a month. And he can get me a part-time job washing dishes at Mills Cafeteria downtown. I think that's what I want. I'd like to have a career and a family. I don't have any great desire to live in Morgan County my whole life. But this is my home, and I'd surely like to be close enough to come down."

He snuck up behind me and wrapped me up.

"And I'd truly like to be your man, and your husband and father of your children. And if that doesn't scare you away, I think maybe we can be happy together."

1937

Charlotte Ross

<u>October 5, 1937</u>: US President Franklin D. Roosevelt gives the Quarantine Speech outlining a move away from neutrality and toward "quarantining" all aggressors.

Not everyone who grew up in Chesterfield was a Quaker. Nor was everyone in favor of equal rights for Negroes. But, Chesterfield's history as an important part of the Underground Railroad in southern Ohio resulted in a high percentage of residents classified as Negro or Mulatto. Some of these families had been in Marion Township for generations. More than a few of these folks had 'mixed' with white residents, which resulted in a fair number of separations and divorces. Some of which resulted in the parlance of the time so-called *mixed marriages*.

Most folks in Chesterfield let bygones be bygones; others, not so much. Some of those folks with the deepest grudges hadn't even been alive when the supposed miscegenation occurred. Still, the "N-word" stirred powerful emotions and, sometimes, actions.

The Ross family experienced a peripheral episode of mixing. Edgar, father of Claude, Twyla, and Minta, packed up his things in 1899 and moved in with a black woman, Reba Johnson, on Fischer Howard Lane. He stayed there, one mile from the farm where he'd lived and worked for all years until his death in 1928. By all accounts Reba and Edgar were a happy couple.

In the same way that some medical conditions run in families but don't affect all the offspring uniformly, enmity toward Edgar manifested itself differently among his descendants. Twyla and Claude rarely visited their father and, only rarely, spoke disparagingly of him and his behavior. However, Claude's wife, Nanny, decided that their children—Penrose, Twyla, and Charlotte—needed to know their paternal grandfather. Nanny announced that she and the children were going to start visiting Edgar and Reba. Claude and Nanny had a good marriage, and she knew that her husband didn't hate his father.is failure to visit was a kind of backward way of supporting his mother, Virginia, who passed in 1917. Deep down, Claude was a gentle soul.

His sister, Minta, on the other hand, was high-strung and mean spirited. She never married and became the default babysitter for her nephew and two nieces. Her concern for her mother, Virginia, manifested itself exclusively as a virulent, verbal hatred of her father. Her tirades—delivered mostly while babysitting the youngsters in their extended family—were legendary. She used the Nword regularly and never understood why town folks shunned her and not her brother, Claude.

The three people who spent the most time with her reacted quite differently. Penrose certainly developed no love for Negroes. He used the N-word with his male friends from grade school into old age. He ignored Reba Johnson when Claude took them for visits. Pen could be prickly, but it was more of a way to keep people at a distance. He had a loud bark at times but no real bite. Deep down, he was a good man and a good provider.

Charlotte loved going to her Grandpa's house. She was a cute little girl who could sing and dance and tell jokes. Nanny worried about Charlotte. Folks in the family talk about girls revealing the Young' in 'em. Grandma Virginia, Edgar's mother was a Young had a history of insanity among their women, including a number who died up in Columbus on the Hilltop at the State Asylum. Charlotte was certainly high-strung, but she made it into adulthood before exhibiting serious problems. And Lord knows, she had some tough breaks in her life.

Twyla showed her "Young from an early age. She and Minta were joined at the hip. Neither of them ever connected with other folks much. They both treated colored folks like dirt. The two of them spent a good part of their adult years living with Nanny and Claude. They must not have grasped how distasteful all their coarse talk about colored folks was. If they did, I suppose they just didn't care.

The ironic thing was they both looked down their noses at everyone—not just colored folks either—family, church members, neighbors, everyone. They made their bed and had to lie in it. Twyla slipped into serious mental illness in her mid-20s and was taken to the Hilltop where she died shortly after the War. Minta spent her last ten years alone rambling around a tiny bedroom in Nanny's last house on Marion Street. Claude died in '49 the year before Minta.

For an only child, Nanny had a long life full of friends, family, and loved ones. And she nearly outlived 'em all—children, grandchildren, friends, preachers at the Methodist Church, choir directors, doctors, dentists and librarians. On her 100th birthday, May 20, 1983, a florist from Athens gave her a bouquet with 100 red roses. She took it to the high school and donated the flowers to make prom corsages for couples who couldn't afford one. When she died two months later, they had her service in the old high school gym in Windsor and a caravan of more than 100 cars came to Chesterfield for burial in the town where she lived for nearly 80 years.

1938

Gabby Thurlow

<u>August 12, 1938</u>: German military mobilizes.

[Item from *The Portage Weekly News, 5/28/1938*]

> Portage High School teachers and staff were happy to celebrate the forty-fourth-class graduation. The ceremony and the dance afterwards took place in the Masonic Lodge in Kalamazoo. Thirty-nine graduates—twenty-one girls and eighteen boys—and their families enjoyed music provided by Rosy McHargue and Ted Weems and their combo. Both men played with Bix Beiderbecke in the 1920s. Principal Ted Jones assured this reporter that: "a good time was had by all."

May 28, 1938 My English teacher, Miss Laverne Osgood gave me a very nice leather notebook with a zipper and a lock for a graduation present. She always encouraged me in class and said I was a good writer. She told me many of the greatest writers kept a journal. She hoped that I would keep writing. So, this is my first entry.

June 3, 1938: We buried my Father today. He was 68, but looked like he was 86. As the youngest of 15 children, I don't remember Dad as anything but old and worn-out.

Ten of his 13 children still living came to the funeral. Vernal and Joseph had gone to Montana after they quit high school and never come back. Ma got letters from Joseph now and again. I'm not sure Vernal could write, or maybe he's dead. The other living child that didn't attend the funeral was Miranda. She killed a young man who had raped her daughter, Sadie. The boy's father was a deputy sheriff, so Miranda got a 20-year bid. She is serving out her last five years in a state penitentiary in Flint.

June 18, 1938

Even though we weren't close, I had heard stories about Pa. I guess he drank a lot as a young man. Nothing shocking there. He had also been anxious to go to war. The youngest of 12 children, and wanted to make a mark for himself. He enlisted in the Army and was getting ready to ship over to Cuba when the fighting ended.

I know something about who survived infancy. People have joked my whole life about my Ma and Pa both bein' give out by the time I came along to explain my size.

As I was leaving the cemetery, I was surprised to see Miss Osgood. She was standing away from the gravesite and dressed in Sunday clothes. She gave me a little wave and I walked quickly over to her.

"Miss Osgood, what are you doing here?"

"I saw the notice in the newspaper about you father's death and thought I would come and pay my respects."

We looked at each other. She had on an outfit that I'd never seen her wear to school. It wasn't exactly what you'd wear to Church. But more like what you might wear to a Speakeasy. Kind of a cross between the two.

After an uncomfortable silence, she noticed the journal she'd given me.

"Why, Melvyn, it does my heart good to see you carrying your journal with you."

"It was a swell present, Miss Osgood," I replied.

"You may call me Laverne, Melvyn."

"Thank you, Laverne, "I said turning away lest I blush.

"Do you have big plans for the summer, Laverne?"

"I plan to visit my mother in South Bend for a week in July. And I am working on my Master's Thesis. I hope to have a completed draft done before school starts."

"That sounds very interesting, Miss Laverne. What is the subject of your Thesis?"

"I am exploring concepts of beauty and disfigurement in American literature of the first half of the 19th century. Using writers like Hawthorne, Melville, Poe and others."

"That sounds very interesting Miss—uh, Laverne. I'd love to read that when you're done."

"I would be happy to share that with you when it's completed. If you want to get in touch with me, I plan to be at the Downtown Branch of the Library in the Archives in the basement every Saturday from 10 AM to 6 PM."

I turned away again, not quite sure whether she was inviting me to meet her on Saturday afternoons or simply explaining her plans for finishing her Thesis.

"Now, enough about me. What are your plans, Melvyn?"

"Well, Laverne, I may have a job at the big dairy farm seven miles north of town. I should find out next week."

"That sounds lovely, Melvyn, to commune daily with fecund nature. To both witness and facilitate the procreative process that is at the heart of life itself. It sounds so positively something out of D.H. Lawrence."

I remember listening to Miss Osgood in class and being swept away at times by her orations. She'd gotten to me again.

"Yes, ma'am it is good be a part of that, especially if you are able to avoid stepping in the waste product of all that fecundity!"

She gave a giggle and grabbed my hand. "Oh, Melvyn, I am so happy right now. I will look forward to more visits over the summer."

I walked Laverne back to the library downtown. As we parted, she grabbed my hands and held on tight.

"Good luck getting the job you mentioned. Don't forget your old teacher—*c'est moi*? She curtsied awkwardly. And keep writing."

Boy, my head was spinning as I walked home past the dime stores and newsstands. I looked at the trinkets, candies and such. I'd spent my whole life walking down these streets past these stores without a nickel in my pocket. I'd never been aware of feeling any desire to buy things, except for Ma on her birthday or Mother's Day.

I sure felt the urge buy something nice for Laverne, though. And I couldn't, not yet. But I sure planned to once I got my first paycheck.

June 11, 1938: I've never had much. But I have done the best I could my whole life. My oldest brother, Devlin, died in France in the last days of the First World War. I went past his headstone before Dad's service. It's a small stone, but that bronze marker describing his service in the Great War is something no one can ever take away.

I'm not the smartest guy in the world, but it doesn't take a brain surgeon to figure out that this world is a powder keg fixin' to go off. And sooner or later, our country will be involved. I want to see the elephant, as I've read about in books. I'd also like for someone to look up to me and say I'd done alright, and not just talk about how little I was or all the things I couldn't do.

June 26, 1938: I started the job on a big dairy farm outside Kalamazoo last week. They've got a big bunkhouse for the hands and they serve breakfast and sandwiches at lunch. There are about 40 of us hands. Most of the fellows are nice guys. There's a couple of fellows that that don't pull their own weight. I think they're drinkers. Must have a still somewhere. Anyhow—so far so good. We work 12 on and two off, so I'll get to go to Ma's in three days.

June 30,1938: Just got back from Ma's house. They had a kind of party for me—Ma and four of my sisters. It was nice. On the way to the farm—a seven-mile walk—I stopped at the Special K Diner a couple of miles from the farm.

There was a waitress there, Nancy. She's pretty and seeing as there weren't many customers, we talked quite a bit. She told me what her schedule was and allowed that she wouldn't mind seeing me again. Hot Dog!

July 14, 1938 I've been thinking about Nancy a lot. I'm going to try and go see her on my next two days off. I'm thinking maybe we could have a picnic or go to the movies or something. I need to get over to see her and try to make a date this coming Sunday. I sold an extra pair of good work gloves to one of the fellows for $1.50. I can use that to buy something at the diner

July 26, 1938: I managed to get over to the Special K Diner and Nancy and I had a cup of coffee and some pie. She said if I come over Sunday morning, she'll have a picnic lunch packed and we can go swimming at a lake about a mile from the Diner. That sounds like fun. I'll get paid Friday. I can get Laverne a present and take it to her at the library. And on Sunday go swimming with Nancy. I can't wait to see her in a bathing suit!

1939

Doak Benoit

<u>September 1, 1939</u>: Germany invades Poland, starting World War Two.

I was raised up in Carlyss, Louisiana until I was eight years old. That's where my Pap, Clayton Benoit, died. He was working on a well in a rice field and got tangled up in the gears and drowned.

He had kids by his first marriage with a gal from Ohio. They stayed in Vinton County with kin. My mom and I moved back to Ohio, where she'd been raised. She had met up with Pap when he was rough neckin' on the oil fields in southern Ohio. I never did get back down to Louisiana.

My mom was only sixteen when I was born. When we got to Ohio, she left me with her mother in New Lex and she commenced to go to Maumee. They knew folks there, and my mom stayed with her grandmother, helping her with nursin' folks at home and such. She worked with some of the cousins at a restaurant, too.

She ended up getting married and havin' beaucoup step kids and stayin' up there. I stayed in New Lex with my Gram. She was a Le Foret from the part of the family up by Maumee, came mostly from a clan of Indian gals and French trappers from way back. There was also a clan up north of Kalamazoo.

We had relations from down 'round Chesterfield. A group of kin from Maumee moved south and some a dem mixed with some mulattos around those parts, leftovers from the Underground Railroad.

No matter. Anyway, it was me and Gram. Her kids were scattered—some in jail, some dead, most just gone. She told me when I left high school after Junior year, "Doak, you is five-foot nothing, and butt ugly with a pot belly. And you ain't never gonna make no gal swoon. But you got somethin' else will get you through. You are a leader of men. Not like a Big Boss-man, more like a Straw-boss, they'd a called it back in the old days. I use to see you out there with the kids when you all was digging a hole or building a treehouse. You didn't never turn a spade or pound a nail, but you told the others what they'd need to do the job, and den you make sure they got the tools they need to get it done. And they listen to you and do what you say. That will be the way you get by in this life, Doak. You'll be able to make a living. And if you ever going to get you a gal, it'll be because of that gift. 'Cause lots of gals is impressed by someone can get other men to work hard. And they know that foremen make good wages and they don't get all dirty like the workin' stiffs."

1939

John Hunt Simon

January, 1940: 22,000 Polish officers, policemen, and others are massacred by the Soviet NKVD in the Katyn massacre.

"Oh, Johnny, is it true? That you got a full scholarship to USC? Oh, Johnny, that's where movie stars live in Southern California. Wow, would I love to see Errol Flynn or Cary Grant. Gosh!" The girl seated behind the driver shrugged her shoulders and straightened her dress.

"Yes, Sue, it is true. I'll be studying Aeronautical Engineering," the tall young man next to the girl said enthusiastically. He gave a sly wink in the mirror to the driver.

"So, that means you'll be a pilot, then, right?"

"No, I'd be working on designing planes. I mean, I guess I could be a pilot, too, but the courses are for Engineers who design aircraft."

"Gosh, Johnny, I think those RAF pilots are just so dreamy! You could be one of them and wear those scarves and goggles, just like on the newsreels."

The driver, a tall slim woman with the same toothy smile as the boy, caught his eye in the rearview mirror and gave her brother a look of mock horror. "Remind me, Ruthie, when we get to your driveway. Alright?"

"Sure thing, Polly. You've still got about a quarter mile to go. Look for a brick mailbox with a bluebird figure on the top."

"Thanks. I see it. Now I remember." The car fishtailed a little as it turned onto the pea gravel driveway but Polly controlled it and pulled up in a small circle in front of the porch that ran the full width of large frame house.

"Thanks, Polly," the girl said as she playfully punched the boy on his long, bony arm. "Johnny, remember, you promised to help me with algebra at lunch every day until you leave."

"I won't forget, Ruthie. See you tomorrow."

"Not if I see you first, Slim," the girl said with a giggle.

"Get up in the front seat, dreamboat." Polly fluttered her eyelids. "Before I develop a case of the vapors."

"OK, Sis. Don't faint or anything."

"Old Ruthie's got it bad."

"She's alright, Polly."

"I know, Johnny, she's a nice girl. It's just, well, you got your pick of girls around here, Johnny. For that matter, you've always had your pick. We are better off than most folks. And at the risk of sounding creepy, you are a good lookin' boy—man. If you repeat that to anyone, I will hit you over the head with a baseball bat and dump you in the holler behind the barn."

"Repeat what, sis?" he said with a frightful look.

"If these gals had any idea what a goofball you are, they wouldn't be flocking around you."

"I'm not stringing anyone along. I mean, what am I supposed to do?"

"Behave like Dad, and you'll be OK. Remember how the women chased Dad after mother passed?"

"Yes, ma'am. We had desserts coming out the ying yang for that first six months."

"Part of me wishes Dad had found someone, but I don't mind the fact he didn't remarry. Does that sound selfish, Johnny?"

"Not really, sis. But, if he'd found someone, you might have found someone, too."

"Maybe. I use to think about that a lot. Not so much anymore."

"You know, with Merle working in Bowling Green and Dennis in Nashville, you could get out a little more."

With a sidelong glance and slight frown, the woman asked, "And just who do you have in mind for me to 'get out' with?"

"Nobody in particular, although Sweeney Jones has always been sweet on you, and he's got a good business going."

"Some business!"

"There will always be folks looking for moonshine in Kentucky, sister. An economist might call that a case of inelastic demand."

"Sweeney has more ex-wives than he does teeth!" Polly shot back with look of mock horror.

Polly drove along the gently oscillating two-lane road home. Every curve and pothole were familiar to them, as were the towering maples and oaks that crowded the berm and stretched up until they nearly formed a canopy across the road in places.

"Seriously, Johnny. Dad is going to be so proud of you. Are you going to tell him tonight?"

"After dinner, I think. If he doesn't have to make a house call."

"You OK, Johnny? Things are happening quickly. This part about leaving in three weeks is sudden. But I guess they're interested in getting Aeronautical Engineers as quickly as possible."

"Yeah—I guess. It's just, well it's one thing to be a Big Man on Campus in Dunmor, Kentucky. But Los Angeles, that another thing. If it wasn't for Pop, I wouldn't be a big deal here either, Sis."

"That's not true, Johnny. You been at the top of your class in every subject since seventh grade. And you're on Student Council and played sports. And you're not a jerk, either. But I will deny ever having said that." She poked him in the ribs and let out a laugh.

"I'm kind of afraid of going that far away. And I'll miss you and Dad."

"You'll do fine, Johnny," she said as they turned into the long driveway leading to a house fit for a genuine Kentucky Colonel. It belonged to Doctor Hardy Simon, the most respected Doctor and man in Dunmor, Kentucky.

BOOK FOUR:

RUMORS OF WAR: A STORM APPROACHING

1941—1945

An eternal verity from time memorial is that new recruits for new wars will spend time with veterans of the last war, being taught the lore of their Outfit—their Tribe.

<u>May 10 and 11, 1941</u>: Heavy German bombing of London; British bomb Hamburg.

A slim man, not young, but still lean skipped down the three steps from the train onto the pavement at the train stop in Roxbury. His movement was animated, but a certain set to his jaw indicated apprehension. He moved quickly over and into the Roxbury Store. The gaunt figure of Henry Forest met him as he entered.

"Howdy, Virgil," Henry said. He broke into a long series of choked coughing.

"You OK, Mr. Forest?"

"Sure," he said through his handkerchief. "Darned summer colds are the worst. How's school going?"

"Just fine, Sir."

"They teaching you which end of the cow to milk up there at Ag school?"

"Yes, Sir." The younger man smiled a bit. "Do you know what my Dad's doin' today?"

"I believe he's up at the house. Ralph's goin' to do the mail route today."

"Have you got a horse I could borrow to get up home?"

"Why sure. Give me a minute, and I'll ring up Louise at the house." The older man was winded as he shuffled into the office.

Virgil walked out onto the porch. He could just see the stone markers through the tree trunks at Big Bottom Park across the river. How many Saturday and Sunday afternoon picnics had he attended? And how many late-night dances?

He and Louise had spent a lot of time in the back seat of Little Mitch's Old Ford at Big Bottom. They finally consummated things on that big built-in table next to the Forest's house, on a steamy late August night in 1937.

He'd told her then she was the only girl for him.

You got a funny way of showing it, Virgil Thomas," she'd replied," seeing as you're fixin' to move up to Columbus and go to Ohio State with all them *hoity toity* sorority girls."

"Those girls ain't nothin' to me," he'd told her. "Besides, between classes, studying, and working at Mills Cafeteria, I won't have time for those shenanigans, see? I'm planning to get finished as fast as I can. If I go Summer quarters, I can get out in three-and-a half years."

"And then what?" she'd said with a slight quiver he'd never heard before.

"And then—well, after that, I guess I'll just have to come back down here and find a pretty girl to marry," he said softly.

"You got anyone in particular in mind?"

"Well, I ran into Jenny Dingess at the train depot in McConnelsville today comin' in."

"I suppose you got her a sammich."

"No, she had a big old feller, and they were eating out of a picnic basket. Looked like he was on his lunch break."

The two chuckled a little.

"There's only one girl for me, Louise. If it wasn't for the damned Depression, I would have asked you to marry me a long time ago. If you can just wait a little longer, we can still have all those things we've spoken of before—children, a home, love."

Virgil's reverie was interrupted by the sounds of saddlehorses. He turned around. Louise sat astride AJ, an offspring of Ajax. She was leading another of Ajax's line— a seven-year-old horse named Homer.

"What are you goo-hawin' at farm boy? You need a ride?"

"Yes, ma'am. I'd be much obliged."

"Will you take these two out back so they can get some water and grain? I need to speak to Pa."

"Sure, take your time. I'll be out front somewhere."

Virgil led the two horses around back and pumped some water into the mossy trough. He admired the horses and thought briefly of the fun he'd had riding Ajax. Virgil reached for a cigarette but had to retrace his steps and get his jacket from the porch. He flew back down the three steps he'd taken nearly every day of his life. When he was young, he thought those steps would lead him from their small store out and into the big, wide world. He'd gotten away eventually, but not in the way he'd dreamed of when he was a boy listening to the Usher boys at reunions and fairs. He moved across the gravel road and down an embankment littered with extraneous pieces of metal, busted ties, and coal clinkers, then picked his way over the train tracks and settled on top of a bundle of railroad ties. He lit a cigarette and gazed at the Muskingum River.

They'd called it 'The Blue Muskingum, Danube of the West' when he was a boy. It was no longer blue. Fertilizer and other chemicals in soil runoff had turned it grey-brown. He hoped to be able to work on projects that could mitigate this kind of thing. The Soil Conservation Service was working on those issues. He hoped to be able to join them after he finished school. But things had changed and here he was nearing age 27, with his life back up in the air.

In an instant, the plans he'd been making since he started at Ohio State had been scrambled. Suddenly plans that would involve getting out into the big wide world weren't so appealing.

"Permission to come aboard, Sir."

"Permission granted, mate!"

Louise scrambled atop the ties and laid a hand gently on Virgil's cheek. "You OK, Virgil?"

He shrugged. "I'll see in a while, Lou."

"I'm happy to see you. I miss you when you're away. You seem sad, Virg. Can I help?"

"I'm glad to see you, too. I miss you, too. Just being with you helps, Lou."

They embraced tightly. Louise's youngest sister, Opal, approached them slowly. After a long minute, Opal cleared her throat. The pair drew apart and Louise blushed a bit.

"Sneaking up on us, huh?" Louise said with a stern look.

"Sorry," Opal said while looking down at her shoes. "Ma told me to come get you. She needs you to deliver some laundry to Bryant Hook, right quick."

"Opal, don't be embarrassed. Virgil and I haven't seen each other for quite a while. If you can go get a horse and bring him over, we can head back home. I need to speak with Virgil for a minute. OK?"

"Yes."

"If you were to wait up at the store, you might find a chance to get some candy," Virgil said with the first genuine smile he'd been able to muster for several days.

"That would be swell," the girl said.

"Louise, we need to talk, but I need to see Dad first and talk to him. Is it OK if I take AJ?"

"Sure, Virgil."

"I'll come to your folk's house from Dad's."

"How about we get together at the Store? I told my Dad I'd clean up and restock for him tonight. He's not doing so well. I surely hate to see him suffer, Virg."

"He's a good man, Louise. So's my Dad. He's getting older, too. We've had issues over the years, but I've always known he would be there for me if I needed him. Say, we both better get going. I'll see you in a few hours, Lou. Here's some candy money you can give to Opal." Virgil deposited six quarters in Louise's pocket.

"Big Spender with the younger girls, I reckon. Take care."

Virgil reflected on Life, Death and Fate on the ride up the hill from the store to the Thomas farm. He wondered how many times he'd been up this hill—coming home from school on Ajax, a few times on foot in the middle of the night after running the family car into a tree, and the many times with Louise hanging on so tightly he thought they'd surely never separate.

He wasn't sure what exactly to say to his Father or even how to broach the subject at hand. His Mother, Anne, was sitting on a glider on the porch embroidering. Virgil stopped short and quieted Homer. He watched this woman with wonder. He had never known her to raise her voice or speak an unkind word to or about anyone.

She had a way with people, treating everyone with respect and kindness. She and Big Mitch got along well. He had a bit of a temper, but Anne had a way of calming him down with a look instead of an argument. They were a good match.

Suddenly, this old farmhouse Virgil had been so anxious to be shed of looked like the finest place in the world. With a catch in his throat, he gave AJ a little kick and they ambled into the lane that wound past the side porch and on to the barn.

He saw his mother look up and adjust her glasses. She put her embroidery on the porch railing and stood up slowly. Virgil saw the signs of age in the way she moved, particularly as she opened and closed her arthritic hands. He tied the reins loosely to the pipe railing on the steps up to the porch.

"Virgil, what are you doing here, son?"

"I came to see my best girl, Ma," he moved quickly over to her and embraced her.

"What a nice surprise," she said with a smile. "But aren't you missing school?"

"Yes, ma'am, but I need to talk to Dad."

"You aren't—I mean— you're not in trouble, are you?"

"No. Is Dad home?"

"Yes, he's in the back room at his desk. I'll set an extra place for dinner."

"I'm not sure I'll be staying, Mom."

"I'll set a place, just the same."

"I'm going to check the pasture gate and I'll be right back."

Big Mitch set up an office in his daughter Grace's room after she got married and moved away. He'd lined the two outer walls with bookshelves and got an old desk that had belonged to one his wife's uncle at his estate sale. Though not quite as impressive as the rolltop in the store, it was still a good piece of furniture. He had a glider rocker he'd made in one corner of the room with a side table, usually stacked with books by Zane Grey, Harold Bell Wright and James Ball Naylor. Two cane-bottom chairs that had been salvaged from the store after the 1913 Flood sat in front of a writing table.

Big Mitch was showing his 70 years. He was as rail thin as ever but not quite as sinewy. The distance from his chin to his belt buckle had shrunk considerably, a victim of gravity and diminishing bone density. The bounce in his step had faded a bit. When no one was looking, he navigated the steps one at a time. His mental acuity, however, was still sharp. Like many older men in that era, especially those serving on draft boards or having sons heading overseas, the stress and worry exacerbated the natural diminution of their mental faculties.

The casualties of this coming conflagration would not be confined solely to the young men and women serving in combat zones. It also included wives and older parents, from Hoboken to Helena, worrying that their loved ones would not survive and be able to establish themselves as workers, spouses, and parents.

Big Mitch had sent a telegram to his son that morning, but after three calls, the telegraph office still couldn't confirm delivery. Virgil's roommate, Ross Neil, had just gotten off third shift at the bakery where he worked, when Mitch telephoned. He hadn't seen Virgil since the previous day, but said he'd tell him to call home next time he saw Virgil.

Virgil headed straight for the train station after getting the telegram from Ross. He'd spent the train ride considering all the different scenarios that might play out.

The sound of Virgil's footsteps taking the stairs two at a time roused Big Mitch from his reverie. By the time Mitch pulled himself to his feet and stood behind the desk, his twenty-year-old son fidgeted behind a cane-bottom chair only, five feet from his Father.

"Virgil, I've been trying to reach you, son. I talked to Ross a couple of times and sent a telegram."

"I figured it would be better for us to have a face-to-face talk, Dad."

"Have a seat then, son."

The two men were in limbo as they heard the measured tread of Anne Thomas. She ascended the steps one by one. They heard the familiar squeaking of the third and 12th steps and the sound at the top of her slightly labored breathing.

The tall, still-elegant figure of Anne Usher Thomas stepped through the threshold. She carried a platter with a coffee pot, two cups, two saucers, creamer, sugar bowl and two spoons. Before Virgil could rise, she placed the platter on the desk.

"Thought you two might want some coffee," she said with a feeble smile. She turned and left without another word.

Big Mitch poured two cups, placed each on a saucer and set one on the desk in front of the chair his son's hands gripped. Virgil sat down, and the two men stirred sugar and cream into their cups. The china was the set from Mitch and Anne's wedding, a fact not lost on Big Mitch.

"Your Mother got out her wedding china, I guess she judges this to be a momentous conversation, son."

"Maybe you'll have another room available to switch over to a library or for storage pretty soon."

"Your Mom doesn't know about what we're here to discuss. But she will before this day is over."

Virgil nearly choked on his coffee. "I guess you didn't think it was very important, then."

"On the contrary, I believe this will be one of the most important conversations I'll ever have in my life." The older man removed his glasses and cleaned them, gently rubbing them, with a soft cloth between the thumb and middle finger of his gnarled right hand.

"Right up there with the talk Anne and I had about getting married. She gave me an ultimatum—marry her before she turned 30, or I'd lose her. I'd got back from teaching in Central City ten days before her 30th birthday. We were married nine days later." Mitch held the cup to his lips and took a sip.

"You and your older brother each had more than one 'Come to Jesus' talk from me about behaving properly with regards to alcohol and driving and such. Grace and Ralph never needed one of those talks, but that doesn't make them any better or worse than you and Little Mitch. Hell, my brothers George and Joseph never needed "the Talk' from my Dad. But I got two or three of them. This talk will be different, though. This talk will be between two adults. So, let us begin."

Each man took a deep breath.

"Dad, I got a draft notice saying I have to report for conscription on June 30th. That's less than two weeks. And I just started summer quarter last week. I can be finished with my degree after Fall quarter, if I keep going."

"I'm aware of that, son."

"Dad, I got started so late. I'm 27. I've been working hard, too."

Big Mitch nodded. "That is reflected in your GPA, Son. We are all proud of you."

"And, Dad, there's Louise. She—I mean I—we are in love, and I want to marry her after I finish school. She's the one, Dad."

"Louise is a fine girl. I guess she's not a girl anymore, she's a woman now, Virgil. She would be a welcome addition to our family, but now may not be the time for a wedding. I guess we need to get comfortable and have a chin-wag."

"I'm almost done with school. A good life is right out there waiting for me. It's as if I can almost reach out and touch it, it's so close. I wished I'd

54

started earlier, but I can't do anything about that. It just doesn't seem fair, Dad."

"Virgil, as the head of the draft board down here, I can tell you we've had to make some tough calls. Right now, we're just drafting from a pool of single men without children or aging parents to care for. All these fellows are put in a pool and we draw the number of slips for the number of men that the District tells us we need to draft."

"Well, how many folks was that for this drawing, Dad?"

"Thirty."

"Who drew the slips?"

"I did, son."

"Which one was I?"

"You were number 31."

"What! Why did you draw 31?"

"Well, the 30th slip belonged to Leon Dutro. But, he had a bad car wreck just a few days earlier and broke both legs. We had to draw another slip."

"Dad, wasn't there anything you could do for me? To keep me out, or at least let me finish school?"

"Virgil, I could have, and I almost did. But son, I couldn't ask someone else's son to do what I wouldn't ask of my own. This draft is only for 12 months. There's talk of extending it to 18 months, but nothing definite yet. But if you follow what's going on in Europe and in the Pacific, you know what's coming." The old man sighed. "I felt bad when I drew that 31st slip, son. But I couldn't bring myself to draw again. And then I thought, you were paying a high price so I could appear to be honest and upright. But that really wasn't it, son. It's a matter of fairness. We have families in Morgan County who have had two or three brothers drafted. I couldn't make an exception. I hope you understand."

Virgil walked over to the window and looked out at some gray clouds moving quickly east approaching the canopy of the trees on the west bank of the Muskingum.

55

"I do understand, Dad. You're the best man I've ever known. I want to have a family like we have. And a marriage like you and Mom. Louise and I have spoken of these things. But I just thought I should wait until I got my degree and had a job. I guess we could go down to West Virginia to a Justice of the Peace—we almost did that last year."

"You know, Virgil, you are a grown man capable of making your own decisions. I've been paying close attention to the news from this War that is engulfing our World. It doesn't take a genius to figure out the worst is yet to come. Our country is going to be involved. We're already starting to gear up industrially. That's going to help people that have been struggling since the Crash. The other piece of this will involve us putting troops on the ground. This draft is just the start. I could blow smoke and tell you that this draft is just for one year and you'll be home. But the truth is, like I've already said, they're already talking about extending it to 18 months. It takes a long time to get soldiers trained. "I'm not going to insult your intelligence, son. Little Mitch is starting to get more and more hours. This war effort needs engineers to move men and material. Ralph is married with children. He's going to get on with Dupont as a millwright–they make a lot of things the military needs. Grace and her family are staying in Arizona. She'll be helping with induction physicals for the National Guard troops. If I could take your place I would. But they don't need old men. I want you to think about how you'd feel if you wrangled a deferment now and got drafted in six months. Or if you get out of the serving altogether by getting married. "Son, I think this war is important. World War I was important. We didn't do much in that one until it was almost over. The one before that—Spanish-American—was just about grabbing territory. This one is about mass murder, people being forced into slavery and then killed. Our country is not perfect, far from it, but we don't just kill and enslave people because they we have a disagreement with them, or don't like their religion, or because we need cheap labor. Hopefully we've learned from our own mistakes on that score. And as down as we've been with this Depression, here in the United States, folks in lots of those places in Europe and other places have it worse. I read somewhere recently that this War is just the continuation of World War I—The Final Act—you might say. And son, we need to settle it this time, so we can get on with things."

They each sat back and sipped coffee. Big Mitch poured himself and his son another cup.

"You know, Virgil, I never thought of myself as lining up with the Democrats, but I think FDR has gotten us back on the right track, his programs addressing the Depression are working out—we saw what it did for us and the other fellows your age with that paving contract. And it also helped all the folks down here by giving us good roads. FDR is having a time getting the country ready for this war, too. This draft right now is just the smallest start. And that won't be the end of it, either." Mitch finished his coffee and ran his gnarled fingers through his thinning hair.

"So, what should I do, Dad? What do you think I should do?"

"I can't tell you what to do, Virgil. You'll need to do some serious thinking. It would be possible for you to file a request for a deferment based on your schooling. If you and Louise got married before June 30th, I suppose you could put in for a deferment for that, too. But if you do put in for a deferment for any reason, I'll have to recuse myself from the deliberations. That will leave four members voting. You'll need three of four votes. And I wouldn't be discussing your case with the other board members."

"So, I should report for induction, I guess."

"Virgil, I've never felt as conflicted over anything in my life. I love you very much, and I feel your pain. But I also love this country. And every parent of every man whose number we've drawn has felt torn. I don't believe we can win this war if we can't count on families to encourage their sons show up for induction. No one wants their children to be sent off to war, but unless we are willing to do this we may find ourselves in thrall to Hitler's Third Reich."

The room assumed a preternatural silence. Mitch stared at his fingernails and Virgil looked out the window.

"Is it alright if I stay here tonight, Dad?"

"Of course, this will always be your home. We'll make up your bed."

"I'm going to go have dinner with Louise and her folks, and then I'll be back."

"Alright, Virgil, tell your mother you'll be back and that you love her. I haven't spoken to her about this yet. But I will over our dinner, tonight."

"Yes, sir. I'll see you later, Dad."

Virgil took the steps two at a time, turned left at the bottom of the steps, and stepped into the kitchen. Anne turned to face him with a plate of sliced tomatoes sprinkled with sugar and covered with vinegar.

"Bet you can't get fresh tomatoes like these in Columbus," she said with a beatific smile.

"No, ma'am. Got to come back to God's country for tomatoes like these."

"Are you staying for dinner?"

"No. I'm going to eat over with Louise and her family. But I'll be back to stay the night, if that's OK."

"Virgil, you can stay over here any time. This house sure seems empty without any children left."

"Thanks, Mom. I miss being home."

"Is your father alright? He's seemed preoccupied the last few days."

"He's got some things on his mind. But I think he'll be OK. We'll all be OK." "I'll be back by ten o'clock, otherwise I'll call."

"Give Louise and her folks my best wishes."

"I sure will, Mom. I've got to go."

"Take a lantern with you, Virgil."

"Yes, ma'am."

The sun showed as a faint orange smear visible through the dark green canopy in the west. He'd be riding in darkness as he passed the store in ten minutes. His mind raced with thoughts of Louise and how their conversation would end. By the time Virgil hit the steep downhill stretch above the store, he'd decided he would ask Louise to marry him, but he would not seek a deferment. Instead, he'd ask her to wait for him until he returned or died. It wasn't what he had envisioned when he'd realized she was the girl for him some ten years earlier. Twelve or even 18 months weren't that long, he supposed. But his father had talked about a longer war. How long could you ask a beautiful, young woman to wait?

He dismounted and led AJ into the small enclosure behind the Forest's cabin. Homer was grazing in the far corner-.

"Zat you, Virgil?" Mrs. Forest called through the back window over the kitchen sink.

"Yes'm, it is. I'll be right in." He stopped briefly before closing the gate, watching moonlight play on the dark river rushing along through the dark night.

Louise met him at the gate and gave him a hug and a kiss. "Supper's ready, Virg, and so am I. It's nice out here, Virg. Let's come back out after dinner and talk."

"Sounds good, Louise."

The lovers entered through the front door. All three sisters were sitting on an old rope bed that had been jerry-rigged into a couch.

"Thanks for the candy, Virgil," Opal said with a smile.

Barbara, Merlene, Louise and Mrs. Forest chimed in with similar offerings.

"You ladies are all very welcome," Virgil said with a tired grin.

As he waited for the womenfolk to be seated around the kitchen, he felt a tug at his sleeve.

"Virgil, I ain't a lady, on account a 'cause I'm only six."

"Age's not got anything to do with being a lady. You most certainly are a lady in my book, Opal. And don't let anyone tell you different. All you Forest women are ladies."

"Gosh, so does that mean that I'm very welcome, too?"

"You betcha. Now let me escort you to dinner, m'lady." Virgil executed a low bow and the beaming couple entered the kitchen.

Harriet Forest had a green thumb in the garden and a house full of lean and hungry people. Meals in the Forest household were frantic affairs, involving the clatter of chipped bowls containing fresh vegetables in season and savory canned food in the winter.

"Is Mr. Forest going to be joining us for dinner, ma'am?"

"He's a little under the weather. I'll take him a plate later," she replied with a forced grin. "I'll tell him you asked after him, Virgil."

"Please do, ma'am."

"How's school going, Virgil?" Harriet asked.

"Pretty well."

"Are you going summer quarter?"

"I'm signed up, but I may have to withdraw," he said staring at the coleslaw on his plate.

Louise pursed her lips and gave him a sharp look.

"How much longer do you have to go until you graduate?" Louise asked with a frown.

"Two quarters and I can be finished."

"That's wonderful, I hope you'll be able to finish soon."

"Thank you, ma'am. Something has come up, and I may have to help my uncle out with some things this summer."

"Helping out family is important. I'm sure if you do have to miss school this summer your uncle will appreciate your efforts."

Virgil shoveled a forkful of slaw into his mouth and looked at Louise. "This slaw is wonderful, Mrs. Forest."

Virgil had seen women's eyes *flash* in the movies at the Opera House in McConnelsville and at the Ohio Theater in downtown Columbus. As he looked at Louise, he ignored the trickle of slaw dressing moving down his chin and witnessed the phenomena for the first time in real life.

By the time he'd wiped his mouth with the napkin, Louise had exited the kitchen with a mumbled: "I'm gonna check on Dad."

"Will you excuse me, Mrs. Forest?"

"Surely, Virgil."

"Thank you, ladies, for a nice dinner.'

"Mom, Virgil told me even though I's only six that I'm a lady, too."

"That's true, Opal. You are a perfect little lady." Her eyes followed the path out of the kitchen. "But, please don't grow up too quickly, dearest little Opal."

Louise stood in the doorway of her parent's room, with her arms crossed tightly, listening to the strangled syncopated snoring of her father. Virgil approached slowly, his feet seeking the loose board that creaked during summertime. Finding it, he stopped and waited.

Louise dropped her head and arms and turned slowly toward her beau.

"Let's go outside, Lou."

"Go ahead, I'll be out directly."

He nodded, and took a seat at the heavy wood picnic table next to the pen holding AJ and Homer. He thought about the story, how Big Mitch and Anne had begun the table the winter after they were married. After the first big snowfall, Big Mitch had jury-rigged two twelve-foot sections of rails under an old wagon bottom and rigged it to pull a big piece of concrete with a heavy eyebolt from the old train depot at Windsor, up and onto the bottom with a four-horse team. The team pulled the whole contraption over to the cabin.

In the Spring, they dug a hole and buried the concrete with the eyebolt above ground. Mitch built a four-sided frame connected to the four vertical legs out of heavy timbers from an old barn that had collapsed in Dale on Old Adam Sheets' place. Then he ran eyebolts centered inboard through each of the four timbers and connected heavy chain through the eyebolts.

That is where it stood for several years after Big Mitch and Anne moved to the farm up the hill. After Henry and Harriet moved into the cabin, they completed the table using railroad ties and added tensioning nuts to adjust the chains and keep the table level and in place.

This jury-rigged table had served as everything from the Blennerhassett Mansion to Fort Necessity to the blockhouse at Big Bottom, to a flatboat negotiating, currents, pirates and Indians down the Ohio River to the Mississippi.

It was also the location where Louise, Barbara, Merlene and Opal Forest each experienced their first kisses as young women.

Virgil wondered if this place that held so many good memories would become forever spoiled with the taint of disappointment and sorrow.

Louise came out and sat across the table.

"How's your Dad, Lou?"

"Not good. But that's the way he's been a long as I can remember. He's just getting so thin."

"He's a good man. I remember my Mom was a little leery of having you folks move in and start working with Dad and all. But she is not one to judge folks by material things and such. She thinks the world of your family, especially you, Louise."

"I appreciate that sentiment, especially coming from Missus Anne."

"Louise, I think the world of you, too. Things we've said over the years about how we feel and what we want—marriage, family, and a life together. I still want those things with you."

"So, what's going on, Virgil? This trip, talking with your Dad. Coming back with summer term underway. Whatever you were sayin' about your uncle and all that?"

Virgil moved around the table and straddled the bench next to Louise.

"My name was picked for the draft. I report for induction nine days from now—June 30th."

"What? But you're in school, and your Dad's head of the Selective Service down here."

"That's all true."

"What are you going to do, Virg?" She moved over and reached for his hand.

"Dad said I could seek a deferment as a student. Bu, he would have to recuse himself from the deliberations and that means it would take a 3 to 1 vote."

"And that's it?"

"I could also get married and seek a deferment for that."

Louise moved closer. "Would you be more likely to get deferred for that?"

"I'm not sure, I doubt I'd get a deferment either way."

"But you just have two more quarters until you graduate. What are we going to do? How long do you serve if you're drafted? Twelve months, right? Or if you turn 28 you're let go."

"Yes, right now. Dad says there's talk of extending that to 18 months."

"What are you going to do? You only have a few days."

"Louise, this has all happened so fast. Talking with Dad helped. And I had time to think riding back from the farm. I'd be happy if you would do me the honor of becoming my wife. Before you answer, though, you need to know that if we do get married, I will not seek an exemption or a deferment."

"Why not try it?"

"What if everyone played the angles and weaseled their way out? My family has four kids. Little Mitch is a railroad engineer working 80 hours a week now that the factories are manufacturing munitions and such. Grace will be working in Columbus with the National Guard in the infirmary. Ralph is married with kids and starting in a few weeks with Dupont in Belpre. He'll be working 80 hours, too, I suppose. Seems only right that the person with no wife or children serves in the Army. "This war hasn't really affected the United States very much. Yet. But it will. We need to be ready. And that means we need men to serve. I've decided I will do my part. "Lou, I've never had anyone else that I wanted to marry but you. The Depression delayed things or I'd have asked you six years ago. And then going to school delayed it three more years. But I've never stopped loving you. The really crazy thing is that they drew 30 names, and Lance Dutro was on the 30th slip. I guess he was in car accident and got busted up pretty bad a couple days before the drawing. So they had to draw another slip, and it was mine."

"I read about that wreck in the *Herald*. The story said he was coming into McConnelsville on Route 60 and swerved to avoid killing a rabbit and lost control. And because of that, you're getting drafted." The young woman turned away with a shrug and a sigh.

"Did he kill the rabbit?"

"I don't know, they didn't say. So, we'd just go to a Justice of the Peace and then you go away for a year or 18 months or forever."

"I know this is not the way we envisioned it, but it's all I can offer you. I'll probably get leave at some point, but I don't know right now."

"Do you know where we could get married?"

"There's a JP in West Virginia that Ralph and Cloris went to—in Parkersburg."

"Wow, Virg! This is like a story out of one of my Mom's magazines."

"I know it's sudden and everything. But I don't want to marry you just to get out of the Army. I want to marry you because you're the only woman I've ever even thought about marrying."

"You better kiss me then," she said with a smile. "Right over here, just like the first time."

She stepped over by the bench, sat on the tabletop facing the river, and patted her hand next to her right hip. Virgil stood and stretched his back a bit.

"Come on, old man. Step up and claim your bride!"

Virgil jumped onto the bench and then onto the top with his arms snaking around Louise's slim waist. They came together and embraced as lovers have since the dawn of time, lost in the moment.

"I can't believe we're finally going to do this, Louise. I've been thinking about this for a long time."

"Me too."

"I need to get back home and tell the folks. Can I take AJ?"

"Sure. I hope this won't disappoint your folks."

"My Mother and Father will both be thrilled! I'll be back as soon as possible."

His ride back was pleasant. Few people were stirring in Windsor or Roxbury. Scattered lights from shacks and houses on the river peeked through the trees. AJ was a fine specimen of horseflesh, like his father, Ajax, had been. Virgil remembered all the rides he'd taken on Ajax and smiled. He'd just finished Freshman year when the Forests put Ajax down Virgil had pined over the loss a bit, but knew better than to get too attached to anything on four legs.

A quarter mile from the top of the hill, Virgil slowed down and dismounted.

"Here, boy, here's some grass." Virgil unzipped and urinated. He lit a match and checked the time: 9:45. He should be home by 10. As he patted AJ, he heard a vehicle through the trees careening past down the hill.

He'd had a few of those 60 miles an hour, one-eye shut, trips down this road. He was glad those days were over. He felt like he'd been searching for something since he'd arrived back in Windsor after that two-month stint in Akron; looking without finding. But now he found what he'd wanted all along. The words he'd spoken to Louise had been honest expressions of his love for her. Now all he had to do was see this whole induction into the military thing through, and he'd be able to come back and finish school, have some kids, and a enjoy a good life.

When he pulled in the lane, he saw Mose sitting on the porch in Big Mitch's chair. He was reading the Bible by the light of a coal oil lamp.

Virgil tied AJ loosely to the railing on the porch steps. "Evening, Mose. You're up late."

"Your folks asked me to stay up 'til you got back. They had to go down to the Forest place. Mister Henry took sick—another heart attack maybe."

"That must have been Dad and Mom I saw coming down the hill. I was just down there for dinner. Henry didn't eat with us, but that wasn't unusual. Were they going to take him to the doctor?"

"Missus Anne called the doctor. He was in Pennsville, his wife said. Your Daddy was going to drop off Missus Anne and den go to Pennsville and tell the Doc that Ralph and Cloris were gonna bring the truck over and see if they need to haul folks to the hospital. I think Missus Anne gonna stay with the three younger girls if'n Harriet want her to."

"I guess I'll go back down and look in on Mom and the girls. First, I need to clean up and change into another shirt. You can stay up here, if you don't mind. That way there'll be someone to answer the phone."

"I sure will do that, Virgil. I'm gonna go down and git my blankets and such while yer cleanin' up."

By the time Virgil got back to the Forest's house, no one was home. A note tacked on the door stated that three girls had been taken to the Cheadle's house just east of the high school. The rest of the folks—Big Mitch, Anne, Harriet and Louise—had gotten a ride to the hospital in Zanesville from Ralph and Cloris. Louise left a note taped to the window of the kitchen door, but it had fallen on the door jamb and been blown out by the wind.

As Virgil trudged from the Forest's house toward the store, Gillen Jobes pulled over and asked if he needed a ride.

"Jobie—well, I'm in kind of a pickle. I came back to see my Dad about my draft status. Even though I'm in school, I'm still draft eligible. I've got nine days to report for induction up to Columbus. I got to get up there and box up my stuff in my flophouse and get it sent back down home here. And then I got to go to the Registrar at Ohio State and get disenrolled and maybe get some of my tuition back."

"Man, I thought I was havin' a bad night, Virg. I was planning to get a jug at Roosterville and maybe get some female company. You're welcome to join me."

"Sounds good, Jobie. I appreciate it."

Roosterville was hopping. They had to park a long way from the barn where the dancing, drinking, card playing, and cockfighting were taking place. Leaf springs in old jalopies were popping, and muffled moans from backseats wafted through the dark night air.

Virgil had cut back on this kind of activity since he started college. But given the circumstances, he decided he might as well have some fun. Virgil had never been much of a gambler, but he liked to drink and dance. Virgil felt old and wished he had a car.

Before Virgil could leave, when he ran into some fellows from Noble County who had worked on the paving crews a few years earlier. They were glad to see Virgil. And happy to buy him a beer. They recounted some of the stories from their paving days.

June Foster, from Chesterfield pursued by one of the Boles boys from Dale wandered over toward Virgil. "Hi, Virgil," she said with a big smile. "Good to see you. I heard you were going to Ohio State. How's that going?"

"Pretty well, but I just got drafted. So, I'll have to finish up after the war."

"That's too bad. I bet Louise is sad."

"I suppose she is. Her Dad had another heart attack today."

"I'm sorry to hear that. Remember my friend Charlotte?"

"With the Baby Ruth bars at the fair? Yes, I remember her."

"Her Dad passed recently. Had a heart attack out in the fields."

"Hey, gal—what you reckon you're doin' over here?" Lonnie Boles asked. He limped as he approached.

"Just talking with Virgil."

"We'll see about that, gal."

"Howdy, Lonnie."

"Howdy yourself, Virgil," he said with a scowl.

"Got a little hitch in yer giddy up."

"You betcha—one that'll keep me out the Army right here at home keeping the gals satisfied, I reckon."

"Virgil just got drafted. He'll be reporting soon."

"The Army is for suckers. You wait here, June. I gotta go see a man about a horse."

Lonnie limped off in the direction of a poker game.

"When was his number called?" Virgil asked

"Just a couple days ago. He's got a cousin that's a chiropractor in Amesville. He give Lonnie a letter verifying he had scoliosis or some such thing."

"If you two are going to be keeping company, you might want to help him learn to limp on the same side. You could do better, Jane."

"I guess, maybe. But men are going to be getting scarce."

A sudden shout from the poker table Lonnie Boles jumping up and down with the crumpled contents of the pot he'd just won. He raised his arms triumphantly,

"Take care, June."

"You be careful, Virgil. God speed."

It had been a good six years since Virgil Thomas watched the sunrise as he stumbled home on a dark Friday night bleeding into an early Saturday morning from Roosterville to Windsor. On this trip, he was neither drunk nor fleeing the scene of an accident. He was angry, however—at himself, Lonnie Boles and shirkers in general, Louise (a little), and at the world. He'd made peace with idea that he would serve out his term in the Army. If all went well he'd come home, finish school, get a job and raise a family with Louise. Twelve hours earlier, he had been certain he and Louise would be able to marry before he was inducted. Mr. Forest's heart attack put this in jeopardy. Virgil still needed to go to Columbus and clear out his apartment.

His musings were interrupted by squealing tires, bright lights, a loud horn and a string of profane threats emanating from an old Model T. He stepped off the pocked berm and straddled an old telephone pole wedged in place against a good-sized rock. He lit a Lucky Strike and conjured the possible trajectories of his life. He could be killed in the war before he'd been able set down roots. If anyone thought of him at all, it would be as a pretty good fellow who could have made something of himself, if only things had been different.

By the time he crossed 792, the eastern sky evinced a faint pink glow. Virgil decided to go first to Louise's house. If no one was home, he'd go to the store and see if she had gotten back in time to restock.

The Forest's house was empty. Virgil lit a Lucky Strike and proceeded south on Market Street and then East River Road to the store. He saw AJ's white rump in the enclosure behind the store. His pace quickened, and he ran up the steps and opened the door.

"'Bout time you got here."

"How's your Dad?'

"He's alive, but it looks like he'll be in the hospital for quite a while. What have you been up to, Virg?"

"I went up to Roosterville with Jobie. That place doesn't hold any interest for me anymore."

Louise had been slowly circling the open area in front of the cash register, getting closer to Virgil. "Well, what exactly does interest you?"

"I'm looking at what interests me the most right now," he said with sly smile. "They still got that sofa in the back room, Lou?"

"We could go find out. Let me lock that door. Never know what kind of riff-raff might wander inside."

They smiled and stared.

"I'm almost done restocking. We might need to settle on somethin' else to do. Guess we'll get along alright."

They closed the distance between them and walked arm in arm to the back room.

After the first few times, their lovemaking was good. This time it had a little more riding on it, and they lay in each other's arms for a long while. Louise got up and disappeared into the laundry area. Virgil stared at the ceiling with a big grin. After Louise returned, Virgil headed for the laundry and cleaned up.

"Let's have a smoke and watch the river. I got a feeling we're not going to have another chance any time soon."

"You go out and pick us a place to sit and I'll be back with some coffee."

"Sounds good. You know how I like my coffee, like I like my gals—sweet and creamy."

"Comin' right up. I put coffee on an hour ago."

Virgil moved a small table over between the two rocking chairs and found an ashtray on the railing that he set on the table.

"Coffee, monsieur," Louise said with a big smile.

"How much do I owe you, mademoiselle?"

"One Lucky Strike is sufficient, monsieur."

Virgil lit a cigarette and handed it to Louis then lit one for himself.

"Virgil, Mom is going to bring the car back to the store here around noon. The three girls are going to stay with Effie Engle. Mary Lou, Mom and I are heading back to the hospital."

"Who's going to mind the store?"

"Ralph and Cloris said they'd come over at one o'clock. Your folks are pretty worn out. They should be up to the house."

The couple sipped their coffee and smoked.

"Lou, we said a number of things yesterday—feels like it was a month ago. I'm not sure which of those things we talked about has a chance of happening. I know I meant everything I said. But I had an experience at Roosterville that strengthened my resolve to serve out my time in the Army. Lonnie Boles was bragging about how he'd managed to get an exemption from some shyster chiropractor due to scoliosis. Scoliosis my ass! "I resent the idea that he should get a deferment due to his *alleged* infirmity, but I couldn't get one that would allow me to finish college."

Virgil pushed his thinning hair back and drained his coffee. "I should probably go see Mom and Dad. Can I take AJ up the hill?"

"Sure, I've got to stay here and wait for Mom."

One of the things Anne Thomas loved about their farm was its elevation. She and Big Mitch reckoned they were a good 600 or 700 feet above the Muskingum River. Their church, Oakland Methodist, was just up the road. Windsor was not a big city, by any means, but it was a river and a railroad town.

The two older Thomas boys had their share of scrapes as teenagers, but none of it had been really serious—mostly driving too fast and behavior while under the influence. Virgil had spent a night in the Windsor Jail a few years back.

Virgil rode hard and AJ was struggling by the time they turned in the gravel drive at the Thomas farm. Mose took the reins from Virgil and led AJ to the back pasture.

"Mose, are Mom and Dad inside?"

"Sure are, Virgil. Your Daddy is 'bout give-out."

Anne and Big Mitch had spent the last 12 hours driving from Windsor to McConnelsville to Zanesville and back. Mitch was exhausted. His frail childlike figure lay on the couch in his office as he sawed logs.

"Are you alright, son?" Anne asked from her small sewing room.

"I guess I'm OK."

"Where were you last night, if you don't mind me asking?"

"Well, I passed you and Dad comin' home on Blackie. And when I got back to the Forest's place, everyone was gone. Jobie gave me a ride to Roosterville. I saw some of the fellows from Noble County that had worked on our paving crews. I'm not sure what I thought was so great. I had a couple beers and danced a couple times. Then I walked back to the store and helped Louise restock the shelves. I slept a little."

"Son, your Dad and I discussed your dilemma while we were driving. He feels awful bad about things."

"I know Dad feels bad. But I had a good bit of time to reflect on school, Louise, and the Army. I've decided I'm going to raise my right hand and do my best. As I was walking back to the store, I thought about other folks who have had it a lot worse than me. I guess things will turn out alright."

"Virgil, are you and Louise still thinking about getting married?"

"We were talking about it. But with her dad being sick and all, I think we should back off. Maybe we could wait until I get leave, but that could be a long time coming, and I might be a long, long way from home."

"Virgil, you have had a wild streak in you since you could walk. You have grown up a lot in the past few years. We are proud of you, son. If we can help, we will."

"Thanks, Mom. I am going to go back to the store Bryce can give me a ride to catch the train back to Columbus. I'll box up all my things in the apartment and hopefully get someone to help me get them back down here. If that's OK with you and Dad."

"That's fine, son."

"I also need to go to the Registrar's Office and see if I can get some of my tuition money back. Hopefully, I'll be back down here by sometime on Wednesday."

"That'll be fine. We should be able to pick you up if necessary."

"OK, Mom. I'm going to head down the hill to the store."

"Thank you. Your Dad really needs his rest."

"I'll see you in a few days, Ma."

"Give us a call and let us know how things are going."

Virgil had never considered the number of OSU students who were drafted that month. He spent a full day to get disenrolled and another day waiting to get his pro-rated tuition refund. It was a lot of time spent to get back a check for $15. On Wednesday, he rode the bus downtown to get his last paycheck from Mills Cafeteria. He cashed the two checks from OSU and closed his savings account at the Huntington.

On Thursday, he boxed up everything worth saving at the apartment he shared with Neal Wilson. He'd gotten rid of most of his clothing. He boxed up his two suits, a couple of jackets and some shoes in one box and his textbooks in another. Neal gave him a ride to the Post Office. Virgil sent them to the store in care of Big Mitch. Neal threw Virgil a surprise party at the apartment Thursday night. Word got out, especially among the other fellows being drafted. The party got started Thursday around ten PM. It broke up just before Friday midnight, not for lack of interest, rather, for lack of funds. The draftees in attendance had spent all the money from their tuition refunds.

1941 Gabby Thurlow

<u>May 10, 1941</u>: Nazis invade France, Belgium, Luxembourg and The Netherlands; Winston Churchill becomes British Prime Minister

May 10, 1941: Journal Entry

Starting on May 1st, 1941, I became what they called a top hand, which got me a raise to $40 a month plus room and board and a bed and a dresser of my own in the top hand bunkhouse. It's a lot nicer than the main bunkhouse—warmer in the winter and the beds are a lot better. Top hands also get to stay in the bunkhouse even on days off.

Laverne and I have grown close. I think she would marry me in a heartbeat. She is not, however, interested in having marital relations with me or anyone else. Something bad happened to her when she was young, something with a male cousin. He's been jailed in a prison for folks that are criminally insane, and he isn't ever getting out. Not with his nuts, anyways. But the damage that was done to Laverne is irreparable. She's interested in raising a child, just not one that she conceives, carries, and delivers.

Laverne was very excited when she heard the news about my promotion. We celebrated with a big spaghetti dinner and a bottle of wine at Leonardo's Restaurant in Comstock over by Morrow Lake. We borrowed her Mom's car. It snowed hard and we got a room in a boarding house for the night so we didn't have to drive home in a blizzard. Laverne was excited when I told the lady we were newlyweds.

When we got ready for bed, Laverne was acting silly, dancing around doing the Hoochie Coochie and all. We'd done plenty of vertical kissing but none of the horizontal kind. The top half petting was fine, but when I slipped my hand inside her panties she had a kind of a breakdown or something. I took my hand out of her britches and took my clothes off. I thought maybe she'd like to help me out. Well, that made things worse. So, we both got dressed and lay down in the bed with our hands on top of the covers and went to sleep.

On the other hand, Birdie Le Foret, a waitress at the Diner has been quite interested in exploring numerous sexual positions, vertical and horizontal, in various barns, haystacks, and arbors. I'd "'dated'" her cousin Nancy the first year I was at the dairy farm. The Le Foret clan—six brothers and their families—had a big farm north of Kalamazoo in Cooper Township with livestock, hay, wheat and corn. They also owned the Diner. Their girls typically got one year waiting tables to find an acceptable husband. If they didn't get connected in that time, they were shipped back North to make do with whatever old bachelor they could find. The family also had a branch outside of Upper Sandusky, Ohio. The whole brood was descended from French Trappers and Indians from way back.

The girls in that family are beautiful, with long dark hair and a clear dark complexion. They sprouted early, too, as my Dad might have said. Nancy was just shy of 13 when I met her. She was already receiving her "monthly visitor." She ran off with a long-haul trucker who lived in Flint and, according to Birdie she has a six-month-old baby and is doing well.

June 23, 1941: Gabby's Journal Entry

I received "Greetings from Uncle Sam" informing me that I must report to the Kalamazoo County Courthouse on June 30th, 1941 by 12 noon to be inducted into the United States Army.

Even though I knew it might be coming, the letter was still a jolt. I had to clear out my bunk and dresser at the dairy. I also had to store my things at Mom's place. And there were goodbyes to be said to Laverne and Birdie.

Birdie had started talkin' a little bit about us getting married. Laverne had been talking about marriage since the night we stayed at that boarding house. One of the bright spots of being drafted was getting away from this situation.

Laverne was very sad that I was going away, but she promised she would write to me every day. She said her mother would pray for me.

Birdie wasn't quite as understanding. The day I told her I was going into the Army was the first time she refused sex to me since we'd started in at it six months earlier.

The day I left they had buses take us to Indianapolis. Birdie and Laverne were both at the bus station. Laverne and I were talking. Birdie came over and interrupted our conversation. I saw her father leaning against his old truck in the parking lot.

"Hey, Gabby. I'm pregnant," she said with tears streaming down her face.

"What?" I said. "How far along are you?"

"Four months. I guess you didn't notice that I hadn't had a period for a while."

"Birdie, I don't know what to say."

"Don't say nothing. I'll get by." She walked away, toward her father's truck, climbed in. and they left.

Laverne came back over and hugged me. "Are you all right, Melvyn?

I shook my head. "No, Birdie's pregnant, Laverne. It's mine."

"How far along is she?"

"Four months, that's what she said."

"Are you sure the baby's yours?" she asked.

"Pretty sure. We spent a lot of time together during the week. The Diner is only a mile or so from the farm."

"And you were, um, pretty active that way, the two of you?"

I nodded.

"I'm going to get us a couple of Cokes. OK?"

I nodded again.

She came back a few minutes later. Her eyes were glassy, and she had a strange smile. "Everything's going to work out for us, Melvyn. This could be our chance to—."

"All inductees are ordered to board the buses marked Indianapolis," shouted a man with a megaphone was shouting. "All aboard!"

Laverne ran along with bus for a little while, giving me the OK sign with her thumb and index finger on each hand.

1941

Dogs of War

Columbus, Ohio: Railroad Depot on North High Street

<u>July 1, 1941</u>: Channel Islands occupation is completed by German forces. French government moves to Vichy.

Hundreds of men aged 18 to 27 wandered around, up and down High Street. Most smoked, and those who had been bussed in from small towns in Ohio, Michigan and Indiana stared in awe at Lincoln Leveque Tower. This building soared over downtown Columbus a mile or so south and just east of the Scioto River.

A group of uniformed soldiers—MPs— walked slowly up and down High Street and through the station itself.

Men milled about the store in the depot and bought cigarettes, cigars, dirty books, girlie magazines, kewpie dolls and candy of all sorts—all under the watchful eye of a large fat man with a black patch over his left eye. He was perched on a high stool behind the counter by the cash register, and his head scanned the space slowly, inexorably. An occasional— "Hey fella, mind where you put that magazine" —kept the men honest. People with sharp senses spotted the civilian floorwalkers milling about the vicinity of the two doors, one to the station, the other to the sidewalk on the east side of North High Street.

A short unprepossessing man carrying a small valise looked up at the pinnacle of the Tower. "Sure, is a tall building," he murmured.

"You can say that again, friend." The speaker pulled out a pack of Lucky Strikes, shook one up, and offered it to the younger man. "Smoke?"

"Sure, that's mighty kind of you." He put the fag in his mouth and fumbled for a lighter in his jacket pocket.

The older man stuck a cigarette in his mouth. "My name's Virgil—Virgil Thomas."

"Pleased to meet you, Virgil. I'm Melvyn Thurlow. Most everybody calls me Gabby." He lit Virgil's cigarette and then his own. "I never saw a building that high, did you?"

"Well, I've seen this one a bunch. Before I was drafted, I was going to school about four miles north of here at Ohio State. I worked part-time across from the state house, about a mile south of here."

"Wow, that must have been something to grow up here."

"Well, I didn't grow up here. Where I grew up, in Morgan County, we didn't have a building more than two stories high, except for some grain elevators and the mill."

"That sounds familiar, I grew up north of Kalamazoo, Michigan. I was working on a big dairy farm."

"What kind of cows?"

"Holsteins."

"I grew up on a farm with Jerseys. We milked about 40 head."

"The farm I was on had about 300 head."

"Well, I guess we won't have trouble getting up early like some of these city boys."

"Amen to that."

Men funneled back to the station from both directions on High Street. Uniformed soldiers herded them into the depot.

"I heard it's over 1000 miles to Camp Polk," Gabby said with a big smile.

"I heard that, too. My older brother, Mitch, is an engineer on the C&O and lives in New Castle, Pennsylvania. You got older brothers, Gabby?"

"Yes, but none that I see regular. I'm the youngest of 15 kids. My oldest brother, Devlin, fought in France in World War I. He was killed there just before the Armistice, got a medal. I don't remember him. He was dead and buried by the time I came along. But I visited his grave two years ago. "Most of my brothers either moved away or died. I was what my mother called a surprise baby. My closest sibling is a sister, Leona, six years older than me. She lives in Gary, Indiana. I visited her with Mama three years ago. Leona has five or six kids. Her husband works at a steel mill. Mama said he's a *good provider*. I guess that's important. "I reckon someday I'll want to settle down with some gal and have a family. But right now, I'd still kind of like to see the world. I suppose we'll get to do some of that, providing we don't get our heads blowed off."

"Yeah, Gabby. I always thought I'd travel after I got out of high school. I even got a job at a factory in Akron for a couple of months. Then came Black Tuesday, and I was back in my old rope bed and then up here in Columbus at college for the past couple of years."

"Say Virgil, we best get back on the train unless we want to be considered AWOL."

"Lead on, Gabby."

After all the men had taken seats, they were given spiels by sergeants in their respective cars. Virgil and Gabby were in the first row of their car. They gazed up at a tall sergeant who looked a little like Victor McLaughlin in some old war movie set in India.

"Men, welcome to the United States Army, my fine recruits. About three days and 1000 miles from here we'll be arriving in Camp Polk, Louisiana—a truly godforsaken piece of land in the Bayou. You, my fine friends are now officially Bayou Blitzmen. Each of you's should have a packet with your orders. You will be members of the 3rd Armored Division. You'll be broken into Companies —A through I— when we arrive at the camp. Another Sergeant began their introduction to military speak.

"Gentlemen, your time in Camp Polk will be spent learning to eat, drink, fight, fuck, shit, shave, shoot and shine shoes like a soldier in the United States Army! Your main job for the next three days will be to stay with your fellows, don't fall off the train if you step out for a smoke and get to Camp Polk in one piece."

"This should be quite an adventure, Virgil. I've always wanted to travel. The only ones in our family who ever travelled never came back home. Didn't write, either. My Dad never learned to write and he distrusted people with too much education. He was 52 when I was born, in bad health and unable to work. Ma sent me to school when I was four. She was afraid he'd hurt me if I was underfoot. As you can see, I'm still waiting for my growth spurt."

"Do you have a gal back in Kalamazoo?"

"I do, kind of. Two of them. My high school English teacher, Laverne Osgood, and Birdie Le Foret, a girl that works in the Diner close to where I worked."

"Two-timer, huh?"

"Kind of. See, Laverne and I dated and went out to dinner and such. We got to be good friends, but she had something happen to her when she was little. A cousin of hers did somethin' to her. He got locked up in a prison for crazy people. Laverne's real nice and smart, too. She's writing her Thesis to get her Master's degree in English. Now Birdie, on the other hand, is kinder the opposite of Laverne. She's 13 and beautiful with long black hair and kind of a dark complexion. And she likes to get frisky. But I found out while I was waiting for the bus that took me to the train in Indianapolis that Birdie was pregnant. And the kicker is that Laverne told me she'd look after Birdie."

The train pulled into the station in Lebanon, just north of Cincinnati.

"Gabby, let's go stretch our legs and have a smoke."

"Sounds good."

We leaned out over the railing at the back of the car.

"What towns do you reckon we go through on our way to Louisiana, Virgil?"

"Well, we should go through Cincinnati, Louisville, Nashville, Memphis and Jackson."

"How many states is that?"

"Five—Ohio, Kentucky Tennessee, Mississippi and Louisiana."

"So, that'll take me up to seven states I've been through. Before today, I'd only ever been in two—Michigan and Indiana"

"You gotta gal, Virgil?'

"Yes, and no." Virgil shook his head. "We were planning on getting married before I left, but there wasn't any time. I had been down home to talk to my Dad after I got my notice from Selective Service. I'm only a little way from finishing college. I thought I might get a deferment for that, or for my age, being as I'm 27, or if I got married. My Dad is the head of the Morgan County Draft Board. After we talked, I figured I'd better go ahead and accept conscription. But I wanted to marry Louise, 'cause she's the only gal I've ever loved. I had to go back up and bring all my stuff from the rooming house I had been staying at in Columbus, back home. And by the time I had done all that there wasn't any time for me and Louise to get to a Justice of the Peace. I hope she waits for me, Gabby."

"I just hope we make it home in one piece, Virg."

1941

3rd Armored Division

The 3rd Armored Division was formed in July 1916, and spent a year on the Mexican border. Although some men transferred to other units and served on the Western Front in Europe with General Pershing, 3rd Armored Division did not serve overseas as a Unit in WW I.

They were reactivated April 15, 1941, at Camp Beauregard in Pineville, Louisiana with men from General George Patton's 2nd Armored Division. On June 2nd, 1941, an advance detachment proceeded to newly opened Camp Polk near Leesville, Louisiana. Recruits received 13 weeks of boot camp and other training at Camp Polk.

Louise

Louise and Harriet stopped for a late lunch at the restaurant next to the train station in Marietta. They recognized the group seated at a large table in the corner. It was the Usher family from Washington County. The group included Anne Thomas, Virgil's mother; her sister, Virgie Pearson; and their four bachelor brothers.

Before they were seated, Harriet and Louise moved over toward the table.

Anne stood and embraced Harriet, then Louise. "Folks, these are Harriet and Louise Forest," Anne said with a big smile. "Their family lives in the house by the store. They run the store and have a laundry they operate out of an out building they built on behind the store. With the men gone to the Army, Louise here is about the handiest mechanic in Windsor."

Louise smiled and dropped her head.

"These are my brothers and sister. Virgie here lives in Amesville. These first three men are Jess, Rob, and Lynn." The older men nodded and grinned. "They all skedaddled right after high school and worked out West. We're trying to get them to move back here now that they're retired. And the feller on the end, Mervyn' is my baby brother. We're kinder celebrating a promotion he just got. He's the new Plant Manager at Monarch Bearings in Akron."

"That's the plant where Virgil worked after high school," Mervyn said.

"He worked on my line back in '29. That was my first supervisory position. I felt badly about not being able keep him on, but with the Depression and all, I didn't have a choice. Boy, things have changed. With the men going overseas, we can hardly find enough people to keep the lines going. And we sure could use some country folks that know a thing or two about machinery and working hard."

Mervyn fumbled in his shirt pocket and pulled out three business cards. "If you know anyone looking for honest work and all the overtime they can get, have them give me a call." He handed the cards to Louise with a nod and a smile and sat down.

"It was a pleasure to meet all of you," Louise said as she tucked the cards carefully into her purse.

Harriet stared at a hole in the floor.

"What brings you two to Marietta?" Virgie asked.

"Well ma'am," Harriet said softly, "we're looking for some glass we can send to my niece in Upper Sandusky. She's getting married next month."

"And we thought we'd go try to get some glass in Parkersburg," Louise said." "I 'spect we should be getting over to get our present and skedaddle back home. Pleasure to meet all of you."

After the obligatory winks, nods, and farewells, the two women slipped out.

"Anne, is that the girl we spoke of before Virgil started at OSU?" Virgie asked.

"Yes, it is. She's a fine girl."

"She's a woman now, Anne," Mervyn said.

"I've always hoped she and Virgil would end up together, Virgie. If it wasn't for this war, I think they would have married after he graduated from Ohio State. But everything is up in the air, now."

***

"I don't know about you, Louise, but I'll be happy to get a sandwich somewhere and get off my feet."

"Suits me, Mother. We can find a place in Parkersburg."

Louise had been closer to her Father than her Mother for most of her life. The pair had been thick as thieves ever since Louise learned to talk and walk. Louise shared a sense of humor with her mother that verged on the grotesque. Harriet had been driven to tears on several occasions after she'd overheard them. Louise also shared her father's sense of sentimentality and melancholy.

As time had passed, however, Louise and her Mother had grown closer. Part of it involved the natural need a girl has as she becomes a woman. In Louise's case, her Father's Franks chronic health issues had been a factor in the gradual estrangement of father and daughter. Louise had taken over more responsibility at the store and with the mail route. This eased Henry's workload but also, perhaps, made him feel like he was no longer needed.

And when Louise found herself 'in trouble' she shared the whole truth with her Mother and no one else. Louise had skipped her period after Virgil's trip home in June, prior to his induction in the Army. She had never missed a period before. Mrs. Forest had scheduled an appointment for her with a doctor in Marietta. "Going to Parkersburg for a wedding present" was a spur-of-the moment ruse. No need to provide grist for Windsor gossip mills.

The doctor seemed confident that she was pregnant. He promised to send the results of the rabbit test in a sealed letter as soon as he had them. Even though Louise had dated several men while Virgil was at OSU and after he was drafted, the only man she'd had intercourse with was Virgil. They'd got on together from the time he'd first kissed her. And he was a good man, from a good family.

Mother and daughter decided to postpone further discussion until she got the test results. The letter came five days later. The rabbit died. Harriet and Louise adjourned to the laundry shed.

"What are you thinking of doing, Louise?"

"I don't know, Ma. I guess I could write to Virgil and tell him. Or, I could give the baby up for adoption, but might make things kind of tense around home here in Windsor. I've also been thinking about trying to get a job at Monarch in Akron."

"Not if you're pregnant, Louise. Who would there be to help you up there in Akron?"

"Ma, I'd be OK. I could make money, work all the overtime I could get. And save enough to get through the delivery and have it up there. Then I'd either give it up for adoption or raise the baby myself. I could tell folks the baby's father died in a car accident."

"Or, you might find a husband, if you get up there right quick."

"Ma, I couldn't."

"The hell you say, girl! Desperate times call for desperate measures." Harriet took a deep breath and continued. "Another thing—it's easy to label that living person in your belly 'it' before the birth, and another thing to hold that baby in your arms and think about giving it up."

"But I couldn't trick a man into marrying me if he's not the father."

"There's lots of things you don't think you can do, until you have to." Harriet turned and looked out at the river through the leaded glass window above the washer. Her sturdy shoulders began to move, and she buried her face in her work-worn palms.

"Mother, are you OK?"

"Yes—dear," she gasped between convulsed sobs." I just need a minute." She wiped her eyes with a faded blue bandanna pulled from her apron pocket.

"What is it, Ma?"

"It's Dwight. You had a brother, Dwight. He died when he was three days old. He was such a pretty little boy."

"But you never said anything about him."

"Well, your Pa and I decided there wasn't any use in telling you girls."

"But you should have—."

"Should have what?" Harriet said as she turned and faced her daughter. "Your Pa said it was up to me. And I decided there weren't no use in all that."

"All that? Now who's treating people like things?"

"The only person who has a right to even speak of Dwight, that's who!"

"What about Dad?"

"Your Dad married me when I was about six weeks along. He didn't know it wasn't his. I'd been dating a boy—Jonah— who worked in the oil fields they had going in Noble County. We'd see each other on weekends at dances and such. He was a lot of fun to be around. But when I was about a month along, their crew packed up and headed to northern Ohio around Findlay. Never did see him again."

"Did Dad know?"

"I've never been sure. I don't think so. I'd known him since I was in grade school, and I knew he was a good man. I knew he was sweet on me, too."

"So, you tricked him into marrying you?"

"I guess you could say I did. When Dwight came out with blonde hair, I was mortified. Old Doc Whitfield said that it was not unusual for an infant to be born a towhead. He said that most end up with darker hair after a while."

"I could have hugged him for sayin' that."

"So, did—does Daddy know?"

"I don't think so. After a while, it didn't seem to matter much. We had you four lovely girls. And I love your Daddy. And we love you girls. And every year on Dwight's birthday, I go down to the river, just up from Luke Chute, and toss a bouquet of flowers in the water where we scattered his ashes."

Louise looked troubled.

"I know how you're feeling. But this isn't end of your life, Louise. I'll help you as best I can, darlin'.

"Ma, I don't know where to start."

"First off, you got to decide if you're going to contact Virgil. What are you thinking about that?"

"I'm not sure why, but I don't want to let him know. His outfit is getting ready to go to war. They're going to California. And then, I suppose they'll be heading to Europe."

"He wouldn't be the first soldier to get this kind of news during a war. Louise looked at her mother, trying to read her expression. "Can you picture yourself married to Virgil and raising kids?"

"I guess I could."

"You don't sound so sure, girl."

"Well, it's just, I've spent the whole time since we moved to Windsor thinking about marrying Virgil Thomas. But, I'm not so sure now. You know, when he went to college, he didn't ask me what I thought about that. And then he got drafted and he said he wanted to get married before he was inducted. And we probably would have, except for Dad having that heart attack right before Virgil was inducted."

"I remember that."

"The thing is, he never really asked me my thoughts on such things. It was kind of like—"Here's the deal, Louise'—and that's what we were gonna do. When he was back from school, we had a good time, but it was still like that first time we met. Big old Virgil on horseback, looking down at little Louise and protecting her from the boys in her grade. "Only problem is, I don't need to be protected from 'the boys' anymore. Do you mind if I use the phone in the backroom to call Mr. Usher in Akron?"

"That will be fine, Louise. Seems like going up there might be good for you."

"Thanks, Mom. I hope you don't think poorly of me after all I've told you today."

"That'd be the pot calling the kettle black, darlin'."

Letter from Louise to her parents

Dear Mother and Father,

I hope you, Dad and the girls are doing well. I just finished my first day at Monarch. I spent most of the morning filling out paperwork for payroll, insurance and other things like that. They also got me some uniforms and gloves to wear at work.

I finished with that stuff just in time to eat lunch. They're running three shifts here on most of the lines. For some of the lines they're running two 12-hour shifts. I got done in time to get a sandwich and some coffee at the dining hall. You can pack your lunch, but for $2 a week, you get to eat in the cafeteria. I think I'll do that. It's a pretty good deal for just 40 cents a day and they aren't stingy with the portions.

I got to eat with the fellow who is the foreman on the second shift bearings line. His name is Doak Benoit. He was born in Louisiana and he talks kind of funny. But he was raised in New Lex by his grandmother. He seems like a nice fellow. There was another woman about my age, Devora, who also started today on our line. The two of us spent most of the shift going over different jobs on the line with Doak.

The reasons they are adding folks on the line is because this line is going to be running 24/7 starting right after Labor Day. So, I guess I'll be busy.

Love,

Louise

A smaller sealed envelope with Mom on the front was inside the bigger envelope This is just for your eyes, Mom. I've been thinking about the situation we discussed before I left for Akron. The work on the line is fairly fast-paced, but not heavy work. When I was eating with Doak, he asked me how I was with math in school. I told him I had straight As. With the ramp-up in production coming, they will be opening a position that takes care of ordering parts and subassemblies to ensure the line keeps running. I'm going to try to impress Doak, so I can get this job.

The other thing you and I talked about, well, Doak isn't exactly a dreamboat, but he seems like a good man. The other women on the line seem to think he's a straight shooter. They say he doesn't get fresh with them.

He lives about two blocks away from where I'm staying. He said I could catch a ride back and forth to work with him. I feel kind of bad putting the moves on him right off, but this baby is becoming real to me. And I don't plan to raise it alone. I feel bad when I think about Virgil, too. I know those boys are getting ready to cross the Channel eventually. Doak said that there are over 2000 of our bearings in each one of those landing crafts you read about in the newspapers.

I better go now. Doak said he'd pick me up at 10:30 tomorrow and show me around Akron a little. In case you're wondering, I am surely grateful that we had our talk before I left.

Don't forget to put this card out of sight.

Love,

Louise

Letter One

August 10th, 1941

Camp Polk, Louisiana

Dear Mitch and Eleanor,

Sorry I haven't written since my telegram after we first got here. They're keeping us busy, that's for sure! Gabby, the fellow I met on the train and I have become fast friends. We're in the same squad and we bunk together. He's a good guy. Worked on a Dairy Farm north of Kalamazoo before he was drafted—several hundred head of Holstein.

If we mind our ps and qs we'll get a twenty-four-hour pass in a week or two. They've got a bar in Leesville I've heard about. And, boy am I thirsty! We are working hard.

Some of the fellows, those who are coming up on twelve months in October are getting edgy. Grapevine has it that we'll all be extended to eighteen months, and probably beyond if and when we get in the War. It all seems a little unreal right now.

Tell Mom and Dad I'm OK. Let me know how Louise's Dad is doing. We'd been talking about getting married in that last week I was home, but with her Dad and all it didn't happen. We've got a term for situations like that in the Army. SNAFU— 'Situation Normal, All F*#cked Up!

Take Care and give Sarah and Carl my best,

Virgil

Louise Forest skipped lightly down the three steps from the train to the platform in Akron, Ohio, on July 15, 1941.

"Where can I get a cab, Porter?" she asked.

"Down to the end of the platform, just past those luggage carts, ma'am."

"Thank you," Louise said. She had a big smile as she pressed a dime into the large dark hand. "Thank you, sir. Is this enough?"

He held out a nickel and dropped it into her hand. "A nickel is plenty, ma'am. I thank you."

The young woman made her way toward the cab stand amid a crush of porters pushing carts full of luggage and people hurrying with children. Folks were smoking as they walked—even women! In the stations at McConnelsville and Windsor, there were smoking areas for men only.

Louise felt as if she'd landed in a foreign country.

The line at the cab stand extended back just shy of the telephones. She put a nickel in a phone and dialed home, collect.

"Ma, it's me, Louise. I'm in Akron and getting ready to get a cab to go to the boarding house. Everything is fine, don't worry. I'll call you tomorrow night."

Her thoughts quickly returned to the bustling station. She'd never seen so many people or felt so much raw, kinetic energy. She gave her ticket to the man at the luggage desk. He offered to take it to the cab stand, but she thanked him and carried it herself.

The cabbie hopped out and put her suitcase in the trunk. "Where to, miss?"

"Five thirty-one Belmont Avenue, please."

"You got it! Velma's got a new boarder!"

When they reached their destination, her driver grabbed the suitcase from the trunk, then scooted around and opened the door for Louise. He moved quickly up the steps and rang the bell.

A tall attractive woman in her mid-50s opened the door.

"I got you another boarder here, Miss Velma," the driver exclaimed as he entered the house.

"Thank you, Jimmy. Just put the bag by Room 205."

Louise waited to be invited into the house.

"Come in, dear. You must be Louise."

"Yes, ma'am. That's me."

"And where are you from, dear?"

"Windsor, ma'am. in Morgan County."

The older woman's face lit up momentarily. "I believe there was a young man who stayed here for several months back in, oh, must have been 1929. He was from Windsor. He was hoping to get on full-time, but then Black Tuesday hit. I believe his name was Vernon—no—ah, Virgil. Don't suppose you know him, do you?"

Louise looked away and shook her head. "No, can't say as I do."

"I was just boarding here at that time. I bought old Miss Williams out in February of 1930. Things were slow then. I barely hung on. But now, well, people can't hardly find housing what with all the factories runnin' around the clock. Shoot, in some of the lower-class places, they got folks on different shifts sharing beds, at different times. I had a retired Navy man staying here, said they called that hot bunking on submarines. You won't need to worry about that here. Now, let's go up and get you situated, Louise."

The two women walked up the carpeted stairway and turned left. Velma unlocked and opened the door and invited the younger woman in with wave of her left hand. "Here we are, dear. Now, this is one of our smaller apartments, which I believe you requested."

"Yes, ma'am."

"Now, you have a bathroom of your own, and down the hall we have three shower stalls, each in private rooms. We have a laundry facility in the basement that is for our guests. We also have an icebox for our guests. Which shift will you be working?"

"Second shift from three to midnight."

"We have a couple of folks working at Monarch on second shift. I believe they have a bus to take their late-night workers home.

"Do you have any questions?"

"I don't think so."

"I'll let you get unpacked, and I'll get you your keys to the house and your room. I'll be back in a few minutes."

Louise looked around. All the shades were drawn. She opened them. The upper level of their house in Windsor where the four girls slept had four windows without any coverings. She'd never thought much of that. She guessed folks that work the land need to be up when the sun's out and asleep when it's dark. City folks must have different schedules and more things to hide.

Louise unpacked her suitcase and lay down on the bed, rearranging the pillows and the unfamiliar sheets and blankets. She'd never slept anywhere but their farm in Chesterfield and then the house in Windsor. She wondered how many different folks had slept on these sheets and what other strange things had taken place within the cramped confines containing this lumpy full-sized bed.

Homesickness crept into the corners of Louise's mind. Thoughts of her parents and sisters. As the shadows lengthened, she imagined them all sitting in the living room, listening to the radio. Soon the girls would go upstairs and brush their teeth and hair. Her three sisters would probably miss having their big sister brush their hair and tell them stories. missed her family. The ostensible reasons for her move to Akron—to help the war effort and send money back home—had seemed reasonable to friends and neighbors, considering her father's illness and his mounting medical bills. She would have expenses of her own coming up in the months ahead.

A sharp rap on her door was followed by a high-pitched: "Louise? Louise?"

Louise was roused from her reverie. She moved quickly to the door and ushered Velma inside.

Velma carried a manila folder under her left arm and she seated herself in the small dining nook. "Well dearie, are you getting along all right? Are you getting all moved in?"

"Yes, ma'am. I will have a box delivered sometime next week. I was hoping you could let the delivery person in and have him put it in my apartment."

"Well, I'll be happy to do that, darlin'," she said with a big grin.

"Thank you, Velma."

"You're welcome. And look here what I found," she said with a flourish, placing the manila folder in the center of the small, rectangular table. "I've got calendars for every year I've lived here. And look what I found from July,1929." She pointed to a square on the calendar. "See what it says? 'Virgil Thomas Room 205, Windsor.' Same home town, same apartment. Isn't that a coincidence?"

Louise flashed a tight-lipped grin. "I guess you're right, Velma. It sure is a small world. I guess I may have heard about some Thomas's from up around Oakland—that would be a Windsor mailing address."

Velma pointed back at the square again. "You can get lots of information in one of these squares, little girl."

Louise figured she better ask a question, in hopes of moving Velma out the door. "What does that smiley face mean, Miss Velma?"

"Well, that's for me to know and you to find out, smarty-pants! And I'm not gonna tell you what the five stars mean, either."

"Well, I'd like to thank you for all your help, Miss Velma. I'm just about tuckered out. I think I'll turn in. I've got be at Monarch tomorrow morning at eight o'clock sharp. I'll be seeing you, and thanks again for everything, Miss Velma."

"You're very welcome, Louise."

"Miss Velma, one more question, and then I'll stop pestering you. Do you have any two- bedroom apartments available?"

"Yes, we do have a two on the third floor. They'd be $60 a month. Do you have a roommate in mind?"

"No, not really. I'm just thinking if there was another girl getting to Monarch from out of town, like me, well we could save a little money by doubling up."

"Well, let me know sweetheart. Take care, now. Bye."

Velma moved quickly down the worn stairs. Her feral mind was chewing on a thought like a skinny rat might chew on fat piece of cheese. *"She tried to play that roommate idea cagey. But something tells me there's more to it. We'll see about that. Yes, we will definitely see about that!* Velma said to herself in a ragged whisper as she scurried down the hallway

Louise

Louise showed a great aptitude for her job. She had a good head for figures, was quick on her feet, and was not prone to fits of pique. She and Doak became good friends and made a good team.

With a single exception, everything was going swimmingly. She had managed to get Doak into bed several times in mid-July. He had backed off a little after that, expressing the feeling that he shouldn't be taking advantage of girls working under him. If he'd only known how desperate Louise had been was to have him take advantage of her. She'd be showing soon, and felt time was running out for her.

Sure, Virgil's eyes flashed, and he knew all the moves, but there had never been a realistic chance at a future during those early, fumbling days. The last time she'd seen him, in June, they'd had a chance. But her father's third heart attack meant daily hospital visits and the precious time vanished. Louise had been disappointed at the time, not only because Virgil had to report for duty before they could marry. But she was also disappointed because her Dad was now an invalid, propped up on a pile of feather pillows in the small back bedroom.

Louise told herself that Virgil would write and let her know they still had a future. Her Mom had written that he'd sent letters to his folks and his brothers, but he'd sent nothing for Louise. He left at the end of June, and now it was September. She wondered how soon he'd be on his way to England and get ready for the invasion of Europe.

The discovery of her pregnancy completely changed things. Why wouldn't a man in love send his fiancé a letter? Louise believed his marriage proposal was a lie, and she wondered how she could have loved him.

She and Virgil had that "Oh, baby! Baby!" thing in spades. And what had that gotten her? When they made love, it was passionate, whether on a picnic table at Big Bottom Park to the lapping sounds of the Muskingum River or in the back seat of a car behind a barn at a bootlegger's in Roosterville or Coal Run.

Louise had escaped the prying eyes of the friendly gossips of Windsor. She missed her family, particularly her father. She was worried he'd die before he got to meet his first grandchild. On the other hand, she liked her job and she was good at it. She'd made a few friends. And Doak had been the biggest surprise of all. He didn't have Virgil's intensity or looks, but he had something a lot more important to Louise in her present state. He made her laugh and let her know, in little ways, that he was thinking of her.

On Labor Day weekend, the whole plant closed for three days. Louise invited Doak over for dinner. She plied him with alcohol, and they danced to her Victrola. He stayed over the whole weekend. Louise knew that Velma could pick up the smell of a bachelor like a bloodhound tracking an escaped fugitive, especially when her landlady attempted to insert herself as a third wheel on a couple of occasions. Doak did not mind the attention of two women one bit. But Louise knew she had to seal this deal quickly.

Monday arrived, and she made her final plea at lunch in a small cafe. "Doak," she said with a quiver in her voice, "I know you don't want to take advantage of me, being my supervisor and all. But don't you know how I feel about you?"

"Well, Cher, I know we is friends and such. And I know we had some fun skittering around a while back. But I never thought a girl like you could really fall for a broke-dick, butt-ugly mug like me."

"You know that ain't true. You got two women after you, me and Velma."

"I ain't returnin' that favor to Velma, Cher."

"Doak, you sure ain't no broke-dick mug. I know that!" The both laughed.

Louise realized she needed to storm up Doak Mountain and establish a beachhead in her small bedroom. For the balance of the weekend, Velma's periodic knocking was ignored. As they went to bed on that Labor Day Monday evening, Louise told him her suspicions that she was pregnant. "You are the only man that I've been with, Doak. This child is yours." She said they might be able to get a two-bedroom apartment in the building after they were married.

By the time they went back to work Tuesday, Doak was firmly in love with Louise. And more surprisingly, Louise realized that she was in love as well. This wasn't the kind of love she'd seen in the movies, or what she'd felt with Virgil, but she wouldn't complain.

They were both happy.

1941

Louise

A fellow from the plant, who was also a Baptist minister married Doak and Louise during their lunch break Sept 28, 1941. The folks from the cafeteria baked three sheet cakes and the different lines took turns coming over to congratulate the newlyweds and have a slice of wedding cake. After brief congratulations and a few bites of cake, the workers hurried back to their lines. As banners announced in various locations inside the plant: "We've Got a War to Win—And the Battle Begins Here!"

"Mom, is that you?"

"Louise? Yes honey, it's me. You're up early."

"Doak and I got married yesterday At the plant. There's a fellow on our assembly line, Bill. He's a Baptist minister. They had cake for us. It was real nice."

"I sense a little let-down in your voice, honey. Not exactly like in the movies."

"No, it's not. I remember when I first met Virgil—the first day of school. He rode Ajax down the hill and put him out to graze behind the store. Then he hopped on the train and took it to school. After school, he came back to get Ajax and the Sheets boys were pestering me. He told them to be nice to me or he'd give 'em what for."

"Things don't always work out like in books or the movies," Harriet said. "I heard someone say one time that all this romance and sentimental stuff doesn't really have much to do with love and romance. It has more to do with what he called the *biological imperative*. That was at a graduation at Windsor High School in '37, the year Merlene graduated. We sat at a table with Big Mitch and Anne, Virgie and Clarence, and Little Mitch and Eleanor. Clarence was a teacher at Amesville High School, and his wife, Virgie, was Anne Thomas's sister. We saw her in Marietta when we went to Doctor Hellner. We got to talkin' about evolution, which was a real controversial topic at the time. And most folks around that table were on the fence, but no real Bible thumping was going on.

"Big Mitch had been a teacher. He was a Mason, like your daddy and he allowed that he thought there must be something to evolution. He said that it doesn't mean the Bible's got it wrong, necessarily, just maybe things changed over long periods. Clarence piped in then and said something to the effect that he was convinced that evolution was the only way to make sense of what fossil records are telling us.

"Could be the Good Lord has his hand on things after all.

"And then he raised a glass of iced tea and proposed a toast. 'Here's to the ladies, without them, our species would have died out years ago. Despite the trappings of sentiment and romance, the biological imperative requires very little of the male of the species for propagation.'

"His wife Virgie had a mischievous grin when she said, 'That's a fact. But it's nice if they put groceries on the table occasionally.

"Are you doing well, Louise? Everything OK with the baby. And with Doak?"

"Yes, Ma. Doak is a good man. We get along really well. And he makes me laugh. And he comes home at night and puts those groceries on the table. And he loves me."

"That's good, Louise. At the beginning, we might like those flirty boys. But eventually, all that drama can wear on a body. Your Daddy still makes me laugh. And I sure hate to see him suffer like he is now. You take care of yourself, baby girl."

"I will, Ma. They got me so I don't have to spell folks on the line through their breaks. So I'm mostly keeping track of inventory and ordering parts and raw materials. I'm off my feet quite a bit. I'll send a letter addressed to all the family, soon."

Harriet decided against telling the girls or Henry about the wedding. He was back in the hospital in Zanesville and not doing well. There would be time to discuss these things later. Perhaps.

1941

Virgil

<u>August 12-17, 1941</u>: Germans evacuate Sicily

<u>August 15, 1941 Camp Polk, Louisiana</u>

Two figures tramped along the dirt road running parallel to a high fence running roughly south on Camp Polk's western boundary. The men wore civilian clothes, but their haircuts and shoes gave them away. They were enlisted personnel, Privates on their way back to the camp after their first 24-hour pass. They were buck Privates, returning from a two-hour session at the Dog Face Lounge in Leesville.

"Well Gabby, looks like we're going to see some new real estate."

"Says who, Virg?"

"Says Sergeant McMullen—that's who! The scuttlebutt is that we'll be heading for the Mojave Desert to train. And that's not far from Los Angeles or Hollywood. The Sarge is going to be chaperoning us GIs out there."

"When will we be going, Virg?"

"He didn't know exactly, just that's where we're likely to go next, after we finish here. We'd be crossing Texas, Oklahoma, New Mexico, and Arizona before we enter California."

"California? Now, that's a long way from Kalamazoo."

"Gabby, neither one of us is going to get within 1000 miles of home until we've gotten further along in training."

"I suppose you're right, Virg. But I'm worried about Birdie and Laverne. And I wonder what's happening with Birdie's baby—my baby!"

"I hear you, Gabby. At least you've gotten a couple letters. I haven't heard one word from Louise."

"Virgil, let's take a load off. We can sit down on that log over there. My dogs are barkin'!"

"Yeah. Mine, too. I kind of wish we'd saved bus fare, instead drinking it all up. We've got 40 minutes to be back in the barracks. Shoot, we can probably sit long enough to have another smoke. But then we'll have to hightail it!"

Both men lit cigarettes.

"Shit, I just can't stop thinking about Birdie and the baby."

"Same here with Louise. I know my brother gave her my address but even if she sends it now, we'll be out in the desert eating sand and her letter will be back here in Louisiana. Damn the bad luck!"

"Let's go, Virg." The younger man crushed his fag in the dirt and began to run.

"Alright, Gabby. Last one there's a rotten egg."

The two took turns in the lead. With ten minutes left, they had a good three-quarters of a mile to go. They ran side-by-side passing and passed through the gate with a minute to spare.

After proceeding through the gate, they walked briskly to their barracks and got into their racks, with Gabby in the top bunk and Virgil in the bottom.

"Hey, Virg," Gabby said in a low voice, "Would you try to get out if we got to 12 months?"

"I don't know. I'm just trying to get through each day here."

"Me too, Virg. But I kind of like it here, being in the Army and all."

"The only thing I miss is Louise. If I could have married her, I wouldn't mind any of this stuff. But, I guess that's not going to happen. My Brother Mitch sent her several letters. And a couple weeks ago, he talked to her at her folk's place. She's moving to Akron. I guess she's got a job lined up. And get this—it's in the place where I worked right after high school, right up to Black Tuesday. Then it was back home to baling hay and milking cows."

"Hey, ladies! could you hold down the pity party? Some of us have to get up early tomorrow. Understand?"

"OK, Gino. Sorry."

***

The headline of *The Chicago Tribune* Graphic Section, on Sunday August 31, 1941, stated: Camp Polk—"Home of the Bayou Blitz".

August 22, 1941: North Gate, Camp Polk

"We ain't gonna make it back in time this week, Virgil. We'll surely get punishment—work detail or something."

"Probably so, Gabby. But it was worth it. That redhead put me on cloud nine, sure 'nuff. That bus could have waited for us. We were only ten feet away when they shut the door.

"Hope that redhead has a sister or a friend."

As they approached the gate, two MPs, a sergeant and a corporal, motioned with their rifles for Virgil and Gabby to approach.

"That's about close enough, maggots!" the corporal barked. "Did you two have a good time"

"Yes, sir," Gabby said with a smile.

"Don't call me sir, maggot, I work for a living. I'm glad you had a good time. Aren't you glad they had a good time, sergeant?"

"I am so pleased that I almost wet myself. They may have had such a wonderful time that they wandered off into a different time zone. If they had somehow drifted into the Mountain Time Zone, they would have 15 minutes before they missed curfew. But doggone it, they's still in Central Time. And that means they are 45 minutes late. What do you think we should do about that, corporal?"

"Well, Master Sergeant McMullen has the Duty. He might want to make sure these two broke-dick hombres are OK. Sergeant McMullen has seen just about everything."

"Speak of the devil, there stands the Master Sergeant now."

A tall, slightly stooped man with a broad grin leaned against the side porch and whittled on a piece of wood. His worn fatigues were bereft of any medals or ribbons

The two MPs finished giving their report to the Sergeant Major. And after some banter, the Sergeant Major and MPs came out through the door of Duty Shack.

The three chevrons and three rockers forming the insignia of a Regimental Sergeant Major— the closest thing to God on Earth, for the two recruits now giving each other frightened looks and doing as good an imitation of standing at attention as any E-1 a couple of months into training could reasonably expect to muster, stepped in through door and on into the backroom where the MPs were removing their weapons.

"Atten-hut," Gabby yelled."

The MPs laughed while pulling they pulled cigarette packs out the pockets in their jackets and moved swiftly away from the door and down the steps into the equatorial night.

"You two may stand at ease."

"Thank you, sir!" the two recruits said in unison.

"A good first lesson for the two of you is to stop calling enlisted men 'sir', except for the Sergeant in charge of your training.

Now, let's try that again. "You two may stand at ease."

"Yes, sergeant major!"

"Better. Anyone with three chevrons is a sergeant of some kind. If you are in doubt about what flavor of sergeant they are, just use the term 'Sergeant. Some fellows, particularly the ones who have just got a rocker may decide to tell you something like— 'That's sergeant major to you, maggot!' To which you would reply: Yes, sergeant major.' "I am Regimental Sergeant Major McMullen. And you are?"

"Private Virgil Thomas, Regimental Sergeant Major!"

"Private Gabby—er—Melvyn Thurlow, Regimental Sergeant Major!"

"That's better. Now, I came out here to get a cup of coffee while I ponder a situation that I need to resolve. Would you two care to join me for some coffee?"

"Yes, Regimental Sergeant Major."

"Good. Help me bring the coffee out and we can sit under the fan and pretend like it ain't a 110 in the shade."

The three took out the coffee, cups, cream, sugar, and spoons.

"Where you fellows from? And we can dispense with the sergeant major stuff when we're just talking like this. OK?"

Both men nodded.

"I'm from Michigan, north of Kalamazoo," Gabby said as he stirred cream into his coffee.

"I'm from southeastern Ohio—Windsor—on the Muskingum River," Virgil said with a grimace.

"What did you do before you were drafted, Gabby?"

"Well, I was a top hand on a big dairy farm running about 400 head of Holsteins"

"And you, Virgil?"

"Well, I was an ag student at Ohio State University. I had two more quarters to go when I was drafted. Before that I was a kind straw boss on a paving crew. We got a grant for Public Works to build roads in Noble and Morgan County. Before that, I grew up on a dairy form. We had 40 or 50 Jerseys."

"Two farm boys, sounds like."

"Yes."

"Yes."

"Well, you see the problem I was talking about involves the dairy cattle here on the base. We have gone through three crews and none of them have stayed more than two weeks. They can't stand the weather and the bugs. Trouble is, they were free to go, if they put in their notice. But this last group just skedaddled, with no notice. The other factor in here is that we've got some officers here that's pretty picky about the cream for their coffee and their ice cream and such. Anyway fellows, I could use help from you two. There just aren't many folks among this first group of Bayou Blitzmen who would even know which end to start with when it comes to milking cows."

"Cows can be finicky. They's kinder like people in that way. They like to know who it is that is playin' with their titties," Virgil said with a smile.

All three men laughed.

"Exactly. I need some help getting this dairy situation ironed out."

"I don't mean to be impertinent, sergeant major, but is it possible that you did some checking on the backgrounds of new recruits and looked at those of us from farm country?"

Sergeant McMullen got a twinkle in his eye and nodded. "Yes, Virgil. You are right about that.

"Doggone, Virgil," How'd you figure that out?" Gabby asked.

Virgil shrugged. He and McMullen exchanged glances. "If I may ask one more question, sergeant major?"

The sergeant nodded.

"Did you, by any chance have red hair when you were younger?"

"Yes, I did."

"One more, please. Do you, by any chance have a daughter or granddaughter who might have been at the bar tonight?"

"It was not by chance that she was there," the sergeant said with a broad grin."

"Doggone, Virgil," Gabby said. "You're pretty quick."

"As you surmised, Virgil, this whole thing was a set-up. My granddaughter gave me a call and said to take it easy on you two. You will not be written up. But if you will agree to it, I'd like to get you two spending time you'd normally spend on other things—cleaning up the barracks, policing the grounds and such—in the dairy barns. You fellows will still be training for the Armored Division. What I'd like is for you to help the fellows from the mess to get up to speed with these dairy cows. What do you think, fellows? Let me step out for a minute so you two can talk."

"What do you think, Virgil?"

"As long as we don't get put on permanent KP, I'm OK with it."

"I guess I am, too. Shoot, I can milk a cow with both eyes closed. And it'll be a good thing to get on the right side of Sergeant McMullen. He's a good guy."

"Master Sergeant, we've talked," Virgil said. "We'd be glad to help out any way we can. But we still want to train to be Armored."

"Absolutely. You are showing your e*spirit de corps*. Any more questions?"

"Just two," Virgil said with a sigh.

"Shoot, Virgil.

"First, what time have they been bringing the cows into the barn?"

"About 5:30."

"OK. And second, can we go hit the sack so we're ready?"

"Yes. I told your sergeant about all this. He says that's fine with him. He'll have the MPs on duty wake you up at 5 AM.

September 1, 1941 4:45 AM

Two privates who clearly knew their way around a barn were lighting lanterns and opening gates in the dairy barns at Camp Polk.

"Gabby, drop yer cocks and grab yer socks! I'm gonna go bring 'em in said matter-of-factly. He walked out between the pens approaching the central lot. "Bo-o-oys, sig bo-oys, repeated, each time with a deeper timber and a little louder. "Bo-o-oys, sig bo-oys. Bo-o-oys, sig bo-oys"

By the time first cow approached the gate that led through the pens and toward the barn, the sound of bells and the lowing of cattle hit a crescendo.

The other man, shorter but no less sure around cattle, had set the gate to the barn off the latch. He moved outside and comforted the passing cows. "Good girls," he repeated as each rump got a gentle touch and heard a soothing voice. Good girl.

By five o'clock, all 200 Holsteins were in their parlor stalls being fed and having their udders washed and rinsed by a team of 20milk maids. Twenty men—civilians—were bringing empty buckets and retrieving full ones. By six-forty-five6:45, all 200 head had been fed and milked and were being released from their parlor stalls back to the pasture.

September 8, 1941

"Hey, Virgil. Do you think we might get something for doing' this stuff with the dairy?"

"You mean like a longer Pass some weekend?"

"Somethin' like that."

"That'd be OK, pard."

"Right now, I'm still happy to be workin' with the cows instead of cleaning toilets in the crapper."

"Amen, brother."

The two men left their barracks and headed for the dairy barn a half-mile away.

"We're startin' to lose the light, Gabby."

"Who knows how long they'll keep us on this dairy duty"?

When the men reached the barn, Regimental Sergeant Major McMullen was sitting on the open tailgate of a wagon and waiting for them. "Hey, fellas. Days are getting' shorter."

"Yes sergeant, they are," the two commented in unison.

"I wanted to let you know what a good job you two are doing. The straw boss of the milk maids is very happy."

"We're having a good time, sergeant," Virgil said with a nod of his head.

"It's something we've each been doing for most of our lives," Gabby chimed in with a big smile.

"Well, good. I was thinking you two might be in line for a little longer ass this coming week, if that would interest you.

How would a 48-hour pass commencing on Friday afternoon at 4 PM suit you?"

Sergeant McMullen jumped up and reconnoitered a man walking toward the barn. "I'll be damned if that don't look like—but it can't be—."

"Who is it, Sergeant Major?" Virgil asked. "Who's the fellow in the riding pants?"

"By God, that's him. Boys, that man coming this way is Colonel Maurice Rose. And he'll be wearing stars before this War is through. I had the great honor of serving with him at St. Mihiel and in the Meuse-Argonne Offensives in the past war."

As the two men approach the barn McMullen stood up and yawned. "Are we keeping you up, Sergeant Major?" the colonel shouted.

"Make way for a tanker!" the Sergeant responded with a broad grin. "Attention!"

The three snapped to attention.

"Stand at ease men," the colonel barked.

"Colonel Rose, it is great pleasure to see you again. I heard you were in command of the 3rd Battalion last year in the Louisiana Maneuvers."

"Yes, Sergeant. And now we're here to participate in 2nd Army Maneuvers here at Camp Polk. How are your recruits faring, sergeant?"

"Fair to middlin', colonel. We're stretching them out on our hikes, and most of them have figured out which end of the rifle you aim at the enemy. Colonel, here are two of our recruits that are helping out in the dairy barn. We know how particular some of your officers may be about cream for your coffee and ice cream and such."

"Outstanding, sergeant. Now that you mention that, Georgy may be coming through here. He ordered 20 head of Jerseys to be sent here. The milk and dairy products from these beasts will be separated from those in the main barn. You got any hands experienced with Jerseys?"

"I believe we do, sir. Private Virgil Thomas was raised on a farm in Ohio that ran Jerseys," Sergeant McMullen said with a smile.

"Is that right, PrivateThomas?"

"Yes, sir. We had 40 or 50 head at any given time."

"Very good, we can use a man like you."

"Begging your pardon, sir. My bunkmate, Private Melvyn Thurlow here is also a very good dairyman. He was a top hand at one of the biggest dairy farms in Michigan, before he was drafted."

The colonel turned and eyeballed Gabby. "How long have you two been serving?"

Gabby swallowed hard and opened his mouth. "Colonel, we were both sworn in on June 30th, 1941."

"That's the kind of bond we need to have in our Army, if we're going to beat those Nazi sumbitches! These two men are examples of comradery, operationally defined. Excellent!"

"Begging your pardon, sir," Virgil said. We should be getting those cows in the barn."

"Right you are. Carry on, men. And keep up the good work. You two are dismissed."

"Yes, sir." They each saluted, turned on their heels and headed for the dairy barn.

"Master sergeant, you still have a way with recruits," the Colonel said with smile. "You turn 'em into fine fighting stock, eager and ready to learn the technical details they'll need when they get to the Front."

"Thank you, sir. And if I may say so, you've got away with men that makes them want to follow you. You had that as teenager 2nd Lieutenant in France."

"Sergeant, I'm not happy about the things that are going on in Europe and Asia—civilian atrocities, concentration camps, and God's knows what else. But since it is happening, I'm excited to be heading back into action. I've got that same feeling in the gut I had when I hitchhiked out to that rifle range on Old Golden Road in 1916. This is what I was made for, Master sergeant."

"Thank God we have leaders like you and General Patton that can take the troops we prepare and lead them to victory."

Colonel Rose turned to the east and squinted at the sun just peeking over the horizon. "Remember our motto at St. Mihiel — 'Lead from the front!'"

"Aye, sir."

"Take care, master sergeant. Keep up the good work."

September 13, 1941

"Two thousand men Wow! Maybe I'll be able to get a date now, Virg."

"Maybe. Don't get your hopes up too high, Gabby. They're not going to disappear overnight. I'm just hoping the lines in the chow hall get shorter for a while."

"So, those guys aged out, huh? You turn 28 and you're gone. Guess we might get out at 12 months. When do you turn 28, Virgil?"

"December 30th this year."

"Do you want to get out?"

"Not really. If we're going to stay in, I'd just as soon get over there instead of doing maneuvers and such stateside. This training has been good, really. I feel pretty good."

"For an old man, you mean."

"Yes, sir. And as an old man that can still run rings around you, Shorty. I'm fixin' to get me a new garrison cap." The older man jumped up, snatched the cap off his friend's head and ran out of the mess tent."

"Hold up, buddy," Gabby yelled.

"Come on, let's not miss the first bus."

Letter Two

Camp Polk Louisiana

December 09, 1941

Dear Mitch and Eleanor,

Well, any ideas anybody in the 36th Armored Infantry had about jumping ship at age 28 or after they hit twelve-month point, are kaput! After the attack at Pearl Harbor, nobody is talking about getting out. I think every man jack here would re-up for ten years at this point.

Things are fine here. Keep those sailors at Pearl Harbor in your prayers.

Virgil

Camp Young: Desert Training May to October 1942

In late spring of 1942, the 54th Armored Battalion was sent to Camp Young in the Mojave Desert to train under General George Patton. The rest of the 3rd Armored Division followed soon thereafter. They bivouacked 1.3 miles west of Freda, which, was a name on a weathered board in the middle of the desert. Essentially, there was no camp.

It was a key training facility for units engaging in combat during the 1942–1943 North African campaign. It stretched from the outskirts of Pomona, California, east to within 50 miles of Phoenix, Arizona; south to the suburbs of Yuma, Arizona; and north into the southern tip of Nevada.

In early summer of 1942, General Patton was assigned to Northern Africa in preparation for Operation Torch. General Alvin C. Gillem assumed command. Desert maneuvers were described as having done more to toughen the 3rd and prepare them for ultimate combat.

These commenced in early summer. Sardines, known to the troops as 'goldfish and camp biscuits were the staff of life for the troops.

During this time that the 3rd Armored Division became part of the VII Corps, an association that was resumed and continued throughout the European campaign. After two weeks of maneuvers, which commenced in late September, 3rd Armored Division was transferred, in mid-October,1942, to Camp Pickett Virginia, located 60 miles southwest of Richmond.

Letter Three

Mojave Desert

September 10, 1942

Dear Mitch and Eleanor,

I am ashamed for not having answered your letter sooner. But we are kept busy as hell now. We work Saturday and Sunday now. Some weeks we get a day off in the middle of week. Last week we had Tuesday off. So, I went to Los Angeles.

We go out on maneuvers and stay out for several days then come back to camp for a day or two. We leave again Sunday morning and will be gone a week so I won't have chance to write or get any mail. We have always been on blue side, but this time we are going to be on red.

It is pretty tough staying out there for very long. We take all our water and food along. Just canned food is all we have to eat, nothing hot.

Yes, Eleanor sent pictures. I wrote her a letter yesterday. A fellow took four of our pictures in Florentine Gardens at Hollywood. I mailed it to Eleanor for it was so large it was hard to carry. Picture wasn't so good but it will be a souvenir. I bought a Masonic ring last time I was in L.A.

I had a letter from Ray about a week ago. I also got one from Dickey last week.

Well, Mitch, there isn't much to write about here. Will try and not be so long next time.

Virgil

"When do you suppose we'll get leave, instead of just 24-hour passes?"

"I don't know, Gabby. If I had to guess, I'd say before we get to Virginia or maybe Pennsylvania and get ready to go to Europe. I hope we'll get at least five days."

"That would be swell. I could go see about things back home. Haven't heard from Birdie, but she can't hardly write much except for taking orders at the restaurant. I finally got a letter from Laverne, came yesterday. She tracked down Birdie at the diner. And she said Birdie is definitely pregnant. Laverne's got this idea that if Birdie doesn't want to keep the baby, maybe she can adopt it. She says maybe we could raise it. But I don't know how that would work out."

"There's a lot of 'ifs' in there, Gabby."

"That's for sure. But I'd kind of like to have a chance to raise one of my own children. My folks were so old and sick by the time I came along, they were more like my grandparents. I felt like I had to raise my own self."

Letter Four

Rice, California

10/01/1942

Dear Mitch, Eleanor, Jim and Donna

Just a line to let you know that I am on my way and what my new address is. We are going to Camp Pickett, Virginia. I don't know where it is but close to North Carolina line I think.

We left Rice at six o'clock Friday night and are in New Mexico now close to Texas line. We will just go across the corner of Texas into Oklahoma, Kansas to Kansas City and on to Chicago. From there I don't know but probably right through

Columbus. That is going to be bad to go through there and not be able to get off. It will take us about 7 or 8 days to make trip. It is over 3000 miles.

I am on the first train that left and we have all our vehicles on it. Just brought enough men for guard duty. You see a guard must ride on each flat car. So, I have to stay back there about half the time. I get off at noon and go back at midnight. The farther we go the colder it gets. Boy, it sure gets next to a fellow after being in heat of the desert so long.

I only hope I like Virginia as well as California. I really hate to leave. I am lucky in a way to get to see so much country. So far, we have come the same route we went out. But will soon turn north into new country for me.

My buddy, Gabby, got on the same assignment as me on this train. He's a fine fellow. I hope you'll get to meet him some day.

Will write more when I get to Virginia.

Love,

Virgil

PS: *this will be my new address*

Company A, 36th Armored Infantry

A.P.O. #253

Camp Pickett, Va.

BOOK FIVE:

Of Tribal Lore and Seeing Elephants

During 12 on and 12 off, two soldiers were stretched out in a Jeep tethered to a grinding flatcar, gazing alternately at the retreating, black western landscape and the brilliant western desert sky.

"Hey, Virgil I always wanted to drive through the Southwest. And now I'm doin' it—except for the part about the Jeep being on a flatcar and us looking at where we have been and all."

"Sometimes I wish I could be an engineer like my brother, Mitch. You'd like Mitch, Gabby. I've told him about you and me being buddies and liking traveling and such. I hope we'll see some sights in Europe, if and when we get there."

"Boy Virg, I hope we can get some good quarters in Virginia. And I hope we get some leave. I'd like to go to Washington DC. I haven't heard from Laverne in a coon's age. Last thing I heard, Birdie gave up her baby—a little boy—to the Carmelite Sisters. And Laverne was going to try to get custody. I need to get back there, Virg."

"I don't think we're going to be getting 'Over There' until we're done fiddlin' around in Virginia, Gabby. I heard we might end up in the mountains in Pennsylvania after Virginia."

A sergeant hollered to them. "Hey, fellas. We're gonna have a 12-hour layover in Gallup, New Mexico. They're bringing in some New Mexico National Guardsmen to watch the train. We'll be able to get off and go into the station, grab some chow and sit around the stove."

"Sounds good, sergeant," Gabby said with a grin.

An hour later, just after midnight, the train pulled into the yards north of Route 66 in Gallup. It was cooling off and the sounds of drunken men in heavy coats—laughing, expectorating, screaming, crying, dying came from behind a tangled pile of busted up railroad ties.

"Boys, we're not going over there," Sergeant McMullen said as he shook his head. "Those poor souls over there. There's men dying in the alleys just up off Route 66."

"Who are they, sergeant?" Gabby asked.

"They're Indians who traded life on the reservation for desperation and debauchery here on the mean streets of Gallup."

"Even the Indians I knew back in Kalamazoo didn't seem to hold their liquor very well," Gabby said with a frown."

"It's not their fault, private; not by a longshot. There's something different in Native Americans, and they can't process alcohol like most people. I mean, it's a cultural thing, too. If you watch them when they get a new bottle, they open it, throw away the cap, and drink it straight down or hand it over to their buddy. I find it interesting, being an old Cavalry man myself, when folks start bragging about how we folks from the United States drove the Indians out. If it hadn't been for liquor and disease, we might never have crossed the Ohio River. You look at it that way and we don't seem so tough, after all, maybe."

"Sergeant, I think we'd both like to hear about your life. How you got in the Army. Things you've done, your family and such," Virgil said.

"Well, be careful what you ask for—you might get it and wish you hadn't asked." The older man produced a long cigar from a jacket pocket and lighter from his pants pocket. "Well, I attended a reunion of my grandfather's old outfit in 1895 with my father and my Uncle Caleb. I guess I was awed at the time. It was at Willard's Hotel close to the White House in Washington. The facilities, like most of the attendees, were getting a little threadbare. General Sheridan had passed a year or two before.

"The glory of those days, though, when the Grand Army of the Republic was rolling inexorably toward victory, was still in the air. The applause for their deceased comrades was heartfelt. In that ballroom I caught the bug, or whatever you want to call it—thirst for Glory, desire to see the Elephant. It led me to join the Army a few months later.

"I rode up Kettle Hill with Teddy's outfit, got through that campaign without being shot or contracting malaria. Along the way, my Uncle Caleb taught me most of things I would need to know to for the next 40 years as an NCO in the US Army. "I'm glad I listened while I was in his platoon, because he was one of the men who didn't make it down from Kettle Hill.

"The older I've gotten, the less I've cared about the *Cult of Glory*, as perceived by civilians. Our family traces a battle-hardened tradition back to the days of Robert the Bruce and William Wallace in the British Isles and later, on the Continent. For *Glory*, we McMullen men have marched from home and family, slogging back and forth across various European wastelands created by other earlier men from sunnier climes. They left home and family suspecting they'd never return. And all for the *Glory* of causes and empires many, if not most of them, had never seen and only a few could have pointed out on a map.

"Beginning in the 1780s, those emigrating countrymen traveled to the so-called New World and helped kill the French, Spanish, English, Indians, and each other in our new home. 'Our more recent forefathers, latter-day legionnaires—fouled and besmirched in steerage—left the starvation of the Great Famine and found a new continent on which to hone the skills associated with the pursuit of a *Glory* we seemed to have been born to chase after. They arrived in time to fight for both sides in the American Civil War. While the Union won the war, the respective Irish units fought to a draw.

"Those that survived that most uncivil war in one piece found a place in the ongoing slaughter of the Red Men in the West.

"After all the enemies in this hemisphere were neutered, penned up, or killed, nearly 500 years into this North America project, we who'd told ourselves we wanted only to lay down our arms for plowshares and pruning hooks found ourselves pressed yet again into service and handed back our swords and rifles.

"And when enough brown rebels in Cuba were neutralized, we celebrated—briefly. Then the generals and politicians turned their sights on the next target. Most of us who survived Cuba and the Philippines wanted a rest.

"Some of us got a chance to chase Pancho Villa around Mexico with General Pershing and the 8th Brigade. It was sold afterward as a tune-up for the war in Europe. Several of us got a chance to go with Black Jack to Europe, where we would have a chance to return to the killing fields on which our forefathers had marched, lived, killed and died for 1000 years. We had the chance to die back in the Old World—in the trenches and the forests, on and under water and in the rarified air.

"Everyone in my family had ties to the military. The men all enlisted and the women stayed home and brought new recruits into the world. Even my daughter, Gabriella, served as an Army nurse in France in 1917-1918. She died while saving lives during the last month of that conflict.

"According to the older folks, my ancestors in Ireland probably served as well. As the saying goes—' rich man's war is a poor man's fight.'

"My grandfather, Wynton George McMullen was born in 1841 on the ship that was bringing his mother over to America. She died at 16 and was given a burial at sea shortly after her son's birth. She'd probably been impregnated by a priest or one of the sons of the Protestant landowner of the estate the McMullen's all worked on at that time.

"Fortunately, a neighbor lady from the Old Country was on the ship and could wet nurse him. She kept him with her family when they settled in Boston. And when The Hunger started a few years later and the McMullen clan arrived in droves, Wynton was located by his Aunt Margaret and raised in New York City among his aunts, uncles and cousins.

"Wynton George McMullen died of septic shock after losing his left arm in Virginia. He'd been a sergeant in Sheridan's cavalry in the Shenandoah Valley and was wounded while leading a counter attack that helped turn a skirmish around, temporarily.

"My uncle on my mother's side, Sergeant Andrew Murphy, had come to New York from Ireland in 1854 when he was 11. A few years later, he joined a group of young men travelling west into Colorado to work in the gold fields at Cripple Creek. Andrew ended up working in a blacksmith shop.

"When the Civil War broke out, the whole gang in the shop, including soon-to-be Private Andrew Murphy, enlisted in Company K, 1st Colorado Infantry of the 1st Regiment of Colorado Volunteers. That outfit fought under Major John M. Chivington at the Battle of Glorieta Pass in New Mexico in March of 1862. Silas Stillman Soule, who Andrew worked with at the blacksmith's shop, was cited for bravery in that battle and began working his way up the ranks. Glorieta Pass effectively ended Confederate activity in Colorado.

"Chivington's Volunteers remained intact and Sergeant Murphy was present at the Sand Creek Massacre on November 29, 1864, in southeast Colorado. He served in Captain Soule's D Company, the only Company of Chivington's force that refused to participate in that unprovoked and unnecessary slaughter.

"Andrew joined back up when the business in Cuba and the Philippines started and served under Roosevelt in Cuba. My Uncle Caleb and I saw him several times before the action started, but we were in different outfits going up that Hill.

"Uncle Andrew mustered out of the Army in 1899. I only got to visit a couple of times—early summer in 1901—at the VA Hospital in Chillicothe, Ohio, after he'd been put on disability. He'd been wounded, shot in the ass at Glorieta Pass and also suffered serious shrapnel wounds in Cuba with Teddy's Rough Riders.

"He was a tough old guy and a true enlisted man, from his calloused, flat feet to his bald, freckled head. And the use of the word 'sir' aimed in his direction always elicited a loud, 'Don't call me sir. I worked for a living!'

"The only officer that he ever had a good word for was Captain Soule. Uncle Andrew considered Soule to be the finest man he ever knew. And it didn't hurt that Soule had come up through the ranks.

"My last visit was 1903, the year he died. He was 60, I think. But he had a lot of miles on him. I think he sensed that this would be our last visit. It was a nice day in late spring. An orderly pushed him out to a courtyard that looked out on low green hills in the distance.

"You know, Kettle Hill wasn't much bigger than that ridge out there, Philip."

"Close, I'd say, Uncle.'

"He shook his head and sighed. I've got six cigars one of the orderlies give me a couple days ago, you want one?"

"That sounds good, Sarge.'

"He pulled a bag out of a pocket in his robe and handed it to me. 'Here's the stogies. Do you have somethin' to cut the ends off and a light?'

'I sure do'.

I pulled out two cigars, cut the ends with a pocket knife and handed him one. It took a few matches, but we got 'em lit finally and sat back and watched the smoke trail off chasing a pack of cumulus clouds that were charging toward the low hills to the east.

"This ain't exactly a deluxe Cuban cigar, but it tastes good. Thing about cigars, it's more about who you're smoking with and where, than it is about the cigar itself. Best cigar I ever had was with Captain Soule and some of the boys from Company D after he'd testified at that Congressional Hearing. No, sir, it ain't the cigar, it's the company. Andrew, think you could find someone who could use these other two?'"

"Yes, Uncle, I believe I could think of something.'

He handed two cigars to William, the orderly. 'Maybe you've got someone to share these with, William.'

"Thank you, sir.'

Don't call him sir, William. This man worked for a living!"

"The three of us smiled. Uncle Andrew picked up the envelope he had in the pocket of his robe and gently removed the brittle pages. "This is some papers and a letter one of the majors under Chivington sent me. Would you read this aloud, Phillip? Best man I ever knew, Captain Soule."

"It would be my pleasure, Uncle Andrew. Here goes:

"Captain Soule was an abolitionist and a friend to all people, Indian, White, Negro. It's funny, Chivington made a big deal about being an Abolitionist, too. He was also a Methodist minister. What I never understood was how someone could be an abolitionist and butcher those Indians that way at Sand Creek.

"He didn't just oversee a wholesale slaughter of hundreds of peaceful, unarmed Indians, he allowed his men to commit terrible atrocities. And in some ways the worst part was bringing scalps and other body parts that had been mutilated back to Denver and parading them around downtown. Chivington was the true savage.

"He was a jackass at Glorieta Pass, too. He wasted over an hour after we'd gotten scouts reports of a Confederate supply train before acting on those reports. And then he took too much credit for the outcome.

"In the end, it was a tactical win for the Confederates—but a strategic victory for the Union—that essentially ended any meaningful Confederate presence in the Rocky Mountain West. Chivington strutted about, wringing as much Glory as he could as the so-called Victor of Johnson's Ranch. He'd been sent to execute a flank attack. He conveniently ignored the fact that he had not attempted, let alone achieved his mission. The discovery of the supply train was a lucky accident—one of those—*even a blind hog stumbles over an acorn once in a while*—moments.

"The final acts of John Chivington's life played out in a succession of tawdry vignettes reported in public records from newspaper articles to minutes of that Congressional Hearing.

> "'Damn any man who sympathizes with Indians! ... I have come to kill Indians, and believe it is right and honorable to use any means under God's heaven to kill Indians. ... Kill and scalp all, big and little; nits make lice.'
>
> —Col. John Milton Chivington"

From the Report issued by the Congressional Committee:

> "'As to Colonel Chivington, your committee can hardly find fitting terms to describe his conduct. Wearing the uniform of the United States, which should be the emblem of justice and humanity; holding the important position of commander of a military district, and therefore having the honor of the government to that extent in his keeping, he deliberately planned and executed a foul and dastardly massacre which would have disgraced the worst savage among those who were the victims of his cruelty. Having full knowledge of their

friendly character, having himself been instrumental to some extent in placing them in their position of fancied security, he took advantage of their inapprehension and defenseless condition to gratify the worst passions that ever cursed the heart of man. Whatever influence this may have had upon Colonel Chivington, the truth is that he surprised and murdered, in cold blood, the unsuspecting men, women, and children on Sand Creek, who had every reason to believe they were under the protection of the United States authorities.'

"United States Congress Joint Committee on the Conduct of the War, 1865 (testimonies and report)".

"Chivington resigned from the service in February 1865. In 1865 his son, Thomas, drowned and Chivington returned to Nebraska to administer the estate. There he became an unsuccessful freight hauler. He seduced and then married his son's widow, Sarah. In October 1871, she obtained a decree of divorce for non-support.

His Long Life Ended". *Denver Republican.* October 5, 1894

"A particularly heinous outcome of Chivington's actions and the climate of hatred it helped to engender involved the assassination of Captain Soules in Denver, shortly after his marriage. No one was ever arrested or prosecuted for this crime. Chivington, however, was either directly or indirectly to blame—you can be sure of that.'

"Chivington] lived a miserable, rootless existence dying finally at the age of seventy-three back in Denver alone and forgotten."

"I folded up the papers and handed them to Andrew.

"Captain Soule was as good a man as I've ever known. Smart and educated and he cared about the men serving under him. Poor fellow, he just got married, too,' Andrew said with a catch in his throat.

"When my Uncle Andrew and I shook hands, I think we both knew that would be our last visit."

"My service under Pershing in New Mexico, chasing after Pancho Villa and his bandits was interesting. And I got to meet some fine men—Pershing and Patton. I got to serve with a bunch of fellows in France in World War II. That's where I got to know, Lieutenant Maurice Rose. He had 'it' then. And he has it now. He connects with his troops. Omar Bradley dresses plain and likes to talk with the enlisted folks. And the men like him.

"Colonel Rose dresses up with those riding pants and all. But for him, that phrase of his, Lead from the Front, describes what he does. Men in the trenches saw him do that. And GIs in this war will see it, too."

Letter Five

Company a, 36th Armored Infantry

A.P.O. #253

Camp Pickett, Va. 10/18/1942

Dear Mitch,

Well here I am back east in Virginia. We got in here yesterday. Were on train for six days making trip. Some trip, practically coast to coast. Came through thirteen states but I had been in all except four.

I just got a letter you sent to California today. I knew you had moved and didn't know your address or I would have written. We didn't know what our address would be here until we got on the train. In fact, we didn't even know for sure where we were going.

Haven't been here long enough to know much about camp. But from what I've seen I like it fine. Seems strange to be back in barracks after sleeping out on the ground or tents for so long. This camp is located between Petersburg and Lynchburg not far from North Carolina line and about 250 miles from Washington, D.C.

Well I can say one thing for the Army—I am getting to see some country. Coast to coast and through 20 states so far. I rather hated to leave California though. It was getting cooler on desert and I really liked Los Angeles.

On the way out here, we travelled all over Ohio but it was night and of course I never had a chance to get off. We came through Chicago to Toledo, down to Columbus, Portsmouth, Ironton and crossed into West Virginia.

Will write more after I get settled down here. Our company hasn't all got here yet. Just a few of us came on ahead on train with all vehicles. Expect rest tonight or tomorrow. Glad you like your new place and hope everything is O.K.

Virgil

PS: Here's the kicker. I got a postcard from Orpha informing me that Louise is in Akron and will be working in **t**hat bearing factory I worked at after high school, the job that Mervyn Usher got me. Guess he's a big shot there now, vice-president or something.

Letter Six

Camp Pickett, Virginia

11/15/1942

Dear Mitch,

Just a few lines to let you know that I got back from my furlough OK. Sorry I didn't get to see you or Ralph. Don't think that I blame you for not coming down though. From the way Eleanor said you are working.

I thought about trying to come or go that way. But you see I could catch a train straight to Columbus from Blackstone. It was by Norfolk Western and went through West Va. And Portsmouth, Ohio. To come to New Castle, I would have to change several times and go on different roads.

I had a pretty good time home but things surely were dead. I was down home from Wednesday until Sunday evening. Spent Sunday nite and till evening on Monday in Columbus.

Fred and Doris planned a party for me Saturday night. My assignment guarding the equipment kept me from attending. I heard Louise was down over the week end and went to the party. I managed to get over to see Eleanor Sunday morning. I thought Eleanor and the kids looked swell. Donna sure has grown.

I suppose you are surprised to know that I'm still mooning over Louise but damn it there is no one else back there for me to run around with. And when a fellow is on furlough he likes to have a date or two.

I have seen Paul Childs twice since I got here. He is stationed here. Has had all his teeth pulled. I also ran into Ambrose McDermott one night. But his outfit has left here now.

I made out a $25 a month allotment to mother. I also raised my insurance from five to ten thousand. If we ever go across my pay will be raised 20%. Then they won't be much to spend for over there. So, I decided to have $25 a month sent home and I will have it when I get back. If I stay here and need it, they can send it to me.

My insurance would entitle folks to $110 a month if anything should happen to me. I also have a $25 bond that I am paying for out of my pay. I just want you to know what folks are entitled to.

We may never go for all I know. But it is only natural to not expect to always stay in the US. We have been pretty fortunate to have not gone before.

I want you to do with the school bus as you want to and think best. Whatever you do is OK with me. If anything happens to me my share of bus belongs to you and Eleanor. I intended to tell Grace and Ralph Sunday but it skipped my mind. However, I will write them and hope they understand.

It has always been more of a worry to you than me so think you deserve it. I don't suppose it is worth a whole lot anymore anyway.

Now don't let this letter worry you. I just tell you these things so everyone will understand. If, and when we go across it will be too late to write after I know it.

Glad you are having good work. But don't try to work too hard. Hope you have a Merry Christmas.

Virgil

Camp Pickett, Virginia —October 1942 to January 1943

The Division history notes that a "strange feeling of hurry, hurry finality pervaded Camp Pickett. The men who went home on furlough or leave decided that 'this one' had to be good because it would be their last before overseas shipment."

Original plans called for embarkation in January 1943, but German submarine activity resulted in postponements. The men trained and waited. A favorite song for the men here was, *"Take It Off."*

Letter Seven

Camp Pickett, Virginia

11/28/1942

Mitch and Eleanor,

Hope you had a good Thanksgiving. We had a good one here at Camp Pickett. Turkey with all the trimmings, potatoes (mashed and sweet), fresh vegetables and cornbread. For dessert, we had pumpkin pie with whipped cream and some really good ice cream (must have come from Jersey milk).

After we finished eating they brought in a Band that played swing music. With hundreds of men and only few dozen girls we all got a chance to get out on the floor. Some of the guys danced with each other while they were waiting for their turn with a female. Not me, though.

I couldn't help thinking about Louise. We're good partners dancing, and in other ways, too. We got real close the last time I saw her. I thought we had an understanding, but I haven't heard anything from her. I guess she's moved on.

Love to all the folks,

Virgil

PS: I finally got promoted to Private First Class

"Hey, Gabby, how long you been back?"

"Virgil, good to see you. I've been back about an hour. How was your leave?"

"I volunteered to stay at the last minute. I'll be able to add those four days to my next furlough. Did you get to see Laverne?"

Gabby grimaced a bit. "I did get to see her and stay with her for two days."

"Did she get custody of the baby?"

"She did. The Carmelite Sisters had asked her to give them a $75 donation. She only had $50. I kicked in 25 bucks. But' I'll tell you, little Jake is quite a kid. Just turned 13 months the day I first saw him."

"Laverne had to give up her job teaching after she adopted Jake."

"Why? That doesn't seem fair."

"That's what I thought, too. I think I'll set up an allotment of $20 a month to be sent to Laverne. And have her as beneficiary for my life insurance. I think she's doin' alright. But, that's a tough adjustment for her."

"Gabby, you're about the best friend I've ever had. I hope things work out for you and Laverne and Jake. And I want you to know that if anything happens to you, I'll do my best see that those two are provided for."

"Thanks, Virg. I feel the same way. I know this situation with Louise— not hearing from her— is hard on you."

"Alright, I guess we'd better knock off this *sorry sister* stuff and get you checked back in, buddy."

Letter Eight

Camp Pickett, Virginia

Dec. 25, 1942

Dear Mitch,

I just came back from Christmas dinner. We certainly had a swell meal. Each man got a flat fifty of cigarettes and a sack of candy. Several of the fellows had their wives here for dinner. Seemed strange to have ladies in the mess hall but it made it seem a little more like Christmas.

It warmed up yesterday and melted all of our snow so Christmas came a couple days late for us to have a white Christmas. We aren't working today but it doesn't seem much like Christmas. Nothing to do here. The PX is closed so we can't even get a bottle of beer.

I suppose Eleanor and the kids are with you now. You probably didn't get down home. I got a lot of cards from people back home.

I got pictures that I had taken. They weren't so bad. Am having some more made. We'll get them next week. Having enough made so that I can send all of you including Ralph and Grace one. Sent the one I got to the folks. Will send yours as soon as I get them.

Yes, I got cigarettes and thanks a lot. I may try for a pass on New Year's and go to Washington D.C. I have only been there once.

Love to all,

Virgil

Indiantown Gap, Pennsylvania—January to September 1943

"In mid-January, 1943, the 3rd Armored Division transferred to Indiantown Gap, a Pennsylvania National Guard Camp, 30 miles from Harrisburg, Pennsylvania. In the coldest weather they'd seen, the troops began accelerated training, which included long (25 miles with full equipment, road marches, 25 miles with full equipment. Exercises and new infiltration courses were also on the schedule.

Harrisburg was "taken over" by the 3rd Armored Division during off-duty hours. Some 40&8 buses ran each day at 5 PM and Saturdays at 11 AM. The hot tune for dancing in Harrisburg was the *Pennsylvania Polka*.

Training continued in earnest. The physical fitness test included 33 push-ups, a 300-yard dash and a five-mile hike in full field gear in 60 minutes or less."

Spearhead page 51

Letter Nine

Indiantown Gap

Military Reservation

Pennsylvania

1/15/1943

Dear Mitch and Eleanor,

I am in charge of quarters tonight, so will write a few letters in my spare time. This is payday and lots of fellows have gone into town. Won't get much sleep, as they will be checking in all night.

What are still in camp are mostly shooting craps and playing poker. I will have to run them out of the dayroom and latrines at eleven o'clock. That is a job too for they don't like to quit.

We are working all day tomorrow and Sunday. Guess will have a day off next week some time.

I got notice today that I am entitled to wear 'Good Conduct Medal'. You must have served at least one year of active service while the US is at war and have no black marks whatsoever on your record. That is never missed a formation unless excused, never picked up by MPs and so forth. Sixty out of a company of 200 got them so it is somewhat of an honor.

I am enclosing a clipping from the paper that is about our division. Might be of a little interest. If you happen to be writing the folks, you might send it on.

How did you like everything at Windsor? As quiet as ever, I suppose.

This will be all for this time.

Love to All,

Virgil

"April 15, 1943, the second anniversary of the reconstituted Armored Division was celebrated with a review that included lots of brass," as well as Governor Martin of Pennsylvania.

The following week, individual firing qualifications, as well as platoon combat firing and tactical proficiency qualifications, were undertaken."

Spearhead page 50

Letter Ten

May 16, 1943

Indiantown Gap, Pa.

Dear Mitch and Eleanor,

Received your two letters O.K. The pictures were unusual but not too good. Oh well you can't expect something from nothing. I enjoyed the articles you sent. The boys wound up things pretty quick once they got started in Africa.

I suppose it sounds foolish and boastful for me to say I wish I had been there. But I like most of fellows often wish they would send us. After almost two years of it gets tiresome. We don't feel like we are doing any good here and after all we came into this army to fight. I know that it is hell over there and if I ever go, I will probably wish I were back here. But I can't help but want to and feel I should go. When this war is all over, I will feel like a heel to think I was in the Army so long and never got out of the US.

I have gotten so I am almost ashamed to go home. So many have come in long after I did and are over there and I am still here. I know people must wonder if I am in the Boy Scouts or the Army.

As for how boys are going to feel after war. It is hard to say but I know the longer you stay in the wider is the gulf between you and rest of the world. It is going to be hard for ones of us who don't have something definite (job or family) to come back to, to adjust ourselves to civilian life.

One of the biggest questions in every soldier's mind is how will things be after war. Will we be assured a job and right to make a living? I often wonder just what I will ever find to do when I get out. I often feel that I have made pretty much of a mess of my life. But then I have no one to blame but myself.

I expect by now you are wondering if I am preaching a sermon or what. So enough of that and on to something else.

Had a day and a half off last week and went to Scranton. It is really pretty up there now. Just up one mountain and down another. I don't believe we will have any summer here either. We went in our summer uniform yesterday and like to froze last night.

Some talk that we will get furloughs soon. It is about time they start. But hasn't been any official announcement yet.

I am feeling fine and hope you all are same.

Love to all,

Virgil

Letter Eleven

7/01/1943

Dear Mitch and all,

I guess I haven't written you since I was home so a few lines tonight.

I got Friday, Sat. and Sunday week before last off. I left camp Thursday night at six. Got the New York and St Louis train in Harrisburg at 00:20 and arrived in Columbus at 5:30 Friday morning. Took McConnelsville bus at 6:30 and caught a ride to Windsor with Les Wooten. Stopped in bank and Maxine was just leaving for lunch and offered to take me home. So, I got down home for dinner. Really made swell connections.

Saturday the folks and I went to Grace's for dinner. I went down home for supper. Neal and Mary Lou were home so we went by and got them and went up to see Fred Kennard for a while.

Sunday morning the folks took me to McConnelsville and I caught the ten o'clock bus. I left Columbus at 6:30 that evening and was supposed to get in Harrisburg at 3:30. However, train was two hours late. I got to camp just as boys were falling out for reveille. Maybe you think I wasn't sweating. Five minutes more and I would have been late. That is what I call using a pass completely up. But I had a good time and was glad I went. It still seems strange to be home and not see Louise.

I won't be able to get another pass for at least a month. Maybe then I can get back over to see you. I enjoyed my last leave down home, but I found it hard to go back and forth past the Forest place. I'd really like to see you and Eleanor and the kids.

PS: Sorry if I sound confused about Louise. I got a letter from Orpha. She said Louise was married and had a baby. I guess if folks had heard about all that you didn't tell me because I'd get my Irish up. Well, I'm in good company here in the Army. Seems like folks back home think we can't figure out what's happened when our sweethearts stop writing. I guess I'm one up on most guys. My sweetheart never did write. Look at me getting all weepy. I guess I better stop crying in my beer. Nothing will ever be exactly settled for me until this damn mess is over.

You know how I feel about Louise. It just doesn't seem that things will ever work out with us. I envy you—Eleanor is a great gal and you two have a fine marriage and family.

My buddy, Gabby and I are going to Washington D.C. tomorrow. We've got a 48-hour pass. He's having woman trouble, too. We can take turns crying on each other's shoulder.

Hope everyone is O.K.

Love to all,

Virgil

Camp Kilmer, NJ: August 10 to 27, 1943

"August was a busy month for 3rd Armored Division personnel. On August 9, 1943, an advanced party transferred to Fort Hamilton in Brooklyn en route to overseas deployment. The following day, August 10th, Lt. General Leslie McNair, Commanding General of Army Ground Forces, declared, "This division is ready to fight as soon as it gets off the boat." These men would prove the veracity of this statement, albeit from different boats, nearly eight months later, on the beaches of Normandy."

Spearhead page 52

Camp Kilmer, NJ: August 10 to 27, 1943

BOOK SIX:

The End of the Beginning: 1943

Letter Twelve

Sept. 19. 1943

Cpl Virgil Thomas

Dear Mitch,

I have arrived in England and am right in the pink. The trip over was very interesting. Much to my surprise I didn't get seasick. The country here is very beautiful. Hope to be able to get a pass later and see some of the towns.

I haven't gotten any mail yet. When you write, you should use V mail for it comes through much quicker than regular mail. I must try and get Ray's [Bachelor] address for I might accidently have chance to see him some time.

I wrote Dad and Mother but couldn't tell them I was in England then. So, if you happen to write you could tell them for, I won't write again for a few days.

Tell Jim and Donna I said hello.

Love to all,

Virgil

<u>Sutton Veny, England 9/1/1943 to 6/24/1944</u>

"Ships embarked on September 5, 1943 and arrived in England September 16 on 9/16/1943. The 36th Armored Infantry settled in Sutton Veny, one hundred miles SW of London.

Soldiers of the 3rd Armored soon learned the "Canadian Crawl," the "Polly Glide," and the "Okie Dokie." They also learned *Roll Me Over* a lusty wartime ballad best suited to the barracks and marching columns.

Across the downs of Britain in late 1943, all the great armies of the Western allies were gathering for the much-discussed assault on Europe. Division officers went along with the 5th Canadian Armored Division to maneuvers in the area east of Andover and north to and beyond Hungerford. Throughout their nine-month stay in Great Britain, hundreds of "Spearhead" soldiers visited the various British and colonial units to swap ideas and techniques. On the "aircraft" carrier anchored off the shores of fortress Europe, the allies learned to respect each other. They began to cement the ties of that first team that swept onto Normandy beaches in June of 1944.

Initially in England, the 3rd had been attached to the V Corps. In early November, when Lt. General Omar Bradley's 1st Army was activated, the division was assigned to Major General Hugh Woodruff's VII Corps, later to be commanded by Major General "Lightning Joe" Collins on the western front.

Training in England was hard and complete. Road marches, obstacle courses, maintenance, and all of the familiar Army drill routines were dusted off and put into practice. Schools which catered to various subjects, such as aircraft recognition, camouflage, waterproofing, and chemical warfare. New weapons were issued and tested. Command post exercises on the downs were not uncomfortable in the early fall, but as raw, winter weather approached, they became a trial. The division slowly assimilated greater knowledge of terrain and its advantages. Continual maneuvers helped, and the men learned the art of shrugging off limitations of blackout, weather, and discomfort. Welcome 48-hour passes were issued to the men after they had been in Britain for six weeks, and the tricolor patch began to turn up in such places as London, Bournemouth, and Bristol. Troops sweated out air raids in the English metropolis. They traveled the byways of Leicester Square and saw the terrible bomb damage in London. And they saw the dead enemy for the first time. Slowly, as a by-product of all these things, men of the future "Spearhead" became aware that the war was close, that the byword in Europe was "kill or be killed." They trained with a solemn thoroughness.

During this time the division was doing a great deal of range firing. Field problems became the order of the day in November. The 36th Armored Infantry, "Parks' Own", went out on a six-day workout. Division Headquarters made its first overnight bivouac on the coldest of early fall days. All the other units participated, and the downs of Salisbury Plain were awakened as never before in history with the rumble of motors. Command Post Exercises were frequent, and no amount of cold or wetness served to postpone them. Maneuvering over the chill downs, in frost or raw, driving rain, 3rd Armored Division soldiers learned to disregard the elements to accomplish their primary missions.

The training highlight of December was a combined arms problem on the range west of Chitterne northeast of Sutton Veny), This was planned and supervised by General Hickey and the Combat Command "A" staff. In this operation, a tank battalion, plus an infantry company, an artillery battery, and an engineer platoon, demonstrated the employment of a covering force in lieu of an advance guard when contact is imminent. They demonstrated the occupation of attack positions and the detailed fire plan necessary for a coordinated attack, and the employment of battalion supporting weapons in the initial stages of the attack and as security against counter attacks during reorganization. Under the guiding hand of General Hickey, the problem was extremely successful."

[Spearhead pages 54-56]

Letter Thirteen

England 9/23/4

Dear Mitch and all,

Got my first letter yesterday, from Faye Bachelor. Today I got yours and several more. Boy was I sure glad to get them. Can't write much on a V-mail so will write a regular letter tonight. Let me know how long it takes.

The article you sent is a very good account of what I went through at Port of Embarkation. Haven't received any Heralds yet ['Morgan County Herald' weekly paper] but hope to soon.

I walked into a small-town last night. It was a beautiful walk. The countryside was so pretty and historic looking. Just like you see in the movies and pictures.

The towns are quite different from ours in a rustic sort of way. Of course, it was a complete blackout every night, and is it ever dark! Lots of business places were sold-out. The Pubs (bars to you) didn't open until eight o'clock and only sold bitter (beer), ale and stout which is a real dark beer kind of drink. It is served warm and rather flat tasting so it didn't take much to do me.

Almost everything is rationed here. We have ration cards and go once a week and get our allotment. Seven packs of cigarettes, 1 soap, 2 razor blades, a little gum, 2 candy bars and a little bag of cookies. I brought a pretty good supply so don't need anything very bad yet. You can send me packages if marked 'Christmas' until October 15, after that if you send anything you must have a letter from me asking you to send certain articles. This is merely information and not a hint Ha!

I certainly enjoyed your long letter. You might send this on to folks, as it would probably interest them.

Guess I have told you about all I am allowed to tell. I'll bet Jim [nephew] is proud of that bicycle. Tell him that everyone over here rides them. Some of the boys and officers already bought one. They are hard to get though.

Well, as the English say

Cheerio (goodbye).

Love to all,

Virgil

Letter Fourteen

Oct. 15, 1943 England (L)

Dear Mitch and all,

I received your letter today and your V-mail yesterday. So, I guess V-mail is faster, but then you can't write so much. And I really enjoy the long letters. So, go ahead and use both kinds. Mail is best morale builder we have here. As long as we can hear from home, we get along pretty good. I enjoy the clippings and other letters you enclose, too. I have only received one Herald (Morgan County Herald) so far.

Faye wrote me a nice letter giving me Ray's address. I hope we can get together some time, but it is doubtful. Mother said she thought Doc Kinney and Nira would be married. No fool like an old fool.

Too bad about Mary Ruth. She always seemed like such a likable kid and I can't picture either she or Barbara as anything but kids. But we are liable to let our foot slip at times so I guess we shouldn't blame her, but rather feel sorry for her.

Enjoyed Turner's letter and guess she did seem rather lonesome and ready to go back to Windsor. But guess we all are. Even when we do though it won't ever be the same. I guess we didn't know what good times we were having. It's funny how little incidents that I hadn't thought of for years keep popping into my head.

I have been on one short pass (48 hours) to Bristol and hope to get to London sometime before long. Most of the people are friendly and I enjoy talking to them. They all ask about things in the US. Boy, they sure go for our cigarettes and chewing gum. Especially the girls. If I had been smart, I would have brought some ladies' silk hose from the States. They can't get them here. A fellow could have his choice of the town almost if he had a pair to give her. Ha.

As long as I stay in camp, I don't realize so much that I am across. When you go to town though you do. Soon everyone is aware of fact that it isn't good old US. The pubs are only open from ten to two and six until ten at night. And no jukeboxes or dancing. They seem so quiet compared to ours.

Everyone seems to drink beer and smoke. Blackouts make it hard to get around at night. You don't see many cars. The bicycle seems to be the main way of travelling. So, tell Jim that he has something in common with these people.

Tell Orpha I got her letter and will try to get around to answering it someday.

I can't write all that I would like to so guess will just have to wait until you get me wound up on a few beers sometime. It hardly seems possible when I think back where I was a year ago. [On train from Mojave to Camp Pickett, Va.] almost as far the other way from you as I am now. As the old saying goes there has been a lot of water run under the bridge (boat) since then.

Love to all,

Virgil

Letter Fifteen

10/27/1943

Cpl Virgil Thomas (V)

Dear Folks,

Tomorrow I am making a trip which I have often thought I would like to take, yet I never expected to. I am going to London on a 48-hour pass. I certainly wish I could take some pictures but guess they will have to be just mental ones.

Imagine me if you can, going by 10 Downing Street, Buckingham Palace and Windsor Castle. Hope I get a glimpse of the Princess. Ha. Am looking forward to a good time.

Yes, you write large enough for V mail. It is easily read. Your letters are subject to censorship, but aren't always—probably just spot censored. Received five letters today. They usually come in bunches that way. It sure makes life a little brighter to get them. Will write again after my pass but probably can't tell you much.

Love,

Virgil

Letter Sixteen

10/29/1943

Cpl Virgil Thomas (Vmail)

Dear Folks,

Received a letter from you today. Hope by now you got some of mine. I had a wonderful trip to London. So many things of interest we couldn't see them all, but we really got around for the time we had. I was indeed fortunate one day attended the funeral of Sir Dudley Pound, Admiral of British Fleet, conducted at Westminster Abbey. You can imagine the nobility that would be there. Got a glimpse of the King as he went past in his car. I have a program of services which I cherish very much as a souvenir. Five of us took a tour and saw most of buildings and historic places. I went through where all the Coronations take place. Stood in the exact spot that King Charles I was executed. The cathedral there is one the most beautiful places I ever saw.

There is nothing that I really need. Hope everyone is OK.

Love,

Virgil

Letter Seventeen

11/13/1943 (Card)

Mitch, Eleanor, Jim and Donna,

The song "White Christmas" seems to be running through my head tonight. So, I'll just say, "May your days in the New Year be merry and all your Christmases be white."

Virgil

Letter Eighteen

12/19/1943

Cpl Virgil Thomas (V)

Dear Mitch, Eleanor, Jim and Donna

I am back home as I write this letter. I have a picture in my mind of the front room and all of us there. Remember how excited we, as kids got when it came time to open presents. Would give most anything to be there and see you all. But when I think how fortunate I am compared to many other fellows it makes my Christmas seem merry. We had a swell dinner, turkey and all the trimmings. Some English children are going to eat with us tonight.

Enjoy the clipping you sent. He writes some good stuff. No, probably people back home haven't been touched much by the war. But we don't want you to be. We want, expect and believe most everyone is doing their part and would do more if duty called. Other than that, we want you to have a good time and enjoy life. When I get back, I want things to be as when I left and not to a war-minded, war-conscious people. It is a date for next Christmas. Cheerio.

Love to all,

Virgil

Christmas 1943

"Christmas in Britain was properly celebrated by troops of the 3rd Armored Division. They celebrated with English beer and an occasional bottle of scotch, with parties for British children, and with roast turkey and cranberry sauce in the old tradition. Some of the men visited friends in the hospitable little suburban towns, or spent the evening with WAAFs or Land Army Girls dancing.

For most of the men there was a strange pathos in this wartime Noel in a foreign land. They heard the children of Britain singing Christmas carols beneath the blacked-out windows of thatched cottages in Somerset and Wiltshire, their voices thin and clear, innocent and joyous with the age-old melodies that challenge death and fear. Many of these youngsters had never known a peacetime Christmas, and yet they lifted wan faces to the stars and sang. The tankers of America pooled their rations; then in every hamlet where the soldiers of the new world were quartered, the gum, the chocolate and the Christmas candy of America found its way to these children of war who still felt the exaltation of good will.

It was the same spirit in the old, dark varnished taverns of Britain. Scotch whiskey was almost nonexistent and yet, for this day, a small amount miraculously made its appearance. The busy, blowsy barmaids of England bobbed in and out with great mugs of ale. Yank and Tommy Atkins sang the ageless Christmas carols and roared together into the ribald wartime ditties *Roll Me Over* and *There'll be No Promotions, This Side of the Oceans!*

Shoulder to shoulder, men of the United Nations drank and, while drinking, sang the lovely old cosmopolitan carols that ally themselves with no one nation. Outside in the blue-black night, the searchlights of Great Britain fingered a starry sky in search of Jerry raiders. There was no peace in England, but there was a great brotherhood of free men poised for the endeavor that should guarantee that peace."

[Spearhead pages 56, 59]

Letter Nineteen

11/13/1943 (Card)

Mitch, Eleanor, Jim and Donna,

The song "White Christmas" seems to be running through my head tonight. So, I'll just say, "May your days in the New Year be merry and all your Christmases be white."

Virgil

Letter Twenty

12/19/1943

Cpl Virgil Thomas (V)

Hello All,

Every so often I sit down and make myself write some letters. I often think it would save a lot of work if I made a form and used carbon copies. For I guess I say about the same to everyone. I had a pleasant surprise last week, was going on a pass when who came in and sat beside me but Clair Zumbro. We were both almost too dumbfounded to speak for a moment. We rode on in together and spent the afternoon and evening together.

So, had a nice visit. Had a letter from Orpha and several Christmas cards from folks back home. I see that you are having cold and snow in the States. So maybe you will have a white Christmas. Guess all we can do is dream of one.

Did Jim get the letter I wrote for his birthday?

Love to all,

Virgil

Letter Twenty-One

12/27/1943

Cpl Virgil Thomas (V)

Dear Mitch, Eleanor, Jim and Donna,

I am back home as I write this letter. I have a picture in my mind of the front room and all of us there. Remember how excited we, as kids, got when it came time to open presents. Would give most anything to be there and see you all. But when I think how fortunate I am compared to many other fellows it makes my Christmas seem merry. We had a swell dinner, turkey and all the trimmings. Some English children are going to eat with us tonight.

Enjoyed the clipping you sent. He writes some good stuff. No, probably people back home haven't been touched much by the war. But we don't want you to be. We want, expect and believe most everyone is doing their part and would do more if duty called. Other than that, we want you to have a good time and enjoy life. When I get back I want things to be as when I left and not to a war-minded, war-conscious people. It is a date for next Christmas. Cheerio.

Love to all,

Virgil

Letter Twenty-Two

1/13/1944

S/Sgt. Virgil Thomas (V)

Dear Mitch and all,

I am leaving tomorrow to spend a short furlough in Scotland. Won't have very long but needless to say I am looking forward to it very much. At least I will see where some of 'me ancestors' come from. Ha. Have talked to several who have been there and they all liked it fine. Will stay at Red Brass in Glasgow.

As for my duties, am not allowed to write of them or organization of our units so there isn't much I can tell you. I do have several men and quite a bit of equipment in my charge, though.

I got an announcement of Mervyn's marriage from Uncle Rob and Aunt Mabel last week. Also got a letter from Aunt Susie. Guess Uncle George is in pretty bad shape. No, I have never seen Clair or anyone else again. Guess the bus didn't make us much, but then I didn't expect it too. Certainly, hope Mr. Forest holds out until next Spring. Hope all is well.

Love to all,

Virgil

Letter Twenty-Three

1/19/1944

S/Sgt. Virgil Thomas (V)

Dear Mitch and all,

Just got back from spending a short furlough in Glasgow. I certainly had a swell time. I can't imagine how the people got the name of being stingy. I never saw more hospitable people in my life. Really beautiful country, too. Only wish I had more time. Am certainly going back if I have more opportunity. Spent one day in Edinburgh and the rest of the time in Glasgow. Will send a picture I had taken there later. Will also try to send you a copy of Stars and Stripes which you asked for.

Had a letter from Faye in Sacramento, California where she and Jobie are now living.

Oh yes, I forgot to tell you that the girls in Scotland are very nice and easy to get acquainted with. Maybe it's best that I can't get there often. Ha. I had such a good time and found it so different from what I expected that I can't get over it. Like my buddy, Gabby, kept saying all the way back. Great country. Fine people.

Love to all,

Virgil

Letter Twenty-Four

Virgil

1/19/44

Dear Dad &Mother,

Just got back from Scotland. I certainly had a wonderful trip and a good time. Can't imagine where Scotch people got name of being so stingy. I was never treated better or saw more hospitable people. Don't think I ever had any better time away from home.

Some beautiful scenery there, only wish that I could have had more time. Spent one night in Edinburgh and rest of the time in Glasgow. Both are very modern and much like our own cities. Of course, I got a big kick out of listening to the people talk. I really like their brogue and they all seem to like to talk to Americans. Guess that I am pretty enthused over Scotland but like my buddy kept saying on our way back—Great country—Fine people.

I am sending two cards which I want to save as souvenirs, also a picture I had taken there. I broke one lens out of my rimless glasses and don't like the looks of ones I have with rims so I didn't wear any. It has name and address of place on back so will be a good souvenir. Tried to buy a few to send but so many things rationed that I couldn't find anything suitable.

Had a letter from Jobie and Faye from Sacramento, California where they are now living. Hope all are well and that you and Shirley had a nice birthday. She wrote me a letter telling me about it.

Loads of Love,

Virgil

Letter Twenty-Five

1/23/1944

S/Sgt. Virgil Thomas (V)

Dear Jim,

Will answer your letter which I received some time ago. I was certainly glad to get it and surprised to see how well you can write. Glad that you had a nice Christmas and got to go down to Grandma's. I had a big turkey dinner that day. It wasn't as nice as we used to have when we all went to Grandma and Grandpa's though. I thought a lot about all of you that day and would have given most anything to be with you and Donna.

When you said that Donna couldn't remember when I wasn't in the Army, it made me realize just how long it has been. But I will be back some day before too long and then what times we will have.

Hope all of you are well and have escaped flu epidemic I hear you have had over there. I haven't been sick a day since I got here.

Love,

Virgil

BOOK SEVEN:

War on the Homefront

1941

Birdie

Birdie Le Foret had her baby, a five-pound boy, on August 30, 1941. The baby's father, Melvyn Thurlow, was in training at Camp Polk. Six months after the birth, Birdie and her mother left the infant in the care of a Carmelite Sisters Orphanage in Kalamazoo. Birdie was sent to live with an uncle from her mother's family in Ohio. They had a large farm specializing in produce and fruit. They operated a farm market near Celeryville, Ohio, in the warm weather and a restaurant that was open year-round.

Laverne

Laverne Osgood attempted to insert herself into the lives of Birdie and the boy they called Jake shortly after his birth. Birdie and the boy moved temporarily onto the farm close to the diner, north of Kalamazoo. Her Aunt Rose helped with the child and Birdie filled in at the diner when they needed an extra waitress. Laverne began spending time at the diner on weekends, looking for Birdie. When she finally ran into her, Laverne could hardly speak. She identified herself as Gabby's former teacher and friend.

"Gabby's down in Louisiana in the Army," she told Birdie. "I heard you had a baby a few months ago."

"Yes, a boy. Jake. He was three months old last Saturday."

"It's just, you see, I promised Gabby I'd look in on you from time to time. If there is anything I could do to help, just let me know, dearie."

"You're that lady from the bus station—Melvyn's teacher, aren't you?"

"Yes. Melvyn and I have a special bond, you might say."

"If Melvyn hadn't got drafted, I reckon we'd be married now and raising a family. See, that's what I thought. Several of my older sisters found husbands workin' at the diner. But not me. When you started hangin' out with Gabby I should a figured that would queer the deal. Gabby and I was gettin' along swell before you started chasing him."

Laverne squirmed on her stool and frowned at the girl.

"Don't be giving me that look, lady. What were you doing going after a boy that much younger than you? Gabby told me about the stuff you two done. Also, what you two never done! You got to give a man what he wants, make him feel special."

Birdie looked around as if making sure they were alone. "Men don't want to just play with yer titties, Laverne. You got to please 'em, or they won't stick around."

Laverne blushed and stood as she fumbled with her purse. "I'll be going, Birdie. I was hoping we could be friends. I'd love to help, if I could, with Jake."

Birdie stood stiffly behind the counter.

"Birdie, you're right that I am old. Laverne dried her eyes with a lace handkerchief. I'll probably never please a man in certain ways. But that doesn't mean I don't deserve to find a partner. I grew to love Melvyn very much, before he left for the Army. I told him I'd try to help with your child after you gave birth. I guess I'm just a foolish woman who missed her chance. "I'd love to see that child sometime. Does he favor his father?" Laverne asked with a tremor in her voice.

"Well, Miss Laverne, that's none of your business. I'm sorry if I've been rude to you. I know you care for Gabby, and I 'spect you do care about his child."

"I beg your pardon, Birdie. I'll be going." The older woman shoved a $5 bill into the girl's hand and ran out the front door.

Melvyn and I had stopped here once, in another age and another world. We'd eaten sandwiches sitting at the same spot. That had been a good day. We'd held hands and kissed, early in our courtship, before the inevitable piling up—misunderstanding, dishonesty and fabrication—had built up like slats on a rail fence.

"I must be getting on home now. If there is ever anything you can contact me at the Library.

Laverne had walked out to the diner that day, four miles from her apartment. Halfway back she stopped and rested on a smooth rock overlooking a swimming hole formed by a beaver dam. A dozen teenagers were goofing off—boys with locked thumbs splashing girls' hair. On the far side of the hole, a sycamore tree stretched out a stout horizontal branch, eight feet off the water. A cobbled mess of grey boards robbed from abandoned gates and fastened tenuously with assorted bent nails formed a platform of sorts. Near the middle of the hole, a heavy hemp rope swung slightly in the wind, its knotted end a few feet above the surface of the water.

Charlotte

After graduating from high school in 1936, Charlotte Ross went to Bliss College, a two-year business school in Columbus. Still being prone to erratic behavior, she was suspended early in what would have been her last semester. Charlotte and her advisor, Myra Green, become good friends. But somehow, Charlotte got the idea. Mr. Green planned to leave his wife and run off with her.

Things escalated and the police were called to the Green's home on Neil Avenue in the wee hours of a Sunday morning where Charlotte was throwing rocks at the living room window and screaming obscenities. After a few hours in jail, Charlotte was released and given a bus ticket to McConnelsville.

She worked for a business supply company in Amesville for a few months as a bookkeeper and part-time secretary. She stayed with a second cousin, Doreen Yoder. After Doreen got engaged, Charlotte moved back to Chesterfield. She managed to work out a deal with Bliss College and Marietta Business School that allowed her to transfer credits from Bliss

College to Marietta Business College. She attended classes for one semester and graduated in May of 1939.

Charlotte got two part-time jobs as a bookkeeper for the Chesterfield Methodist Church and Fawcett Furniture and Mortuary in Chesterfield. She and Nanny grew closer during this period, especially after the death of her father. Claude had been raking hay and didn't show up for supper. Charlotte took their old truck over and found him lying in the field. The tractor and rake had run down the hill and were piled up against the fence.

After attempting, unsuccessfully, to get her father's body into the truck, she headed back toward Chesterfield. Before she got to the gate, just off Route 555, her brother, Pen, showed up with his truck. The two of them managed to wrap Claude's body in a canvas tarp and into the bed of Pen's truck.

"Eddie and I will get the tractor and rake out tomorrow, Char. I stopped at Ma's. She said she'd call Doc Whitacre. I guess maybe I should go to Fawcett's."

"OK, Pen. I'll go to the house. It never occurred to me that Dad would die."

"Me neither."

May 13, 1943: German and Italian troops surrender in North Africa.

"Aunt Minta!" Charlotte shouted into the telephone. "I've got a job. Bookkeeping at the Landmark Grain Elevators outside of Buckeye Lake."

"Well, that sounds good, Charlotte. Where will you stay?"

"They've got a real nice rooming house for girls about a quarter mile from work. I can walk to work. And we get our meals at the rooming house. Sharon Dutro from Pennsville works at Landmark and stays at the rooming house. She has a car and said I can get a ride with her, if I give her a dollar each way for gas."

"That sounds fine, Charlotte. Are you OK for money?"

"I'm OK. There's a big place by the lake where they have dances in the summer. That's the biggest tent I've ever seen. That'll be opening in a couple weeks. Tell Mom I called, OK?"

"I will, dear. Goodbye."

"Bye, Minta."

"Well, Minta, I'm glad Charlotte found work."

"I hope she'll settle in and settle down. "Sharon said with big smile.

It will be nice if she can get home regularly. Not so keen on her having a dance hall close by. That's what got her started in Columbus. She started going out, drinking and dancing with that advisor of hers and her husband. Like Delbert Green used to say about dancing, 'it's a vertical expression of a horizontal intention'. I believe Charlotte would be better off settlin' down and having a family. We'll see."

May, 1943: USC Graduation

<u>May 22, 1943</u>: Donitz suspends U-boat operations in the North Atlantic.

"Oh, Johnny, I wish Mom could have been here to see this. Dad's about busting his buttons. We're all so proud of you. Merle and Dennis sent letters. Dennis planned to be here, but his squadron had a change of plans, and he couldn't get back in time."

"Well, Merle and Dennis have something to be proud of, not just sitting in a classroom and doing homework."

"Johnny, you are going to help the war effort by helping the Air Corps to fight more effectively. I don't want to hear that from you. Just stop it, OK?"

"OK, sis. I'll stop."

Polly gave him a hug. The two siblings, each tall, leggy and rangy, were peas out of the same pod. They favored their mother, who'd died giving birth to Johnny. Their brothers, Merle and Dennis, took after their father. Doctor Hardy Simon, shorter than his wife by half a foot but solidly built.

1943

Johnny Simon

<u>June 10, 1943</u>: Pointblank directive to improve Allied bombing strategy issued.

Dear Polly,

I am starting to settle in at the house we rented in Buckeye Lake, about 30 miles from Columbus. The local history is interesting. The lake was a swamp—Buffalo Swamp. When the Ohio and Erie Canal was built in the 1820s, they built a dike to block off the south fork of the Licking River. This provided water for the canal.

There is an amusement park that has a big canvas dance hall that is open Wednesday and Saturday nights. We're only a five-minute walk away from the park. We've been really busy at work, but I'm hoping I can get over to the dance this coming Saturday. That is, if I can get rid of one of my left feet.

We are getting busy at work. The bigwigs in the Air Corps are calling for a complete rethink of many things (I can't really get specific). Depending on their findings, we may have to come up with further modifications of our equipment.

Hope you and Dad are OK. Let me know if you hear from Merle or Dennis. It's probably best to give them my address at work. My Supervisor said even though we aren't in the military, we can use the military mail and it will get delivered quicker.

Address is:

Mr. John Simon Engineer II

Air Force Combat Command

Tactical Wing Design & Development

Columbus, Ohio

I've never been much for prayer, but I find myself praying for Dennis and particularly for Merle. From what I've heard, the situation in the Pacific is getting worse.

I know you don't want to hear this, but, Uncle Sam put me through school and sent me here to work on aircraft design, but I can't help but wonder if I shouldn't be more actively involved in the fighting aspect and not just pushing a pencil and a slide rule.

Love,

Johnny

PS: I met a girl two weeks ago, at the Library. We kind of agreed to go to the dances together starting next Wednesday.

Charlotte Ross

<u>July 22, 1943</u>: Americans capture Palermo, Sicily.

"—and he is tall and handsome. He finished his degree at USC in less than three years."

"What did he study, Charlotte?"

"Well, Ma, he studied aeronautical engineering. And he works for the Army Air Corp designing things for use in warplanes."

Minta Ross, a scatterbrained woman whose lean body suggested nothing so much as a long bone bleached a good while in the sun, opened the screen door and stepped into the house. A faint fold of skin between her misshapen nose and a loose pile of ragged curls just above her wrinkled forehead put one in mind of a caricature a sketcher at the Ohio State Fair might draw of a spinster chicken.

"Where is this joker from?" she asked with a raspy voice

"Well, Aunt Minta, he's from Kentucky," Charlotte answered.

"Does he wear shoes?"

Charlotte and Nanny stared in disbelief.

"Yes, as a matter of fact he does. And he has a touring car with a convertible top, too."

"Well, Effie Ott was from Kentucky, and she always said that you got to—."

"Enough, Minta! If you can't carry on a civilized conversation, go back out on the porch and play solitaire,"

Charlotte sagged back against the yellow flowered wallpaper. Nanny gave Twyla a nod of the head indicating she should join Minta on the porch. Twyla pulled the oak door closed on her way out.

"I've got some tea in the icebox, Charlotte. Would you like a glass?"

"Yes, thank you, Mother."

Mother and daughter went into the small kitchen. Nanny put out a sugar bowl, two lemon wedges, two glasses, and a small ashtray on a worn wooden tray.

"Shall we have our tea out back, hun?"

"That would be nice."

They reached the backdoor via a mud room precariously perched off the back of the house. Five steps down led to a small landing that looked out west across pastures stretching a good half mile until they reached a fence just shy of Henman Road. A longer set of steps came off to the south and settled on a patch of disintegrating concrete with a low table and two chairs facing the sunset.

A weathered door under the steps led to the basement. A jerry-rigged coal chute went through the exterior wall a few feet from the door. The old coal furnace provided heat straight up through a single grate that straddled the threshold between living and dining rooms. The three small rooms on the second floor were as cold in the winter as they were hot in summer.

"Mom, I wish Minta would stop being so spiteful."

"She can't help it, Charlotte. Mom use to tell her to stop being a pill! She's not really a mean-spirited person. She struggles," Nanny said and she wiped her glasses with her apron and shook her head.

"I know that I'm like that, too—sometimes. Lots of times, I guess."

"That's true, dear. But you have a good heart, Charlotte. And I hope that you will find someone like your father, may he rest in peace, to marry and to raise children with."

Charlotte fumbled with a pack of Lucky Strikes in her jacket pocket. "Do you mind if I smoke, Mom?"

"No, dear. Go ahead."

"Thanks. Mom, I know I've been a handful for you from time to time. And I've had some trouble with men. That situation at Bliss College with my advisor's husband. I don't know what got into me. I do want those things you were talking about—a husband and family. But, I'm scared. I haven't had any real trouble since that stuff up in Columbus.

"And Johnny, he's a nice boy. He's three years younger than me. But he is the smartest person I ever met. He got a scholarship to USC in Los Angeles. He got a full scholarship paid for by the Army, and he got his degree in aeronautical engineering, and he finished in less than three years.

"But he's not stuck up. His Dad is a doctor in Kentucky in a poor county. When Johnny talks about his father, it puts me in mind of the way folks use to talk about Doctor Naylor here in Morgan County.

"Johnny and I have been to four dances at Buckeye Lake. They have them on Wednesday and Saturday nights. He and three other fellows he works with in Columbus are renting a house on Route 40. They all work for the Army Air Corps, but they are not 'in the Army'.

"He's a good man. And he's not fresh, either. He's a gentleman. I'd like to bring him home sometime, to meet you and show him where I'm from."

"I'd like that very much, Charlotte." The women looked out across the pastures, and Charlotte lit another Lucky Strike.

They watched Mr. Arthur Willard, the neighbor two doors down, drag a galvanized trash can down the steep hill that comprised ninety 90% of his back yard and then up to a flat patch with a metal ring like someone might see at a campsite. He spread the trash around, removed a flask from his back pocket, and sprinkled the contents liberally inside the ring. Then Willard pulled a small flare from his pocket, what looked like a fuzee of the type used on the railroad. He took off the cap, scratched it against the body of the flare and dropped it into the ring.

The man stood still and watched the fire for a few minutes. *As men have done for millennia*, thought Charlotte. When he seemed to be satisfied it was under control, he turned around, waved at Nanny and Charlotte and walked over toward them.

"Evening, ladies. Sure has been nice weather here lately. Almanac is calling for an early freeze this year."

"Well, perhaps we'll get a few more good weeks of Indian Summer, Arthur."

"That would be nice," he said. He turned back, probably to check the fire and glance at the sunset. "Say Charlotte, how are you liking your job up to Buckeye Lake?"

Charlotte stubbed her cigarette into the ashtray. "I like it very much. All the folks at Landmark are nice. Sharon Dutro from Pennsville works there. I've been riding back and forth with her. So, that's worked out real nice."

"Well, good. Glad to hear that." He turned again and appeared to eyeball the fire. He nodded his head and turned again to the ladies. "I better get back to Myrville," he said with grimace.

"How is she, Arthur?" Nanny asked.

"'Bout the same. Doc said if she doesn't improve in a few weeks we might have try something else. Talkin' 'bout sending her to the hospital down to Marietta. Funny, all those years I worked the railroad, away from home, I just wanted to get back home. Myrville always wanted to travel after I retired. I will tell her you asked after her, Nanny."

"You do that, Arthur. And if there's anything I can do to help, you let me know."

"Will do. It sure is nice seeing you, Miss Charlotte. I'm glad you're liking your new job."

"Thank you kindly, Mr. Willard."

Arthur disappeared around the side of his house.

Twyla and Minta broke out in laughter and peeked their heads around the north side of the house. "Thank you kindly, Mr. Willard," Twyla boomed sarcastically.

Minta followed shortly and said in a loud voice, "Johnny's such a ni-i-i-ice boy, Ma. I cain't wait to marry him." Minta walked around the concrete pad, wrapped her boney arms around her back, and making loud kissing noises.

"Enough! Both of you! Get out of here!" Nanny said sharply. "Leave us alone!" Nanny yelled. "Now!"

1943

Charlotte and Johnny

<u>October 1, 1943</u>: Allies enter Naples, Italy.

An incongruous couple emerged inside the flap of the canvas dancehall at Buckeye Lake. A few men straightened chairs at the tables on the periphery. A group of four others swept leaves, paper and other trash through the opening behind the bandstand.

The young man—all legs and elbows—snaked a long arm down around the waist of his petite partner. An older man in a rumpled suit carrying a clipboard looked at the couple with a weary smile.

"Johnny, would you like me to put on a record?"

"That would very nice, Mr. Potter."

"Is *In the Mood* OK?"

"Yes, sir. Thank you."

The older man put on a 78. Glenn Miller's unmistakable sound echoed through the nearly empty space. And the two figures meshed beautifully on the dance floor.

As the music stopped Johnny called out, "Thanks again, sir."

"You bet. See you kids tomorrow night."

"Oh Johnny, this is going to be such fun, getting to spend the weekend together."

"How late do you have to work tomorrow, Charlotte?"

"They said we should be done no later than 2 o'clock."

"It's supposed to be nice again tomorrow. How about if we rent a boat and explore Buckeye Lake?"

"That would be fun. You mean a rowboat?"

"We could get a rowboat. Or we could get a motorboat. Whatever you'd like."

"I've never been in a motorboat."

"If you're game, I'll get us all set up with a motorboat. And we can get dinner. I know a good place in Lancaster, if you like steaks. And then we can come back to the dance."

"Oh Johnny, I've had such a good time. But I've got to be back to the boarding house by ten o'clock."

"I'll walk you over, you've still got 25 minutes."

"OK, let's walk on the path through the garden. It's so pretty."

"So are you, Charlotte." He bent down and kissed her.

They walked the rest of the way in silence, holding hands, with the drone of cicadas providing background music.

"Here we are Miss Charlotte," he said with a sweeping bow.

"Pinch me, Johnny, so I know this is real."

He gave her a gentle pinch on the cheek. "It's real, Charlotte. I'll see you tomorrow. I'll bring the car over to Landmark, and we can go to the lake from there."

"OK. I'll bring my bathing suit and a towel to work, so we won't have to come back here."

The house mother opened the door and cleared her throat before the two could kiss again.

"Good night, Charlotte."

"Good night, Johnny." She pinched him on his cheek and ran inside.

***

"What time is it, Joann?"

"Fifteen minutes since the last time you asked, Charlotte."

"I'm sorry, I can't see the clock from the back room in here."

Joann, a plain woman in her mid-30s, rolled her eyes and said, "It's 1:30."

"OK. Thanks, Joann. It's just, I haven't ever been in a motorboat before. I can't wait."

"You got it bad, girl. Hope this feller is worth all the hubbub."

"He is, Joann. He's smart and good looking. You'll see. He's picking me up at two and we're going boating at the lake and then go to a steakhouse in Lancaster and then go to the dance."

"He wouldn't be a tall guy with wavy brown hair and a convertible, would he?"

"Well, yeah."

"Looks like Prince Charming has arrived early."

Charlotte ran out of the back room and over to the window. "Oh, I'd give anything to get out of here a little early."

"Darlin', I can cover for you with Abigail when she gets back from lunch. It's a quarter to two. Why don't you take off if you want?"

"Thanks, Joann. I owe you."

"No problem. You have fun."

Charlotte ran out the door and over to the car

Joann followed with her beach bag. "You might need your bathing suit, Charlotte."

"Oh! Thanks, Joann. Johnny, this is Joann. I work with her."

Johnny took a few steps and shook her hand. "Very nice to meet you, ma'am. Charlotte has spoken of you."

"It's nice to meet you, too. Have fun at the lake."

"I love your car, Johnny. You must have been a big man on campus out in California."

"Not really. I was too busy studying. Otherwise, I wouldn't have been able to graduate in three years."

"In high school, then. You must have had girls chasing you in high school."

"Sort of. But, well, I have never been caught, if you know what I mean. Shucks, now I'm embarrassed." The boy hung his head down, blushing.

"That's OK, Johnny. Don't be embarrassed."

They drove in silence to the boat ramp. Johnny had put the boat in the water at anchor that morning. They stopped at the boat rental and changed into their swimming suits. Johnny was out in a few minutes, but Charlotte didn't appear for 15 minutes.

"You alright, Charlotte?"

"Yes, but now it is my turn to be embarrassed. I have to —well—you've seen me in blouses and sweaters, but never in a swimming suit. I enhance my figure with Kleenex. And I can't do that with my bathing suit. So, I guess you'll notice that I look different." It was Charlotte's turn to grimace and blush.

After a minute, they looked each other in the eye, and broke out laughing.

"I don't care if you've never been caught, Johnny."

"And I don't care if you don't have a figure like Betty Grable."

"Race you to the boat, Highpockets! Last one in is a rotten egg."

Johnny cruised around the lake for an hour or so. There were a few boats out, but not many.

"Would you like try to water ski, Char?"

"I don't know, Johnny. I'm not the most coordinated person."

"It's OK if you don't want to, but this is a perfect chance to try. There aren't very many boats out, so you won't have to worry about getting run over. And I'm a good driver. We had about the only ski boat around, and I've taken dozens of folks out the first time." He smiled and added. "Didn't lose a one of 'em."

"OK, but you've got to tell what I have to do—and not do," she said with a frightened look.

"Well, first thing, you need to put on a life jacket." He handed her an orange jacket. "When you get in the water, doggy paddle out and grab the tow bar. When you get to the point where you just have a little slack, face the boat with the tow rope lined up. With both hands spread out on the bar, imagine you are sitting on a rolled-up rug and lean back a little until you can get the front end of your skis up out of the water.

"The biggest problem first timers have is the tendency to try to pull yourself up. Don't do that. Leave your arms extended with just a little bit of bend in the elbows. Let the boat pull you up. The other problem is keeping the skis in the proper position. You don't want to get the tips crossed. But you also don't want them diverging outward. Finally, if you end up on top of the water on your belly, let go of the tow bar.

"What do you think, want to give it a try?"

"I guess."

"Don't worry. I'll be keeping my eye on you. Why don't you get that life jacket snugged up, and then you can get in the water? I'll get the skis and the tow bar to you. Are you ready, sweetie?"

"Yes."

"After you get up and ski a while, if you want to stop, give me an index finger motion across your throat. Then I'll slow down, and you can let go. I'll come and pick you up. Let me check your life jacket. That's good. Now, jump in and work your way back 20 feet or so behind the motor."

"Here goes nothin'." She jumped in and bobbed up and down a couple of times.

"You OK?"

"Yes."

"Here are the skis, one at a time—here's left."

She got her left foot in.

"Here's right."

She got the ski tips out of the water and close to parallel.

"That looks good, Char. I'm going to toss the tow bar back. Are you ready?"

"OK." She grabbed the bar.

"Good. Hold on. Remember, your arms should have just a little bit of bend in the elbows. That's it. Now I'm going to pull the slack out of the line. You'll feel it. If you're ready, give me thumbs up, and then grab the bar and I'll pull you up. Here goes."

Charlotte gave him thumbs up. The boat jumped and Charlotte started up smoothly. Johnny had set up a mirror so he could keep track of her. Halfway out of the water, she smiled. He gave her a thumb's up. She stayed in the wake with the rope between her skis. Johnny was looking back and smiling. Just seconds from being up on the water she pulled the bar to her chest and found herself face down in the water.

Johnny pulled the boat around next to her. "You OK, Char?" he said, trying to suppress a big grin.

"Yes. This lake water doesn't taste very good."

"You almost had it. But just about everyone does that the first time. Do you want to get out?"

"Not on your life, Johnny Simon. Let's do it again."

She gave him thumb's up, the boat jumped, and she came up smoothly. Johnny picked her up in the mirror. She smiled and he gave her a thumb's up. She stayed in the wake. After a few minutes, she did a couple of experimental left and right slides within the wake.

After another ten minutes, she gave the cut sign and let go of the tow bar.

"That was great, Charlotte. You looked like a pro out there"

"Thanks. Oh, Johnny that was fun."

"I put some beer in the cooler and some Cokes, if you want one."

"A Coke would be good."

He pulled her up out of the water and cradled her in his long arms. "You're a natural, Char." He cut the boat to a slow idle, and they drank their Cokes.

"Johnny, it looks like someone is waving at us from the dock."

"That looks like Teddy one of my roommates. I told him to come down if he felt like skiing. He's a swell guy. You'll like him."

"That sounds like fun."

"Hold on," Johnny yelled. He pulled the boat around and opened the throttle full bore. He turned the boat so that it tapped the dock directly in front of Teddy's bare feet.

"Incoming!" Teddy yelled as he leapt off the dock behind the boat. Johnny pushed the skis back to him.

"You ready, slick?" Johnny asked as he pushed the throttle wide open. Once up, Teddy began moving back and forth across the wake on both sides. Johnny managed to wring a bit more horsepower out of the engine and Teddy spent 15 minutes jumping clear across the wake, before finally dipping a ski and performing an unplanned triple somersault.

Johnny was up next and he did Teddy one better, with half an hour back and forth over the wakes with longer jumps and more elevation. Charlotte smiled broadly and waved at her beau.

When Charlotte went to movies in Columbus and McConnelsville, she always imagined herself in the position of the young heroines coming out of nowhere to catch the handsome leading man. And now, six months after the debacle in Columbus, she stood on the cusp of realizing her dreams.

Life, suddenly, seemed wonderful!

Johnny

Johnny dropped Charlotte off at her rooming house so she could get out of her bathing suit and dress for dinner. He found a flower shop and got her a big bouquet of flowers. After filling up his car, he used the sink in the men's room to clean up. He put on the graduation suit his sister Polly had picked out for him in Los Angeles.

He had enjoyed the day. Despite his popularity in high school and college he still felt awkward in certain social situations. But he felt very comfortable with Charlotte. Work was going well. He enjoyed being around his housemates. And he was dating a girl he was crazy about.

Life, suddenly, seemed wonderful!

Polly

The rest of the weekend went smoothly. Charlotte and Johnny were each secretly thrilled that the other wasn't pushing for sexual consummation. Charlotte didn't want another debacle like her break-up/ breakdown in Columbus with Myra Green's husband.

Johnny had many opportunities at USC, but he had demurred. Part of his reluctance involved his sister. Polly was 16 when their mother died. Doctor Hardy found wet nurses to get Johnny past weening. But otherwise, for Johnny's first 15 years, Polly was his surrogate mother. She gave her full attention to his care. What was left over went to their father. In the process, Polly's social life shriveled up and died. An Honors Student, she'd been active in Band, Choir and Student Council. After her mother's death, the summer after tenth grade, she dropped out of school.

After Johnny's tenth grade year, Polly declared she thought she'd go to weekend classes for Adult Education in Clarksville, Tennessee and finish her high school diploma. Polly was the only white person in the class of 20. She was acing the academics and becoming good friends with the teacher, Charles Jackson.

Mr. Jackson was a mulatto, in the parlance of the day. He taught English and history at an all-black high school in Clarksville. He was also a Deacon at the Clarksville A.M.E. Church. Mr. Jackson was a widower whose wife and two daughters had been killed in an auto accident a few years earlier.

The accident was caused by Dewey, 17-year-old son of the Clarksville mayor. The boy was drunk at the time and driving his father's new Cadillac. He'd survived with bruises and a broken arm. The police tracked him down at a bootleggers' place a couple blocks from the accident. He'd jerry-rigged a sling from one of the working girl's nightgowns and convinced police to send an ambulance.

"Just send 'em here, boys. No rush," he said.

Dewey managed to avoid punishment. He wasn't even cited. In the "round up the usual suspects" *modus operandi* of the times the Chief of Police concluded that Mrs. Jackson had been speeding through the intersection. Dozens of witnesses—white and black—told the investigators that she had been stopped at a four-way Stop sign when the Cadillac swerved left of center and hit her car head-on without slowing down at all through the intersection. The crowd also witnessed Dewey leave the scene of the accident while holding his left arm. A silver flask protruded from his back pocket.

He'd been registered to attend Vanderbilt University, where classes were scheduled to begin in three weeks. His mother bought him a new car to take to Nashville. Police estimated Dewey hit a bridge abutment on Route 13 while crossing the Cumberland River at over 90 miles an hour. And the resulting fire left no remains to bury or cremate.

Dewey's mother and her friends grieved. His father bullied the District Attorney into charging the late Mrs. Jackson posthumously with Vehicular Homicide.

The meeting of Polly Simon and Charles Jackson appeared opportune at first. They spent time before and after classes and shared meals at several restaurants in the colored quarter. As winter approached, Polly became reluctant to drive the two hours it took to get home in the dark.

His pastor arranged for a few women from the congregation of the A.M.E. United Methodist Church in Clarksville to put up Polly on Saturday nights. Things went smoothly until classes resumed in the second week of January.

After class, Polly and Charles exchanged presents.

"I noticed that the chain to your watch had a damaged clip. I got you a new one. I hope it matches, Charles." She handed him the small box.

He opened the box methodically and removed the chain. "A perfect match," he said, smiling.

"I took the liberty of getting you two hankies with your initials, Miss Polly." He handed her a box.

Polly reached for the box and their hands brushed. Her gaze lowered, and a slight flush appeared on her sturdy face. She removed the paper slowly, folding it two times and laying it on the table. She opened the box and removed two linen handkerchiefs, each with the initials, "PS" in a fine violet embroidery.

"I thought that color would favor you, Miss Polly."

"They are lovely, Charles. Such fine work, I will cherish these." She put the paper and one of the handkerchiefs back in the box, which she slid into her purse. The other handkerchief she folded twice and slipped into a small pocket in her jacket. "I wish we could have dinner, Charles, but I'm expected at the parsonage in a half hour. I left my car there this morning and walked."

"That's the Methodist Church on Maple, isn't it, Polly?" A grimace flickered across his face. "I'll walk with you."

"Thank you, Charles."

The mileage to the church, a dozen blocks at most, failed to capture its true distance. From their current location in the outskirts of a colored neighborhood, they moved into several blocks of redneck taverns, package liquor stores, and diners. The couple walked briskly. But before they reached a large boulevard that seemed to mark the end of the four blocks of 'Hillbilly Heaven" they had hurried through, they came to a ramshackle structure that looked like an abandoned warehouse.

It was a bowling alley and a Saturday afternoon league was exiting, spilling out onto the sidewalk. Groups of men wearing different brightly colored team shirts were heading to the taverns that Charles and Polly had passed. Most of the bowlers gave the couple dirty looks and muttered a few unintelligible remarks.

The final team, sponsored by Dukes' Sporting Goods and Shooting Range, moved slower and appeared to be angry about their bowling performance. They blocked the sidewalk, and when the couple detoured onto the grass, the whole team encircled them.

"You can't walk on Mr. Jones' grass, boy. That's agin' the law!" said the ringleader, a short fat man with a mouth full of ruined brown teeth.

"We will be happy to wait until the sidewalk is clear and then we'll be on our way," Charles said with restraint.

"We may not want to clear the sidewalk. And if we do, we may not want you two to use our sidewalk. It is a sidewalk for Whites Only. And around here, we don't consider any women that have truck with niggers to be white."

"We don't want any trouble," Charles said very deliberately.

A younger man from the team walked over to their spokesman. "Willy, let's just go eat, like we was planning to do."

"We don't want any trouble," Charles said, again, deliberately.

"You keep sayin' that, boy. But you sure as hell have found a big heap of trouble, boy. And I don't see how y'all are gonna get out of it."

"Just let us go, please," Polly said in a small voice. "If you want money, that can be arranged."

"She don't talk like a coon, does she?" another man asked. "We don't want your money, bitch. But that pocket watch your boyfriend has sure would look good on me. What do you say, boy?"

"I'll be happy to give you the watch." He unclipped the chain from the watch and let it slide back into in his pocket. "Here you go." He handed Willy the watch.

"And the chain, boy," Willy said loudly. Producing a switchblade, Willy moved quickly over to Charles, cut the belt loop and back pocket and snatched the chain. Charles put his hands around the cracker's neck. But Willy moved the knife up and sliced Charles' left ear nearly clean off.

Charles pulled a white linen handkerchief from his pocket and held it to the side of his head. Willy moved over to admire his work. Polly hesitated, but when Willy leaned in, she told Charles to step back. She threw a right hand that dropped Willy. All three of her brothers had boxed at the YMCA. She had been trainer and coach for each of them. She had not forgotten what she had learned.

As she was helping Charles to his feet, Willy recovered and just missed Polly's left eye with the knife. He traced a wide, but not deep, arc down to her chin. She stumbled to the ground and pulled her new monogrammed handkerchief from her coat pocket.

Willy grabbed it. "PS, huh?" Maybe I should give a matching scar on your other cheek, PS."

A fat man from a nearby bar stuck his head out and shouted, "Willy Jones, get on outta here. The police are on their way. One more warrant for you, and you'll be gone a long time, boy." He pulled a revolver out his back pocket and waved the barrel. "Now git, you redneck piece a trash."

Willy looked for his team. They were in the shadows of a big maple tree near the corner of the bowling alley. Willy started in that direction. Charles began pulling himself up, and Willy went back.

"Hey, coon. Guess I showed you that a white man can use a knife, too."

The sounds of sirens grew stronger. Charles had regained his feet. "You certainly are white, but I'm not sure I'd call you a man."

"Why you uppity—."

"Put the knife down, Willy," a large policeman yelled. "We're done here. Get out of here, Willy."

"Alright, I will." He walked over by Charles. "PS, huh? Well boy, I got a PS for ya'. PS, don't come 'round here no more with a white gal 'less you want somethin' besides that other ear cut off." He skulked off to join his team who were smoking and grumbling under a large maple tree.

Four or five policemen were speaking with the bartender.

Another patrolman spoke with Polly. "What happened, ma'am?" the young officer asked.

"I have been taking weekend classes at the Bragg High School. I had arranged to stay at the Methodist Church just a few blocks from here. Mr. Jackson, our teacher, offered to walk me to the church. When we passed the bowling alley, the last team to come out harassed us. Those white trash cowards skulking up there under that tree. That one called Willy stole Mr. Jackson's watch and chain and cut him with a knife. And he came at me, just missed putting my eye out."

"I see, ma'am. My name is Officer Dillard. Now, could you describe the ways in which Mr. Jackson provoked these boys? Willy in particular?"

"There was no provocation from Mr. Jackson. Willy pulled his knife out and demanded Mr. Jackson surrender his gold watch. Mr. Jackson gave it to him, and then Willy demanded the chain. When Mr. Jackson refused to give him the chain, Willy cut it off his belt loop and then cut his ear."

"I see. It was a disagreement that got out of hand. Willy here was provoked by an uppity colored man squiring some white women around in the white part of town."

Polly was flabbergasted. She shook her head.

"If you'll excuse me, ma'am. Where are you from?"

"Dunmor, Kentucky."

"That explains a lot. Why didn't you drive to the Methodist Church?"

"I left my car there this morning and thought it would be nice to take a walk."

"Well, there's another provocation. You just didn't know where you could walk here in Clarksville. We won't charge you, but your colored friend, whoever he is, knew better. He'll be charged. You could have been killed. He can be charged as an accessory to your assault."

"Unbelievable," Polly said softly. She looked around for Charles. "Where is Mr. Jackson?"

"Don't you worry your pretty little head about that coon," the officer said with a patronizing tone.

"Where is he?" she demanded.

"They took him to the workhouse on the north end of town."

"Is that normal in this town? To take an innocent man, who hasn't been charged with a crime, let alone convicted of one, straight into incarceration?"

"Sure is. If a colored man causes a disturbance involving white people, he is guilty, 'specially if he should've knowed better."

"I would like to make a phone call."

"For what purpose do you need to make a phone call?"

"Well, to call my father in Dunmor so he can get a lawyer for Mr. Charles Jackson, for one thing."

"I believe you can only make a phone call if you are taken into custody."

"So, Mr. Jackson would have gotten a phone call, is that correct?"

"Niggers taken into custody don't get to make phone calls."

"The reason for that being, exactly what?"

"The reason being, that's the way it has always been, lady!"

"Same as the reason that uneducated white men seem to get all the jobs in law enforcement in the South. Do you agree?" Polly said, shaking her head.

"Why, no! No, I do not agree and I'm goin' to get you your phone call right after I book you for prostitution. How do you like that?"

"Just fine. Now, please take me to the station and book me."

"If that's what you want, I'll be happy to take you—in handcuffs in the back seat of the squad car. So, stand up with yer hands behind yer back and we'll get this party started." He cuffed her and gave her a not-so-gentle shove into the car.

The police station was a ten-minute drive. Polly noted the Maple Street Methodist Church, where she and Charles been headed, just two blocks away from the scene of the crimes. She said a silent prayer for her friend, Charles.

When they reached the station, her captor seemed unsure of himself. He left her in the backseat of the unlocked car and went inside. The desk sergeant listened to his questions, nodding mostly.

Finally, he cut the young man off and suggested that if his prisoner was really the dangerous madam and prostitute the young officer described, he might want to go get her and bring her nto

The duty captain and all the other officers came out to get a gander at this dangerous *femme fatale*, as Officer Dillard led her through the front door. Then the duty captain took Dillard aside and called a reporter with a camera over to take a picture with the two men and Polly.

As they broke up, Polly asked Dillard, "When do I get my phone call, officer?"

"Where are you calling, lady?" the duty officer asked.

"Dunmor, Kentucky."

"Well, we'll have to see about that. Where exactly would you be calling in Dunmor?"

"Probably a bar or a whore house," Dillard said with a snigger.

"Be quiet, nephew."

"I would be calling my father, Doctor Hardy Simon. And he will call his cousin, Sheriff Luther Watson, who happens to be my godfather. And if we get that far, I will make sure that Sheriff Watson hears about things such as not getting medical attention for Mr. Jackson or myself."

"He didn't need no more medical attention. His ear was two-thirds off, so Delbert just finished the job and taped a big gauze pad over it."

"Dillard, don't you have some paperwork to file?"

"Well, no. Not really."

"Go find something to do, OK?"

"For God's sake, no one even asked me my name or anything else!"

"Don't raise your voice at me!"

"And don't assume I'm a prostitute just because I'm walking a few blocks with a colored man. Fair enough?"

"What is your name, ma'am, if you don't mind me asking?"

"Polly Simon, pleased to meet you." She waited a long 20 seconds and continued. "And you would be?"

The officer ignored her, while sorting through some folders.

"And you would be—good Lord, people think folks from Muhlenberg County have no manners. And you would be—?"

"I am Sergeant Dingess. We can make that phone call in my office." They went into an office next to the office of the chief of Police.

"I see you are a Mason," Polly said with grin. "I recognize your certification in the frame there."

"Yes. I was appointed Secretary of the Clarksville Lodge last month," he said with a big smile.

"That's nice. My father is a medical doctor and the Worshipful Master in the Greensville, Kentucky, Mason's Lodge. Here is the phone number for my father—Worshipful Master Hardy Simon."

Polly smiled malignantly at the sergeant as he waited for Doctor Simon to pick up. After a half-minute, the sergeant's eyes perked up.

"Yes, is this Doctor Simon?" There was a brief pause. "This is Sergeant Dingess with the Clarksville Police." After a wide-eyed look from the sergeant, he continued. "No, sir. Your daughter, Polly, is just fine, sir. There has been some trouble, but everyone is alright."

Polly grabbed the receiver. "Everything and everyone are not OK, father. Charles Jackson was assaulted by a group of rednecks and had his ear cut off. He was walking me to the Methodist Church and these drunken reprobates assaulted him. I'm OK. I got a cut on my cheek, but I'll be OK. Charles needs help, father. They took him straight to the workhouse without charging him. And his ear was nearly cut off." There was a minute-long silence on Polly's part with some nods and frowns. "OK, Dad. Here is Sergeant Dingess. By the way, he is the Secretary of the Clarksville Lodge. Yes, sir. I'll put him back on."

The Sergeant picked up the receiver. "Yello, Sergeant Dingess here." From this point to the end of the call, the sergeant was reduced to head movements and short rejoinders. "Yes, sir." Affirmative nods. "I understand, sir." Yes, sir. We have a doctor on call." More nods. "He'll get in touch first thing." Sergeant Dingess gave the receiver to Polly.

"Yes, Dad. They are treating me reasonably well. We must get Charles out the workhouse, before he disappears." Polly nodded her head. "OK, here he is."

"Yes, sir," Dingess said with a sour look on his face. Shaking his head, he sighed. "We have never done that to my knowledge, except if the colored person was badly injured. The station is closer to medical care. No sir, we haven't gotten the doctor yet. The officer handling that is on his lunch break. Well, yes, he is in the building." More shrugs and head shaking. "I suppose that call would take about three minutes. Yes, sir. I'll do what I can for the colored man. I'll do what I can, but I can't make any promises about getting him out tonight. Those boys over at the workhouse have their hands full. Yes, sir. Here she is."

Her Dad cleared his throat. "Polly, you wait three or four minutes from the time we hang up and tell this Dingess person two things: First, Sheriff Luther Watson, Senior Warden in the Muhlenberg Lodge, and a deputy left Dunmor 30 minutes ago. They will be at the workhouse in 20 minutes. Second, they will be transporting Charles Jackson to either the hospital or the police station in Clarksville. OK?"

"Yes, Dad. Will do. Thanks"

"Satisfied, ma'am?"

"Not really. I've been here for half-an-hour and haven't been offered the use of a bathroom."

"There is a ladies' room just up the hall. I'll show you." They walked together. "Here you go, ma'am."

Polly used the commode and then turned to examine the cut on her face. It ran from just below her right earlobe to just above the corner of her mouth. It wasn't deep, but it would leave a noticeable scar.

"Ma'am, I apologize for not offering you the use of the facilities sooner."

"Are you familiar with Scripture, sergeant?"

"Some, ma'am."

"Do you remember the story of Jesus and the woman at the well?"

"Yes."

"Did you ever consider the idea that if our Savior could treat that woman with love and kindness. perhaps we—white folks— could treat people not so fortunate with some respect and dignity? That knife-wielding peckerwood, Willy, was treated better than the two people he attacked and robbed. Has he even been arrested?"

"Not to my knowledge."

"And you are waiting for what, exactly? The officers seemed to know him, and they just let him walk off."

"We will be investigating this case. But—."

"But, what!"

"Not right now. You see he's, well, had trouble. He's been in trouble before, and he's kind of a shirttail cousin to one of the judges here in Montgomery County. So, he's kinder—."

"Kinder what? Just given a pass because his cousin doesn't want to get Willy's mother, his sister, riled up?

Dillard shrugged.

"Interesting. The only people taken into custody are the two victims. You should be ashamed of yourself, sergeant. My Father asked me to pass along a message for you. Sheriff Luther Watson, Senior Warden in the Muhlenberg Masonic Lodge, and a deputy left Dunmor 30 minutes ago. They will be at your workhouse in 15 minutes. They will be transporting Charles Jackson to a hospital in Clarksville."

The denouement of this tawdry tale, if it had been a sporting event, would have been a tie. The charges against Charles were eventually dropped; likewise, for Polly. After three months of stonewalling by the sheriff and Willy's uncle, the judge, Willy was charged with aggravated assault and became a guest of the Great State of Tennessee for three years.

Polly finished her diploma requirements through the mail. She and Charles still exchanged letters regularly. By this time, her three brothers were gone, and she could get the letters without any prying eyes raising questions.

In a better world, Polly and Charles would have been able to marry, or at the least, move somewhere away from nosy neighborly suspicion. Although Doctor Hardy Simon was an enlightened man who did not play the race card often, there were still unwritten strictures against miscegenation in Kentucky and Tennessee.

The result of this unfortunate situation left Johnny with a profound feeling of regret, but not guilt, regarding his sister. He felt a certain sense of responsibility for depriving Polly of her adolescence and seriously hampering any chance she had to meet, marry, and have a family with a man she loved.

Johnny, unlike most 16-year-old boys, was considerate and paid attention to things going on around him. He certainly realized the dislocation brought about by his mother's death. When Polly started attending weekend classes, he was roughly the same age she'd been when she left school to provide care for him. He tried to imagine what it would be like to quit school at 16 and stay home for the next 16 years. He couldn't.

And as a young man, starting to think more about young women, he could also feel sympathy for his sister's virtually cloistered existence. The thought of her brief flirtation with Mr. Jackson and its abrupt end added a poignant exclamation point to their ill-fated friendship.

Johnny's reservations about sexualizing his courtship with Charlotte too quickly was attributable, in part, to his lack of experience. More importantly, it was out of concern for Charlotte's well-being. Being a good listener, he'd surmised that Charlotte's difficulty in Columbus had involved the loss of a good friendship caused by her becoming the "other woman" with a friend's husband. He didn't know the details of stalking her friend's husband or breaking into their home.

He was starting to see Charlotte exhibiting signs of guilt. He didn't want to exacerbate these feelings. Instead, the boy wanted to reassure her. He looked forward to being intimate with her, but he was not desperate to somehow seal the deal because he was afraid of losing her.

Charlotte had made more than a few bad choices in her 24 years. Few people in Morgan County had ever been surprised when a female descendant from the Young Clan exhibited mental instability. Whether the cause was some inherited mental defect or just a result of households long on disturbed women and short on balanced nuclear families is anybody's guess.

In this respect, Nanny Ross's home was representative. Her husband, Claude had died at 48. Nanny was a good woman with no signs of any mental issues. She lived to be 100. Her two spinster sisters, Twyla and Minta, lived with Nanny for over 50 years.

Charlotte was thrilled to be dating Johnny. He was a nice young man with a big future ahead of him. She was interested in moving along and developing the romantic aspect of their relationship. But she told herself to be careful and avoid the scandal she'd created with her behavior in Columbus. There were many things to like about Johnny Simon. The fact that he was not a local yokel and privy to the gossips of Chesterfield was also a bonus in Charlotte's eyes.

1943

Johnny and Polly Simon

<u>November 1, 1943</u>: In Operation Goodtime, United States Marines land on Bougainville in the Solomon Islands. The fighting on this island will continue to the bitter end of the war.

The tall, handsome woman wore a faded dress and kept her long hair pulled back in a tight ponytail. She gazed serenely at the sun dipping low and orange on the surface of Lake Malone. As a young girl, she couldn't wait to be tall, like her mother, so she sees the sunset while doing dishes without standing on a chair. She'd caught up to her mother's six-foot height just before Idene Simon died.

While Doctor Hardy Simon may have been the most prominent citizen of Muhlenberg County, his wife, Idene, had surely been the most admired. No one in the county had ever seen anyone like Idene Hardy; in person. She was a movie star among a herd of extras.

Most people in the county attributed her elegance to her roots. She was born in New York—Buffalo. When her father lost his job, they moved to Newburgh in southern Indiana. She got a scholarship to IU that included work study in a dining hall. Hardy Simon met her in the Graduate Students' Dining Hall at Indiana University, where he set-up shop when cramming for exams. Idene Dingess lingered late on those long evenings with Hardy Simon. When Hardy was accepted to medical school in Chicago, Idene had just finished her sophomore year in high school.

Idene signed up for four classes that summer session and overloads for fall and spring semesters. This allowed her to graduate early. It also reduced their separation to one year.

Idene was accepted into an English Master's Program at DePaul. She and Hardy were married over Christmas Break and set up housekeeping in an apartment overlooking the lake on Chicago's Near North Side.

In February of 1905, Doctor Hardy Simon took over a practice in Muhlenberg County, Kentucky. Idene was three months pregnant when they moved. After the birth of Polly and then Merle, the following year, it was 11 years until Dennis was born.

On February 02, 1921, Idene died while giving birth to Johnny, who was born prematurely. Doctor Hardy was away, delivering twins in Wolf Lick.

The doctor was inconsolable. He engaged the services of a recent graduate of the University of Chicago Med School to help him with his practice for two years. In spite of his grief, he continued to serve his patients well.

Polly calculated in her head estimates of the number of times she'd washed dishes while gazing wistfully at the lake. Her math teacher, Miss Wohlman, told Polly she was the brightest student she'd had at Dunmor.

"Try doing calculations in your head," Miss Wohlman told her. "It will increase your proficiency—like doing push-ups for your brain."

Polly was sad when Miss Wohlman got married and moved to Nashville. She wondered why men didn't move to where their wives lived after they got married. When she voiced this idea aloud, Miss Wohlman hugged her and shook her head. "Maybe someday, Polly."

As she began to multiply number of years, times 350, plus number of years, times 15, the phone rang. "Hey, sis. It's me, Johnny. Can you hear me, Polly?"

"Yes, sir."

"What are you up to?"

"Doing dishes. Dad got a call from Bridie Jones. Her husband stoved up his knee in the mines, but that doctor they got there gives 'em aspirin and turns 'em out and back to work."

"What's the number?"

"Plus, or minus, 10,950."

They each laughed.

"How's Ohio treating you, Johnny?"

"Fine as frog hair— as Asa Willard use to say."

"Did you get my letter about Merle and Dennis getting leave, and us thinking that we could get together in Columbus or at Buckeye Lake?"

"I did. I hear things are getting pretty hairy where Merle is. I wouldn't be surprised if his leave isn't cancelled."

"I hope not, Johnny."

"We'll see. Will Dad be able to come up?"

"Health-wise, he can come with no problem. But—I don't know if he can get away. Most of the younger doctors are in the Service. And a lot of the older fellows are working in Lexington or Louisville at Induction Centers. He said he'll try to get Doc Wilson to come back for a week so we can all come up your way."

"I've got something else to tell you, Polly. I told you about Landmark having a bunch of grain elevators. Well, I've been going out with a woman, and I think you'll like her. I sure do. She's the girl I met at the library. "She grew up on a farm in Chesterfield. That's about 40 miles from here. She's got a two-year degree from Marietta Business College."

"Well, that's all well and good, I suppose, but let's get right down to brass tacks, little brother. Can she dance?"

"Well—shoot—yes, she can. And she can sing, and she's a lot of fun. She's three years older than me, but I'm used to having older women tellin' me what to do."

"Does this woman have a name?"

"Of course, she does."

"Is it a secret or something?"

"Well—shoot—no, it's not a secret. Her name is Charlotte Ross."

"I hope we'll get meet her in three weeks when we visit. I'm happy for you, Johnny. If this one doesn't work out, Ruthie Jorgenson is still available."

"Ugh! I can't wait to see you, sis, I better get off here. Tell Dad I said hello."

"Take care, Johnny."

November 6, 1943: Russians recapture Kiev in the Ukraine.

"Mom, I'm going to stay up at Buckeye Lake next weekend. Johnny's family is going to be visiting. Dennis, his next older brother has a three-day pass. He's heading over to Europe in a week or so. He's ball turret gunner in a bomber. Johnny's Dad and sister are driving up from Kentucky. So, I'll get to meet his family, except for Merle, his oldest brother. He's on a destroyer in the Pacific."

"Alright, Charlotte. That'll be nice. Will his mother be coming, too?"

"No. She died in childbirth with him. His sister, Polly, pretty much raised him."

"That's a shame. I'd love to meet his family. If they have time, maybe we could meet in Zanesville for lunch on Saturday or Sunday—at that restaurant by the Y-Bridge."

"I'll see, Mom. They're getting in on Wednesday. I'll call you Wednesday night."

"Yes, Charlotte. And I'll see if Pen or Eddie could drive me up."

A car horn sounded on the street.

"That's Sharon, Mom. Gotta go."

1943

Charlotte Ross

November 28, 1943: Roosevelt, Churchill, and Stalin meet at Teheran.

Johnny's roommates decided to spend the week in the old barracks at the airport in Columbus. This presented an opportunity for Johnny and me to get better acquainted. Johnny was exhilarated, and I was relieved. I think we both felt that we'd reached a new level in our relationship, though neither of us expressed those sentiments in so many words.

The roommates' decision to stay in Columbus for the whole week gave us some privacy. We rehearsed on Monday and performed on Tuesday.

Johnny was ecstatic. I was relieved. We talked long into the night about matters large and small.

"I'm worried about Merle," Johnny said with a sigh. "The guys on the ground in Bougainville are being mowed down. New replacements are being taken in around the clock. Merle's job is taking the boys in on landing craft. Those guys are Spam in a can until they get on the beach. Then Merle has to take the craft back for a refill. It's a dangerous job."

I put a thin arm up and onto his angular shoulder. "We can pray for him."

"I do—every night," he said. "My family is important to me. I'm grateful to have such good folks. Not everyone has support like me."

"You're right about that, Johnny. I hope to have a good family someday."

"Maybe we could have a family, Charlotte. I mean you and me, together. What do you say?"

"That sounds wonderful, Mr. Simon. I'm game."

"Me, too. I could get use to sleeping with you, Char."

Johnny and I were each a little nervous about his family's visit. He was worried that I might be uncomfortable. I was worried that Johnny's family would look down on me or think he could do better.

Within five minutes of meeting them, though, I felt completely at home. I thought Mr. Hardy might be stuck up, seeing as he was the most prominent citizen in Muhlenberg County. He wasn't. Polly and Dennis were both friendly and down-to-earth.

I felt bad for Johnny. Merle's leave had been cancelled. Polly told me Johnny had always looked up to Merle. With their age difference of 15 years, and with their Dad traveling so much with house calls, Merle taught Johnny how to play baseball and football. And he took him to the creek and taught him how to swim and dive.

Eddie picked up Mom, Minta, and Twyla and we all met up in Zanesville at Mueller's Restaurant on Thursday. It was a nice night and we walked over to the Putnam House on the 6th Street Bridge.

Mom gave us a little history lesson. "This part of what's now Zanesville was settled by folks from New England—it was originally a separate town from Zanesville. They were anti-slavery. Zanesville, back on yonder side of the bridge, was settled by folks from Virginia. They were pro-slavery and secessionist.

"Those two groups had quite a time. Folks in Putnam would have meetings that lasted a week or more with Abolitionists and such. They didn't just talk about freeing the slaves. They were a station on the Underground Railroad line that ran right through here, too. A lot of them came up through Chesterfield and Deavertown.

"One of those meetings they had here, a bunch of pro-slavery folks crossed the bridge and tried to burn the house down. Good thing brick doesn't burn."

We walked back across the bridge. Eddy helped the ladies into the car and headed for Chesterfield.

Johnny and Dennis spent lots of time talking about airplanes and such. Dennis was supposed to be leaving Ohio and heading straight over to Europe very soon. I could tell Johnny was feeling that he should be in the service, not just designing equipment for airplanes.

We rented a motor boat. Johnny and Dennis donned wet suits and wore themselves out skiing, but I remembered the jubilant expressions that Johnny and Teddy had earlier in the summer. The wetsuits gave them a decidedly soldierly look, producing a grim aspect.

On Saturday, just as we were getting ready to take Dennis to the train station, a telegram arrived from Doctor Simon.

It read:

> We regret to inform you that your son, Petty Officer First Class, Merle Simon was injured November 7th in the Pacific Theater. He will be evacuated to a hospital ship. You will be contacted after he is evaluated.

This telegram put a damper on the rest of the visit. The mood of our group went from celebratory to downright funereal. By the time the Hardy family left, Johnny was a basket case. He told me after they left that he was glad they were gone. I knew he felt that he should be in the Army, not just working for them as an engineer.

I don't think Johnny ever got over that telegram. He tried to get more information from the Navy personnel at Columbus. For the next 40-plus days, I watched Johnny twist on a rack of anger, guilt and despair.

The war, that great looming thing, had finally become real for the Simon family.

BOOK EIGHT:

The Beginning of the End

Letter Twelve

Sept. 19. 1943
Cpl Virgil Thomas (V)

Dear Mitch,

I have arrived in England and am right in the pink. The trip over was very interesting. Much to my surprise I didn't get seasick. The country here is very beautiful. Hope to be able to get a pass later and see some of the towns.

I haven't gotten any mail yet. When you write, you should use V mail for it comes through much quicker than regular mail. I must try and get Ray's Bachelors address for I might accidently have chance to see him some time.

I wrote Dad and Mother but couldn't tell them I was in England then. So, if you happen to write you could tell them for, I won't write again for a few days. Tell Jim and Donna I said hello.

Virgil

Letter 13

Dear Mitch and all,   Wed night—England

9/23/43

Got my first letter yesterday. It was from Orpha. Today I got yours and several more. Boy, was I sure glad to get them. Can't write much on a V-mail so will write a regular letter tonight. Let me know how long it takes

The article you sent is a very good account of what I went through at Port of Embarkation. Haven't received any Heralds yet ['Morgan County Herald' weekly paper] but hope to soon.

I walked into a small-town last night. It was a beautiful walk. The country side was so pretty and historic looking. Just like you see in the movies and pictures. The towns are quite different from ours in a rustic sort of way. Of course, it was a complete blackout every night, and is it ever dark! Lots of business places were sold out. The Pubs (bars to you) didn't open until eight o'clock and only sold bitter (beer), ale and stout which is a real dark beer kind of drink. It is served warm and rather flat tasting so it didn't take much to do me.

Almost everything is rationed here. We have ration cards and go once a week and get our allotment. Seven packs of cigarettes, 1 soap, 2 razor blades, a little gum, 2 candy bars and a little bag of cookies. I brought a pretty good supply so don't need anything very bad yet. You can send me packages if marked 'Christmas' until October 15, after that if you send anything you must have a letter from me asking you to send certain articles. This is merely information and not a hint Ha!

I certainly enjoyed your long letter, you might send this on to folks as it would probably interest them.

Guess I have told you about all I can. I'll bet Jim [nephew] is proud of that bicycle. Tell him that everyone over here rides them. Some of the boys and officers already bought one. They are hard to get though.

Well, as the English say

Cheerio (goodbye).

Love to all,

Virgil

Letter 14

Dear Mitch and all,   *Oct. 15, 1943 England*

I received your letter today and your V-mail yesterday. So, I guess V-mail is faster but then you can't write so much. And I really enjoy the long letters. So, go ahead and use both kinds. Mail is best morale builder we have here. As long as we can hear from home we get along pretty good. I enjoy the clippings and other letters you enclose, too. I have only received one Herald (Morgan County Herald) so far.

Faye wrote me a nice letter giving me Ray's address. I sure hope we can get together some time, but it is doubtful. Mother said she thought Doc Kinney and Nira would be married. No fool like an old fool.

Too bad about Mary Ruth. She always seemed like such a likable kid and I can't picture either she or Barbara as anything but kids. But we are liable to let our foot slip at times so I guess we shouldn't blame her, but rather feel sorry for her.

Enjoyed Turner's letter and guess she did seem rather lonesome and ready to go back to Windsor. But guess we all are. Even when we do, it won't ever be the same. I guess we didn't know what good times we were having. It's funny how little incidents that I hadn't thought of for years keep popping into my head.

I have been on one short pass (48 hours) to Bristol and hope to get to London sometime before long. Most of people are friendly and I enjoy talking to them. They all ask about things in the US. Boy, they sure go for our cigarettes and chewing gum. Especially the girls. If I had been smart, I would have brought some ladies silk hose from States. They can't get them here. A fellow could have his choice of the town almost if he had a pair to give her. Ha.

As long as I stay in camp, I don't realize so much that I am across. When you go to town though you do. Soon everyone is aware of fact that it isn't good old US. The pubs are only open from ten to two and six until ten at night. And no jukeboxes or dancing. They seem so quiet compared to ours.

Ever one seems to drink beer and smoke. Blackouts make it hard to get around at night. You don't see many cars. The bicycle seems to be the main way of travelling. So, tell Jim that he has something in common with these people.

Tell Opal that I got her letter and will try to get around to answering it someday.

I can't write all that I would like to so guess will just have to wait until you get me wound up on a few beers sometime. It hardly seems possible when I think back where I was a year and a half ago. [On train from Mojave to Camp Pickett, Va.] almost as far the other way from you as I am now. As the old saying goes there has been a lot of water run under the bridge since then.

Love to all, Virgil

Letter 15

10/27/1943

Dear Folks,   *Cpl Virgil Thomas (V)*

Tomorrow I'm making a trip which I have often thought I would like to take, yet I never expected to. I am going to London on a 48- hour pass. Certainly, wish I could take some pictures but guess they will have to be just mental ones.

Imagine me if you can, going by 10 Downing Street, Buckingham Palace and Windsor Castle. Hope I get a glimpse of the Princess. Ha. Am looking forward to a good time.

Yes, you write large enough for V mail. It is easily read. Your letters are subject to censorship, but aren't always—probably just spot censored. Received five letters today. They usually come in bunches that way. It sure makes life a little brighter to get them. Will write again after my pass but probably can't tell you much.

Love,

Virgil

Letter 16

10/29/1943

Cpl Virgil Thomas (V)

Dear Folks,

Received a letter from you today. Hope by now you got some of mine. I had a wonderful trip to London. So many things of interest we couldn't see them all, but we really got around for the time we had. I was indeed fortunate one day attended the funeral of Sir Dudley Pound, Admiral of British Fleet, conducted at Westminster Abbey. You can imagine the nobility that would be there. Got a glimpse of the King as he went past in his car. I have a program of services which I cherish very much as a souvenir. Five of us took a tour and saw most of buildings and historic places. I went through where all the Coronations take place. Stood in the exact spot that King Charles was executed. The cathedral there is one of the most beautiful places I ever saw.

There is nothing that I really need. Hope everyone is OK.

Love,

Virgil

Letter 17

11/13/1943(Card)

Mitch, Eleanor, Jim and Donna,

The song "White Christmas" seems to be running through my head tonight. So, I'll just say, "May your days in the New Year be merry and all your Christmases be white."

Virgil

John Hunt Simon

"Charlotte!" A big fist at the end of a long arm threatened to unhinge the door to Charlotte's room.

"Coming," a muffled voice responded. The deadbolt turned and the door opened. "Johnny, what's wrong? You've been crying. Come in."

He entered the room and stared at the floor.

"What is it, Johnny?"

'It's Merle. Polly just got the telegram. It had today's date—December 12th. But after all the 'regret to inform you' stuff —it said he'd died—and his body hadn't been found. That's a FUBAR if I ever saw one. He was surely dead when we got that other telegram. He's gone, just the same. They're having a service down home for him. I guess they'll bury the flag they send or something."

"When's the service, Johnny?"

"Two o'clock on Friday afternoon in Dunmor, at the Methodist Church."

"Do you want me to go, Johnny? I'd be happy to be there for you. I love you, John Simon."

"I was hoping you'd want to come. But I don't want to get you in trouble at work."

"I haven't taken one day off since I started at Landmark. They'll understand. I'm sure of it."

"We should get started tomorrow by noon or so. I guess I'll head back home. But I don't think I'll be able to sleep."

"Johnny, let's go downstairs. Elsa is house mother tonight. They have a room with a big couch, maybe you could bunk there and we could get going in the morning after I explain things to my manager."

The couple sat on the couch, holding hands and speaking in low tones. About a quarter of ten, Elsa came down the stairs from her second-floor apartment.

"Hey, you two," she said with a pretend frown, "What are you doing? It's almost lights out."

"Elsa, we found out Johnny's older brother, Merle, who's been Missing in Action has been declared dead. The funeral is in southwestern Kentucky day after tomorrow."

"I'm so sorry to hear that, Johnny. How can I can I help?"

"Well, Miss Elsa, we need to leave tomorrow morning."

"Yes," Charlotte said softly. "I am going to try to get two days off so I can go with Johnny. He hasn't slept since he heard the news yesterday. Could he sleep on the couch in that back room with the fireplace?"

"I can sleep in my car if you think that'd be OK. I don't trust myself driving without some shut eye, Johnny said"

The couple eyed Elsa nervously.

"Well, it is kinder nippy out there. You can stay on that couch in the back, Johnny. I'm so sorry to hear about your brother. We just got word my first cousin Wilbur was killed in the Pacific."

It was Elsa's turn to eye Charlotte and Johnny. "Get some sleep you two. But, no foolin' around. OK?"

"Yes ma'am," Johnny said with a big smile. "We won't do anything to get you in trouble. I promise."

"OK, I'll get you two up at 6:30 tomorrow, so you can be on your way. There's a necessary room on the porch just outside the door to your room, Johnny."

Charlotte ran over and hugged Elsa. She ran over to Johnny, and grabbed his hand. He picked her up off her feet and hugged her like a ragdoll.

"They exchanged mumbled good nights and Charlotte headed upstairs behind Elsa.

The drive down was a blur. Johnny wasn't himself. We were passing nearly every vehicle on the road. It was the most afraid I'd ever been in my life.

Johnny had been awful quiet on the way home. I didn't know how to help him. And I started feeling scared. I didn't want to have one of my spells, as Mom called 'em. I didn't want Johnny or his friends or family to see me like that. Once I get started down that slippery slope, I never knew how long it will last.

The service was attended by hundreds of people. Polly said she'd never seen that many folks in the cemetery. Doctor Simon was stoic. He maintained his composure until we got back to the house. The following day he asked me if I'd like to visit his wife's grave. I said I would like that very much.

A year after her burial in the Dunmor Cemetery, he had her moved to a smaller graveyard on the back of their property. It was about a mile from their house, at the end of a gravel lane flanked by big oak trees overlooking a good-sized creek. He'd put in a bench on a little knoll by the creek that looked down at his wife's grave.

"I don't get down here as much as I use to, but I'm glad we got a chance to come down, Charlotte," he said softly.

"I am very pleased you asked me to join you."

"What we have of Merle will be moved down after things calm down. And I hope I don't have to bury anymore family members taken before their time."

BOOK NINE:

To The Beach: Run Up to Normandy

Letter Twenty

12/27/1943

Cpl Virgil Thomas (V)

Dear Mitch, Eleanor, Jim and Dad,

I am back home as I write this letter. I have a picture in my mind of the front room and all of us there. Remember how excited we, as well as kids got when it came time to open presents. Would give most anything to be there and see you all. But when I think how fortunate I am compared to many other fellows it makes my Christmas seem merry. We had a swell dinner, turkey and all the trimmings. Some English children are going to eat with us tonight.

Enjoy the clipping you sent. He writes some good stuff. No, probably people back home haven't been touched much by the war. But we don't want you to be. We want, expect and believe most everyone is doing their part and would do more if duty called. Other than that, we want you to have a good time and enjoy life. When I get back, I want things to be as when I left and not to a war-minded, war-conscious people. It is a date for next Christmas. Cheerio.

Love to all,

Virgil

Letter Twenty-One

1/13/1944

S/Sgt. Virgil Thomas(V)

Dear Mitch and all,

I am leaving tomorrow to spend a short furlough in Scotland. Won't have very long but, needless to say, I am looking forward to it very much. At least I will see where some of 'me ancestors' come from. Ha. Gabby's going with me. We have talked to several soldiers who have been there and they all liked it fine. Will stay at Red Brass in Glasgow.

As for my duties, am not allowed to write of them or organization of our units so there isn't much I can tell you. I do have several men and quite a bit of equipment in my charge, though.

I got an announcement of Mervyn's marriage from Uncle Rob and Aunt Mabel last week. Also, a letter from Aunt Susie. Guess Uncle George is in pretty bad shape. No, I have never seen Clair or anyone else again. No guess the bus didn't make us much, but then I didn't expect it too. Certainly, hope Frank holds out until next Spring. Hope all is well.

Love to all,

Virgil

Letter Twenty-Two

1/19/1944

Dear Mitch and all,   *S/Sgt. Virgil Thomas(V)*

Just got back from spending a short furlough in Glasgow. I certainly had a swell time. I can't imagine how the people got the name of being stingy. I never saw more hospitable people in my life. Really beautiful country, too. Only wish I had more time. Am certainly going back if I have more opportunity. Spent one day in Edinburgh and the rest of the time in Glasgow. Will send a picture I had taken there later. Will also try to send you a copy of Stars and Stripes which you asked for.

Had a letter from Faye from Sacramento, California where she and Dickey are now living.

Oh yes, I forgot to tell you that the girls in Scotland are very nice and easy to get acquainted with. Maybe it's best that I can't get there often. Ha. I had such a good time and found it so different from what I expected that I can't get over it. Like my buddy, Gabby, kept saying all the way back. 'Great country'. 'Fine people.'

Virgil

Letter Twenty-Three

1/19/44

Dear Dad & Mother,

Just got back from Scotland. I certainly had a wonderful trip and a good time. Can't imagine where Scotch people got name of being so stingy. I was never treated better or saw more hospitable people. Don't think I ever had any better time away from home.

Some beautiful scenery there, only wish that I could have had more time. Spent one night in Edinburgh and rest of the time in Glasgow. Both are very modern and much like our own cities. Of course, I got a big kick out of listening to the people talk. I really like their brogue and they all seem to like to talk to Americans. Guess that I am enthused over Scotland but like my buddy, Gabby, kept saying on our way back—Great country—Fine people.

I am sending two cards which I want to save as souvenirs, also a picture I had taken there. I broke one lens out of my rimless glasses and don't like looks of ones I have with rims so I didn't wear any. It has name and address of place on back so will be a good souvenir. Tried to buy a few to send but so many things rationed that I couldn't find anything suitable.

Had a letter from Jobie and Faye from Sacramento, California where they are now living. Hope all are well and that you and Shirley had a nice birthday. She wrote me a letter telling me about it.

Loads of Love,

Virgil

PS Please give Frank and Harriet my best wishes. I'm not sure what happened or didn't happen with Louise and me. I hope she is happy in Akron.

Letter Twenty-Four

1/23/1944

S/Sgt. Virgil Thomas(V)

Dear Jim,

Will answer your letter which I received some time ago. I was certainly glad to get it and surprised to see how well you can write. Glad that you had a nice Christmas and got to go down to Grandma's. I had a big turkey dinner that day. It wasn't as nice as we used to have when we all went to Grandma and Grandpa's though. I thought a lot about all of you that day and would have given most anything to be with you and Donna.

When you said that Donna couldn't remember when I wasn't in the Army, it made me realize just how long it has been. But I will be back some day before too long and then what times we will have.

Hope all of you are well and have escaped flu epidemic I hear you have had over there. I haven't been sick a day since I got here.

Love,

Virgil

Letter Twenty-Five

3/12/1944

Staff Sgt. Virgil Thomas **(V)**

Dear Mitch and Eleanor,

Yes, I guess that I have received most of your letters. But they seem to be slower coming through lately. I got one about bus and believe that I answered it.

Glad to hear that you got a new classification. Mother wrote that Ralph had been put in 1-A. Is Carl going to have to go? Personally, I can't see why they are taking so many with families and essential jobs, too. It looks to me like they have about reached the point where they are needed worse at home on the job than in the Army.

I sometimes wonder if they aren't paying more attention to elections than to war. Of course, I believe that we certainly have the right to vote, but can't see why so much argument over it. I guess Ohio has it settled now, so we can. Well it is almost

Spring and I suppose by now you are beginning to have more warm days. Mother said lots of kids were having measles. Have Jim and Donna had them?

Love to all,

Virgil

Letter Twenty-Six

3/28/1944

S/Sgt. Virgil Thomas(V)

Dear Mitch,

Glad to hear that the bus did so good for February. Maybe it will make out O.K. for rest of term. Sorry to hear about Carl. It just doesn't seem right.

I got a box of candy from Grace Clutter today. Also, had a letter from Faye with a picture of Jobie and Billy. Boy, the green grass, trees and California sunshine looked good to me. I suppose you are having nice spring weather by now.

I spent the past weekend in Bath. It is quite an old and historic place. I really enjoy seeing all these historic places and guess so far, I have been pretty fortunate, although at times you would have a hard time convincing me of it. Ha.

Right now, I am listening to some good music coming from Chicago. Don't get to hear it very often and it makes me kind of homesick. Makes me think of other times, places and people. But hell, I think I better stop and get into a bull session before I start getting sentimental.

Virgil

Letter Twenty-Seven

4/17/1944

S/Sgt. Virgil Thomas (V)

Dear Mitch,

Received your Easter card O.K. also got a box from mother which I had requested. I went to church this morning. Had a nice Easter service. This is the first Easter that I ever remember that I didn't have all the eggs I could eat. I have had only two fresh eggs since I left the States. Didn't buy a new suit this time either. Just decided to make old one do. Ha.

Glad you received the paper and enjoyed it. We certainly like it here for it seems like a connection with home. And anything that does that to a soldier strikes a tender spot.

I finally had a letter from Harriet last week. She said Louise had a bit of good fortune. Harvey Knight and wife, a relative of hers both died recently. They had no children so left house, contents and automobile to Louise. It is a swell property in one of the nicer districts. I have been there several times and knew them both. She said work was going well for Louise in Akron.

Tell Jim and Donna I would give anything to see them. Hope you all had a lovely Easter.

Love,

Virgil

Virgil in England prior to landing in Normandy.]

June 1944: Channel Crossing and the Second Front

1944

Johnny Simon and Charlotte Ross

The air war in Europe, and all the variations and permutations thereof, was underway. In spades!

As Allied planes were destroyed and damaged by the thousands, Johnny's section added troubleshooting to its original developmental mission. The brilliant minds that had developed such elegant procedures and equipment found themselves now on "cob job" duty—figuring out the optimal way to apply duct tape to prevent $100 hinges from failing.

In the lull between Allied landings in Normandy one of the air wings in England stored pieces of wreckage from various airplanes in huge containers and shipped them back to Columbus for evaluation. Surviving members from some of the planes came along.

The reality of war hit home for Johnny with every bloodstained and pretzeled piece of steel. Both ball turrets in each of the two B-24s sent back had been damaged. The plexiglass cover in the front turret of one had sustained damage to its hinges.

As Johnny examined the hinges a sergeant who had accompanied the wrecks across the Atlantic spoke up. "Corporal Billy Jones manned this turret, sir. He left behind a wife and two children. He kept their pictures taped where he could see them. When those hinges blew out he was extruded right through that opening. The picture of his family must have followed him. You can see four small pieces of tape where the picture was. And you can see Billy's blood on the hinges."

"I have a brother who is a gunner on a B-17," Johnny said as he examined the blood pattern.

"It's a hell of a job, Mr. Simon. Some of the designers told us that those guns in the turrets, that added extra weight, don't really improve the crew's chance of survival. But those officers up in the cockpit want some gunners. No one wants to get their nuts shot off. Some of them pilots fly while sitting on helmets or iron. That leaves us gunners as the first line of defense. And we don't want to get our nuts shot off, either. But there isn't really much room in there for gunners to protect the family jewels. It's a hell of a thing."

Johnny was listening, but his thoughts drifted away to his brother, Dennis, cramming his short but sturdy frame into this turret. He felt powerless to help these expendable gunners. They were like cattle queued up in a slaughterhouse waiting for their turn.

Johnny's job was to design and/or modify these components to protect the crews. But he couldn't even help his own brother! Christ! How, with a straight face, do you tell men that this slight modification of the hinge or the turning gears could improve their chances to survive? Christ, their tiny turret had only plexiglass! A properly aimed slingshot from 20 feet away could breach that barrier. It was all a probability problem. And the odds were stacked against them.

Johnny might have been able to blow smoke about improving the safety of those gunners in the aggregate, but when he thought about just one gunner, his brother Dennis, he felt like crying or picking up a gun and sacrificing his life.

Meanwhile, Charlotte had been suffering, waiting for the right time to tell Johnny the "good news." He had been working late for two weeks, ever since they delivered that plane wreckage to Columbus. She had to be back in the dorm by ten o'clock. And he wasn't getting off work much before midnight.

When he finally took a day off, she was so worried she could hardly speak. "Johnny I've got some news. I hope you'll think it's good news."

"Fire away, Char," he said with a tired grin.

"Well, its just—well. I'm pregnant."

The boy's grin faded.

"What do you think, Johnny? I've been waiting to tell you. I hoped you'd be glad."

"Wow, Charlotte. That is good news."

She came over and hugged him. "I love you, Johnny. I've been an old worry wart waiting until I had a chance to tell you in person."

"I love you too, Charlotte. We should get married."

"I'll do my best to be a good wife and mother. Oh, I'm relieved that you're happy, too. At least, I hope you aren't just saying that. I hope you mean it, Johnny."

"I do, darling. And I think you'll be a wonderful wife and mother."

On June 14th, 1944, Johnny and Charlotte were married in the dance tent at Buckeye Lake. It was a small ceremony. His roommates attended. Johnny's sister, Polly, got her first ride in an airplane, thanks to the Army Air Corps. She hitched a ride up and back with one of the test pilots from Columbus.

Charlotte's mother, Nanny, attended along with the bride's aunts—and Charlotte. Twyla was her maid of honor.

An Army Air Corps chaplain—a Lutheran— married them. Twyla and Charlotte were scandalized. For them, that Lutheran minster might as well have been the Pope. Nanny put her foot down hard with those two and managed to avoid a scene.

Charlotte was just happy to be married. The nagging feeling that she was not good enough for Johnny diminished slightly, after the ceremony.

The couple rented a small house in Duncan Falls on Route 60. Charlotte cut back to part-time at Landmark—two days a week and other day if folks needed time off. She enjoyed having enough time to keep the house looking good. And she did her best with the cooking.

Johnny and Charlotte went back to Nanny's house on Saturdays. None of the beds were big enough for Johnny. He'd sleep on quilts piled on the floor.

Twyla and Minta nagged incessantly that the newlyweds should move in to Nanny's house and not squander money on rent. The scene was always the same when Charlotte and Johnny prepared to leave on Sunday after lunch.

"You two could save a pant load of money if you stayed here," Minta would say.

"Johnny already has a 70-mile drive each day. If we moved here, it would be over 90 miles."

Twyla would snigger and whisper to Charlotte, "You just want to be able to do the nasty things at night, don't you, Charlotte?"

Nanny sent Twyla upstairs.

"Don't pay attention to her, Charlotte. She can't help it. Whatever is wrong with her is not gonna change."

"OK, Mom. tell the girls we said goodbye."

Nanny gave Charlotte a hug and a big smile. Johnny bent over and gave his mother-in-law an awkward hug.

"Lordy, you need a stepstool to hug this feller. You two be careful. And thanks for coming down. We all enjoy seeing you. And I think Pen and Eddie are going to come over for church next Sunday. You're always welcome here, both of you."

June 24, 1944: 3rd Armored Division with 36th Armored Infantry lands on Omaha Beach

Letter Twenty-Nine

6/22/1944

S/Sgt. Virgil Thomas(V)

Dear Mitch,

Happy birthday. Just happened to remember that you are having one soon. It is almost eleven o'clock here and not dark yet. Will be light again by five. Makes a short night of it.

News from Italy seems pretty good now. Certainly, I hope this second front soon gets started. I am tired of sweating it out. Want to get it over with and get home and really live once again. Guess getting home is the big thing in all the boys' minds over here. It's a lot different than being stationed in the States.

Did you hear what caused a riot in the old maid's home? Someone found the toilet seat turned up. Hope everyone is O.K.

Virgil

6/29/1944: Villiers-Fossard

"Hey, Virgil think we dug deep enough?"

"Maybe a little more, Gabby."

They continued digging, the only noise gentle grunts as they threw the sand and mud up and out of their foxhole.

"Gabby, I think there are some busted up skids down by the mess tent. I'm gonna go look and bring one back so we're not sleepin' in the mud."

"OK, Virg. If they got any busted-up biscuits, maybe you could bring a couple of them back, too. And as long as you're gonna be up by the brass, see if they can do something about this rain. OK?"

"I'll see what I can do, pard."

Ten minutes later Virgil returned, dragging a two-foot wide section of a skid with heavy cardboard shoved between the top and the bottom.

"Incoming," he said in a soft voice. Gabby pulled himself out. They dropped the skid to the bottom of hole and put the cardboard on top.

"Here you go, Gabby." He handed him two biscuits.

"Thanks, Virg. Now 'bout that other thing—."

"Two out of three ain't bad, Gabby."

"Reckon you're right, Virg. Thanks! This hole ain't too bad, Virg. Getting this skid was a good idea."

"Not bad."

"I used to think bein' in a tank would better than infantry. But seein' those tanks stuck on that hedgerow yesterday, laid out like a doggone target, kinder changed my mind."

"Yep, those fellers got it tough. They might as well be Spam in a can once they take a well-placed shell."

"Yes, sir. They got those tank dozers coming in now. Maybe that will help."

7/24/1944: Carantilly

"More rain. Man, I could go for some sunshine, Virg. My feet are getting to look like an old lady's ass.

"I hear you, Gabby. Remember that night we spent in the underground with those two old English gals?"

"I'll never forget those two. Right friendly old birds they were. I never knew you could have so much fun with all your clothes on. Those two were experts."

"Pros more like," Virgil said with a wink.

"Yeah, that was a good time, Virg."

"Well, keep your powder dry, Gabby. This rain has got to let up soon. I found a good-sized piece of canvas we can use for cover if the rain gets worse.

7/26/1944: Carantilly AM

"Do you hear that, Virgil?

"The sound of it <u>not</u> raining. Downright beautiful, ain't it?"

The two men stirred, climbed up and out of their foxhole and inspected their feet and toes. As they were digging for dry socks, food and cigarettes the cloud cover that had dogged them for days lifted. The rumble of Allied aircraft—Mustangs first and then wave after wave of Fortresses and Liberators--was hypnotic, soothing even. The implications, however were anything but comforting. The 36th Armored Infantry would be moving on against German troops. And these experienced troops were regrouping, not giving up or heading East.

One of those B-17s carried a tail gunner from Muhlenberg County, Kentucky. Dennis Simon was 27 years old; a veteran of 15 missions without incident. This would be his 16th and last mission. Machine gun fire from a German Fouke Wulf FW 190 nearly cut him in two.

He hung on in a field hospital after they amputated both legs a few inches below his scrotum. A month later, on his first wheelchair trip outside the hospital, his squad leader, Lt. Jason Christy, pulled a heavy object wrapped in a towel from inside his flight jacket.

Dennis unwrapped the towel. It held a loaded 45 caliber pistol.

"Sergeant Simon, if this can be of any use to you, it's yours. In addition to the gun, I have arranged for a young lady of my acquaintance to meet you at hotel just down the street. She knows your condition, and she is a professional."

The man in the chair shook his head and took several deep breaths.

"Denny, we've been together nearly from the beginning. I'm not trying to push you one way or the other. It has just occurred to me that if I was sitting where you are, I might want to have some options."

Dennis broke out into a big grin. "Don't suppose there's a bottle of good Kentucky bourbon in that hotel room is there?"

"Roger that, sergeant. That bottle cost more than the gun and the girl combined."

"I don't want anyone else getting into trouble. Can this look like a suicide?"

"I think folks at the hospital are understanding about these things. I'll do everything I can. I can also explain to your sister, if I make it back."

Dennis swallowed hard with a stricken look in his eyes, something like the look a white mouse might get after being placed in a snake exhibit in the zoo.

"OK, it's your call, pardner."

"You know, I always wondered what it be like to have a cock as long yer leg. Guess I'll find out. Just make sure the lady doesn't get in trouble. I'm a tail gunner, and I'll finish this off myself. I appreciate what you've done. If I had enough of my legs left to be able to use prosthetics, I'd probably give it a shot. But I don't think that's realistic. I can't imagine living without being able to ride a horse or play with my children. I'm satisfied. You tell my brother, Johnny, not to feel bad. He is an engineer in the Army Air Corps, and he works on design fixes for the B-17. He'll blame himself."

"Ready to go, Denny?"

"Yes, I am."

Letter Twenty-Nine

7/29/1944

S/Sgt. Virgil Thomas(V)

France

Dear Eleanor,

If I remember right, I believe you are having a birthday before long. So, I want to wish you, the best Sister-in-law any fellow ever had a happy birthday and many returns of the day. Believe me, I think of you all a lot.

I know that you all are wondering and keep asking what I have been doing. Am sorry that I can't tell you as much as I would like. About all I can say is that I have seen some action but am all right in every way. And if you don't hear too often from me, remember that no news is good news.

So, your new neighbor has two good looking daughters. I'll have to get on the hustle and pay you a visit.

Does Donna start school this Fall? Hardly seems possible, but when I think of it, she must.

Love to all,

Virgil

Duncan Falls, Ohio: 07/30/1944

Johnny's car pulled into the gravel driveway. He killed the engine but stayed in the driver's seat, staring at the rusted swing-set in the back yard. He thought of Dennis, who always talked about having a family with lots of kids. He'd never realize that dream.

A corporal he knew from Dennis' squadron had contacted him. He sent a telegram to Johnny asking him to call.

"Corporal Jenkins?"

"Yes, this is Corporal Jenkins."

"It's John Simon, Denny's brother."

"Yes, sir. I wanted to let you know that your brother was severely injured on his last mission. He died in a hospital in France."

"What were his injuries?"

"He was tail gunner in a B-17 that took heavy fire from enemy fighter planes. His legs were amputated when he got to the field hospital. He was later sent to a hospital in Belgium. They thought he was stabilized, and he got a pass.

"But they found him dead at a hotel not far from the hospital."

"What was the cause of death, corporal?"

"Official cause of death was heart failure due to a blood clot. Sir, can I speak freely?"

"Yes, please."

"Sir, lots of men who are on these bombers worry about getting shot—in the private parts. It's especially bad for tail gunners. The pilots can sit on a helmet. But tail gunners? Well, there's just no room in there, unless you're a midget. Anyway, again, this is strictly off the record."

"Yes, fine. Off the record. Go on, please."

"OK. Corporal Simon had both his legs amputated, according the report, 16" above the knee. His stumps were too short to allow him to get prosthetics. In many cases, these fellows help each other. Every man jack that gets into one of those bombers knows it could happen to them. The speculation is that one of his fellow crew members might have offered to help him."

"What would that entail, corporal?"

"Seeing as Dennis got a two-day pass and he was found in a hotel a mile from the hospital, I'd say one of his buddies offered to get him a hotel, a bottle, a gun, and a girl. And I want to remind you again that this is not uncommon. If you were just a civilian, I would not have told you any of this. But seeing as you work for the Air Corps, I figure you got a right to know. Those tail gunners gotta feel like a worm on a fish hook in a pond full of sharks."

"Well—thank you, corporal. I appreciate your candor. Under no circumstances will I ever say anything to anyone else about what you've told me."

"Thank you, sir. I'm glad I told you. May God, bless you and your family."

"Thank you."

The desire to share this with Charlotte was intense. They had been each other's sounding board since they met. This would be the first time he kept something important from her, but not the last.

Chatillon: August 10, 1944

"I'll be glad to get some shut-eye in a proper foxhole," Virgil said as they climbed into the four by four by four-foot deep hole. "Those slit trenches aren't worth a damn! They put me in mind of the gal with a short dress and no underwear. Not much is covered up, for long!"

"Hey Virg I grabbed a couple of them French baguettes and two tins of stew when I was checkin' mail. We can have a good supper. Heard we might get some R&R tomorrow. That'd be nice."

"Anything from Laverne?"

Gabby shook his head and frowned. "I haven't heard from her in a coon's age. About all I knew was that Birdie give up the boy to the Carmelites when he was six months old. And then Laverne give the Sisters bucks as a donation and they give him up to her. But now I don't know where she or Jake ended up."

"I'm awful sorry about that, Gabby."

"It's a SNAFU, alright."

"I still haven't heard from Louise. I think about her every day, Gabby."

They sat in silence 'til the latent heat in their uniforms dropped, and a slight chill started crawling in around their collar and cuffs.

"Virgil."

"Huh? What, Gabby"

"You're the best friend I've ever had."

"I feel the same way about you Gabby."

"I—I'd like for us to make a deal. If anything happens to either of us, the other one will go and see the other's family. For me, that would be Jake and maybe Laverne and Birdie. They should be up around Kalamazoo or in Upper Sandusky, Ohio."

"That's a good idea. My folks—Big Mitch and Anne Thomas—are in Windsor, Ohio. Louise is working at a factory in Akron. I've loved her since I first saw her in 1925."

"Deal?"

"Deal!"

[8/11/1944 Virgil injured in Chatillon, France—shrapnel in his head. Returned to his Unit on 9/02/1944 just south of Mons.]

Mons 9/02/1944:

"Hey buddy" Gabby said. He ran over just as Virgil climbed down from a Red Cross truck. "Man, some guys will do anything for a free haircut." The two men embraced warmly. "You OK, Virg?""

"Yes. Nothin' left in my head to damage. So, they sent me back."

"I haven't rented out your half of the hole yet. Come on and follow me. Wow, I'm glad to see you, pard. I thought I'd jinxed us talkin' about what we wanted each other to do if one of us didn't make it. But it looks like you're OK."

"I am. I just laid around on a cot in a tent. Every hour or so some nurse or a doctor would stick their head in and look in my eyes and make me follow the light from a flashlight. But the good part was—the fellow I shared a tent with didn't have stinky feet like you. Ha!"

"Your feet don't exactly smell like rose bushes, either, Virg!"

"I know. I'm glad I'm back, where I belong."

Letter Thirty

9/10/1944

S/Sgt. Virgil Thomas(V)

France

Dear Mitch and Eleanor,

Haven't received any mail for a long time. Hope I get some soon for I can't help but wonder what is going on back there. If I don't answer some question you might have asked it is because I haven't received your mail. I am all right though and completely over the little accident I had. [Shrapnel 8/11/1944]

I saw Bing Crosby in person. I sure enjoyed it. Was almost like a ray of sunshine from the good old States. Yet it made me rather sad for it recalled other times and places. I am seeing quite a lot of country, but will have to wait to tell you of that.

Boy when I get back nobody wants to say anything about any part of the States to me. As for women, well, I have seen some really beautiful ones here. However, this language business makes it rather unhandy. Ha. Don't have much time for that, anyway, yet.

Love,

Virgil

Letter Thirty-One

10/19/1944

S/Sgt. Virgil Thomas

Germany

Hello Everyone,

A few lines to let you know that I am O.K. and still kicking. I am acting Platoon Sergeant right now and being kept plenty busy.

Sorry to hear that Mitch is off work with his hip. Certainly, hope he gets all right. Be sure and let me know. Had a letter recently from Kent Bachelor. He is over here somewhere, too. We got a replacement in my platoon who is from Zanesville. He used to drive a truck on some of the same jobs I worked on. We sure did some heavy trucking. In our 'spare moments.'

Did you ever hear from Louise? She asked Grace Clutter for your address and said she was going to write Eleanor. But, hell you know these women. Ha. Boy, I believe Goldie Burkhouse would even look good now.

Have you seen any articles in paper about my outfit? A few of the boys received some nice articles. Because of censorship they haven't let much out. Just wait until final history is written, though. I am not caring for any glory. All I want is to get home. God, I never realized what a wonderful place it was.

I get plenty to eat and am not having it too hard. So, don't worry. Just get sort of homesick at times.

Believe mother said you were taking your vacation at Thanksgiving. Tell Donna I am sorry that I didn't get a letter written for her birthday. However, at times it is just impossible to write. I thought of her and she is still my best girl.

Love to all,

Virgil

Letter Thirty-Two

10/20/1944

S/Sgt. Virgil Thomas

Germany

Dear Mitch and Eleanor,

Just wrote you a letter a short time ago. Received one from you today and will drop a line to set you straight. You are getting my Regiment mixed up with a Division of the same number. <u>I am in the 36th Regiment which is part of the 3rd Armored Division</u>. *Will enclose a little clipping which might be of interest. Look in papers for news of my division to follow me. Yes, your last hunch was right as to my Army.*

Believe Frank Brill is in the same one, although not positive.

You mentioned something about a bed. What is that? I am an authority on foxholes. I have dug, slept, ate and lived in all sizes, shapes and forms. While a poor substitute of a home they can be mighty comforting at times and those times aren't too far apart. I suppose when the war is over I can get a job digging a ditch. Boy, I have plenty of experience.

Yes, I know all about the hugging, kissing, flower throwing populace through France and Belgium. It is rather thrilling at the time. But when it is all over one stops and wonders. I have been cheered and treated swell by some Germans. I am not sucker enough to believe they are sincere or to trust them. None of them claim to be Nazis. Never yet have I met one who would admit it. A few years ago, they were sticking chests out and giving the old salute. Now it is a much different story.

Well must close for now.

Virgil

PS I was referring to civilian population above.

Stolberg: 11/27/1944

"You reckon this rain will ever let up, Virg?"

"If it does it does, we could get worse. Watch what you pray for."

"I guess you got a point.'

"A big turkey dinner would be nice right now. With mashed taters and gravy. And biscuits dripping with butter."

"I'll take my biscuits with apple butter on 'em. And cornbread. And some ham with red-eye gravy."

"I'm getting full just thinking about Thanksgiving, Virg."

"Me too, Gabby. I am thankful to have you for my buddy. All the way through, pardner."

"We better get some sleep. Not everybody just had a week of R&R in a tent with some feller with good smellin' feet, you know."

"OK, goodnight."

"Goodnight, Virg."

Letter Thirty-Three

Card from Third Armored Division

12/1/1944

Dear Jim and Dee Dee,

Another Christmas has rolled around I can't be with you. My thoughts are sure back there though. Next year I'm going to be there and we will sure have a time then.

Uncle Virgil

Pictures taken at Big Mitch and Anne's' farm in Oakland Virgil with Jim and Dee Dee on furlough in 1943]

Echtz: 12/11/1944:

"Virgil, them Jerrys hain't run out of ammo, that's for darn sure."

"They'll have to let up some eventually, I suppose."

"Hey, Virgil. Remember our trip to Scotland?"

"You better believe I do."

"That was something. The folks were nice and the scenery, too. I really liked going up on that hill, they called it King Arthur's Seat and looking at the castle and the old part of Edinburgh. And I really appreciated being treated like an upstanding human being, too. My family was treated like white trash back home. But bein' in the Army has given me a sense of pride. Something I never thought I'd have. And I guess I feel like when I get back, I'll be able to hold my head up with the best of 'em."

"I know what you mean, Gabby. My Dad was an upstanding citizen, but I got in a lot of trouble in high school. I guess I feel like I've finally grown up some, too. I just hope when this is over— and after we do a little world traveling'—I just want to go back to Ohio and find a gal and settle down and have some kids."

"Me too, Virg. I thought I had that all worked out with Laverne, but I think she has more problems than I suspected. I hope I can find her and Jake when I get back. I wish I at least had a picture of Jake."

"At least you got a son. Someone to carry on your name."

"Yeah, but I got to find him first."

They lapsed into silence. Only the exhausted plumes of their breathing interrupted their reverie.

"How much longer will this war go on, Gabby? I can feel my life slipping away. I feel like if I ever get out I'll be old and used up. Who would have me for a husband? Maybe some old maid. If I ever get to finish school. I'll be older than my professors! "Enough of that sob sister stuff from me, Gabby. This is the finest foxhole I've ever had the pleasure of inhabiting. I think I need to get some rest."

"Don't want you to overdo it, Virg. Got to keep you healthy, buddy. We'll get through this. We've got plans after the war ends, and I want to make sure we're able to go."

"Yes, we do! Thanks, buddy. I feel the same way."

[12/12/1944 ECHTZ: Gabby Thurlow was killed on 12/12/1944, and Virgil was shot the following day, 12/13/1944, just west of the Ardennes— 'The Bitter Woods'. This occurred during the run-up a few days before the Battle of the Bulge commenced in earnest.

Battle Honors were awarded to Company A 36th Armored Infantry Regiment, on February 20, 1945. The citation described their accomplishments: "Company A, 36th Armored Infantry Regiment, is cited for outstanding performance of duty in action during the period 10 to 13 December 1944 in Germany. On 10 December 1944, Company- A was assigned as the only infantry company of a task force which launched an attack on Echtz. Aware of the superiority of enemy troops which were dug in and heavily fortified, the men and officers of Company A attacked vigorously, and with great determination routed the enemy from its defensive positions and secured the village prior to nightfall. On 12 December 1944, Company A, as part of a reconnaissance force, joined with tanks to reconnoiter a small village on the Roer River. The sector assigned to Company A required an advance of 1500 yards over flat and open terrain and under complete enemy observation from the east bank of the river. Though the company on its left was driven back in its attempt to cross the fire-swept field, the officers and men of Company A, ignoring heavy explosive shells, direct tank fire, and withering automatic weapons fire, and suffering heavy casualties, unhesitatingly advanced across the fire-swept field to reach the edge of town. With very few leaders remaining and its ranks thinned by casualties, Company A continued to push forward aggressively and successfully captured the village, clearing the approaches to the town in preparation for the advance of another rifle company. The heroic action and esprit de corps displayed by officers and men of Company A. though weakened by heavy casualties are worthy of high praise.

[Staff Sergeant Virgil Thomas 35034728 was awarded a Purple Heart, and a Bronze Star: For heroic achievement in action against the enemy in Germany on 13 Dec 1944.]

From the *Morgan County Herald* 12/13/1944

> Henry Forest of Windsor, Ohio died quietly in his sleep on December 7, 1944—nearly twenty years after Doc Whitacre convinced him to sell his farm because of poor health. He was survived by his wife, Harriet, four daughters—Barbara, Merlene and Opal of Windsor and Louise Forest Benoit of Akron—and one grandchild, Pierce Emile Benoit of Akron.
>
> Services will be held at the Oakland Church on December 15th Internment to take place immediately following the Service conditions permitting. The Oakland Women's Auxiliary will provide a buffet luncheon afterwards in the Church open to all.

Louise and Doak faced a conundrum concerning the funeral. Harriet had met Doak briefly during their two-day visit at Thanksgiving. Frank had been too sick to travel. The other girls, aged 15, 24, and 27, had been busy.

Louise would have liked for Doak to come with them, but she understood, only too well, the problems with keeping those lines rolling 24/7. After several discussions, Louise and Doak agreed he would stay, and Louise and Pierce would go.

When Mervyn Usher heard about Louise's father's death he came over to the bearing line and expressed his condolences.

"Sorry to hear about your Dad, Louise."

"Thank you, Mervyn. I'd like to get a couple days off, if I could."

Mervyn nodded his head. "How would you like to get three days off, with pay, both of you?"

"Well," Doak said with a shrug, "we figured you'd want somebody to stay on the line."

"I've got somebody else in mind, has experience on the bearing line."

"What dat be?" Doak asked with a toothy grin.

"Me," Mervyn said. "I ran this line for five years from 1929 to 1934."

"I guess I heard dat before."

"It would be nice to get three days off," Louise said with a tired grin. "What's the catch, Mr. Usher?"

"Well, we figure this push to the end of the War will last until the end of 1945 and maybe longer. Depending on how things go in the Pacific, maybe longer. We are starting to see attrition with our employees, particularly the women. If you have one child, you don't mind working and having Junior in the nursery. But add another one or two and lots of gals want to stay home. Especially if they've been good with their money. And some of them have husbands returning. "What I would like you to do is see if you can find some folks familiar with machinery and see if they want work. If they do, we'll supply them with railroad tickets and the first month's rent on an apartment at Velma's. What do you think?"

"Well, I guess we'd be kinder killin' two birds with one stone. Long as Louise don't have to spend all her time recruiting, I'm OK with that. How 'bout you, Cher?"

Louise nodded her head. "I think we can work this out. I just want to focus on the funeral on the first day."

"That sounds good," Mervyn said with a big grin.

"How many folks you lookin' for, boss?"

"About 30 or 40 for jobs on the line. And we could use ten or 15 with some kind of supervisory experience, Doak."

"We can do our best. Now, I was raised up in New Lex and got family there. If we don't line up enough folks in Morgan County we could swing by New Lex on the way back."

"That sounds good. Again, I'd like to offer my condolences. If you see my Mom, give her a hug from me. But don't tell her how fat I'm getting," He patted his belly over his suit coat with both hands. "She'd worry."

"So, let's see. The funeral is Saturday, the day after tomorrow. So, you folks work tomorrow, Friday, and then be off Saturday, Sunday, and Monday, returning Tuesday at noon. Sound, about right?"

"Yes sir," Doak said. "I'll call my Gram, tell her to round up folks for Monday in New Lex."

"Good, I got a good feeling about this. Country folks make good workers. I'll stop down tomorrow. Y'all take care now."

For the next 24 hours, Louise's mind was burdened—anxiety—operationally defined. Her Father's death was not a surprise, but the intensity of her grief shocked her. She looked forward to seeing her Mother and sisters.

When Louise and Doak first married, she was reluctant to take him down home. This was partly out of shame surrounding the circumstances of her marriage, even though her Mother was the only one who had all the facts, and she was not about to divulge that information to anyone.

After their marriage and especially after Pierce was born, the worrying *vis-à-vis* paternity was, for the most part, laid to rest. She gave birth on February 6, 1944, but managed to have all the documents dated February 26th. These papers were placed in a safety deposit box in a bank in McConnelsville, under Louise's maiden name. Doak was very happy to be a husband with a new baby. He wasn't interested in playing sleuth.

Louise had spent the last few months of her pregnancy casually mentioning that all her mother's children had come early and other comments in a similar vein.

Any residual worries Louise had concerning Doak and Pierce were laid to rest after she woke from a nap and overheard Doak's side of a phone call he had with his sister, Lucinda.

"Gram was right about me and 'bout all that. When those assembly lines started gearing up before the War, I got on as a lead man and then supervisor in a ball bearing plant up in Akron. And I'm doin' good, at work and otherwise. I got me a good wife and a boy. Dat boy sure don't look like me. But that was OK with me, too. I've never fretted over things I didn't have. My Cher and I get along just fine. I is a lucky man—not bad for a five-foot tall. Coon Ass Cajun! You take care now, sis. We'll send you a picture of our boy, Pierce."

About the only variable Louise couldn't control was Pierce Emile Benoit himself. He was growing like the proverbial weed. As he got longer and thinned out, the appearance of a slightly cleft chin under his baby fat revealed a definite clue about the identity of his father. Fortunately for Louise only two other people were liable to recognize that clue—Harriet Forest and Anne Thomas— who resided in Windsor.

Louise and Doak were fortunate to have the nursery at the plant for Pierce. As they loaded the car in preparation for their trip to Windsor, Louise had a momentary wish that she could leave her darling boy in Akron away from the scrutinizing, divining eyes of family, friends, and gossips. She felt a twinge of guilt as she took Pierce to the nursery and realized she trusted these strangers with him more than she trusted the family and neighbors she'd known her whole life.

Such mixed feelings by women in her situation had to have been in play almost from the beginning of time. Certainly, it has been that way since people could leave mud huts or rickety cabins and move to a city and trade their time and talents for cash, currency, or credit, while reinventing themselves away from the loving but intrusive eyes of their elders.

The folks back home worry and wait. Letters can lie. Phone calls can be finessed. Those windows of the soul are another matter. People down home, many of them, remember these returned exiles before their reinvention — from a time before the lies and finessing came quite so easily.

Louise's original sin began with circumstances beyond her control—her Father's third heart attack prevented a marriage to Virgil before he reported to the Army. He had to be with Uncle Sam. It germinated, like Pierce, as a secret shared only with her Mother.

Her play for Doak had been desperate and seemed more than a little foolish at first, but it had worked. An ironically, as their marriage unfolded and blossomed into parenthood, she found herself extremely happy with her two boys—Doak and Pierce.

Still, some nights, when Doak had to drop off reports up front, she sat in the car and let her mind drift back to good times she'd had with Virgil— the nights they acted out their silly Heathcliff and Catherine Earnshaw skits. Nights on the table by the Forest's house and in the backseat of cars parked behind a bootlegger's barn.

She had an envelope full of addresses for Virgil at his different Army camps given to her by members of the Thomas clan. But she never sent any of the letters she wrote. They resided beneath Pierce's altered birth certificate and an 8x12-inch page covered with Virgil's addresses in Louise Forest's personal safe deposit box.

The Friday night before the funeral, they left straight from work. Louise put Pierce in the crib Doak had made that nestled securely behind the driver's seat. *Three days*, she thought. *I can do anything for three days.*

"OK, Cher. And with Hi*s* Majesty's permission, let us head south. We is goin' in among 'em."

Four hours and three stops for gas and diaper changes later, they pulled up next to the big built-in picnic table just downriver from the Forest's home in Windsor. Harriet came out and fussed over Pierce and Louise. She showed Doak where to take the baby and their luggage. Louise sat on the table's familiar planks and watched a nearly full, but waning, moon glisten obliquely off the river's still surface. She pondered, reflecting on the last time she been at this table alone with a moon, a river, and her thoughts.

It was that long night of the soul, waiting for Virgil to return from the Thomas house. She'd been on the table when her Mother came out and told her to call the doctor.

An hour earlier, she had been on a horse blanket on the table on her back, consummating the approaching nuptials. Before she had time to button her blouse, Virgil had left for his folk's house, and Frank Forest had a heart attack. Between the time Virgil left to ride up the hill to his family's farm and his return, Louise had gone with her mother and father to the hospital in Zanesville.

Effie Engle had come over to watch the girls. She related the events to Louise the following morning. "Well Louise, Virgil stuck his head in the kitchen and checked to see who was home and if the girls were OK. I told him yes, they just needed sleep."

Louise closed her eyes as she remembered more of Effie's conversation.

"Then I asked him when his leave was over. Virgil said that he had to catch the train Saturday at 6 PM in Columbus. Big Mitch was supposed to drive Virgil, but now he's gonna be give out with all the running around he's doing. So, I said that Bryce could probably take him up to Columbus. I offered to call Bryce to see if he could swing by here, Virgil thanked me, and I said it was a pleasure. my pleasure. After all, we've got to support our boys."

Louise recalled that Effie always wanted to help out others. "Then I asked where he was heading to from here, and he said Pennsylvania. I said that if he could stick around for a bit, I'd call Bryce. He was on third shift that month but he should be home in 15 minutes or so. And Virgil thanked me, then said he'd go outside and watch the river."

***

Virgil sat on the bench and buried his face in the folds of the forlorn horse blanket. The musky smell both excited and sickened him. His Aunt Virgie use to say, "Sometimes things just aren't meant to be. No use beating your head against the wall."

Virgil hopped up on the table, put his feet on the bench, and watched a pink eastern sky shading toward orange until the leading edge of the fiery orb peeked just over the horizon from the other side of the big bends that sent the Muskingum through two loops. The first loop sent the channel past Luke Chute. The second sent the channel back east and then southeast through Beverly and Waterford.

Neither Louise nor Virgil knew that morning that they were on the edge of one of those irreversible inflection points on life's curve. Louise didn't know she was pregnant. Virgil didn't know that dark night when he hopped onto AJ and headed to his Dad's farm, that he might never see Louise again. More importantly, the invisible tie that both Virgil and Louise had felt since their first meeting had been stretched past the breaking point. Neither party knew at that time. Fortune, distance, age, and circumstance contrived to shatter a bond that had once seemed indestructible.

Louise appeared to have dealt with the fallout from these events better than Virgil. At first, this could be attributed to staying home and continuing with her normal routine. Once she found out she was pregnant, though, she couldn't just continue treading water. She shifted into high gear and figured out a way to have a safe, secure place when her baby arrived. Few forces in this mean old world are stronger than maternal instinct.

Virgil, on the other hand, found himself treading water until the end of the war and beyond. He'd been anxious to get overseas. After his outfit got to England, he was anxious to get into action. For the rest of the war he mooned over Louise, wondering what went wrong and why she never wrote. While he was in the hospital after being shot, he was anxious to go back to combat or be sent home. When he got home, he was anxious to finish his last two quarters at Ohio State and get on with finding a career.

As Louise lay awake on her old rope bed, she felt the anxiety returning. Pierce would be eyeballed by the townsfolks. Old friends would be glad to see mother and son. She hoped not too many of Virgil's family would be in attendance. Big Mitch and Anne would be there, she was sure of that.

Ralph and Cloris came up from Belpre. Little Mitch and Eleanor got off the train in Windsor five minutes before the service started and reached the cemetery at a quick trot.

Birdie Le Foret, a young woman from Upper Sandusky and a distant cousin of the Forests, came in on the same train. She held a pad of paper in her hand about the size of a waitresses' pad. She walked back and forth between the train station and the mill as if she was looking for something she'd dropped.

After a short while, Ruth Janes approached her and pointed to the Forests' house. "That's their house, but they're up at the cemetery. all of 'em, except for Louise. Mr. Forest passed away last week. They're burying him later today."

"Reckon they'd mind if I waited for them here at this big old table?"

"Are you kin a theirs?"

"Yes'm, I am second cousin to those four girls. My granny fixed it so I could come to visit and see if I can't get a job around here."

"I suppose it'd be all right then. Now, what was your name again?"

"Birdie. Birdie Le Foret—means 'Forest' in French."

"OK, hun, I'll tell Louise you're here. Just wait at the table here. OK?"

"Yes'm. Thank you," Birdie said quietly. "You don't have a cigarette, do you, ma'am?"

"No need for that, ladies. Did I hear we have a relative from Upper Sandusky visiting?" Louise said as she emerged from the front door.

"Yes'm. I'm Birdie Le Foret."

"You can go on, Ruth. I'll stay with Miss Le Foret."

Louise took a pack of Lucky Strikes from her apron pocket, extracted one, lit it, and handed the pack and some matches to Birdie.

"Thank you kindly, Louise. I'm obliged." The girl lit a cigarette and placed the pack into her coat pocket.

"Birdie, I may be able to help you get a job in Akron in a defense plant where I work. Would you be interested?"

"Oh! Yes, ma'am."

"Call me Louise. My husband, Doak, and I work at the plant, and we are looking for good workers. What kind of employment experience do you have?"

"Well, I worked as a waitress for two years in Michigan. And I worked off and on at my cousin's dairy farm milking cows and cleaning out the barns. I'd be a good worker, Miss Louise, if someone shows me what to do."

"OK, Birdie. Just a couple more questions. How old are you?"

"Well, next October I'll turn 17."

"OK. Are you married?"

"No."

"Do you have any children?"

"Well, I had a boy. But his father went in the Army, and I gave my son, Jake, I called him, to the Carmelite Sisters in Kalamazoo."

"That must have been a difficult decision for you, Birdie."

"I guess—yes—it was. Not a day goes by that I don't think of him. I just pray that he is getting better care than I could have given him."

"Bridie, I think we can get you a job. If you'd like to, you can come back with us. New employees get a month's free rent in the building where we live."

"I don't know what to say, Louise."

"Just say yes. That will do."

"Yes!"

Doak and Louise didn't have time to get proper funeral attire. They each wore black armbands over their only "good clothes."

Harriet had spent the past 20-odd years expecting her husband to die at any moment. She seemed preternaturally calm. The three younger girls had spent their lives rolling their eyes and ignoring the warnings from their Mother and Louise that their Father might pass at any minute. Now that it had happened, the Gang of Three seemed to be in shock. Louise had expected Pierce to be trouble, but he was "good" and happy to be in loving, familiar arms.

The Forest family processed past the burial plot and tossed handfuls of southeastern Ohio soil into the open grave. Big Mitch and Anne Thomas came next. They moved over in the vicinity, but not too close to the Forest family after processing. Little Mitch and Eleanor made a beeline for Big Mitch.

Anne Thomas, regal as ever, smiled and focused on the bundle in Louise's arms. Louise waved her over. "And who is this little man, Louise?" Anne asked softly.

"Pierce Emile Benoit, Mrs. Thomas."

Anne was brought up short when she heard the child's first name. "He's a big fellow. And that's a pretty name."

Louise held the blanket so it covered Pierce's chin.

"Has he been healthy, Louise?"

"Yes, ma'am. He has been."

"I understand you're working for Cousin Mervyn. Is that right?"

"Yes, ma'am. He said to send his best to all the Ushers."

"And your husband—."

"Doak."

"And Doak works with you. Is that right?"

"Yes, we both work on the same line that Virgil worked on after high school. Is he—is he alright?"

Anne shook her head slowly. "We got a telegram last night telling us he had been wounded. But there were no details yet. He was hit by some shrapnel in August, a few weeks after they landed on Omaha Beach. That wasn't too serious, apparently. We'll be waiting to hear about this after they get him to a hospital."

Louise looked stricken and pale. "I'm so sorry, Missus Anne. So, sorry."

The two women looked at each other.

"Dear," Anne said softly, "do you suppose I could hold Pierce for a bit? Maybe in one of those chairs over there? Just this one time, dear."

"Yes, ma'am. Of course."

Anne sat in the folding chair, and Louise gently lowered Pierce onto the older woman's lap. "It's warming up, isn't it?" Louise said as she pulled the blanket beneath the child's chin.

"Such a beautiful boy. If you'd like to go rescue your husband, I'll be happy to watch this young fella."

"Of course. Thank you." Louise said softly.

Anne smiled and brushed back the child's hair and then extended her little finger for Pierce to squeeze. The boy smiled. Anne tickled his neck and made a funny face.

Louise introduced Doak to several people. Each of these introductions included a brief pitch about the jobs available in Akron.

Doak's accent threw some folks off. But when he told them he'd lived with his grandmother and finished high school at New Lex, everyone relaxed.

Doak and Louise stepped back a bit and watched Anne play with their son. She bounced him on her lap. Cloris went over to see Anne for a bit. Ralph went over to see the two Mitch's.

Cloris hoisted Pierce on her ample hip. "Puts me in mind of Virgil's pictures when he was little."

Anne sighed and shook her head. "Things happen kinder unexpectedly sometimes, Cloris. No use spreading blame around. We all fall short at times, dear. I 'spect I know what happened."

"What did the telegram about Virgil say?" Cloris asked.

"It was like the first one— 'We regret to inform you that your son has been wounded' and then— 'You will be informed of his condition after he is seen by medical personnel'. I just hope Virgil's injuries aren't too bad. He's been through a lot. And he's not out of the woods yet."

"We'll all be praying for him, Anne."

"I just hope we'll hear soon. I've heard stories about folks left for months without hearing. One friend of mine, Orpha, said a Ross girl from Chesterfield who'd married a feller that worked for the Army Air Corps had a brother in the Navy, in the Pacific. They got a telegram in October that said he'd been injured. Two months later they got another telegram saying they had never found the body, and he had been declared 'Missing in Action and Presumed Dead'."

Columbus, Ohio: December 25, 1944

Christmas Day had been an awful ordeal for Charlotte, Johnny, and the rest of the Simon family. Hardy and Polly took the train to Columbus, and

Johnny and Charlotte came up on Christmas Eve. They got two suites at the Neil House and had a low-key Christmas Day, exchanging a few small presents and eating dinner in the hotel dining room.

Hardy, Polly, and Johnny suffered from some kind of stress-related malady. The idea that Merle and Dennis were both gone was hard to fathom.

"I just don't understand what happened to Dennis," Doctor Simon said bitterly. "I spoke with doctors who treated him. The amputations were only six inches from his hip sockets, but they were healing nicely. Out of the blue, he gets a three-day pass and ends up in a hotel with a hooker, a bottle of bourbon and, supposedly, dies of a blood clot that caused cardiac arrest! It doesn't make sense. How did he get to the hotel? And how did he end up with a hooker and a bottle? For God's sake! How can this happen to us? What have we done?"

Polly was visibly shaken by her father's words. Charlotte moved over and comforted her. They adjourned to the other suite, and the men stayed behind.

"Johnny, do you know any more about this? Maybe something you might not have wanted to say in front of Polly and Charlotte?"

The younger man took a deep breath and grimaced. "I don't have any solid evidence about Dennis's death, but I have heard some scuttlebutt from a few of the pilots. No one wants to lose their testicles, but pilots and gunners are all at risk. These people are a brotherhood. No one wants to go home to their wives and family as a eunuch. In some cases, I guess, these fellows help each other out, literally."

"My word, they call that helping? What hath God wrought?" Polly said in a sad, low voice.

"I don't have any evidence that this is what happened to Dennis, but some of the boys say that kind of thing happens sometimes."

The older man stood slowly and ran his fingers through his silky, white hair. "I guess if we live long enough, we will all run up against things that make this world seem like a place that we no longer wish to inhabit."

The next three days were more somber than festive. Johnny and Doctor Simon took a walk around downtown Columbus on the 26th. The cloudless blue sky and bright sunshine almost masked the background desolation of these two men.

The whole country seemed mired in despair. The heady days after the breakout from Normandy through Paris and on toward the Ardennes had seemed to portend a quick end to what was becoming a long slog. But now, Allied casualties were piling up in Europe.

The German retreat had resulted into a reorganization. And while many of the replacement troops were teenagers or pensioners, the Third Reich seemed to be back. Back, moreover, on ground that had been contested for millennia by Germanic tribes. This home field advantage, if you will, further added to their renewed vigor.

The Pacific Theater was a horse of a different color. The action in New Guinea at Bougainville, from November '43, when Merle disappeared under the waves, to November '44 resembled nothing if not a year-long, interminable replay of the Normandy landing crafts dropped fresh troops and supplies seemingly every day. The Marines on the beachhead took heavy causalities while fighting for yards and, sometimes, inches.

"When will this war end, Johnny?"

"I don't know, Dad. We are making progress, but whenever it looks like we've got them on the run, they come back. This business in the Ardennes is a good example of that."

"Johnny, those turrets—where the tail-gunners are—are they protected?"

"You know, Dad, when you get down to it, the answer is no. They're plexiglass with a light aluminum frame. This protection doesn't weigh much, but when you add it all up, it's enough to affect the plane's performance. "Here's the deal. The Brass in the Army Air Corps are almost all pilots. They flew in World War I, sitting on a helmet. Air Corps has dozens of studies that indicate that any advantage gained by having men and guns in turrets is lost with the extra weight and the effect it has on speed, acceleration and maneuverability. If they had enlisted men flying and officers in the turrets, tail-gunners would have been eliminated years ago. The fact is, Dad, I was assigned to a team trying to improve the various components of those turrets. The only way to beef up the design added so much extra weight, it wasn't practical. We could either leave the turrets as is and hope the extra speed would lower casualty rates, or beef up the design but live with less speed and maneuverability. Christ, I feel personally responsible Dennis' death. Why did I study aeronautical engineering, if I couldn't help my own brother survive?"

"Don't start down that road, John. It only ends in heartbreak. I've spent the past 23 years wondering why I didn't stay home on the day you were born. And before you chime in, let me assure you that it wasn't your fault, either."

Letter Thirty-Four

England in Hospital

1/15/1945

Dear Mitch and Eleanor,

Now that I have been able to get air mail envelopes will write something besides v-mail. It is hard to write much though since I don't receive any. Should start getting some soon. I hope Dad and Mother are all right. I worry about them.

I went to a show a couple of times last week and yesterday went to Church. One of the fellows pushed me in a wheel chair. Could make it on crutches but is a little far. Don't think it will be long before I can start walking on it a little. Have a swell bunch of fellows in my ward. Some of them can be up and around and they sure take care of the rest of us. That is one thing about the Army over here. It brings out an unselfishness and friendship among fellows that one seldom sees in civilian life.

Of course, I would like to get back in that cruel civilian world and take my chance. Ha. It seems so long ago that I scarcely even remember being a civilian. Suppose I must have been once, though.

Is Carl still in the States? You and Ralph never have heard any more from the Draft Board, have you? God, I hope not. Hope Ralph Robinson is all right. I do lots of thinking about boys up there. In fact, now that I have time, I do lots of thinking and daydreaming about everything. They say it is a sign that you are getting old when you start reminiscing.

Thought I would make this a long letter but hell there just doesn't seem to be anything to write about.

Love to all,

Virgil

Duncan Falls, Ohio: 02/11/1945:

John Simon

We received mountains of data regarding failure frequency and mechanisms from Army Air Corps Headquarters. We have been tasked to perform FMEA analyses for the top 50 failure modes. This is data for all types of aircraft from calendar year 1944.

Our group decided to camp out in our conference room for two days to get familiar with these datasets and begin to come up with classifications to use when we divvy them up.

Charlotte was very upset. She is due in March and not feeling very happy about carrying all that weight. I told her I would come home if she insisted, but she said she'd figure something out. I hope her attitude, which I would characterize as pissy, improves after the baby is born.

I am still grieving over Dennis's death and feelings that I should have been able to design something to help those gunners in turrets on our bombers.

I've never been one to worry and mope, but my feelings of inadequacy concerning Dennis, Charlotte, and how little good I'm doing for the war effort, have been growing exponentially in the past four days.

The first pass through the failure data was distressing. Of the top 50 failure modes that could lead to catastrophic failure identified in June of 1942, only 12 of our fixes showed any significant improvement.

Two days stretched to four. I called Charlotte to explain, but she hung up on me after a rather graphic explanation of what I could do with my failure analyses.

When we finally broke up our conclave on Sunday afternoon, I headed straight home. Charlotte was fast asleep on the couch. The carpet was covered with cigarette ashes and Lucky Strike butts, as well as the waxed paper wrappers from an empty box of chocolate-covered cherries. I put this trash in a small wicker trash can.

Charlotte did not stir as I plumped her pillows and covered her with a comforter. As I tucked the cover into the cushions of the couch, I found two empty whiskey bottles shoved behind the cushions.

Her pajama bottoms were damp. I got a warm wash cloth, some soap and a towel and cleaned her up. As I stripped off her soiled pajamas, she awoke with a snort. Her breath was foul. She asked for a cigarette.

"Wait just a second, and I will join you, Charlotte."

As I rinsed things out in the bathroom, I noticed a razor blade with traces of blood on top of the sink. I got a pair of her flannel pajamas and returned to the couch. She had passed out again. I looked at her arms and saw shallow cuts on the wrist of her left arm. Further up her arm, I noticed faint scarring that extended just short of her elbow.

I lit a Lucky Strike. She jerked awake again. I let her have a drag. She let me pull on her pajama bottoms and then demanded another drag. As I pulled her top on, my hands brushed her breasts.

"Fellers like big titties, my Aunt Minta always said," she slurred before nodding off again.

Her belly was distended. I looked in the kitchen. The sink was full of dirty dishes sitting in curdled gray water. I opened the cupboard under the sink. The trash can overflowed with empty beer bottles.

I had slept very little in the past four days. I made a pallet of sorts with blankets and comforters on the living room floor and went to sleep.

Our neighbor's chickens awakened me on Monday morning. Charlotte was still on the couch, snoring. There was no food in evidence except three black bananas and a half empty carton of chocolate ice cream. I wrote her a note telling her I was going to Zanesville to get groceries. When I came down after a shower, she was sitting, smoking, with a nearly full beer bottle on the table in front of her.

"Hair of the dog?" I asked softly.

"What if it is?"

"Do you want anything in particular from the store?"

"Beer and cigarettes and a magazine or two."

"What sounds good as far as food?"

"Cocktail peanuts and some dark chocolate."

"OK, Charlotte. Do you want to talk about anything?"

"No, just write me a letter. You might as well be in the Army, you're never home anymore."

"Charlotte, we had to put together a study and a report that will, hopefully, help us keep more airplanes in the air and more airmen alive."

"Little late for that isn't it, for your family?"

"What are you saying?"

"Little late for Dennis!"

"This isn't just about my family. It's about all the airmen and all their families. What is wrong with you?"

"Don't you ever say that to me again! I'm sick of hearing that—like I'm some kind of retard or a crazy person. Stop it!" She picked up the beer bottle and drained it in two gulps. After emitting a loud belch, she waggled the bottle back and forth. "You could add a case of beer to the shopping list."

"OK, I'll be back in a jiffy," I said with a grimace.

"Take your time, Slim."

Johnny jumped off the porch, reached the door in three strides, and hurried to the car. He drove slowly through Duncan Falls. As he cleared the intersection at Miller Lane, he saw Gibb Jones pulling a tractor out of his barn. Johnny waved and Gibb raised his index finger of his left, and only, hand off the top of the steering wheel. Gibb had been a tank mechanic and lost an arm in Africa.

Johnny put his foot into it and headed north.

Zanesville was awakening. They had a table set up in front of the grocery. Johnny fumbled in his wallet.

"You in the service, young man?" a man in his 60s asked as he pulled out a red boutonniere.

"I'm an engineer with the Army Air Corps in Columbus."

"Well, that's good. We need folks to help keep our fighting men safe. That's why we are raising money for our disabled veterans, when they get home."

Johnny pulled a $5 bill out of his wallet and put it into the bowl.

"Here you go, young man." He handed Johnny the paper flower. "Thanks for helping our fighting men."

As John walked into the grocery, he stuffed the flower in his coat pocket. He bought the food items that Charlotte requested. As he passed the old man at the table he began to sob, softly at first, then harder and harder until his broad shoulders heaved, and his hands covered his face.

An older woman in a Model T with Kentucky plates had just pulled in behind him. He put the bags in the back seat and got behind the wheel with his head in his hands.

A knock on the window got his attention. He rolled the window down.

"You awright, young man? I saw your tags. What part of Kentucky you from, son?"

Johnny looked up. "Dunmor in Muhlenberg County, ma'am."

"These folks up here shor do talk funny, don't ya know?"

"I guess they do, now that you mention it."

There was a pause.

"You lost someone hain't ya?"

Johnny nodded.

"Me, too. My youngest, Denton Ridgley Junior. He's jist 19. He ain't dead but doctors say he hain't got long to go. I'm heading up to Cleveland to the VA to see him."

"I'm awful sorry about your boy. I've lost my two brothers in the war."

"Your folks still alive?"

"No ma'am. That is, my mother died when I was born. My father is a doctor, and he's still in good health. I also have an older sister, Polly."

"Family is important, 'specially as their numbers dwindle."

"I hope you get to see your child and that he has God's comfort at the end, if it should come."

Their eyes met briefly, and she left him.

After a few minutes spent going back and forth, he decided to take the groceries back home. Surely Charlotte would be up. If not, he might go to Buckeye Lake or to the office. He wanted, no, needed to talk to Polly.

Charlotte was not on the couch, but a few more beer bottles were scattered around. He bounded up the stairs and looked in the two small bedrooms. No sign of Charlotte. He peeked through the curtains looking out on the backyard. Charlotte was sitting on the bench of the picnic table. Her arms and head were on the table, and she wasn't moving. John figured the temperature must be 40 degrees.

He ran back down the stairs and out the back door.

"Charlotte!" he screamed and ran over to her inert form. He picked her up, carried her into the house, and placed her on the couch. "I'll draw you a warm bath," he said, still not sure if she was awake or coherent. He ran to the bathroom and opened the hot water tap in the tub. When the water warmed a bit, he put the plug in the drain.

Hearing a thud and a curse, he went back to the living room. Charlotte was trying to find a light for her Lucky Strike.

"I've got a lighter, Char." He lit her smoke and got one for himself. "What were you doing outside?"

"It was stuffy in the house. I wanted some fresh air, and I was hungry."

"You get in the bath, and you'll feel better. I'll go get the groceries and bring them in."

Johnny Simon had been the kind of boy and young man upon whose butt the sun had always shone brightly. In Muhlenberg County, everyone from the US Representative to Congress, Wilbur Clark, to the moonshiners who lived and worked in the caves and hollers around Lake Malone liked Johnny Simon.

It's not unusual for regular folks to defer to the children of prominent men. Powerful people—politicians, sheriffs, businessmen—can all make life miserable. In a remote county with only two doctors to cover nearly 500 square miles and only two road that weren't as crooked as a dog's hind leg, a doctor is just as powerful. He's the priceless man who will take that call in the middle of the night, get dressed, drive 40 miles through the snow, and deliver that baby, set that that broken bone, or comfort your dying mother. And if that same doctor accepts butter, chickens, eggs, IOUs and occasionally, moonshine for his services, it was understandable that a certain radiance grew around Doctor Hardy Simon.

He had become almost a legend in his time in Kentucky. People were in awe of Doctor Hardy Simon. *Awe* in the early meaning of <u>*awe*</u>: *"an emotion variously combining dread, veneration and wonder that is inspired by authority."*

And this veneration, if you will, extended beyond the doctor's medical ministrations. He joined the Masons in Chicago while in Medical School and moved up a few rungs. When he got to Dunmor in 1920, he joined the local Lodge in Greensville and didn't make any waves. He stayed still and volunteered for the lower-level activities, biding his time.

In 1920, the Dunmor Lodge had more in common with a half-drunken 18th century posse composed of half Hatfields' and half McCoys' than a 20th century Masonic Lodge. Leaders came and went. Evenings were considered successful if no one was injured during the course of the meeting or bushwhacked on the way home.

By 1930, Doctor Hardy Simon was Worshipful Master of the Greenville, Kentucky, Lodge. Doctor Simon was not one to lead from behind. He led by example. As a result, he was respected, rather than feared.

Folks may have always given Johnny a break because of his parents. Idene was, if anything, more beloved than her husband. But before he was out of grade school, everyone could tell that Johnny was special. Good at school and sports, well-behaved, but not stuck up.

The only complaint that a few people might have had was a niggling feeling that it must have been easy to be like that if you never faced adversity. Even the one event in his young life that might have qualified as tragic—the death of his mother—was mitigated by the fact that (1) he was too young to remember, and (2) Polly took over the role of mother immediately after his birth.

After the sorrow of Idene's sudden death eased, the Simon family went back to being one of those "happy families that are alike" that Tolstoy wrote about. During the war, many of these families experienced unhappiness with the loss of beloved children on the cusp of adulthood. The Simon family ended up giving more than most.

Johnny awakened from his thoughts to the sound of his wife's voice. It was loud and demanding. "Help me get out of this damned bathtub!"

He complied and withdrew as she began drying herself. When she emerged on the stairs ten minutes later, he stood and asked her to join him on the couch.

"No funny business, Johnny! That's how I got in this mess in the first place," she said as she patted her quite prominent belly.

"Charlotte, I have to go into work and get some files straightened out for a meeting we're having first thing Tuesday morning."

John Simon told his first lie while on his first campout with the Boy Scouts. Around the campfire, he told one of the boys from the Senior Patrol that his older brother, Merle, had become an Eagle Scout when he was 15. Merle had been nearly 18 when he made Eagle.

His second lie, about needing to go into work, occurred 12 years later.

Charlotte frowned and shook her head.

"I have to go today, I could drop you in Chesterfield and pick you up later tonight or tomorrow morning."

"Are you just trying to get away from me, John?"

"No, it's not that, Charlotte." *That's number three.*

"OK, then. Let me call home and see what's going on there." She stood and walked slowly into the kitchen. "Ma, is that you?" She paused. "It's me, Charlotte. Say, could I stay over with you tonight?" She paused again. "What? Well, that's OK. When are you coming in?" She listened for about a minute. "On the train? What train will he be on from Zanesville?" Charlotte wrote something down. "Getting in to Zanesville at 2 PM and catching the Doodlebug to Windsor. Great. Johnny can drop me off at the train station. Yes, I can wait."

Charlotte held her hand over the receiver. "Pen's home on leave. He'll be coming in to Zanesville at two and catching the Doodlebug to Windsor." She paused and continued. "What? Well, that would be great—I'll hold on." Charlotte made a face at the phone. "They are. Thanks, Mom—Pauline, can I get a ride from the train station in Zanesville? At our house? Why sure, that would be great, if you have room in your car. Great! I'll see you at our house. No, he's got a lot of work to catch up on, and he's going to his office. "Put Mom back on, if you can. Thanks." She hung up.

Charlotte put her hand over the mouthpiece. "You're free to go any time, John." she said with her hand over the mouthpiece.

"Are you mad at me, Charlotte."

"No, I'm just struggling a little."

"Yes, I kind of got that impression. I was—oh, surprised and a little disappointed when I got home last night. I want our baby to be healthy."

"So do I, Johnny."

"It's not good for the baby when you are in the third trimester to drink that much. A couple are probably alright."

"That's easy for you to say. Men get all the fun and very little of the work!"

"Charlotte, I love you. You are my first girlfriend and my wife. I guess this is kind of our first fight. I don't like the way this feels."

"Well Highpockets, I guess you can go to work now."

"I will. I'll give you call at your Mom's house this evening."

"Maybe you could come over and meet Penrose. He'd like that."

"I would too, darling."

Johnny drove back through Zanesville. Road construction on Route 60 forced him over onto Main Street, where an Army Recruiting Office caught his eye. They'd put out a sign that read, "Uncle Sam Still Needs You".

A big-shouldered fellow with lots of stripes and chevrons on his green jacket sat on a chair, just inside the door. He was smoking a cigarette and reading a newspaper. Johnny nearly lost control of the car but managed to pull it into a parking space across the street from the recruiter.

The recruiter stepped through the door and down the three steps to the brick sidewalk. Johnny extended his hand, and the two men shook hands.

"Hello, young man," the recruiter said with a big grin. "Are you interested in helping your country finish this war?"

"I'm interested in learning more about helping my country out, I suppose."

"Well, good. I've got eight fellows heading to Camp Chase for physicals on Wednesday. From there, they'll be routed to Basic Training, and then Advanced Training. If you're interested, we can go inside. What do you say?"

"Sounds good."

They climbed the three steps and took seats across the desk.

"I need to ask you a few questions, son."

Johnny nodded.

"Have you ever served as an enlisted man or officer in any branch of the Army, Navy, or Marine Corps?"

"No, sir."

"Have you ever been convicted of a felony?"

"No, sir."

"How about misdemeanors?"

"No, sir."

"Do you have any physical infirmities that would prevent you from being able to walk five miles?"

"No, sir."

"Do you have any children?"

"No, sir"

"Have you ever been married?"

"Yes, sir."

"Are you currently married?"

"Yes, sir."

"Have you discussed enlisting with your wife?"

"She knows that I have thought about enlisting."

"What is the highest level of school you have completed?"

"High school. I've taken college classes, but only for a couple of years."

"Do you currently have a job?"

"Yes, sir. I work at the airport in Columbus as a troubleshooter."

"If you are found to be qualified to enlist, when could you go?"

"Immediately."

"Questions?"

"When could I be done with training and get into action?"

"By April, I'd say. Are you interested?"

"Yes."

"If you'll fill out this packet here, we can get the ball rolling."

Johnny filled out the eight-page packet in 15 minutes.

"Will you be here on Monday, Sergeant?"

"I will. Why don't you stop by anytime from 9 AM to 5 PM?"

"Will do."

Some people lie to seek advantage, and others lie to purge shame.

Johnny Simon told his wife several of the bald-faced kind. And virtually every response to the recruiter's questions contained a mixture of truth and lies.

The truth is, the young man didn't have enough experience telling lies to even feel any guilt. As a novice in this world of deception, he believed those half-truths he'd told the recruiter. The ones he'd told Charlotte had served a purpose. They bought him enough time and space to let him put his plan in motion.

In one day, Johnny Simon had learned to lie. His next lesson applied to lies, rats, and cockroaches, the moral being that there is no such thing as just one of any of these three—they travel in packs. Even though the team had agreed to take the day off, Johnny hoped that his boss would be at the office. He wasn't.

The young man straightened up his desk and bookshelves and put on a pot of coffee. Milt, a security guard who lost an arm in Africa, came through on rounds. He was surprised to see anyone in the office. They'd told him the day before that they were all exhausted. John invited him in for coffee. Milt called the security office and said he was going to take a break in the Air Wing Conference Room.

"Milt, I know you served in Africa. Do you mind if I ask you a couple of questions?" John asked.

"Not at all. Fire away and fall back."

"Were you drafted?"

"No, sir. My number never came up. I was married and had a child—a boy named Franklin—born in 1940."

"How did you come to enlist in the Army?"

"Well, after Pearl Harbor I enlisted."

"How did your wife take that?"

"She wasn't very happy, but she calmed down eventually."

"Where did you get your training?"

"So, I went to basic training in Georgia. And we did maneuvers in Louisiana. And then we went to Africa with General Clark. Operation Torch, they called it. Our outfit landed in Oran in November of '42. I took a couple bullets on the beach. They stopped the bleeding, but that was the end of my active duty. End of my left arm, too."

"How long were you in the hospital?"

"Six months or thereabouts. I didn't have enough of a stump left to get a prosthetic limb. But that's OK. I get along."

"You ever regret volunteering?"

"No, sir! Never have! "I didn't have what you might call a long or illustrious career. But I done my part. Way I figure it, if I wasn't there, those bullets I took may have killed someone else, like an officer or a squad leader and that might have prevented them from leading men in important battles that may help win the war."

"How long until you got back home, Milt?"

"A few months. I spent time in a light duty detail at a hospital in New Jersey. Guess I got back here around Labor Day of '44."

"Must have been good to see your family again."

"Well, kinder. But my wife, Vivian, didn't take much to my 'disfigurement', as she called it. I signed the divorce papers just after Thanksgiving. By Christmas I had got on here and found a rooming house within walking distance."

"Do you get to see Franklin regularly?"

"I was supposed to, but Vivian run off and got married to a long-haul truck driver. He's based out of Grand Isle, Nebraska. He hauls farm equipment all over the country. He's stopped by and seen me a couple times and given me pictures of my boy. I appreciate that. But I think all of us are better off now."

"I better let you get back to work, Milt. It's been nice talking to you."

"You bet, Mr. Simon. The feeling is mutual."

Johnny stayed in the Conference Room—looking lackadaisically over some reports, draining the coffee pot, and going to the bathroom. At 2:30, he decided to call his department head, Ward Gamble, at home and see if they could get together to discuss his dilemma.

Gamble picked up on the 12th ring. "Hello," a tired voice answered.

"Mr. Gamble, this is John Simon."

"Hey, Johnny. You caught me taking a nap."

"I've got something I need to talk to you about, sir."

"OK, shoot."

"It would be better face to face, I think."

"OK, where are you?"

"At the office. I could come to your house."

"My wife has got her bridge club coming over pretty soon. Why don't you sit tight, and I'll be over directly."

"Thanks. I'll be here."

"Put on a pot of coffee, please."

"I will."

The half-hour wait for Ward Gamble seemed interminable. Johnny considered calling home but didn't. The sighing, stomach churning, and clammy sweat—signs of a shame he'd never felt until a few days earlier—paralyzed him. He thought of the release he might feel with a bottle and a woman.

Ward Gamble showed up in a short-sleeved shirt and blue jeans.

"Hello, Johnny," he said with a big smile.

"Thanks for coming, Mr. Gamble."

"My pleasure, John. Like I told you, you rescued me from 16 card players at the house."

"Mr. Gamble, I have a bit of a dilemma. I've certainly learned a lot working here. And I enjoy the comradery this group has." Johnny swallowed and looked down at his shoes.

"But?" the older man said forcefully.

"Sir?"

"There is a 'but' coming."

"Yes sir, there is. Here goes nothing. But I want to talk to you about my desire to join the Army—to enlist in the Army."

"You have been doing great work here, Johnny. Our group has come up with many innovations that have improved the performance of our aircraft."

"Yes we have, sir. But I have lost my two brothers in this war. One of them was a tail gunner in a B-17. Looking at all the failures associated with the hardware, strategies, and tactics is tough on me. The rest of the team can look at these data we're crunching as just equipment and machinery. For me, I see Dennis every time we talk about turrets. I feel like I can see him being shot. And these are problems I've been working on for the last year.

"We had an Air Corps Major General brief our group a couple months ago. His topic was, How We Can Win This Bleeping War? The gist of it was that we can win this war by killing more enemy troops than we are losing. He talked about gaining advantages over the Krauts, and he described in brutal detail the kinds of things that can give our boys an edge—less non-mission essential weight, more reliable components, easier in-air replacement procedures of critical components and enhanced Standard Operating Procedures that contribute to effective missions and safer return flights.

"He got me fired up, alright. But after his talk was done he looked around the room and finished with a brief summation. Men, whether we are in combat on the land, sea, air, or working in facilities like you fellows, we can only do so much. We all must give our best effort. No one wins every battle. The great enemy of all fighting men is despair. When we see our brothers-in-arms fall, we must not hesitate.

"Twenty-three hundred years ago, Pericles delivered a funeral oration in and for the city of Athens after the first year of the Peloponnesian War. 'So, died these men as becomes Athenians. You, their survivors, must determine to have as unfaltering a resolution in the field, though you may pray that it may have a happier outcome.'

"Johnny, I hear you. I'm sorry if you have any doubts that the work we are doing is worthwhile. That being said, I believe that now I understand a little better how you must feel."

"Sir, my older brother, Merle, was in the Navy. He ran landing crafts at Bougainville ferrying troops in and bringing men back to the ship, reinforcements, replacements. My Dad got a letter from one of Merle's shipmates describing their job ferrying those troops as being like D-Day every day. Every day, troops were sent ashore to replace the fellows that had never made it off the beach from the previous day.

"I hear people talk about 'the calculus of war', the way I use to. But I don't believe it's that complicated anymore. It's still a math problem, but it is addition and subtraction. Every morning I go past a neighbor who lost an arm in Italy. And Milt, who cleans up our offices, lost an arm in Africa. They needed replacements. And now a lot of those replacements need replacements. And the guys that have been out there for three or four years who haven't been injured physically need replacements. I need to go, Ward. I won't be able to live with myself if I don't."

A preternatural silence settled over the room. Both men drank their lukewarm coffee and kept their own counsel for a long minute.

Mr. Gamble raised his head and nodded. "John, there are several things that present themselves as issues that may have a bearing on your ability to enlist in the Army. Maybe none of them, by themselves, would be deal breaker. But taken together, they might add up.

"OK, these are the issues that come to mind, in no particular order. (1) your family has lost two sons in combat. (2) you are an engineer with the Army Air Corps engaged in important work. 3) you are a newlywed with a pregnant wife. And finally, (4) the Army Air Corps paid your way through college at USC."

"Sir, not to interrupt, but can I just quit this job?"

"I don't know. I've fired a couple of folks, but I never had anyone quit."

"What would I have to do, short of breaking the law, to be fired?

"I fired one fellow for insubordination. We got into a discussion that nearly turned into a brawl."

"Mr. Gamble, I've learned a lot from you about engineering, leadership, and life. That puts you in a select circle with my Father, my brother Merle, and my stats teacher at USC."

A brief grin flashed across the older man's face.

"So, what can I do to get myself fired?"

"Well. First, please get me all of your classified files and documents in locked filing cabinets. Clean out your desk carefully, getting all Classified documents into one of your locked cabinets. Then type me a letter indicating your dissatisfaction with your job. Do not indicate that you are resigning or quitting voluntarily! You can refer to your aging father, things like that. I wouldn't mention your pregnant wife, it might keep you from getting in quickly."

"Give me until noon tomorrow."

"I'll call tomorrow at noon. And Johnny, talk to your family. Don't go off half-cocked."

With that thought Johnny headed west and pondered, like untold thousands of young men, volunteers, and draftees before him had done. Johnny Simon headed toward Camp Chase, where he hoped to raise his right hand while vowing to Protect and Serve.

Virgil in Germany December 1944.]

Duncan Falls, Ohio 2/18/1945

Johnny bunked at Buckeye Lake that night, where he still had a key. Ward Gamble called it the Frat House. Good name for it. The other fellows had gone to Columbus to see a basketball game at Ohio State. They were going to stay in Grandview at the house of Teddy's uncle.

Johnny had left enough clothes there to get by. He also thought about going to Steubenville. There was a dance club he and Charlotte went to a few times. They played Bix Beiderbecke and *Race Music* on the jukebox and nobody cared if you did the Bo Hog Grind in a dark corner.

He'd watched Charlotte struggle with depression but he'd never experienced it himself, until now. And he felt so helpless he could hardly open a can of beans and cook them on the stove.

He thought about calling home. How nice it would be to talk with Polly and his father. The thought of talking to Charlotte, however, made him feel worse.

What is wrong with me? he wondered. *I'm tired, but I don't want to go to sleep.*

He found a bottle of bourbon in one of the cupboards and left a $5 bill where it had been. The bourbon did the trick, but at 3 AM he woke bathed in the cool shimmer of a full moon peeking in through the bedroom window as he wondered what had happened.

He called Ward Gamble at 11:30, anxious to get on with his hare-brained scheme and then disappear.

"Johnny, you're all set. If you are bound and determined to do this, I won't try to stop you. I wish you'd change your mind. You are a brilliant engineer. And I believe you've been disillusioned by what you perceive to be your failure to make a difference for the airmen serving our country. You've shared your admiration for your father. As a doctor in a small town, he has served many folks and saved many lives.

"The number of variables in setting a compound fracture of an arm or a leg cannot be compared to those involved in aerial warfare. We do the best we can and keep striving for improvement. You are a wonderful young man, and if I may put forward the opinion of an older man who has seen his share of ups and downs, I will tell you unequivocally that no one gets a free pass. Many folks are pummeled by circumstance and failure from an early age. They either live with it or pull themselves up. Others know little but success. The world is their oyster, and life seems to be a non-stop celebration of their brilliance.

"But at some point, however, this unending run of good fortune vanishes. Our hero finds himself in the muck with lesser beings, struggling harder than ever before without any positive results. He questions himself, God, mankind—everything.

"The Greeks knew this. A man named Boethius climbed to the pinnacle of power and served as advisor to Ostrogothic King Theodoric the Great, in the sixth century. He was charged with treason. His jailhouse treatise, *The Consolation of Philosophy*, is perhaps the finest treatment of these issues that we all will face—sooner or later.

"All of the fellows send their best. Good luck and God speed, John Simon. Drop us a line."

Letter Thirty-Five

England in Hospital

2/26/1945

Hi Ya Everybody,

Received the first mail Saturday since I came here. Really hit the jackpot too. Got eleven letters and your air mail where both of you wrote was one of them. Also, one each from Folks, Ralph, Edgar Nott, Aunt Virgie, Uncle George, Susie Wilson and Mabel Maynard. So, you see I had quite a variety. They sure boosted my morale.

Still nothing from Louise, though. Oh, well. If you ever find anything out about her let me know.

My knee still has stiffness and can't walk much or be on it too long. Going to take quite a while, I guess. No, I am afraid there isn't any chance of getting home. This war isn't over and as soon as I am able I will be on my way back to my outfit I guess.

No, I guess I never wrote much about my friends in the Army. Probably because you wouldn't have known any of them. I really had some swell buddies though. Best ones I ever had even in civilian life I think.

My best one was Gabby—Melvyn Thurlow—from Michigan. We were always together. I often wished you could have met him. You would have liked him. I lost him the day before I got shot. That was one of the hardest things I ever had to take. **I have never gotten over it.**

I am sorry if some of my letters sounded critical. I really didn't mean it. I know most everyone there is doing all they can. And I know that you people probably worry more about us than we do ourselves. But some of the things we hear or read do sort of burn us up. Especially when things are going rough with us.

You know it often seems like the big boys spend their time talking about what they are going to do after the war instead of settling down to winning it. When things like Gabby happen, you aren't very apt to have a clear head anyway.

Cloris sent a picture of Shirley and Virginia. My how they have grown. Guess I expected them as last time I saw them. When I stop to think that has been some time ago.

You must be having one hell of a winter. Everyone mentions it and I also read in paper about it.

No, I never got your Christmas box. Maybe they will catch me some time. Or maybe Jerry got them. If so that is just one more thing the next one I see will pay for.

I must write Uncle George. Guess he is in pretty bad shape. He wrote me a nice letter, only mentioned Ivan once. Ha.

I never get the Herald anymore, but then I never have received all my back mail. So, I am behind on the news back there.

Orpha told me Louise has lost both of her Grandpas this winter. And her Father. Henry. was a good man. And I hated to hear of Mr. Strode's death. He was a swell old man and we were quite buddies. I didn't know her Grandpa Forest. You know he was blind. Joan is working in Akron with her now.

Certainly, hope I can be there when you take your vacation. But—well need I say more. You know I even get a thrill out of thinking about it. I just can't imagine what it is going to be like.

Don't worry about me for I am O.K. Lonesome, homesick—yes, but who the hell isn't.

Love to all,

Virgil

Letter Thirty-Six

3/07/1945

Hi Ya Everybody,

I got two letters today so I guess I better get on the ball tonight. One was a v-mail and the other an air mail. It was the first letter addressed here that I had gotten. My mail is coming through well, but my back mail just never seems to catch me. I can tell by the way the people write that there is plenty I never got. So, I am behind on happenings. I didn't even know that Waldine was back in Windsor.

Nash and Goldie must be trying to outdo his Dad.

Glad to hear that Ralph R. is still O.K. So, sorry that I never got to see him. Yes, his wife and kids are probably the very things that keeps him going. I sometimes think mail is more important to a fighting man than food. A man can go through hell if he knows everyone at home is O.K. Then too it is just natural for a fellow to want to know that he is missed back there.

Sometimes I get so homesick for my old outfit. Then when I stop to think of what they are going through and fellows that won't be there. I don't know what I want.

You know sometimes I think what I need is a good loving, American style. This English just doesn't seem to fill the bill. Ha. You had me all worked up about that pajama deal. Right after telling about going to church.

You will notice a slight change in address. Am at same place but transferred to headquarters company. I am helping out at Post Utilities now. I don't do any work, but oversee different jobs around camp. Last week I was in charge of two trucks hauling cinders. This week I have a group of men painting.

Gives me something to do and a few extra privileges. You know me I can't be content doing nothing.

Sorry my letter disappointed you. Sure, wish it had of been true. My leg is some better but slow as hell.

I find now that I have no air mail so will have to send free.

Love to all,

Virgil

Letter Thirty-Seven

3/23/1945

Hello All,

Got your letter of 9*th* today. No, never got the pictures you sent or any of boxes. Have received Ralph's Christmas package since came here but it is only one.

I am glad if you enjoyed my last letters. I know that most of my letters aren't very interesting and I probably don't tell you very much you would like to know. But you know that is an old fault of mine keeping things to myself. I know that I would be better off if I wasn't that way so much.

Telling someone what is on your mind or 'getting things off your chest' really makes you feel better. There are a lot of things one just doesn't care to talk about. Then it is a lot harder to write than talk. Don't think I'm holding out on you though, for I tell you more than anyone else.

You kids have always been my standby. I don't have anyone else back there to tell my troubles to, like most guys. So, I don't know what I would do without you. It isn't so bad now that I am out and can keep occupied. But back there when I was laying in the hospital with no mail or anything. It wasn't that I worried about myself but well—I just had too much time to think, I guess.

I am sorry I never told you more about Gabby. I wish you could have met him. He was a prince. We had great post-war plans.

I guess you better not subscribe to the Herald until I get a permanent address again. Don't know how long I will be here or whether I will be here or back to my old outfit or not. Most of stiffness is gone but still bothers.

I am glad that Jim and Donna are getting along so well in school. At least Jim was being honest when he gave Donna her orders. Ha. Yes, he will have to do worse than that to outdo his Dad or Uncle when they were kids. Ha.

I will enclose a letter that I got from an Australian Nurse, I wish you would write me all of it, purely for curiosity sake. Well, maybe I did have a little soft spot in my heart for her. But don't ever think it is worrying me. I have gone through too many things to let a thing like that bother me.

Love to all,

Virgil

Letter Thirty-Eight

4/9/1945

Dear Mitch and Eleanor,

As you probably know by this envelope, I got your Christmas package today. The cigarettes were a little smashed and candy a little melted but still good. Cigarettes came in handy for I was smoking English cigarettes until I get my rations. We only get seven packs a week which isn't hardly enough especially if you go out on passes. So, I usually end up smoking English last day or so. They aren't rationed but cost two and six (50 cents to you). I don't like them too well but are better than nothing.

I sent you a few clippings about our division and will enclose one. Suppose you saw my Division Commander [Major General Maurice Rose] was killed.

I had a letter from mother today. She mentioned Louise's marriage. That's the first I'd heard about it. Mother said she thought the wedding had been up in Akron. No one seems to know much about it or who she married. If folks know they're not telling me. Ma said that she hoped I hadn't decided to be an old bachelor. Ha. It doesn't look like this Army is going to give me much choice. They have had almost four years of my life. [Virgil is 31 when this is written] and still no relief in sight even after this part of the war is over.

They seem to be making big plans to get us to the Pacific as soon as possible. Doesn't give one much to look forward to. Guess I better just marry an English girl and bring her home when and if that time ever comes. How would you like that?

It was beautiful weather over the week end. Sunday was such a beautiful day. Mary and I took a couple of deck chairs and spent afternoon on the beach.

I am liable to leave here anytime now. Am supposed to be given limited service for a couple of months and then re-examined. So, I don't know where I will end up. Will get seven days' delay en route when I do leave. Don't know where I will spend it. May try to go and see Ray for a day or so and the rest somewhere else.

Love to all,

Virgil

Letter 39

Postcard

Eiger Germany

8/17/1945

I ate dinner at this hotel. Then this afternoon we came up to highest peak you see in background-12,000 feet altitude. It sure is a wonderful trip. Certainly, wish you could see it for it almost takes your breath.

Love,

Virgil

PS: Sure, wish my old pard, Gabby, could have been here.

1945

Dane Pearson

<u>August 9, 1945</u>: Second atomic bomb dropped on Nagasaki, Japan.

My sister-in-law, Virgie Pearson, asked me to write a short obituary for her husband, my older brother Clarence, to send to the newspapers in Washington, Morgan, and Athens Counties. Clarence passed on Memorial Day, 1945.

I suppose a story that captures Clarence, a humble man who did so much for so many, while neither desiring nor receiving much in the way of credit, centers around when he received the news that he was to be recognized with the greatest tribute he received during his lifetime—*Ohio Teacher of the Year*—on December 6th, 1941. The notices never appeared in any of the newspapers on that day or any other. Pearl Harbor was attacked, and the country was finally at war.

The certificate and plaque sat on the mantel of their home in Amesville with little notice from any living thing, except perhaps the spiders who occasionally knit ornate webs running from the top corner of the frame to the bottom edge of their oval wedding portrait hanging nearby.

On May 28, 1945, Clarence died in his sleep of a massive heart attack. Following his request, his body was cremated. At Virgie's request, they waited until the end of August, on the Sunday before Labor Day, to hold the service. At first, we were puzzled by the delay. But Virgie knew what she was doing.

Virgie and her sister, Anne Marie, had a bittersweet laugh in the back room at the funeral home in Amesville. Clarence would probably have taken the delay of his funeral in stride. One time he said, 'Well Virgie,' he said to me with a big smile, after he got that award, 'I guess it figures I can't even get my name in the local paper when I get an award. I suppose I'll have to go rob a bank or something.'

He was never one to draw attention to himself. But I'd like to think he'd smile seeing all those folks at his funeral. Not because it would have made him feel like a big shot. He'd enjoy seeing all those ex-students and finding out about all they'd done. Where they'd been."

"I know Virgie. But you know what, he'd have been just as glad to see old Thornie Phillips show up in his coveralls, telling everyone in earshot that he would never have made a go of his truck stop if Clarence hadn't finally taught him how to add and subtract."

Virgie and Anne knew Clarence as well as anyone else. His father, Old Man Pearson, had a farm that adjoined the Usher place. The use of "Old Man" was not just some vague epithet for Ebenezer Pearson. He was in his late 30s when he and Lizzie Blind married. Clarence was their first child. Over the next five years, Lizzie lost four children in early infancy. In the next five years, she gave birth to two girls, then two more boys—Dane (that's me) and Wesley.

The Old Man was just that. Dad and Clarence did the farm work, and Clarence did his best to stay caught up in school. Somehow, he did. When he graduated from school in 1884, he got a four-year scholarship from the Methodist Church to go to Ohio Northern in Ada, Ohio. But our father was slowing down, and Clarence agreed to wait a year to go to college. He worked with Wes and me, showing us how to do things and, just as important, explaining what was happening to Dad.

For someone who never aspired to spend his life farming, Clarence was a great farmer. That year he stayed home from college, the three of us did the chores every day. At night, Clarence worked in the barn and other outbuildings. He spent all those nights repairing our equipment, making sure it was in good condition. He didn't want Dad or us to have to do that heavy work when he was gone.

By the time he left to go to college, the farm was in the great shape. Clarence also made sure we knew that Dad had input in the work he was doing. When people commented on how good the fences looked or the other outbuildings, Clarence told them that it was all his Dad's idea to get things in shape.

Clarence was great at just about everything he did. He was such an unassuming fellow, both physically and temperamentally, that most everybody underestimated him. Folks just never gave him credit. He was small so they thought he couldn't be a good hand. But he could buck hay better than anybody I ever saw. And he wasn't one to brag or try to boss others around. But he'd get you to do things the way he wanted. Shoot, by the time he got done with you, you'd be convinced it was your own idea all along.

Clarence had always wanted to be a university professor. He loved geology and geography—all the sciences. Sometimes we would wander around out in the woods and he would talk about what you could tell about the underlying rocks and things under the surface by what was on the surface.

That's what he hoped to study in college, but that didn't work out. The scholarship he got was for four years, but he didn't realize he had to start that autumn to get four years. So, when he started, he only had three years. He tried to take extra classes and catch up, but he couldn't take enough without going summer term to get a four-year degree. And he felt that he had to help with the farm in those summers.

Circumstances prevented him from having the professional life he imagined. But he and Virgie had a wonderful marriage. They both were disappointed at never having any children of their own. But all the nieces and nephews loved spending time with them.

One time at the Chesterfield Fair I remembering hearing Effie Fleming and Sarah Jane Thomas talking about big extended families and saying there always seemed to be maiden aunts or childless couples that helped their brother's and sister's families.

Effie wasn't a particularly religious woman, but she said she figured that was one area that the Lord might have got right. Effie sure did help Sarah Jane. And Sarah Jane paid that forward—in spades!

On Sundays that whole year that Clarence stayed home, he prepared us for what we'd need to do when we finally left for college. He'd shoo us off to bed and spend the evening, way into the night, studying. And he never complained.

He introduced me to what turned out to be my life's work. He did the best he could with Wesley. But that's a whole another story. That summer after his first-year teaching high school, and just before my senior year, he took me with him to a symposium on the Teays River, being held down in Huntington, West Virginia, at Marshall University.

Clarence had followed the various findings about this primordial river system that had once drained nearly the same watershed that the Ohio River has since the end of the last Ice Age. As we listened to the lectures on the latest findings by geologists and heard the scientific tools and analyses they were utilizing, for the first time I felt the real power of science.

It was my first long trip in a car. Clarence had borrowed Uncle Charlie's old Ford. After the conference, we drove over to the section of the Ohio River downstream a bit. This was the section that has been identified as one of the few sections where the Ohio flows in the same channel as the Teays. The mighty Ohio looked like a little bitty creek running through the flat land extending for a mile or more on either side of the channel. We drove back along the Scioto River immersed in a reverential silence.

I spent senior year concentrating on math, science and chemistry. I was able to get a scholarship to OSU. I've spent my career teaching geology and chemistry at Denison. When Clarence was hugging me warmly after my graduation, I felt a twinge of sorrow that he had missed his chance at the academic career he desired. It was almost like he had introduced me to his girlfriend and then watched the two of us run off together.

I stayed close to Clarence and Virgie. When I was at school, at OSU, we talked on the telephone every Sunday all the way through until my PhD was completed. They threw a big party for me when I was hired as an associate professor at Kenyon. Virgie introduced me that night to Maggie, a librarian from Amesville.

We started keeping company, and the following summer we were engaged. Maggie's parents died in a car accident when she was 18. Dad had passed a few years earlier, and mom was confined to her bed in a rest home. Virgie and Clarence stood up with us at the wedding. And when Maggie got pregnant, they agreed to be godparents for our child—Winifred.

When the war broke out, Clarence wanted to enlist. He kind of forgot about the age limit. But like always he wanted to contribute. In his own inconspicuous way, Clarence had fought the good fight his entire life. He'd been a good son, brother, husband, uncle, and teacher, and he wasn't about to start slacking in 1941. He ended up on the committee for metal drives, rubber drives, and every other kind of drive they came up with until the war ended. He also kept up correspondence with an incredible number of his students who were in uniform. He and Virgie worked together on those letters late into the night many evenings.

By August, soldiers by the thousands from Europe, Africa, Asia and the South Pacific were being released from active duty. Many of those boys who'd had Clarence as a teacher were home on furlough.

The day of his funeral, the Bartlett Cemetery was filled with Army colonels, Navy commanders, pilots from the Army Air Corps, and nurses from all branches. There was a virtual Division of enlisted men as well, exhibiting Silver Stars, Purple Hearts and other medals. Not all of those fellows had gone to college. But when they got out of high school, they took what they had learned back to their farms and shops. And when they were drafted, they used that practical knowledge and analytical thinking to solve problems from obliterating hedgerows in Normandy to fighting for beachheads in the South Pacific.

And as all the people gathered for the service and internment, finally, Clarence Pearson's efforts and accomplishments appeared, writ large, for all to see. The cemetery was crowded, making it look at once large and small. One of the pilots from the class of '36 rented a small plane and trailed a black pennant three times around the field.

The funeral oration/eulogy was given by Brigadier General Horace Jobes of the Big Red One, from the Class of '32. He paused and looked around at the sea of olive drab and crackerjack blue with a big smile that turned to a wrinkled frown: "Glad I didn't have to look across a beachhead or through those darned hedgerows at you fellows—you're a scary bunch.

"When they asked me to give this eulogy I was honored—I still am. And then I was puzzled wondering how to describe Mr. Pearson to those who hadn't had the privilege of being a student in his classroom. So, rather than trying to give a blow by blow account of his pedagogical approach, I decided to try to describe the overall effect. Kind of like trying explain the way Joe Louis fights. There's no one else like the Brown Bomber. He doesn't have just one style. He adapts, depending on his opponent. You just have to appreciate it. Mr. Pearson's teaching style was like that. He used different approaches with his students. You just had to be there.

"I grew up poor in Dale, not so very far from this spot where we stand. We had a big family—12 kids—and a small farm. Mr. Pearson recognized something in me, a spark, and he fanned that spark and made me hungry for knowledge. The other thing great teachers and great leaders know is that the folks they're leading are not robots. They are human beings.

"There's an old saying that an Army runs on its stomach. The same thing was true for a school, especially a small rural school during the Depression. My Dad use to kid Mr. Pearson, saying, 'You know a lot about farming for a school teacher'.

"And he did. He helped my dad and a lot of the other small farmers in the area. After 1929, the difference between a good crop and a marginal one wasn't just about income. It was about having enough food to feed the whole family.

"He put together programs that helped small farmers increase yield and cut waste. And he did it without insulting anyone about their knowledge or work ethic. By the time these co-op programs got going, the farmers had taken responsibility for helping each other and sticking with the better practices they had come up with. And finally, Mr. Pearson was able to get equipment dealers to help struggling farmers by making some of their older models available for rent at reasonable rates.

"Mr. Pearson also wasn't a guy who would forget about you after you graduated, either. He wrote me a letter of recommendation that helped me get into OSU, and he kept track of my progress. He wrote me letters while I was in Africa with Ike. And he kept writing them all the way through the war.

"The last letter I received was dated April 20, 1945. It finally caught up with me two weeks ago. I'd like to read it for you.

Dear Horace,

I hope this letter finds you well. Virgie and I are fine. We speak of you often. Guess you boys will be returning soon. I hope you know how proud we are of all you men and women who served.

We certainly hope to see you if you get back this way and have time.

Warmest Wishes,

Clarence and Virgie Pearson

PS: I hope you haven't forgotten that *Ode* you promised to send to Virgie. You know how fond she is of poetry.

"The importance of keeping one's promises was another lesson that Mr. Pearson and my Dad taught me. So, with some trepidation and apologies for the length of time it took me to complete, here goes nothing. And another thing, Mrs. Pearson, despite my first name being Horace, this is a *Pindaric* Ode about one of your husband's favorite subjects.

<u>*Requiem for the Teays:* Ode to La Belle Riviere</u>

Once was a time before the ice did scour the heights

When fields, forests, rivers, hills and dale

Endured eternal in Heaven's sights

Yet freeze and thaw o'er eons did prevail

Cold Earth rent and knit, streams near confounded

The very Father of Waters, almost reversed.

Its' streams submerged

While basin bending channels 'cross the range

The Earth's fiery crust itself to rocks and dust did change

And from the mire La Belle Riviere emerged.

"I'd like to get a show of hands from our military folks out there. How many of you received letters from Mr. Pearson?" A sea of hands waved. "Wow, let's rephrase that. How many veterans did *not* receive a letter from the Mister Pearson.

No uniformed arms were raised.

"I rest my case. "Mr. Pearson would have made a fine soldier. His intellect was impressive; his temperament, extraordinary. I've served with many fine soldiers—officers and enlisted men. There is an elite group in each branch of the service, certain select men—sergeants, chief petty officers, warrant officers who are arguably among the most vital leaders we have. They take young men, scared recruits, and build them up, encourage them, push them until they're exhausted, and then train them until they are strong individually and darn near unbeatable collectively.

"That's what Mr. Pearson did with his students. He trained them—us—for college, for service to our country and for life."

The General took off his glasses and wiped his eyes.

"May we—*we happy few, we band of brothers*—always remember the lessons we learned from this great man. And may we pass them on to the next generation."

A military honor guard appeared and the bugler, a jazz trumpeter before the war, played the bluest rendition of *Taps* ever heard in the Lower Muskingum Valley.

"Attention!" said General Jobes and the hundred or so veterans in the crowd turned toward the gravesite and saluted on his command. He walked over to Mrs. Pearson, offered his arm, and the two walked down from the platform and through the crowd, which parted as they smiled and cried, remembering the man who had changed their lives and those of many others.

POST WAR

> *"It is easy to go down into Hell; night and day, the gates of dark Death stand wide; but to climb back again, to retrace one's steps to the upper air - there's the rub, the task." Virgil. Divine Comedy*

Virgil Thomas was discharged in mid-December, 1945. He spent his first Christmas at home since 1940 on the family farm. His father let him use their flatbed truck to visit friends. Virgil refused to take the normal route down the hill past the store. He didn't want to see the Forest family, the store, or the table in the yard by the Forest's house. He figured the odds were slim he'd run into her, but he wanted to be safe, not sorry. She was probably spending the holidays in Akron or with her husband's kin in New Lex.

Big Mitch, Anne, Little Mitch, and Eleanor had all agreed that news about Louise and Pierce would not be brought up while Virgil was present. He'd be going back to school the second week of January to arrange housing and sign up for Winter Quarter classes. He'd be taking his last agronomy class and an independent study with his advisor that basically would cover what to expect when he graduated and began to look for a job.

After that, he planned to come back home and work on the farm and try to put together a career plan. He'd go back for two classes Winter Quarter. The first was a soil science class only offered Winter Quarter and taught by curmudgeonly Dr. Gustavson. Virgil had taken the class as a freshman and gotten a B+. Unfortunately, the records stored in upper levels of the old Sawtooth Chemistry Lab had been destroyed by water and pigeon droppings. His professor had lost his files from that time, as had many agriculture and science professors considered the report cards to be enough proof of passing the class. Unlike most of his colleagues, Dr. Gustavson, refused to accept their grade card as sufficient proof.

A few other veterans were in the same bind. Virgil's advisor suggested the five of them make an appointment with Dr. Gustavson.

They made an appointment on a Friday late afternoon at 4 PM. By 8 PM, only one person from the group stayed. He told them later that Gustavson gave him quizzes from his latest class.

"He gave me 70% on the quiz—a C-! Good luck fellows."

The next appointment was the following Monday at 5:30 AM. That's what Virgil's note read. He sat on the bench outside the department office until 11:30 AM. At that time, Dr. Gustavson emerged with his head back and a reptilian smile on his face, followed shortly thereafter by the three other victims.

"I'd give anything to get that dude one-on-one in a dark alley. Watch yourself, Virgil. He's really got a hard-on for you," a fellow from the Second Armored Corps whispered.

"Gentlemen, we'll be late for lunch," Gustavson said with cacophonous chuckle. "Better get with it, Bub. You've got one more chance."

Bub, Virgil murmured to himself. *Why did the old bastard call him Bub?* He sat back down in the chair outside the department office. A few people left for lunch and came back an hour later.

The secretary brought Virgil a cup of coffee around three o'clock. "Are you still waiting for Dr. Gustavson?" the secretary asked as she buttoned her coat and prepared to leave. "He doesn't always come back at the end of the day."

"I'm waiting right here. I've been waiting four and a half years to finish my degree. I got drafted with three classes to go for my bachelor's degree. I was discharged a few weeks ago. When I came back to see my advisor, I find out that I no longer have credit for a class I took before the war and passed with a B+. I have been trying to see him for the last three days. He has given me the run around, and I'd just like to know why. Does he have something against veterans?"

"It's complicated. Dr. Gustavson served in World War One. He was drafted just before he was set to get his master's degree. He had been accepted to go to the University of Wisconsin for his doctorate."

"So, 25 years later he takes it out on other returning veterans. I get it, that makes it clear as mud."

"Don't take it personally. He treats lots of people badly. I feel sorry for him. His wife left him when he was overseas. She took their son and moved to California."

"That's a bad deal but not my fault. Who can I talk to that can get this straightened out?"

"Wait just a minute. I think our Chair is still here." She walked down the hall and entered the room at the end.

A few minutes later the door opened and a tall man in a cardigan sweater approached Virgil. "Mr. Thomas, I understand you are trying to find out about a class you took in 1940. Is that right?"

Virgil frowned and nodded. "Yes, sir."

"Do you have a copy of your grades for the semester in question?"

"Yes, sir." Virgil handed the grade card to the Chair.

"It looks like everything is in order. Have you made an appointment with Doctor Gustavson?"

"Twice. Both times he gave me a bogus time. Today I had a 5:30 AM meeting scheduled."

"Did something keep you from making these appointments?"

"I was there, both times. The first time I was told to show up at 4 PM last Friday afternoon. I got there at 8 PM. The doctor hadn't shown up. I made another appointment for today at 5:30 AM and didn't see the good doctor until he and three other students came out of his office at around 11:30. They were heading out for lunch. I'm not interested in getting into a pissing match. I just want to finish my degree and get on with my life. I only had three classes to finish when I was drafted. Now I'm back and find out I need to retake this class because your department's records were destroyed. I've had enough bureaucracy in the past four-plus years in the Army to recognize a genuine FUBAR when I see one."

"Well, Mr. Thomas, I certainly sympathize with your plight, but I can't go over Gustavson's head. Perhaps he'll be back shortly. Would you like some coffee?"

"No, thanks. I'll wait him out, and I'll not be shy about using salty language with him. What does he have against students?"

"He had a bad time when he came back from World War I. Maybe he thinks you returning vets have it too easy. He was a decorated soldier, a sergeant."

"If that's the case, I'll settle his hash right quick." Virgil was breathing hard and staring at the Chair.

A door opened down the hall, and Eric Gustavson came through and joined the party. "Whatta you say, Bub?" he said.

"If you call me Bub one more time, I'll put you on the ground!"

"You don't like being called, Bub, do you? Neither did I when you called me that as you turned in your final exam. I guess we're even."

"Not hardly. I passed that class fair and square. I had a 93% going into the final. I want that credit. I need to finish my degree before I'm too old. You do the right thing, right now. Shoot, who holds a grudge for six years anyway?"

"You aren't getting any closer to those credits, Bub!"

"I'm leaving here with a document reflecting the fact that the B+ that shows in my transcript is accurate, and I have completed this class. Now, who is going to make that happen?"

"Let's all take a deep breath," the Chair said. "Eric, you do as he says. There is no question he passed that course. Get him a note on our letterhead explaining that to the folks in academic records."

Gustavson grimaced and stared at his shoes. "I will comply with your request immediately." He executed a crisp about face, marched down the hall, and disappeared into his office.

Virgil spied a chair halfway down the hall. He sat down, back straight, thinking of all the time in the past five years he'd thought about being back at OSU, working again on a degree that would allow him to take his place in society as an honorable man.

His primary interest wasn't learning for learnings' sake. He was interested in applying what he learned. He'd learned lessons about the importance of that kind of tactical knowledge in the hedgerows of Normandy. There was cost, a butcher's bill you might say, that the Third Army paid before learning how to keep their soft-bellied tanks from getting stuck.

Many of the tankers were incinerated after lodging belly-up on the hedges, before they brought in modified tanks to breakthrough. The fellows in the 36th Armored Infantry accompanied the tanks on foot.

As Gabby put it— "Might as well have been staked out with a sign on our belly that read: 'Bait!'"

As the days and miles went by, those who survived learned lessons. Most of them attributed this to skill and knowledge they learned as apt pupils of warfare. But at night, in their foxholes, when the wind or heat or bugs or damp kept them awake, they suspected that probability and luck were really the driving forces that would determine if they would ever return to parents, sweethearts, wives, children, friends—in short, normality.

"Mr. Thomas, here is a copy of this letter you may take to the Registrar."

"Dr. Gustavson, I'm sorry if I lost my temper. I've been waiting for almost five years to get back to school."

"I understand your predicament, Virgil. I lost two years during World War I and a chance to get a PhD from the top ag school in the country."

"I lost my girl too, sir. My fiancé got pregnant while I was on leave before I reported to Camp Polk. And she married her foreman at the defense plant in Akron where she worked."

"I'm sorry to hear that, Virgil. I had a similar experience in the First War. I got through my PhD at Indiana University, married, and had a wonderful daughter. But I don't know. Somehow, it's not the same. I came back a different person, that self-assurance I had was gone. After some of the things I saw, it's been hard to look at—to trust people like I had before the war."

"I understand that feeling. It kind of feels like I had to go to the back of the line. Again, sorry for gettin' my Irish up. "

"I'm responsible for this situation. I've had my Danish up for 27 years. If you're looking for a work-study job for your last couple of quarters. I could find something for you here in the department. What specific field are you interested in, after you graduate?"

"Well, I think soil conservation and contour plowing. My family has a farm in Morgan County. My Dad saved me newspaper articles and a few bulletins from the county agent about contour plowing and things like that."

"We've got a new faculty member in the department, he just got back from the Pacific. His name is Tim Kennard, from New Lex. Soil conservation is his field of interest. Come back after classes start and we may be able to get you a 15-hour-a-week job that would pay for your books. More importantly, Tim might be able to give you some help finding a job after you graduate."

"Thank you so much, Sergeant Gustavson," Virgil said with a smile.

***

Charlotte Simon received a telegram on May 7th, 1945, informing her that Uncle Sam was sorry to inform her that her husband, Johnny Simon, had been killed in Germany on April 21, 1945, by a sniper, while leading German POWs to a holding area behind the Allied lines.

The following day—May 8th, VE Day— dawned as the entire town of Chesterfield celebrated. They were sprawled down Marion Street past the Union Hall Theater and the mortuary. Even old enemies hugged one another, happy to get to the end of this World War II. Unlike its predecessor, this war had impacted everyone. The loved ones of fallen soldiers had grieved as small groups and clans for the past four-plus years. But now, they celebrated, too. All of them. Only a single small craft bucked the pulsating armada that surged down Marion Street. A tiny girl and her frail mother connected tenuously by a rickety handmade baby buggy bucked the trend and managed to get past the throng up the hill. The mother stopped in front of each house and stared vacantly through the leaded glass into these homes of Chesterfield. She spent extra time gazing at the Fawcett House at the top of the hill.

"I'll never have this," she sobbed softly. Literally wringing her hands, she repeated over and over "Why me? Why us?"

It was the first of many such sojourns. On this first trip, no one in the crowd knew the cause. And over the next month people came to understand. But as the days lengthened and temperatures soared, a consensus of family, friends, and neighbors coalesced, and Charlotte Simon was offered a job as a bookkeeper at the Windsor Mill, beginning June 1, 1945. Her brother, Pen, would take her to work after he finished milking in the morning. Nanny would watch little Lurlene Simon, and someone from the Mill would give her a ride home.

Johnny's inexplicably abrupt departure had shocked everyone in the Ross family. Charlotte simmered at a slow boil that spring, but kept her head down and settled into work and motherhood. Nanny let her know she was proud of her.

On those steamy summer nights, though, when the moths and other insects engulfed whatever light source they could find, Charlotte kept Lurlene swaddled and wondered if she'd ever get out of Chesterfield. She had been so sure that Johnny would take her to southern California, where they could live out the American Dream.

Johnny would certainly have had enough money. The very thought of the clothes, cars, and opportunities to go to nightclubs, concerts and other artistic endeavors sent a jolt down her spine. She could almost taste that life—so close. When Johnny came back home, everything would be wonderful. Even after he went to Europe in late March, it was hard for Charlotte to believe he wouldn't be coming home. His last two letters were short but he expressed his desire to restart their marriage and settle down after Uncle Sam was done with him.

It had been enough to allow Charlotte to think better thoughts. He wanted to come back to her and their daughter, Lurlene.

But her Johnny never came marching home.

And Charlotte never understood his departure. She'd had that one weekend when she drank too much. But, surely that wasn't grounds for desertion of her and their baby. And the war had been winding down.

Given her fragile mental health and tendency toward paranoia and depression, Charlotte blamed herself. After Johnny left, she moved back to Nanny's house and awaited the birth of her child. Things got worse. Her two aunts were each prone to pacing the floor at night while holding conversations with ghosts.

After seven-months Charlotte delivered Lurlene, a baby girl the claustrophobic perambulation increased by an order of magnitude. Everyone was praying for an early spring so the inmates could get out on the large front porch and play Flinch in the springtime beauty of southeastern Ohio.

For all intents and purposes, Charlotte was in shock from the moment she found out Johnny left for basic training and would not return until the war ended. Tiny Lurlene Simon was born on a coffee table in the smallest of the three rooms on the second-floor of the little house on Marion Street.

Spring came, and the folks on Marion Street got to witness the joy that Lurlene brought to the eccentric older female residents of Nanny's house. But Charlotte felt no joy. Her legs felt heavy, and her desire for sleep worried her mother, Nanny Ross.

The late winter of 1945 hung on into mid-April. It was a bad one for Charlotte and her baby. The house was crowded. After Christmas, Minta took a job in New Lex helping an elderly woman who had been recently confined to a wheelchair. This gave Charlotte a little more room to spread out.

In May, Johnny's sister, Polly came up to visit her niece, Lurlene. She also wanted to make sure mother and baby were OK. Twyla barricaded herself in her room until Polly left in early June.

Charlotte enjoyed the visit. The two sisters-in-law talked about Johnny. Charlotte hadn't received but one letter from Johnny. His outfit was heading to Germany to help with the German POWs.

"Did you get many letters from Johnny?" Charlotte asked.

"A few. Last one was the first week of May. They were guarding prisoners crammed into what he described as feed lots no decent cattleman would abide. He didn't really complain, but I could tell he was disappointed."

"Polly, I'm sorry if I did something to drive him away. We had a spat over him working four days straight. I got low and drank a little too much. That was the only fight we ever had. I just wanted us to be a happy family, and I didn't want to disappoint him."

"Charlotte, don't do that to yourself. Johnny was so down about Merle and Dennis, he felt like he needed to get over there and fight. The darn thing is, we got a telegram just before I left. It said Merle and a few other sailors had been picked up by a Japanese ship and taken to a prisoner-of-war camp in the Philippines. He's alive! Dad is going to Hawaii to see him and bring him home."

"That's great news, Polly. I hope they are wrong about Johnny. I have been so afraid something will happen to him over there. I don't want to have to raise Lurlene by myself."

"I know dear. Johnny left you at a bad time. We'll be happy to help you out if you need anything."

"That's kind of you. Johnny left me with a car and money in the bank. He set up an allotment. I've got everything I need, except him."

"They may have made a mistake—that could happen—couldn't it."

"This war has to end soon, Polly said with a sigh.

"The Germans are never going to win, but they're just too stubborn to surrender, the same with the Japanese."

Charlotte fell into a routine. Her world revolved around Lurlene and work. Minta continued to work for the lady in New Lex. Twyla managed to get on part-time at Yocum's Store just down the hill from the house. Nanny did her best to watch Lurlene so Charlotte could have some grownup time. But Charlotte didn't seem to take an interest in social activities. She and Lurlene attended the Methodist services on Sunday mornings. But she didn't attend any of the other events—movies in McConnelsville, dances in Zanesville— when her friends from school invited her.

Nanny decided against pushing her to go out. There would be time, and soon the men would return. And Charlotte was a grown woman. She went to work and came home, took care of Lurlene, and kept her head down.

And in the evening sometimes, when Lurlene and everyone else in the house were sleeping soundly, Charlotte pulled out a rectangular makeup case. Not the one with her compact and powder that she carried in her purse, but one that she hid in a book, *Little Women,* whose pages had been hollowed out methodically and precisely with a single-edged razor blade. The interior space was just big enough to store the case, a tiny bottle with rubbing alcohol, a spool of gauze, a small tube of epoxy glue, and a plastic pouch containing extra blades. After the other residents on the top floor had settled down, Charlotte laid out her instruments with surgical precision on a worn off-white washcloth. Next, she removed her nightgown and sliced off two six-inch pieces of gauze. One she wet with alcohol and wiped down a long swath of alabaster skin on the top of her left thigh. The other, she laid aside for later. She carefully wiped the razor blade on both sides.

And very carefully, she picked up the blade between the thumb and index finger of her right hand and cut a V-shape wedge whose pinnacle just grazed the border of her pubic hair. She shivered with a secret delight and gently blotted the cut with the alcohol-saturated gauze.

She repeated this process several times. Each iteration of this process gave her a little more satisfaction. When she stood for a minute or two and gazed at her work in the old oval dressing mirror in the corner of the room, she smiled. The wounds were perfect—the blood formed a single line in the shape of a chevron, like the one Johnny had worn on his uniform when he died.

Then she turned slowly, the side of her left hip revealing a perfectly straight line of chevrons, each one a bit fainter than the previous one. She shrugged and gazed at the beauty of these totems. She checked Lurlene in her crib, squatted on her chamber pot and emptied her bladder. She was under control and she'd be damned if she wasn't going to be a good mother.

***

"Excuse me, ma'am. I'm supposed to see Mrs. Simon, the bookkeeper."

"You found her."

"Well, good. I've got two wagon loads of corn I need ground."

"We can take care of you. Do you have an account here at the mill?"

"My Dad, Big Mitch Thomas, does."

The bookkeeper lowered the glasses on her nose and eyed the man before her. He was a hair above average height with broad shoulders and no belly to speak of. She'd noticed he had a slight hitch in his giddyup when he walked up to the desk. And he had a cleft chin that rang a bell from 20 years before.

"Do you remember a little smart-alecky girl who locked you out of the Chesterfield Fair?"

"I surely do, Charlotte. How are you? I'm really sorry about your husband."

"Thank you, Virgil. I heard you'd been wounded a couple of times."

"Yes, but nothing that keeps me from getting around. I heard you had a daughter."

"Yes, Lurlene. She's 14 months old. Mom watches her when I'm working. Right now, we're staying with Mom."

"Yeah, I'm stayin' up home, too. I'll be finishing up at OSU this fall and getting out and finding a job. Well, I better get those wagons to the floor. It was good seeing you, Charlotte."

"It's pretty late today, but you can get your cornmeal first thing tomorrow. I'll make sure it's ready."

"Thanks. See you tomorrow."

Virgil still hadn't gone past the Forest house or the store since the evening in 1943 when Henry Forest's third heart attack had started the chain of ill-fated events that prevented him from marrying Louise before he shipped out overseas.

He had a hankering for a Baby Ruth bar—a lot of Baby Ruth bars. He stepped in the store. Harriet was behind the counter and flipping through a magazine. She looked up, and a fleeting trace of fear flashed in her eyes before she composed herself.

"Why, Virgil Thomas. It's good to see you."

"Yes, ma'am. I'll be helping out up home until classes start at Ohio State."

"Well, that's fine. Just fine."

"I was sorry to hear about Henry. He was a fine man."

"Thank you kindly, Virgil."

"How is the rest of the family doing, Mrs. Forest?"

"Just fine. Barbara is working as a court stenographer in Marietta. She usually comes home on weekends. Merlene teaches third grade at Pennsville. She'll be getting married later this summer to Clyde Shook from Malta. Opal will be a senior at the high school this fall."

"That hardly seems possible," Virgil said with a big grin. "I almost forgot. I'll take two dozen Baby Ruth bars, if you please."

"The big ones?"

"Yes, ma'am."

"Alright. Six, 12, 18. and six more, for two dozen. That'll come to $4.86 with tax."

He put a $5 bill on the counter and took the bag. "It's been nice talking to you, Virgil."

"Pleasure's been all mine, ma'am. I've missed you Forest girls."

"I bet you have, Virgil. This war has surely thrown a monkey wrench into so many lives."

"You can say that again. Thanks again. I'll be seeing you."

***

"Could you put this bag on Mrs. Simon's desk or give them to her when she arrives, please?" Virgil asked the secretary at the main desk on the first floor of the mill.

"I'll give it to her on her way in, hun."

"Thanks."

"She should be in any time. You can wait on the bench down the hall."

"Thanks, again." No sooner had he taken a seat on the bench when Charlotte arrived, bag in hand.

"Could you get the door, please? Between my purse and this bag, whatever it is, I'm out of hands."

Virgil jumped up and ushered her through the door.

"Your cornmeal is ready, Virgil. I checked with the fellows before I came up."

"That sounds great."

"Will you excuse me just a minute? I need to see what's in this bag."

"That will be fine."

She removed a heavy rubber band, unrolled the bag, and opened the top. Well, I never—." She gently emptied the bag onto her desk.

"And don't go leaving any of those bars on Mr. Bowman's car."

"You remembered—you remember me," she smiled broadly and blotted a few tears with a tissue.

"I surely do remember you, Charlotte Ross Simon. Now, I best be getting my cornmeal and heading home"

"And I hope I'll be seeing you, Virgil. You know, my Dad had quite the sweet tooth. I suppose I inherited mine from him. But I could use some help with these. Maybe you could come over some Sunday after church, and you could join us for lunch. We could have these for snacks."

"That sounds very nice. I'd like to do that."

"Well, how about this Sunday? With Memorial Day and all. My aunts—Minta and Twyla—are home caregivers for folks that need help getting around. They each have patients–Minta in New Lex and Twyla in Deavertown. They won't be there, but you can meet Lurlene. And Mom will be there, too."

"That sounds wonderful, Charlotte. I'll give you a call Friday here at the mill."

"I'll be here. And I take my lunch at noon over on that the picnic table that sits over toward the river. Unless it's raining."

"OK. I'll be seeing you on Friday for lunch, Charlotte."

"I'll put that down in my social calendar."

Friday morning. Virgil was given the day off milking. He'd finished raking the first cutting of hay on the upper field in the gloaming the night before. The family car was in the garage up in Roosterville getting the wheels aligned and the suspension checked.

Virgil decided he'd ride one of the horses down to see Charlotte at the mill. He'd been thinking about her a lot during the week.

"Mother, is it alright if I ride Blackie down to Windsor? I don't want to leave you and Dad without a vehicle."

"That's fine, Virgil. I was just going to come and see if you'd go down to the store. Harriet called and said Barbara had gotten Friday off for a four-day weekend. Barbara wanted to see you about something."

"I can go right now, Mother. I was going to go down to the mill and see Charlotte Simon, have lunch with her."

"Well, you don't waste any time 'bout some things, I suppose. She's had a tough time, from what I've heard. Just don't go off half-cocked, as your Father would say."

"I won't, Mother. I just haven't had a date for a long time."

"OK, be careful. And don't forget to stop at the store on your way down."

"Will do, Mother. I'll be back for dinner."

"Be careful and behave yourself."

Virgil snapped to attention and saluted sharply. "Aye Aye, captain." After a smart about-face, he straight-armed the screen door and shambled down the backsteps and toward the barn.

He used the 15-minute ride down the hill to ponder what in the world Barbara Forest had to say that was so important. The morning air was damp. And the sun illuminated the dew on the thistles. He remembered how stark, dry and desolate the Mojave had seemed in contrast. He'd liked that landscape, liked the difference from the familiar scenery of the Muskingum River Valley.

He'd had a few women while he was in the service. A Cajun gal—a mulatto—who worked at the bar just outside Camp Polk. In California on a pass, at a bar just outside Los Angeles he'd followed a young Mexican girl to a tar paper shack and watched the beads on her Rosary rise and fall in the hollow of her throat as he humped his way to frenzied ecstasy. The two women that he and Gabby had shagged in the tube in London during a blackout in December of 1943. His final assignation had been as the *caboose* on a *train* his squad pulled on a bald Frenchwoman—a Nazi collaborator who had thrown a grenade, fortunately a dud, into a Jeep from a second story window in St. Lo.

Except for the last one, which crossed the line into prurience, Virgil had enjoyed those experiences, for the different sensory stimuli, the look, smell, taste, feel and sound. They were memories, like the faded postcards his Father tacked up over his desk at the store, of his month spent at the St. Louis World's Fair.

Virgil cherished the memories he had of travel and exotic places. But he would have never seriously considered settling down anywhere except in Ohio.

"Bloom where you're planted," his Grandmother Mary Jane would say. He planned to, but it still seemed the faster he chased the life he wanted, the further it receded.

He took Blackie, an eight-year old horse into the lane leading to the Forest's house.

Barbara Forest sat on the huge table, which had assumed near-mythic status for Virgil as he had traipsed across the US in training and then Europe with the Third Armored Division. He tied up the horse on the railing of the porch.

Barbara came out the front door, wiping her hands on a dish towel. "How are you, Virgil?"

"I've been better, but I guess we all have to go on. Your Mom said you had something you needed to tell me."

"It's something, alright. Something kind of bad for all the folks involved."

"Do I have to guess what it is?"

"I don't think you could in a million years."

"Is something wrong with Louise?"

"Yes. She and Doak, her husband, were in a car wreck in Canton a few weeks ago. They were heading to New Lex from Akron."

"Are they OK? They have a child, don't they?"

Barbara nodded. "Yes, they do. A boy—Pierce. He had been staying with Doak's Grandmother in New Lex. They were going to pick him up. They weren't alright. Doak was killed instantly. Louise is in very bad shape in the hospital in Canton."

"Is she going to pull through?"

"Doctor said he thought she had a chance, but I've been talking to him on the phone. She's getting worse. I just got back from seeing her yesterday."

"Were they still living in Akron?"

"They were going to move to New Lex. The thing is, why I really want to talk to you is about something Louise said you needed to know. She has a safe deposit box in a bank in Akron. She gave me the key to give to you. Said you were the only one that had any business with the contents of the box. She had your name put on the account when she opened it shortly after she moved to Akron. She wanted me to tell you this if anything happened to her."

"I don't know what to say. I spent most of my time while I was fighting in Europe, wondering what happened. The last time I saw her was early the next morning at the store after the night after your Dad had a heart attack in '41. I rode one of the horses up from your house, up to Mom and Dad's place. I was going to come back down after seeing them and Louise and I were going to get married. I had to go Columbus to clear out my room and disenroll from OSU. My outfit shipped out for boot camp in Louisiana, a week days later.

"I thought your sister and I always had a kind of understanding about getting married. After I got back from that final stateside leave, I told myself, if I could have just gotten one letter from her explaining what happened it would have put my mind at ease. 'Course I never wrote her either."

"Virgil, I need to get up to the hospital in Canton. Could you go with me? Actually, I need someone to take me up there. And if Louise does pass, you can get the things in the safe deposit box in Akron. Could you get a car?"

"Maybe. Let me check with Weir Kern. I think he's got a car that belonged to his Dad that he's tinkering with. If he's got two cars running, he might let me borrow one. Mom and Dad have their car getting worked on, so they only have the truck. I'll go catch up with Weir or Mary Lou and see if they can let me borrow one. OK?"

Barbara nodded.

"I'll be back in a bit." Virgil climbed up on AJ Jr and rode on toward Windsor. He tied the horse up to a porch rail at the mill and walked down to the empty picnic table. He checked his watch: 11:45. He walked down to the river and watched as stray tree branches launched over the spillway by the roiling brown water, headed downstream. The scraps and detritus roiled and swirled near the western bank just upstream from Silverheels Riffle.

"Ahoy, captain," cried a thin voice barely audible above the water's roar.

Virgil turned and waved in the direction of the table. His first thought was a wish that it might be Louise with her auburn hair glistening in the sunlight. This was followed immediately by a vague disappointment.

"Permission to come aboard, ma'am."

"Granted."

Virgil's steps were more sluggish than they had been before the war, when he would approach Louise by her house on the river. This new lethargy had its roots in his injury, a bullet that somehow entered the side of his knee and passed under without shattering his knee cap. It also reflected a slight disillusionment with the pale, young woman waving and smiling at him from the table.

The last time they had parted, he had been happy, looking forward to courting Charlotte. They'd each been wounded by the war—physically, emotionally, spiritually. But, perhaps, they could support each other. Each been harmed, by the behavior of their partners—feeling lied to, discarded.

He wondered how much he had left to offer anyone other than Louise. Barbara's description of her condition didn't sound promising. Still, the mere thought of seeing her again raised his hopes.

Virgil focused on Charlotte. She was lighting one Lucky Strike from the butt of another. He extracted a Pall Mall from the pack in his shirt pocket and lit it with his Zippo.

"Hello, Virgil. Glad you could make it."

"Me, too. I almost couldn't come. We had bad news about some neighbors. I need to drive Barbara Forest up to Canton. Her sister is in the hospital, in pretty bad shape after a car accident. Then we need to bring her things back down. Long and short of it is, I won't be able to come over on Sunday after church. I hope you'll give me a rain check."

Charlotte had been begun to inhale and exhale like a madwoman. "Rain check, huh? What if it ain't raining Sunday after next?"

"Sorry, it was just an expression."

Charlotte took a last lungful and dropped the smoldering butt into a cracked china coffee cup. "I guess that would be OK."

"Charlotte, I'm sorry. I hope you don't take this like I'm standing you up or anything."

She frowned and shook her head. "Guess you're right. If you need to help folks, that's understandable. Can you call me at home by, say, next Friday?" She pulled out a scrap of paper and wrote down their phone number.

"You bet. I'm looking forward to seeing you and meeting your daughter."

Virgil turned and headed for his horse. The only thing he was looking forward to hinged on the possibility of reunion with a recovering Louise and maybe never seeing Charlotte Simon again.

Virgil rode back to Barbara's house and let her know they were set.

"Ray Kern's wife is out of town for a few weeks, so he's going to let me borrow her car for a week. I'll pick you around about six o'clock if that's OK, and we can head to Canton. Have you heard anymore news?"

"I spoke to the nurse in the ward Louise was on. She had a good day, I guess, that means she didn't need to be resuscitated or anything. They said she appears to be getting stronger."

"That's good. I need you to know something, Barbara. I've loved your sister since the day I first saw her. I dated a few other girls in Columbus. and I've been out with other women at the different Army bases where I've been stationed. But I've never given any thought about marrying anyone but Louise. She was my girl, and circumstances have kept us apart, but I still wanted her to be Mrs. Virgil Thomas someday."

"I know you're sincere, Virgil, but I hope you don't get your hopes up too much. She might pull through this, but if she does, she may not be the same as she was. Could be in a wheelchair or bed-ridden. She has a son, Pierce, he will need to be cared for. Doak's grandmother in New Lex is 85."

"I guess we'll just have to wait and see, Barb. I'll be back in a couple hours and we can go."

"Take care, I'll see yo soon."

Virgil spent three hours explaining things to his folks. Both Anne and Big Mitch liked Louise very much. They had hoped that she and Virgil would marry at some point. But after Virgil shipped overseas and Louise married

Doak Benoit and had a child, they simply wanted her to stay away from Virgil.

Anne was no dummy. When she finally did see Pierce the weekend that Henry Forest was buried, it confirmed suspicions that she'd held ever since Louise beat feet up to Akron in '41 not long after Virgil's last leave before shipping overseas. That child was no more sired by Doak Benoit than the man in the moon. Anne knew with one look that boy was Virgil's.

She had made peace with leaving Louise, Doak and Pierce alone. But with Doak dead and Louise in bad shape, she had the same ideas as Virgil. It was about Pierce. With or without Louise, they needed to be prepared to help that boy.

The telephone in Big Mitch Thomas's study rang two dozen times before Virgil picked up the earpiece. "Hello."

"Virgil, it's Barbara Forest. I just got a call from Louise's doctor. She's been moved back into ICU."

"I got Kern's car last night. I'll be down directly."

"Hurry, Virgil. We may not have much time."

I don't know how we got to Canton. I stopped at the store and grabbed one of Dad's old mail pouches. The weather went from bad to worse with a thunderstorm following us up 77. Traffic was heavy and both of us were at wits end. We got to the hospital after midnight.

I'd become familiar with Army hospitals. But, the ICU in Canton was like nothing I'd ever seen. The frenetic movement, bright lights and loud voices made me feel like I was back on the beach. It took a while to locate Louise. A six-car accident with twelve victims hit the hospital shortly before we arrived.

Louise was in a corner with the drapes closed. A nurse was checking her pulse and other vitals. I grabbed two folding chairs and took them to her bedside. She looked so fragile that I could hardly look at her. Barbara had trouble looking at her sister.

A nurse came in and grabbed the clipboard.

"Are you family?" she asked us.

"Yes," Barbara said. "Is she making any progress?"

"Doctor Ledger will be here any time. We've really been hit hard tonight."

I stood up and gently grabbed the rails on her bed. Louise's eyes fluttered. I placed my hand on her forearm. The Doctor entered the room and looked at her chart.

"You are Louise's sister, aren't you?"

"Yes. And this is Virgil a longtime friend of Louise."

"I'm not going to sugarcoat anything here. Your sister is not improving. We really don't have anything we can do to help her. We've had her on dialysis for five hours. We are running out of ideas and time."

We took turns staying with Louise. I couldn't help thinking that she must be suffering. I thought about Gabby and how he looked just before he died.

"I whispered to Louise— 'I love you.' No answer.

Louise coded just before noon. Barbara was with her.

I felt empty. By the time we finished with the paperwork it was dinnertime. We were closer to Akron than Stockport. Barb had keys to Louise's apartment.

Velma greeted me with an awkward hug.

"I'm so sorry for your losses. You are welcome to stay here as long as you need. I have a whole closet in the basement full of various suitcases and duffel bags people have left. You're welcome to take a couple if you'd like. I'll miss Doak and Louise.

"Why don't you come down and look at my luggage closet, Virgil."

"I'll empty out the drawers," Barbara said "You two go on ahead."

Velma grabbed my hand and practically pulled me down the two sets of stairs.

"Kind of like old times, huh, Virg."

"Yeah, it sure is, Velma."

"If you'll excuse me, I'm going to go find your water closet."

"You do that, it hain't moved. I'll start pulling things out of the closet."

"OK, thanks."

I figured Velma wasn't going to let us go gracefully, but I didn't have it in me to pretend that I was interested in renewing our long, lost intimacy. I heard her rustling in the back of closet. She'd cleaned out about all the various bags and suitcases.

"Virgil, help me. I've got my best pair of nylons on and I've got a splinter catching me on the inside of my leg. Can you help me?"

"I can try."

"I'll hold the flashlight for you."

She pulled her skirt up above her waist, revealing bare skin, hair and a garter belt.

I managed to remove the splinter without too much damage.

She gushed about how nice it was to have a gentleman in the house. I helped her to her feet and out of the closet.

"How about a dance for old time's sake? I've still got my Bix Beiderbecke 78s and my Victrola."

Neither one of us were exactly great dancers, but it was fun to have some human contact. She grabbed me and buried her tongue three—quarters of the way to my tonsils.

Barbara stood stock still at the bottom of the stairs. She turned on the light switch.

"Well, here you are," she said with a queer smile.

"Yes, Barbara, here we are. Velma has offered to let us borrow some bags. Isn't that nice?"

"Yes, that's very nice. Thank you, Velma."

"Let's pick out a few and go back upstairs."

The rest of the day was a tug-of war. Barbara and I were mourning Louise's death. Velma was, well, Velma: one part solicitous and one part invasive.

She let us make a phone call to Harriet. And we took Velma to her favorite Diner for lunch. Fortunately, Velma had three prospective renters comin in mid-afternoon.

Barbara and I lingered for a half hour, drinking coffee. We decided to walk back. On our way back to Velma's place we passed a Mortuary.

"I didn't even think about that, Virg" Barb said with a catch in her throat.

"Me, neither. Let's go see if these folks can get Louise down to Fawcett-Stone in Chesterfield."

They had a car dispatched to the hospital in Canton. They also made arrangements to transport Louise home.

The sun came out and Barb and I took the long way home. We stopped in a Park and watched kids playing.

"Remind you of anyone else, Barb?"

"Yes, the five of us in Windsor."

"Amen, Barb I want you to know that I loved your sister with all of my heart. We had plans to get married before I was sworn in the Army. But with all the rigmarole with your dad's heart attack, well it just didn't work out. I was angry for a long while. About the only thing I heard in my first year was that she got married and had a baby and moved to Akron."

"Louise played things pretty close to the vest with most people, outside of the family," Barb said while shaking her head. "After Louise got pregnant, she confided in me more. Mom had to pick up more of the work at the store and the laundry. Heck, she even subbed the mail route three days a week."

"Barbara, I apologize for that stuff with Velma. I hope you weren't too embarrassed earlier. Velma is not a bad person, but that's just Velma. That being said, I'd like to propose that we tell Velma we need to get back to Morgan County. We also need to get to the bank tomorrow and get into the safety deposit box. You might want to see what you need to do with her bank accounts, what documents besides her death certificate that you'll need."

"I can't believe she's gone, Barb. If you are up to it, we could go to Monarch and find out about Doak and Louise's insurance policies. I've got enough cash to get each of us our own room, in a motel if you don't want to stay at Velma's place."

"It's OK with me, Virg," she said softly burying her nose in a handkerchief. "Things sure get complicated when you get older."

"That's for sure. You know what I bet the plant is running today. Let's go to Monarch now and see if we can find Mervyn or some office people. And then we can pick up Louise's things at Velma's."

The lot was nearly full and we drove around until we found the Main Office.

"That's Mervyn's car," Barb said pointing at a sports car in a space reserved for upper management. He drove that down home when they were recruiting folks.

"Let's go in among 'em, then, Virgil!"

The first thing you saw when you came in the door was a large sign that read:

Mervyn Usher General Manager

I tapped lightly on the sign and heard chair wheels and then footsteps.

Mervyn emerged with his hand out and a hundred-dollar smile.

'Virgil Thomas if you aren't a sight for sore eyes, come on in."

"This is Louise Benoits' sister, Barbara.

We have come to get together her things and papers that the family will need. We'll be going to the where she and Doak banked."

"Anything I can do to help, just ask."

"First off, do the workers here get some type of Life Insurance?"

"Yes, after they've been with us for six months, they get a hundred-dollar policy. That increases with hours worked as long as they're here. It can decrease if the employee misses work doesn't follow work rules, safety and such."

"Could we find out what their policies were worth?"

"Yes! Doak and Louise were good workers responsible no shirking on their line. Is Louise going to pull through?"

"She passed the night in Canton at the hospital."

"If I'm not mistaken, Doak was pronounced dead at the scene of the accident."

"How about the boy, Pierce?"

"He was staying with Doak's grandmother in New Lexington."

"So, we'd like to get as much of the paperwork together as we can."

"Absolutely, Virgil. If you give me a day or two, I'll have one of our secretaries in Human Resources put everything together."

"That sounds good. Could you send it to "Harriet Forest/ Windsor, Ohio Post Office?"

"Will do! Give your best to Big Mitch and Anne. And Barbara, please tell all your folks we are so sorry about your loss. Louise and Doak were such good employees."

Barbara muttered unintelligibly under her breathe and stepped out of Mervyn's office.

"Thank you, Mervyn. I will give your best to all the folks down home. I think Barb is about worn out and me, too. I didn't get home until the end of September."

"Take care, cousin. If you need a job look me up."

Barbara was sitting on a bench at the bottom of the steps rocking back and forth. I remembered her doing that in grade school.

"Barb, are you alright?"

"OK, I'm OK. I wish I was home with our family. But our family is disappearing—Dad, Louise, Doak and Pierce."

"Let's get you back home today, Barb."

"We've got to go to the bank tomorrow, Virgil. And we have to go get Louise and Doak's things from that horrible woman."

"I'll take care those things. We'll be home before dinnertime."

"Good, I don't want to be alone, like Louise was in the hospital."

"I promise to get you home safe and sound."

"OK, Virgil, Louise missed you when you were in the Army. She liked Doak, too. He was funny, too. Pierce looks like you, too, Virgil. Missus Anne thought so to, I think. She cried when she saw him at our house. He's at New Lex with Doak's grandmother. He'll need some winter clothes purty soon.

"Would you like to get in the backseat and sleep. There's a blanket back there."

"OK, please drive careful. I don't want Mom to lose any more kids."

The two-hour trip seemed longer in the mid-October gloaming. I figured Weir Kern would be wondering where his car was and what condition it was in. I picked a radio station that was playing Bennie Goodman.

I had plenty of time to lay out an agenda for myself. I'd drop Barb at her house and then go up to see Mom and Dad. I could use their telephone to call Weir and tell him I'd bring his car back shortly. I'd need another car to go back to Akron and take care of all the loose ends there.

Getting Louise, Pierce and Doak's baggage at Velma's without any of Velma's shenanigans could be tricky.

Go to the bank in Akron to get the contents of the safety deposit box and see how to handle her and Doak's other accounts. Get Louise's death, Virgil certificate in Canton on the way back up.

Something told me I should go back and see Mervyn to make sure about the life insurance for Louise and Doak. And finally, go to New Lex and visit Doak's grandmother and Louise's son.

While I was planning all these maneuvers I almost ran out of gasoline. I filled up in Canton.

Harriet was waiting on the enclosed porch at their house when I pulled in. She ran over to the car, woke Barb up and walked her into the house.

I gave Harriet, a succinct summary of where things stood and my plans to head back up to Akron tomorrow.

"I decided to bring Barb home. She's pretty shook up."

"I appreciate that, Virgil. I know we're all shook up. And I know you've been through so much in the War. And I want you to know, that I have never held a grudge against you or thought you abandoned Louise. "

"Do you want me to go to New Lex? I could take Pierce's things to Doak's grandmother. And you should figure out who the Executor will be."

"Do you think Clyde Bowman would be willing to be Executor?"

"Mom and Clyde are friends. She could talk to him."

Harriet nodded.

"I need to go over to Weir Kern's and see if I can use his car for a few more days. I'll stop back here before I head north, tomorrow."

"OK, Virgil, God Bless you."

My return trip to Akron was less frenetic than my trip with Barbara. Weir said I could keep the car for another week. I got a good night's sleep back home and had a good visit. Mom sweet-talked Clyde Bowman into being the Executor of Louise's Estate. And Dad told me I was doing an honorable thing—said he was proud of me.

I stopped in to see how Barb was doing. She looked rested and offered to go with me. I told her she could help by contacting Doak' grandmother and bringing her up-to-date on things.

I stopped at the hospital in Canton and got some of her things. I talked with hospital to see how to get death certificates for Louise and Doak. They brought both of them to me.

First National Bank in Akron was hopping. I got Louise's large safe deposit box.

"Do not Open" unless you are Virgil Thomas! I extracted the black folder. A large label proclaiming: "Do Not Open" unless you are Virgil Thomas!

I emptied the box. It contained a copy of Louise's 500-dollar Life Insurance policy from Monarch, her Checking account book, a Savings account book and a picture of Louise and Virgil at a dance in Cambridge.

Mervyn's car was in the same spot at Monarch. Virgil approached a Secretary in a large cage in the center of the lobby.

"May help you, Sir?"

"Yes ma'am. I spoke with Mervyn yesterday concerning Louise and Doak Benoits Life insurance. He was going to get one of the Staff Benefits Secretaries to put together a summary of all these things."

"Excuse me, sir. Let me speak with Mr. Usher. I'll be right back. Could I get you a cup of coffee?"

"Yes, black, please."

A few minutes later I was escorted to Mervyn's Office.

"Virgil, this a pleasure, Mrs. Jones, could you see if Rhonda Hart is available."

Miss Hart appeared with a large folder.

"Rhonda, please bring Mr. Thomas up to speed regarding Louise and Doak's pay, benefits, insurance and get someone to gain access to their lockers."

Rhonda looked over her glasses and pulled two insurance packets from her folder.

"Louise had a five-hundred-dollar death benefit, Doak's policy was for seven hundred and fifty dollars. I need death certificates for both of them."

I pushed the two death certificates across the table.

"They each have checks for the recent two weeks' pay period." These checks should ideally be given to the Executor's of their respective estates.

"Clyde Bowman will be Louise's Executor. I'll be stopping at Doak's grandmothers' home in New Lex today. I can get information. Thank you, all of you. I will get you addresses and phone numbers for the Executors."

Two more stops.

Velma had left Mr. and Mrs. Benoit bags on the porch. The front door was locked. The window in her bedroom was illuminated with Bix Beiderbecke blasting on the phonograph. I gave her a loud shout. No response. I turned and gathered the luggage and put it in the car along with Pierce's high chair.

On to New Lexington.

Traffic was heavy heading south. The rain had subsided and the traffic diminished once I cleared Canton. It felt good to just drive and not worry about artillery fire.

After several years of mail and phone calls that danced around the question of the boy's 'legitimacy'. I'd given myself permission not to deal with Pierce until if, or when, we were finally together.

I stopped to get gas and called Harriet.

"When are you getting back to Windsor? "she asked.

I'm not sure. If Doak's grandmother invites me stay, I will. If she doesn't, I'll come home."

"Virgil, another thing. Eleanor is coming home for the weekend. She's going to stay with your folks."

"I'd love to see her, she wrote me more letters me than anyone while I was in the Army."

"Maybe you should come home, Virgil. Is it the boy?"

"I'll play it by ear, I guess."

"Be careful what you pray for. You might get it and not know what to do with it."

"Harriet, how is Barbara doing?"

"She's OK. She slept in until noon."

"Good. I'll see you either tonight or tomorrow morning. I've got most of the things that we'll need to settle their Estates."

New Lexington

Not much happening in New Lexington, Ohio. It took me a while to get to the house. Someone finally told me to go down Madison Street until you hear the sound of a dozen pit bulls. I found the house after a few times around the block. I moved toward the front door carefully skirting the chains holding the dogs.

I parked well away from the dogs and carried the bags around the back of the house. A small woman with a big smile, opened a beat-up screen door and let me come in.

"I'm Virgil," I said while extending my hand. You must be—,".

"Just call me Goody, Virgil, that's the onliest thing people calls me."

"I am so sorry for you and Pierce."

"Likewise, for you and the Forest family, cher."

"I've got all the things from their apartment in Akron. I'll go get Pierces' highchair."

"That boy takin' his nap now. I get him up directly or he be up all night."

I set up the highchair in the kitchen, and took a deep breath.

I put Louise's bag on a chair and looked through it and felt a momentary impulse to get away from everything.

Pierce's voice emerged from the stairwell, followed by Goody's footfalls.

Goody and Pierce entered the kitchen laughing.

Pierce spotted the highchair and made a beeline for it.

"Mom mommy mom."

I lifted him up and buckled him in.

Goody came back in and gave Pierce a teething ring.

"Pierce gonna need some formula pretty soon. You want to feed him?"

"Sure, I'll try."

"Good, I gotta get off my feet."

"You can take him into the sofa and feed him."

"OK. I'll give it a shot."

I removed Pierce from the chair and moved to the couch, he took the bottle eagerly. He spit out some formula. I pulled a bib out of Louise's bag. As I was wiping his face, he pulled the bib up to his face.

"Mom mommy mom."

"Mom mommy mom."

"He can still smell his mommy, on dat bib, Virgil."

"I guess kids need stability when they are little."

"Sure 'nuff, cher."

"Goody, would you mind if I went down home tonight?"

"Reckon not."

"I feel like an intruder here."

"You welcome here, son. But you ain't obliged to do nothing."

"I will make sure you get Doak's life insurance from Monarch."

"Much obliged. You always welcome here. She put Pierce on her hip, Like my first husband would say, you got skin in this game. Nothin' ever gonna change that."

"Thank you."

"Give yo' boy a hug."

I did.

Carry Me Home

The forty-minute drive to Windsor seemed interminable. I saw Eleanor's car at the Mill. I stuck my head in, she was talking with Charlotte Simon.

"Look what the cat drug in," Eleanor chirped.

"Oh, Virgil we thought we'd lost you."

"I just got back from Akron, ladies."

"Did you get things straightened out?"

"Not everything, Charlotte. Louise passed the night before last."

"I brought back Louise and Doak's things from their apartment. And I got copies of their life insurance from Monarch and Death certificates from the Coroner in Canton. I stopped in New Lex and dropped off Pierce's clothes and his highchair.

"That must have been interesting, he's a good-looking boy," Eleanor said.

"Eleanor, have you been up to the house and seen Mom and Dad?"

"I stuck my head in the store. Ralph was stocking the shelves. He said his hours were likely to get cut at Dupont."

"Are you going to stay in Windsor or at your folk's place?"

"Why don't we drive up and see your folks and see if they feel like having company."

"Do you need a ride, Charlotte?"

"If it's not too much trouble. That would be nice, Thank you."

Minta was sitting in the swing trying to crochet in the fading light.

"Virgil, would like stick your head in for a minute?"

"Give me a raincheck, Char. I'm anxious to see my folks. I'll call you tomorrow, OK?

"OK."

"Trinda told me you and Charlotte were sparkin'."

"Kind of, I guess. Don't hold your breath I ain't ready for anything permanent."

"That had to be pretty painful for you, Virg."

"Bittersweet, when I brought Pierce's things into Goody's house, she fixed him a bottle. I grabbed one of Louise's old sweaters to wipe his mouth with. "He started saying— "Mom Mommy Mom."

"Children can differentiate between Mother and the rest of the world up to age five or so."

"I wonder what will become of Pierce."

"How old is Goody," Virgil?"

"Eighty- five, but she is amazingly spry."

"You may have something to say about that. If you have a mind to."

"Eleanor, would you do something for me? And not judge me to be crazy."

"OK, Louise had a safe deposit box and she put about fifteen letters addressed to me. Barb gave me the key. I haven't looked at them yet. I wondered if you'd read them to me to me. When I was being mustered out a shrink told me to face things that were bothering us. The two things that bothered me most were Louise and Gabby. I'll never have a friend like Gabby or a girl like Louise."

Louise's Letters

August 13, 1941: 1

My darling Virgil,

I am writing this letter to you from Akron. I got a job from your Cousin Mervyn working on the bearing line that you worked on after High School. Even though I feel like you are a thousand miles away, it makes me feel a little closer to know that we both have worked on the same assembly line.

My Father is starting to recover from his heart attack. I'm glad he's doing better. I guess we'll never know what might have happened if we hadn't gotten separated that last night.

I was excited about our plans to get married. I guess since that first day I saw you I kind of daydreamed about us riding off into the sunset together some day. I guess I finally realized that dreams don't always come true.

You were the first man I was ever with; and still the only man I'd been with the last time we were together.

I always thought we would eventually be together and raise a family.

Shortly after you left Windsor to be sworn in, I discovered I was pregnant. I guess I shouldn't have been too surprised. You can't dodge bullets forever.

I left Windsor for several reasons. I didn't want to embarrass my family, or have people talk badly about us. And I needed to go someplace where I can be left alone and earn some money to help my family.

Dad may be getting better, but he'll never be able to work full-time again. I also need to find a place for me and little Pierce or Anne Marie to live. I also like the idea that our bearings might be used in the Landing Craft that you are carried in across the Channel. Each boat has over 2000 of our bearings in it.

I hope you are well. And hope you will understand the reason that I will never send a letter to you. Your relatives send me your various addresses. As much as I need to express my feelings, it's not fair to you.

I know that not hearing from me may seem mean-spirited. That is not my intention. I want you to be safe and strong and not worry about me.

I will keep you in my prayers. I hope someday you will forgive me.

Love,

Louise

"That was a beautiful letter, Virgil."

"I was so angry when I left Windsor- about College, Louise, just feeling like I would never have things that I'd always wanted."

September 15, 1941: 2

Darling Virgil,

I have been reading newspapers at the Library and though they don't give all the details as best as I can tell your outfit—3rd Armored Division, 36th Armored Infantry—is now in England. I know you will be busy and that each day brings you closer to an Invasion of Europe.

I hope you have time to do some sight-seeing. Maybe you could visit Peniston Crag and send me some heather. Ha!

I have been working hard. I'm aiming to get myself off the line and into a job more involved with supply chain/parts. I can still work on line at this time, but not for long.

I found out for sure about six weeks after we last saw each other. This was one of the reasons I came to Akron. And darned if I didn't end up on the same line you worked in '29. I'm also staying in the same apartment house you were in and in the same apartment—205. By the way, Velma says 'Hi'. She owns the building now.

Another reason I came to Akron was to find someone to marry. Some women in my position pack up and disappear. I can't do that. I want to go home after the War and raise a family in Morgan County.

With all my heart, I wish it could be with you. But I am not strong enough to have this child and wait for you to return. I'm also not going to send you letters leading you on. That's not fair to either of us.

I've heard some of the older ladies talk about 'things not meant to be'. I guess maybe our plans just weren't meant to be. But I'm not willing to give them up, just yet.

So, I'm allowing myself one letter a month. These letters will be stored in a safe deposit box in Akron under my maiden name.

You are always in my thoughts and prayer.

Please take care of yourself, Heathcliff.

Love,

Cathy

October 16st 1942: 3

Dearest Virgil,

I got married two weeks ago. My husband's name is Doak Benoit. He's the Supervisor on the bearing line. He's not exactly handsome or striking, but he is a good man and he will be a good Father for Pierce or Anne.

Mother is the only one who knows the whole story. Without getting into too much detail, she also understands the situation I found myself in. Nuff said about that.

I think of you every day. And I pray each night that you will be safe. I feel badly about the way things turned out for us. I'll probably end up one of those old ladies thinking about those 'things not meant to be.'

I know that we're not putting our lives on the line, but I like to think we're helping the War Effort. We've got a big banner at the end of each of the different lines. It reads: <u>We've Got a War to Win—And the Battle Begins Here!</u>

People with family and loved ones in Service have been encouraged to write down their names and the Outfits they're with. I'd like to put your name down, Virgil. But I'm not going to. I put Cleveland Cheadle down. He's somewhere in England, too.

I must think of the baby. I've got to jump through some hoops to be sure that Doak believes the baby is his. I made sure we slept together as soon as possible. I got him drunk on Labor Day weekend. But that was more than a month after you and I had been together. I've been mentioning how Forest women have a history of delivering babies before full-term. And I have a friend at work whose brother works for the County here in Akron. She is going to get a blank Birth Certificate with the Seal affixed. I can fill in a date after the birth just in case. I've rented a safe deposit box at a bank in my Maiden name. I'll put the bogus certificate in the box along with these letters.

I keep telling myself I'm doing it for the baby. But I feel like a rat doing all this to deceive Doak and the folks back home. Only Mother knows about this. If things go as planned, it will stay that way.

I'd like to tell you, but I don't think that would be fair. If it was just us, with no baby, I wouldn't be dodging you. Little Mitch has given me your addresses. But I just think it's better if we make a clean break. You are a good man and I know you would do the right thing and assume responsibility for your child—our child.

But I don't want my child growing up under a cloud.

Love,

Louise

November 30st 1942: 4

Virgil,

I'm officially fat. We only got Thanksgiving Day off, so we stayed in Akron. Velma put on a big spread. We had about forty people sit down for dinner.

It was fun. Velma keeps asking about you. You two must have had quite the good time in '29.

I felt a little blue, missing Thanksgiving down home. But then I thought about you and all those other boys overseas. I hope you are well and had a chance to have some turkey and taters.

Everything with the baby is going well. I will probably deliver in February or March. The later the better. I'll be glad when the baby comes. I feel as if every day I live this way is a lie. I'll be glad to be a mother and I only have worry about Anne or Pierce and not about whether people are talking about me. I know that sounds selfish, but it is how I feel.

Love,

Louise

"I never got to know Louise very well. Her letters make me wish I'd gotten to know her as a sister-in-law.

"When Barb gave me the keys to the bank box and told me what was inside, I got my Irish up.

I decided I wouldn't read them, but I am glad to have them. Maybe I can read them to Pierce when he is older."

December 26th 1942: 5

Virgil,

Doak is passed out on the couch after devouring about eight pounds of turkey and most of the trimmings.

I hope you got to have a good Christmas Dinner. I have been thinking about our Christmas Dinners when we were kids. Remember when our Mothers would make desserts and both families would get together at the Store and stuff ourselves. Those were good times.

I don't know if there is any way I could ever explain to you the way things have turned out for us. I don't even understand it myself. I know it may sound like a lame explanation, but I think my maternal instinct kicked in and took over.

Adulthood isn't all I'd thought it would be, when I was a kid. Sometimes I feel like I'm just treading water. I tell myself I'm doing the best I can to be ready for the baby—our baby.

Please take care of yourself, Virgil. You are in my thoughts and prayers.

PS: I'm getting pretty good on the typewriter. I'm going to start typing my letters to you.

Love,

Louise

"She is quite a gal, Virgil. I'm sad you two didn't quite make it."

"I was angry when I left Windsor. I tried to forget her, but after I started getting letters mentioning Louise getting married, I just tried to forget about her and us."

January 25th, 1943: 6

Virgil,

I hope you had a good Holiday season, Virgil. We got a week off and spent Christmas at Doak's Grandmother's house in New Lex and New Year's with my family in Windsor.

I can hardly get in and out of the car. This baby is about ready to drop. I hope!

Doak got me a no-work chit until after the baby is born. I suppose you may roll your eyes when you read the next sentence. I'm sorry. When everything fell apart for us, I was so busy trying to get things set for motherhood that I stopped thinking about anyone else but myself and the baby.

After I got everything set up, I realized that you must have been upset, too. I know you're a good man. I tried to tell my Mom that you'd ignored me when you went away to school, but she just rolled her eyes.

I know how hard you worked at school to get through as quickly as possible. And I knew how much you loved me. Despite these things, you've been doing your duty in the Army. And I'm doing mommy duties. I heard you got promoted to Sergeant. Congratulations. But, don't be a hero.

I have tried to convince myself that I'm over you. No dice.

But I still plan to stay with Doak. He's a good man and he will be a good father.

Please take care of yourself, Virgil. I know you fellows will be hitting the beaches soon. We will be praying for you.

Love,

Louise

"Louise is wise beyond her years, Virgil. With two brilliant parents Pierce is going to to be a man to be reckoned with."

February 28th, 1942: 7

Virgil,

Your son was born three weeks ago. He's healthy and happy. Doak is so happy he's not even doing the Math. My mother knows, but I don't think anybody else does. Your mother might figure it out later. He's got eyes like yours. If he gets that cleft chin of yours, your Mom will surely notice. But that's some ways off.

I wish you could see Pierce, he is a little cutie patutie. Just like his Dad. I hope you don't think I'm an awful person. You may not understand the things I've done. But I'm just trying to do the right things for Pierce.

In a perfect world, we would have gotten married and Pierce and I would be waiting for you back in Windsor. It's not a perfect world. I thought I would go crazy when I found out that I was pregnant.

Mom helped me get through things. After I got the job in Akron from your Cousin Mervyn, I was too busy to dwell on things. I got the hang of things at work quickly. I liked the work. But I felt guilty being happy. I didn't think I deserved to be happy.

I hope you will be able to forgive me some day.

Love,

Louise

March 30th, 1942: 8

Virgil,

Little Pierce is rolling around like a seal. He has such a sweet smile. I'm going to start putting pictures in the box for you. I am putting photos of Pierce with these letters, so you can see how he grows.

We're really ramping up production on our line. Everybody in our plant is working harder now that you fellows are getting closer to crossing the Channel. I'm the one on our line that keeps track of product quality. We are turning out more parts with fewer defects. We are all proud to be providing you fellows with top notch equipment.

Love,

Louis*e*

April 20th, 1942: 9

Virgil,

I have been reading more newspaper coverage of build-up to the invasion of British tanks in Africa. Everybody back home is holding their breath. We know that you boys will suffer many casualties. And we are bracing ourselves as the lists of dead and wounded come in.

Everyone here is sending prayers and good wishes your way.

Another thing. Harvey Knight and his wife, June, passed away. And they left me their house and car. What do you know about that.

They didn't have any children and I spent a lot of time with them and helped them if they were having a party. They treated me like a daughter. Mr. Knight was a lawyer from Beverly. His wife was involved in all kinds of community activities—library, her church, Eastern Star.

Keep your head down—please!

Love,

Louise

"Louise captured the mood of all of us back home in the run up to D-Day. Everyone was holding their breath."

"We were all holding our breath in those landing crafts, too."

June 29th, 1942: 10

Virgil,

I have been following the progress of the 3rd Army with great interest. I only hope that you have not been injured in training. We have heard that the casualty rates on the beaches have been very high for some units.

Mother said that she would stay in touch with Eleanor and Anne. If anything happens to you, I will find out. I don't know what I will do if anything does happen to you.

I decided not to contact you and I intend to stick with it.

Pierce is getting taller and thinning out. He looks like you. I hope he'll be a good man like his father. I hope that when all is said and done, and Pierce is grown, I will be able to look back without regrets.

Love,

Louise

"Louise will be a great mother, Virgil. She seems be getting the hang of working, being a wife and a mother."

"She always was smart and hard-working,"

July 29th, 1942: 11

Virgil,

The newspapers are covering the Allied movements from the beaches into France. Sounds like tough going through those hedgerows.

You wouldn't believe how closely everyone is following the Allied advances. It seems like you are advancing much more quickly in the past few weeks. Hope you can stay safe.

A couple of boys from Morgan and Washington Counties have been MIA for nearly a month. One of them was a Kirkbride boy from over on Wolfe Creek.

I suspect we'll be seeing a lot more funerals before this War is over. Watch your top knot, Virgil.

Love,

Louise

August 18th, 1942:12

Virgil,

Mom just called me. Anne had told her that you were injured a week ago. She said it was shrapnel in your head, but they didn't know how serious it was. I hope you are going to be alright.

Please be careful. Mom will keep track of how you're doing.

Pierce is six months old and he is crawling everywhere. I remember your Mom talking about how 'active' you were when you were crawling.

It's funny, Doak is good with Pierce, but he never says a word about who Pierce favors. The boy favors you from his long eyelashes to his big ears.

Please be careful.

Love,

Louise

September 20th, 1942:13

Virgil,

I was so happy to hear that your injury was just superficial. But, not so happy that you are back with your Unit. We've had a couple of funerals since my last letter. Jake Hook and Randy Zumbro died in the Pacific. They were on Bougainville.

Charlotte Ross from Chesterfield got married to a fellow from Kentucky who is with the Army Air Corps. His brother was at

Bougainville taking Marines from the ships to the beach. I heard they got a telegram about a week ago, but it didn't give any details.

This War is becoming real in different ways. It's one thing when assembly lines started running around the clock. It's another when we start hearing about local boys, like you, getting wounded and others dying.

Please take care of yourself. Pierce and I are doing well. He's such a good boy, not a bit like his father. Ha, just kidding!

Love,

Louise

October 27th, 1942:14

Virgil,

I got some news about you from Mom. Anne told her you were acting Platoon Sergeant. I guess that means you are good at your job. I fear it means you will be right up front and in grave danger.

We are staying busy at work. Nearly every line in the plant is running 24-7. I'm so glad they have a nursery here at the plant. I can check in on Pierce on breaks.

Your boy is getting ready to walk. He can pull himself up at the coffee table. When he does, he stands up straight with the same look in his eyes you used to get when you were getting ready to do something crazy.

I'm glad that I've gotten news about you through Mom from Anne. But it makes me wish things were different. Like the song says: "If wishes were fast trains to Texas, how I'd ride, and I'd ride and I'd ride."

I hope you stay safe. I hope all of you boys know how much the folks here support you. We are all looking forward to welcoming you back home after you finish the task at hand.

Love,

Louise

November 27th, 1944: 15

Virgil,

I hope you fellows manage to get some turkey. Doak, Pierce and I went home and had an open house at the Store with turkey and all the trimmings. We had forty people show up including a couple of local boys from down around Luke Chute who had been wounded at Salerno.

I was thinking about you and the guys in your outfit. I also thought about previous Thanksgivings spent down home. Your folks came down to the store for a couple of hours. It was good to see them. They both seem to be doing well.

Anne wanted to see Pierce, but Merlene had taken him back to the house for a nap.

Doak had dropped Pierce and me in Windsor and gone over to his Grandma's house in New Lex. Vern Addy let me borrow his car So, Pierce and I drove over to be with Doak.

I told Mom I wanted to see Doak's Grandmother.

And that way, Anne won't see Pierce. She's going to know eventually. He looks so much like his father."

I feel bad hiding him from your Mother, but I don't want her to find out. Not yet. Dad is still very sick. He knows nothing about any of this. I don't want to upset him. I It would be nice to have one more Christmas with all of us together.

Love,

Louise

December 8th, 1944:16

Virgil,

Dad died on December 7th, the third anniversary of the attack on Pearl Harbor. The funeral is set for December 13th. So much for having Dad around for one more Christmas.

Doak, Pierce and I will go to the funeral. Mervyn suggested we could try to find some folks in Windsor and New Lex to come to Akron and work. Many of the women, especially those with a couple of kids want to go home and play Mommy.

That's not for me, not yet. But we're going put on a little Dog and Pony Show at the Roxbury Store and at the Grange Hall in New Lex before we head back to Akron.

I'm pretty sure that Anne will figure out the issue of Pierce's lineage before we head back to Akron. I'm also sure she won't make a scene.

PS

I got some news about you from Mom. Anne told her you were acting Platoon Sergeant. I guess that means you are good at your job. I fear it means you will be right up front and in grave danger.

We are staying busy at work. Nearly every line in the plant is running 24-7. I'm so glad they have a nursery here at the plant. I can check in on Pierce on breaks.

Your boy is getting ready to walk. He can pull himself up at the coffee table. When he does, he stands up straight with the same look in his eyes you used to get when you were getting ready to do something crazy.

I'm glad that I've gotten news about you through Mom from Anne. But it makes me wish things were different. Like the song says: "If wishes were fast trains to Texas, how I'd ride, and I'd ride and I'd ride."

I hope you stay safe. I hope all of you boys know how much the folks here support you. We are all looking forward to welcoming you back home after you finish the task at hand.

Love,

Louise

December 16th, 1944:17

Virgil,

Your Mother got the telegram right before Doak and I were going to head to New Lex. Little Mitch and Eleanor said they could drop me off at New Lex when I was ready to go.

Eleanor fussed over Pierce and then Anne came over. Bless her heart. I knew, she knew.

"May I hold him, dear?"

"Yes, ma'am. I'll go see to my husband," I told her.

When I got back, she told me about the telegram. No word on your condition.

We talked for a spell and then a young woman I didn't recognize wandered over.

"Excuse me. I heard that they were folks here from Akron, might have jobs for hard workers," she said with a queer look in her eyes.

"My husband and I work in Akron and we are looking for folks to work on the assembly lines in our plant. Do you have experience working in assembly?"

"Not exactly," the girl said softly. "I have waitressed and milked cows and I's on a clean-up crew on a big dairy farm, for the barns and such."

"We need help in the janitorial department. What is your name?"

"Birdie LeForet. If you are Louise, I am your cousin from up around Kalamazoo, except I've been living in Upper Sandusky for the past year or so."

"Do tell. Do you live here in Windsor?"

"No, I just got here today."

"Well, don't unpack. We may be able to take you to Akron with us in a couple of days."

We did take Birdie back with us. She got on the cleaning crew and seems to be doing a good job.

I waited for Mom's message when they found out your condition. I was grateful you were not hurt worse and hopeful you'd be out of action for the rest of the War.

Love,

Louise

January 20th, 1945:18

Virgil,

I'm so sorry to hear about your friend Gabby. I remember your Mom mentioning him after your last pass at home. You've been through a lot, Virgil. This War has sure put you fellows through the wringer.

I hope you will be able to have a normal life when you get home. I know how much you want to finish your degree at OSU. I know some of the other things we used talk about, too.

You will find someone, Virgil, and settle down, have a family. You have given your share to your country.

I hope you have someone to talk to in the hospital. These letters I write will never be seen by anyone else, but they have helped me to get through with all the turmoil I've faced. I'm not comparing it, in any way, to being in battle or getting shot, but everybody needs someone to talk to.

Mom also told me you got a Bronze Star, a Purple Heart and a Unit Citation. You can be proud for the things you have given this country. And a little sad for the things you've given up. Including what we have given up.

Hope you aren't upset that I used the term 'we'.

Love,

Louise

"Virgil, I hope you keep these letters in a safe place. They are gems," Eleanor

February 20th, 1945: 19

Virgil,

I guess I figured you would have found out from some of your family that I had married. So, when Mervyn and Doak and I ran into Orpha in Columbus and she started talking about Virgil just getting the news, I told the boys to run along and took Orpha to Mills Cafeteria for some coffee.

Initially I was angry, but I guess it makes sense that Anne, Little Mitch and Eleanor would not say anything while you were in combat or in the hospital.

I just assumed you'd have heard. I sure didn't tell you. I guess I treated you poorly and I shouldn't be surprised that you have been angry or hurt.

I know it might seem like I want to have my cake and eat it, too.

I guess this just confirms that I need to keep writing these letters, but never send them. I hope you are healing physically and otherwise.

God bless you, Virgil. And God forgive me.

Love,

Louise

March 20th, 1945: 20

Virgil,

It is starting to look like this War might end after all. I know that things in the Pacific are still going strong in some places. But it seems like things in Europe are winding down.

I don't know what I'll do when the War finally ends. I've gotten used to working eighty hours a week. And most of us women, especially those with husbands or sons in combat, feel like this is our contribution. As soon as the War is over and the men get back, we'll be let go and return to hearth and home, I guess.

Most of the girls are looking forward to going back to being housewives. I never was a housewife, so I don't know if I'll like it. We'll see.

Sorry if I sound like I'm whining. Take care of yourself.

Love,

Louise

May 10th, 1945:21

Virgil,

Well it looks like things are wrapping up in the European Theater for most part. There was a sad story in last week's *Herald*. That fellow that Charlotte Ross, from Chesterfield, married was killed in Germany a couple weeks ago.

He had worked for the Army Air Corps as a Civilian Engineer. But it seems he enlisted—volunteered— toward the end of February and just got over to Germany. Seems he was leading a group of Nazis, who had surrendered, back behind the lines where they were being put in some kind of holding pen before they were shipped to POW camps. A German sniper shot and killed him. He'd only been there for a couple of days.

Charlotte gave birth to a baby girl, two days after her husband was killed in April. She didn't find out until May 7th. It's a shame. I think she was in the Band, played clarinet. Sad about the baby—little girl I heard will never know her Father. I guess there's quite a bit of that goin' around these days.

Back to what I started with concerning Europe winding down a bit. We switched over to making only products used in the Pacific Theater.

They say those Japs won't surrender. They're a different breed, I guess.

There sure are going to be a lot of folks having a tough time readjusting to civilian life.

I hope you'll make a smooth transition, Virgil.

Love,
Louise
May 28th, 1945:22

Virgil,

We are starting to slow down a little bit here at work. We only worked 48 hours last week, instead of 80. I'm not sure how they are going handle the ramping down of production. Probably will lay off most of the women to open up jobs for returning veterans.

I'm not sure what we will be doing. Doak has been talking about taking a long vacation down to Louisiana, where he was born. We'll have to wait and see.

Ma saw Eleanor in Beverly, last week. She said it looked like you wouldn't get home until the Fall. Take care of yourself.

Love,
Louise

Eleanor stood up abruptly and stretched. "These letters must be preserved, Virgil."

"I'll keep them safe. I meant what I said about sharing them with Pierce. Of course, that's not my call. I'd like to be involved with him. I hope Harriet and Goody will be let that happen. As my buddy, Gabby would have said: 'You got skin in this game, buddy.'"

He had left a loved one with child. His girl was Birdie or Bridie from Michigan. We were great friends."

The telephone rang.

"Who would be calling here at this hour, Virgil?"

"Beats me. I'll get it. "Yellow."

"What! When. A heart attack. Where is Pierce? The police station in New Lex, shit!"

"I have a car, I'm here with Eleanor. We could go get him, if Barb could come it might help Pierce."

"Eleanor, would you be willing to help with this situation?"

"Yes, Virgil. Let me go speak with Mitch and Anne and see what they think."

"I'll tell you what we think," Mitch said in his reedy voice as he and Anne stepped into the store.

"Harriet should have the last word on this subject."

"Speak of the Devil," Eleanor said.

"Harriet, what should we do. We are at your disposal."

"I'd like for Virgil and Barbara to go get our boy, Pierce. Poor dear needs some down home loving'."

CPSIA information can be obtained
at www.ICGtesting.com
Printed in the USA
LVHW031139200319
611264LV00001B/320/P